ROTTING BEAUTY

ALSO BY ELIZABETH K. KING

THE HORRIFIC FAIRY TALES SERIES
Rotting Beauty
Beast By Day
The Little Sea Monster
Seven Hexes
Ghoul Girl (forthcoming)

Don't Go Into the Woods (novella)

ROTTING BEAUTY

A HORRIFIC FAIRY TALE

ELIZABETH K. KING

ROTTING BEAUTY: A Horrific Fairy Tale

Published in the United States by Elizabeth King. For inquiries, please visit the author's website: www.elizabethkking.com

Cover Art by Miblart.

Map by Saumya Singh (@Saumyasvision/Inkarnate).

The text for this book was set in EB Garamond.

The Library of Congress Control Number: 2023913971

ISBN 979-8-9888121-0-4 (hardcover)

ISBN 979-8-9888121-1-1 (paperback)

ISBN 979-8-9888121-2-8 (ebook)

First Edition, September 2023.

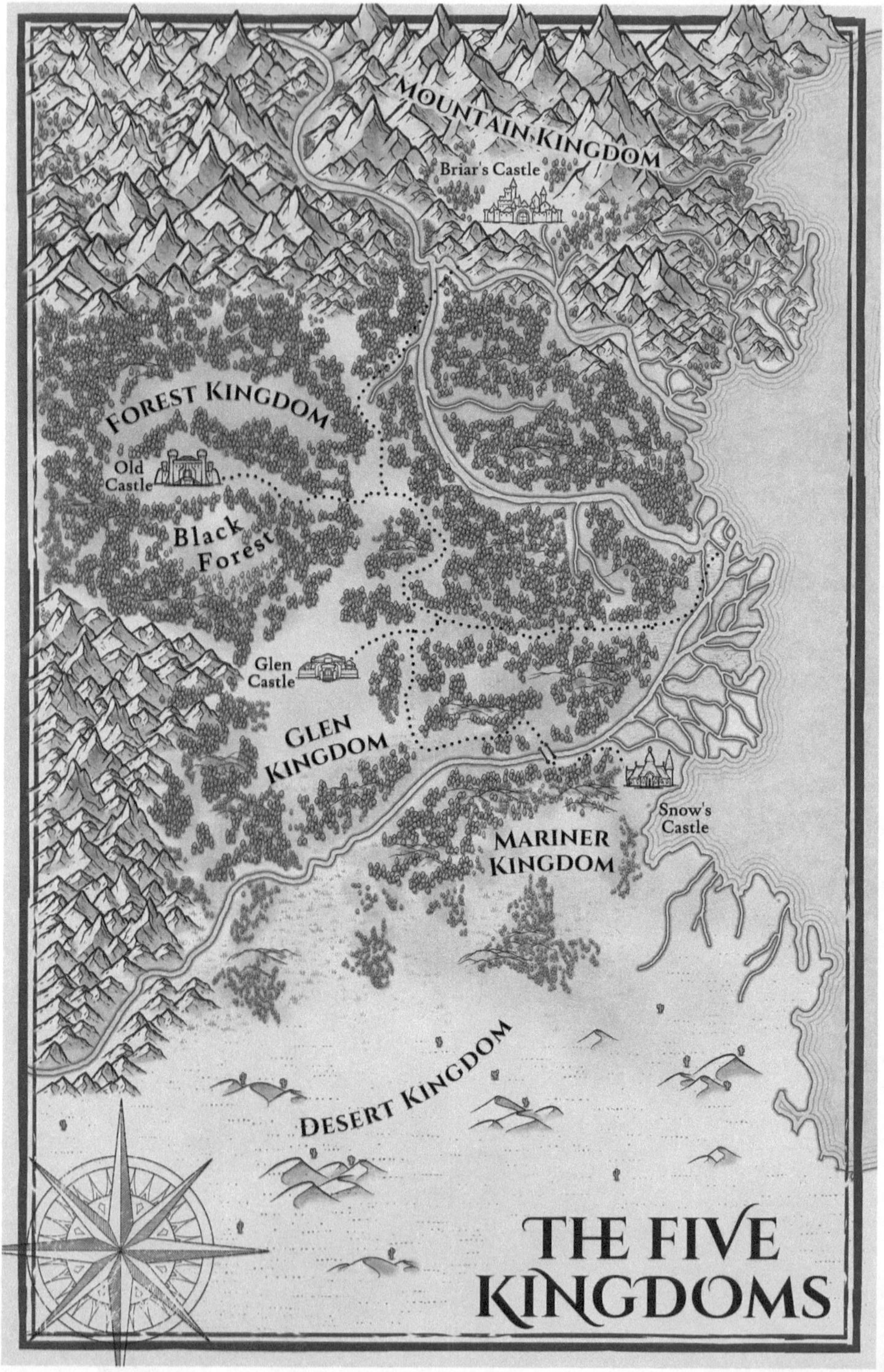

MOUNTAIN KINGDOM
Briar's Castle
FOREST KINGDOM
Old Castle
Black Forest
Glen Castle
GLEN KINGDOM
MARINER KINGDOM
Snow's Castle
DESERT KINGDOM
THE FIVE KINGDOMS

PROLOGUE

S HE WANTED A LILAC ribbon. She couldn't find one.

Princess Briar frowned, lifting a pale blue ribbon to inspect it. The gleaming vanity table before her was a mess of ribbons. In light of what tonight meant—in light of everything—this decision was insignificant. Briar knew that. But it was easier to lose herself in it, to pretend it meant everything. As though the fate of the world rested upon this one thing—what color ribbon she would wear to bind her dress tonight.

She blew out a frustrated breath, letting the ribbon slip from her fingers. There *had* to be a lilac ribbon somewhere in the castle, but Briar had already asked Laurel for one, to no avail. Laurel was Briar's cousin, and the only person in her family who actually spoke to her. The only person in the whole castle, really. So she had already exhausted her options.

"Is that what you're going to wear?"

Briar turned, lifting a sardonic eyebrow. Perhaps she was wrong. Here was someone else who would speak to her, if only to criticize. And only within the last few months—only since Briar had discovered the truth, the reason behind her parents' glacial attitude towards her.

Briar's mother, the queen of the Mountain Kingdom, stood in the doorway of Briar's bedroom. Her ice blond hair was a shade lighter than Briar's, her chin more rounded, and her hips a bit larger, though the volume of her brocade gown disguised that tonight.

Otherwise, they were unmistakably mother and daughter. But in appearance only. Anyone who had observed them together over the years would never have guessed they were close family.

Briar cast a quick glance over herself. "What's wrong with it?"

Her mother pursed her lips so tightly, you would have thought she'd bitten a lemon. But she said nothing, her silence carrying the weight of her disapproval. As always.

Briar stared back stonily. Once, she had strived to earn her mother's praise. That was before she'd learned that nothing she could do would ever get her any. "Mother," she said, her voice dry, "everyone under the age of thirty is going to be dressed in this fashion." Or so Laurel had assured her. Briar hardly knew anything about current fashions, since she never left the castle, and no one talked to her about anything. But Laurel had commissioned Briar's gown, a gauzy dress in the new fashion, which was to say, looser and high-waisted, leaving her arms bare. Much less covered up and much less *confined* than her mother's old-fashioned gown.

Her mother's lips went even tighter. "You look like a ghost."

Briar stifled a laugh. "Very fitting, then."

At that, her mother's face closed off entirely, her expression colder than ever. Of course. She would continue to deny Briar's fate, to pretend it away, even unto the hour of her doom.

Briar reached back for the ribbons and selected one that was blood red. "Perhaps this, then. To give me some color."

"Don't be crass, dear," her mother snapped, and with that final condemnation, she swept from the room, leaving Briar alone again.

Briar stared at the empty doorway, bemused. She wondered what her mother had been doing here to begin with. Come to say goodbye? Come to, finally, impart some words of love to the daughter she would never see again, after tonight? The daughter who would be all but dead?

No. Of course not. That was ridiculous.

Against all her resolve, Briar felt tears gather in her eyes, her vision glazing over. Speaking of ridiculous. It was beyond ridiculous that she should cry, for the loss of a mother who had never cared about her. Who had given her up for dead from the time she was an infant, all because of a curse Briar had done nothing to earn. She had wondered, once, if it was her parents' guilt that kept them from Briar; if deep down, they understood *they* were to blame for this.

That was probably too generous of her. And it didn't matter. They had chosen, consciously or not, to both prepare for the curse by distancing themselves from Briar, and to ignore the reality of it as entirely as they could, continuing with their lives—and Briar's—as though it was never going to happen.

It certainly hadn't stopped them throwing this stupid ball for Briar's sixteenth birthday. Briar turned back to her vanity, crumpling the red ribbon. Her tears flowed freely, steady but silent. She didn't even want to attend this stupid ball. Stars and stones, she was living her last hours in this world—in this *time,* anyway—and she should get to do what she wanted.

She knew exactly what she wanted.

She left her quarters sans any ribbon at all.

There was one other person in the castle—one person besides Laurel—who spoke to her. More than that, he was her friend. No, he was something so wonderful and so dear, Briar didn't have a name for it. Even though she had only met him six months ago, when he came to visit the Mountain Kingdom as part of the betrothal agreement between his parents and Briar's.

Prince Demetri.

Briar and Demetri had been betrothed before the dark fairy cast her dreadful curse upon the princess. There were political reasons her parents chose to maintain the betrothal, keeping the curse a secret from Demetri's family. But Briar knew very well it was another part of their pretense, keeping up with the lie they told themselves.

Yet for once, Briar was grateful for the denial her parents lived in. Without it, she would never have found such an ally as Demetri. It was Demetri who had overheard her parents arguing two months ago and discovered the truth—that the marriage planned between him and Briar was never going to happen, because Briar was doomed to fall to a fairy's curse on the night of her sixteenth birthday. It was Demetri who had revealed to Briar the truth her parents had kept from her all her life—that she was cursed to prick her finger and fall into a death-like sleep, a sleep she would not wake from for a hundred years.

And Demetri—against all reason, all common sense—had not left the Mountain Kingdom. He had not left *Briar*. He had stayed and agreed to keep the curse a secret. He had stayed because he was determined they could avoid it—not deny it like her parents did, but find a way to break the curse before it happened.

Briar and Demetri had snuck out of the castle just this morning and gone to find fairies in the nearby forest, fairies who might help them. But there had been no help to be found. Not from the fairies. Not from anyone else.

Now, they were out of time. And in these last hours, Briar didn't want to parade around the ballroom, pretending everything was all right.

She only wanted to be with Demetri.

She found him in his quarters. Slipping into the anteroom, she found him standing before a full-length mirror, fiddling with his cravat at the base of his throat. "Damn it," she heard him mumble, as something small and metallic slipped from his fingers. He bent to look for it.

"Demetri," Briar said, announcing herself without preamble.

Demetri snapped up so fast, he nearly banged his head against the table on his left. He missed it by a hair, but Briar winced. Still, she could not contain a smile as he whipped around to face her.

"Briar!" For a moment, Demetri looked endearingly gobsmacked, as though she really was a ghost come to haunt him. The thought made her smile waver—soon, she would be as good as a ghost—but she was determined to keep maudlin thoughts from intruding now. "Sorry, I thought—" His gaze flitted to the grandfather clock across the room. "Is it seven already?"

"No. I don't know." Briar stepped inside. "I don't care. Demetri, let's forget about the ball."

A smile twitched over his face. When he spoke, his voice was teasing. "You mean, you don't want to dance with me? I'm shocked."

Briar laughed. Under ordinary circumstances, she knew Demetri loved balls. He loved social engagements of any kind, he loved music, and he loved to dance. He also knew that she, even under ordinary circumstances, hated dancing.

And these were far from ordinary circumstances.

"I'll dance with you." She drifted towards him. "Here. We can dance right here."

Her throat tightened as she swept her gaze over him. Taking in every detail. His mousy hair, even now a little tousled, refusing to lie flat over his head. His elegant hands, fidgeting at his sides. Demetri was a trained violinist, and she loved to watch his slender fingers move along the neck of the violin as he played. His deep brown eyes, often serious, always steady. And fixed upon her now.

"Briar," he said, and his voice sounded tight too. His eyebrow hitched as she came within a pace of him, close enough to touch. His gaze traveled over her face. "Are you...have you been crying?"

Briar cursed silently. She'd wiped her cheeks clean before leaving her rooms, but her eyes were probably still red. "Not anymore." She lifted her arm and realized he was already reaching for her. Their hands met and closed together like the most natural thing in the world. "I don't want to cry anymore. I just want to be here. With you."

Despite her best efforts, her voice shook. She cursed herself again. She was never like this, never emotional, never unsteady. But she couldn't hold it back anymore—the tide of feelings rushing through her, good and bad. All the fear and dread she harbored of what was to come. And all the longing. All *her* longing, for him.

She wanted him to hold her. To tell her everything would be all right, even if it was a lie.

She wanted him to kiss her.

He was the only person in the world who had ever cared for her. Who had ever told her the truth.

The only person who had ever loved her.

"Briar," Demetri whispered. Briar didn't think she'd ever been this close to him before. Demetri was a proper prince. He never breached the strictures of decorum and decency. But he didn't pull away when Briar slid her hands up his arms, entwining them behind his neck. Indeed, his own hands settled on her waist, if a bit tentatively.

"I won't give up, Briar." His voice was little more than a breath. "I won't stop looking for a way..."

Barely breathing, Briar canted her head to the side. They were almost exactly the same height. Demetri's eyes fluttered shut, but Briar kept her gaze fixed on his face. She slid one hand forward to cup the side of his neck.

That was when she felt it.

A *prick* upon her finger. An almost painless jab into her flesh.

Her breath caught. For a moment, she stood frozen. A suspended moment where she wasn't aware of what had happened, and yet she knew, deep in her gut, that something was terribly wrong.

"Briar?" Demetri, too, had sensed the wrongness. "What is it?"

That was when she saw the tiny drop of blood blooming on her finger. As crimson as the ribbon she had picked out earlier.

That was when she saw the pin in Demetri's shirt collar. A decorative pin. It sat there, stuck through the starchy material of his shirt, but its backing had fallen off. Briar remembered Demetri bending down to look for something when she'd come into the room.

At that exact moment—as she saw the pin and understood—she felt it descend over her.

The sleep.

The curse.

It didn't feel like falling asleep. It was no slow drift into unconsciousness. It was a physical thing, a heavy, black curtain stealing over her mind.

"*Briar!*" She heard her name one last time on Demetri's lips, this time a panicked cry.

But the darkness overtook her, sealing her away. And she knew no more.

EIGHTY-TWO YEARS LATER

1

DORMANT

"THIS IS EITHER GOING to be the greatest venture I've undertaken," Prince Garrett said, "or we're all going to die horribly."

Demetri said, "The former, I hope," as his eyes rose to the castle before them. A splintering wooden gate and a grimy stone wall were all that separated them from the castle. The wall was still standing despite the heavy vines creeping over it. Before he could think twice, Demetri reached out and gave the ramshackle gate a solid push.

It swung open, squealing on rusty hinges. The *cr-e-e-ak* of it echoed down into Demetri's soul.

"Doors unbarred," murmured Garrett. "And no guards."

No guards. No people at all, that they had seen. Demetri stared up at the forbidding ruin of a castle. It had once been a shining beacon, the walls so white the sun gleamed off them. Now, the walls had gone gray. Dark moss clung to the fortress, draping itself over the rooftops and slithering down the high towers.

A fearful tension built in Demetri's shoulders. It didn't look like anyone had lived in this castle for many years. In the face of that stark truth, Demetri hoped one of the stories they'd heard about this place was true—that there had been some snowstorm, or some sickness or attack that had driven everyone out. Something normal to explain what had happened. Because if what *truly* happened here had anything to do with Briar's curse, then they were walking into something most unpleasant.

"It doesn't look much like the place you described." Garrett peered at the gate before them, now slightly ajar. His eyes lingered over the damp rot eating at the wood.

Demetri managed an edgy smile, though it felt weird on his face. At odds with the clamminess seeping into him. "Eighty-two years will do that, I suppose."

Garrett chuckled. Even their quiet exchange seemed too loud in this eerie place, where silence stretched before them as in a graveyard.

One of the soldiers, a young man named Spencer, grimaced. "This place is cursed." He was rail thin, with skin as black as the night sky. There were five soldiers, all Prince Garrett's. Forty had come on this venture, but most of them waited below in the lower mountains. Garrett had decided five men should be sufficient to accompany them into the castle.

Standing before these sinister walls, Demetri had begun to question that decision.

"This place isn't cursed," Prince Garrett said affably, resting a hand on his holstered pistol. "Just because it's an old, dark, abandoned ruin doesn't mean it's cursed. Only the princess inside is cursed." He cast Demetri a sidelong glance and murmured, "So far as we know, yes?"

Demetri shrugged.

"And you don't remember anything?" Garrett prodded. "Anything to suggest what might have happened here? After your princess fell to her curse, I mean."

Demetri shook his head. "The last thing I remember is—" The words stuck in his throat. "Briar. Falling at my feet." Falling to the dark fairy's curse. "Beyond that, I've no idea. The only other thing I remember is ..." *The darkness. The solitude.* Being abducted from the castle by a small, hooded figure. Being held captive by parties unknown, in a place unknown. Frozen by some spell that kept him from aging, but also kept him conscious. Worse than the darkness though, worse than the solitude, was the slow, crushing realization that he was helpless, helpless to aid Briar and with no one to help him—

He clenched his jaw.

Garrett did not press him. Though the two had only been friends for about a month, Garrett, Demetri had observed, had a knack for reading people.

"Well." Garrett gestured at the gate. "I suppose the only way to find answers is to go looking for them. It's why we came, isn't it?"

Briar, Demetri thought. Briar was why they'd come. And wary as he was, Demetri wasn't about to leave her moldering in this horrid place a second longer than they had to.

Pushing the gate open wider, Demetri stepped through it and beneath the archway that led into the guardhouse. The way was thrown in darkness, and the heavy smell of mildew hung in the air, grown from the damp layered over stone and wood. It was a wrong smell—not just foul, but *wrong*, the kind of smell that said *Stop now, go back*—

Demetri let out a low, uneven breath. He held his lantern aloft. But the gears spinning beneath the lantern's bulb only mustered a light bright enough to show a few feet in front of him. Beyond that, shadows flickered over the walls like capering creatures in the dark.

The fear curling in Demetri's gut wound itself into a tight, knotted web. It sat inside him like a stone, rooting him to the ground. It was a few seconds before he managed to step forward into the shadowy passage. He stretched a hand out to keep from running into anything.

Unfortunately, it wasn't his hand that hit something in the darkness. It was his foot.

Demetri cringed as he tread upon something that gave a sharp *crunch*. The dread inside him leapt into his throat.

"Demetri?" Garrett called softly. "What was that?"

Demetri's pulse stuttered. He dropped his gaze.

A person sat crumpled at his feet.

Demetri jumped back with a yelp and jumped again when Spencer let out a startled oath beside him. They all goggled at the man slumped against the wall.

"What the...?" Garrett said.

"It's a—a person," said Spencer.

"It's a body," said another soldier. "A corpse."

He was right, of course. "A corpse indeed." Demetri's voice was shakier than he liked, his heart thumping erratically. "One long dead at that. Well, that's a good sign. A great start to this venture. A ruined castle, a long-dead corpse—"

Garrett grinned. "There's your sense of adventure."

"It's not all that long-dead, though," Spencer noted, "is it?"

Clenching his jaw, Demetri looked down at the body. He understood what Spencer meant. The corpse's flesh was mottled in pale greens and inky blues and looked as though it could melt off at the lightest touch. In some places, the flesh was gone, leaving bare bone in its wake. Oddly enough, the corpse still had its eyes, the loosely-shut lids translucent.

"A guard, once," Demetri said. His breathing began to even out as he noted the faded, course wool clinging to the body, remnants of the dead man's black uniform. He could just make out flecks of the golden crest on the coat, the crest of the Mountain Kingdom. "Or someone dressed like a guard."

"It's weird, isn't it," Garrett murmured. "How he's sitting like that. Like he just sat down and died."

Demetri tried to shrug off the cold that had come over him. "Come on." He stepped past the corpse. "We don't know what killed him. It might have been some sickness."

"Or it might have been something else," Garrett added with thinly veiled excitement. "Everyone keep a sharp eye out."

Demetri shook his head, though he smiled a little. Garrett was a strange young man; he seemed to welcome danger. He had been eager to accompany Demetri on this quest to the long-forgotten Mountain Kingdom, not only out of friendship, but out of genuine enthusiasm. Apparently, the prince was a bit of a daredevil; he chased monster stories the way other noblemen hunted stags. Well, everyone needed a hobby, Demetri supposed.

As they crept through the guardhouse, Demetri ran a nervous hand down the scabbard of his rapier, his fingers bumping along the gilded silver. He was the only one here to bear a blade; Garrett and his soldiers carried firearms, pistols mostly. Pistols had been around in Demetri's day, but not the kind they carried now—these were new models called "revolvers." Garrett carried an even newer invention slung over his shoulder, a rifle called a "repeater." Demetri didn't know much about it, except that it was powered by gear work, like their lanterns. He hadn't seen Garrett use it yet and hoped he never would—at least, not until they were out of the castle with Briar.

Briar. Demetri swallowed, trying not to think of her. Which was futile, since he hadn't stopped thinking about her once in the last eighty-two years.

They passed through the guardhouse and into the courtyard, where gnarled, black roots grew in clumps over the flagstones. The walls of the castle rose up on either side, closing them in. Dark curtains of moss hung from the ramparts, and knotted ropes of it wound around pillars. The eerie quiet seemed even more pronounced here, so quiet that Demetri's breath felt loud in his ears.

Then there were the bodies.

"Stars and stones," Spencer swore. "There are more of them."

There were indeed. Pale corpses, strewn among the court-yard as though they had been posed, grotesque dolls arranged for child's play. There were about a dozen of them. Some lay sprawled on the ground, roots creeping over their rotted flesh. Others were slumped over in seated positions. Two corpses sat together, huddled in a corner—a couple maybe, for one wore the tattered remains of a ruby red dress, the silk thread woven among the slime-like flesh beneath it. Demetri even saw one corpse on its feet, leaning upright against a stone pillar.

"By the gift," Jones whispered. She was one of the youngest soldiers in Garrett's company, a year younger than Demetri—or at least, a year younger than the seventeen years he looked to be. "What happened to them?"

Spencer shrugged. "They died."

"But...how?"

"I suppose they *are* dead," Demetri said, "aren't they?"

He and Prince Garrett exchanged a quick look. Demetri knew he sounded ridiculous—of course these people were dead. They were decaying. But the way they were, some sitting, that one standing...

A chilling howl bayed into the quiet. Demetri jerked around, his chest tightening. But it was only a burst of wind, funneling into the courtyard from behind the castle.

He shook himself. "Never mind. We just need to get to Briar. Let's just...stay away from the bodies."

"Sounds good to me, Highness," Jones agreed.

As they picked their way towards the front steps, Garrett said, "Have you any idea why there would be so many dead here? I mean, by the look of them I'd say they haven't been here for the last eighty years. They'd be only dust and bones by now."

Demetri shook his head. "I don't know. I was taken almost as soon as Briar fell to her curse. For all I know, the people here continued to live their lives. For a bit, anyway." He glanced at one of the bodies and shuddered. "Clearly not anymore."

"All the stories suggest otherwise," Garrett murmured, "but those same stories don't say much either, so. Who knows if there's any truth to them."

All the stories. Garrett was not referring to the tales they'd heard on their way here. Those had been plausible stories, rumors the locals had come up with to explain why the castle was deserted. A great storm, a great sickness.

No, Garrett was referring to the *stories*—the reason he, mad adventurer that he was, had never been here before, even though it was the sort of place a person like Garrett would have fancied for a summer holiday. Evidently, after Briar fell to her curse—after Demetri himself was taken—all sorts of mad rumors came out of the kingdom. Rumors that said the whole kingdom was cursed, rumors that said fairies had claimed the land for themselves. Rumors terrible enough that Demetri's own parents, the king and queen of the Glen Kingdom, had ordered their northern borders closed and declared no one was to travel into the Mountain Kingdom.

An edict that had still stood, all these years later. Until now.

"And this fairy," said Garrett, "the one that freed you—"

"I *think* it was a fairy." Demetri had not gotten a good look at the creature. All he remembered was a blue nimbus gleaming from a hooded cloak.

"Well, whoever—isn't it odd he didn't mention the place was littered with corpses?"

"Maybe he didn't know. He only told me where to find Briar."

"Though not how to wake her," Garrett said.

Demetri averted his eyes as he passed near a corpse. "He said it would come to me. Whatever that means."

"Whatever that means," Garrett repeated. There was something strange in his voice, but when Demetri looked at him, the prince's gaze was on the castle doors ahead. Garrett was a comforting, steady presence in such a frightening place. He never panicked, but that didn't mean he wasn't watchful. Looking at him now, Demetri could see the vigilance in his gaze as they stepped into the grand entrance hall.

Or at least, it had once been grand. Demetri remembered the warmth of the entry, and the *light*. The hall had glowed with it, sparkling off the crystal chandelier, burning in sconces in every corner. He remembered the scarlet rug that covered the floor, a plushy wool that was a blessing beneath weary feet. He remembered the tall, oak doors, polished until they shone, standing open in invitation at the back of the hall.

Now, the chandelier lay in shards over the rug, which was no longer scarlet but soiled a mucky brown. Cobwebs stretched across the bare sconces, and the doors were shut tight, their exteriors peeling like an apple skin.

Demetri took it all in, and for the first time, something flickered past his fear—an unbearable wave of nostalgia. This castle had never been his home, but he had lived the best six months of his life here. With Briar.

It felt like another life. As though that time didn't belong to him, but to someone else.

"Bloody—!" Demetri heard shuffling boots and the *click* of a trigger being cocked. He spun around, half-afraid of what he would see. But it was only Spencer, who had ventured so far back into the hall, he had nearly disappeared into the shadows.

"What is it?" Garrett asked.

Ashen-faced, Spencer moved towards them, a pistol in hand. "I..." He licked his lips. "I thought I saw—something moved. Back there." He pointed towards the back of the hall.

Garrett peered into the dark. "Back where?"

Demetri lifted his lantern, his eyes darting along the back wall. The dim light cut jagged swathes through the shadows—but he saw nothing.

He frowned. "What was it?"

"I'm not sure." Spencer's eyes were wild. "Something moved."

"A person?" Garrett demanded.

"Maybe." Spencer darted a glance down the corridor.

"Could it have been an animal?" Demetri asked. That made sense. Or, well, sort of. All the people they'd seen were dead. Was it possible someone was alive here?

Besides Briar, obviously. The thought of her somewhere in this castle tugged at him unpleasantly, and in that moment, the desire to find her rose in him like a storm. To find her, to see her again...

He tamped that desire down. There was no telling what stood between them and her in this dreadful place. No guarantee that he *would* see her again. He needed to stay focused.

"Could've been an animal," Spencer muttered. "But...I think it was—a person."

Garrett flashed a jaunty grin. "No worries. If there's anything here, we'll handle it. What could be worse than that beast we hunted in the Black Forest last year?"

"I don't know, sire," Spencer said dryly. "Since we never actually caught it."

"Details," Garrett said breezily.

Demetri wandered over to the winding steps on the left. The creature who'd freed him had said Briar was in the tallest tower. Demetri had gone over it in his head, trying to remember the castle's layout. If they took this stairwell up, he was fairly certain they could—

He stopped dead.

A figure lay crumpled at the base of the steps.

Demetri's heartbeat skittered. Fear grasped at the back of his neck like a claw.

It was another corpse, curled up on the first step. Like a child tucked away for a nap. Though it was not the body of a child, but of a man. A servant, Demetri thought, as he raised his lantern, casting light over the body. The threadbare jacket draped over its emaciated frame bore the gold crest of the Mountain Kingdom, but it was cut differently than a guard's coat. Yellowed bone peeked through the doughy flesh on its knuckles. Demetri shuddered, his gaze lingering on the corpse's cheek, where bone jutted out like the point of a knife.

He was so fixated by the gruesome sight that he didn't notice when the corpse opened its eyes.

Then he did notice. His heart faltered. He forgot to breathe. Demetri stared at the corpse, and it stared at him.

Then it lunged for his throat.

2

REMAINS

GARRETT DIDN'T REALIZE ANYTHING was amiss until he heard Demetri shout. Then he looked around, and what he saw made his blood run cold.

Demetri lay at the base of a stairwell, struggling with a pale figure that had wrapped a hand around his throat. It was not until Garrett glimpsed the bone poking through that hand that he realized what had attacked his friend.

It was one of the corpses. Come *alive*.

Any thrill Garrett might have felt was vanquished in a rush of concern for Demetri. Leaving the repeater over his shoulder—Garrett didn't want to risk hitting Demetri—he reached for his pistol. Then a shot rang out from another direction. Garrett looked up and spotted Jones across the hall, pistol raised, a tendril of slate gray smoke curling up from the barrel. Her bullet struck the corpse below its neck, and the monster released Demetri, staggering back. Before anyone could get off another shot, it turned—and launched itself at Garrett.

Garrett didn't have time to shout. The corpse was so frail-looking that one solid blow should've shattered it, yet it fell upon him with the strength of a man twice its size. It barreled Garrett into the wall, crushing the breath from his lungs. As Garrett struggled to draw air, the creature sank its teeth into his shoulder with a vengeance.

The pain was immediate, flames erupting beneath his skin and racing down his arm. Garrett felt every shift of the corpse's jaw as it dug its teeth from side to side, razors sawing through his flesh. He lashed out with his legs, his free arm flailed, his entire body heaved to shove the thing off him. Just as he was sure the corpse would tear out a chunk of his shoulder, the monster jerked away from him. Shots cut through the air, and then, silence.

At first, all Garrett could do was breathe and try not to fall over. A muted ringing resounded in his ears. Waves of agony rolled through his shoulder. He breathed in deeply until he began to choke on the metallic tang of gunpowder residue. Once his knees stopped buckling, he looked down at the corpse, motionless, at his feet. Its body was ripped with bullets, and its head had been blasted off, leaving a pink glob on the carpet.

Garrett tangled his fingers in his hair, gripping the ends tight. Trying to ground himself. He had seen plenty of mad things in his last two years, things other people would not have believed. But a corpse come back to life was a little too mad, even for him.

Then his soldiers were there, demanding to know if he was all right, and someone grabbed his shoulder and the pain snapped him into focus. "Don't." He winced. "I'm fine." He was definitely *not* fine, or at least, his shoulder wasn't. But he was more concerned about his guards. As they stepped back, he looked them over and only relaxed once he determined they were unharmed, if a little shaken. Then he looked for Demetri. Garrett slumped in relief when he saw him on his feet, his brown hair mussed, rubbing his bruised throat.

"Is everyone all right?" Demetri's voice was rough.

"Think so," Garrett replied. "Are *you* all right?"

"I'm alive. But then, so was that—thing." Demetri pointed at the corpse.

"That thing was dead," Jones said in a trembling voice. "If it was dead before, how do we know it's dead now?"

"We don't," Spencer said bleakly. "And we don't know the rest of them out there are dead, either."

Garrett looked into the courtyard. His stomach fluttered with unease. Even *he* didn't fancy taking on an army of corpses, not if they were as strong and violent as this one. "Let's get moving." He tried to inject some confidence into his voice. If his soldiers saw he was not afraid, it might ease their fear as well.

"It's this way." Demetri pointed to the stairwell on the left—the same stairwell the corpse had been in. "Up this tower."

They started up the stairs, but one of the soldiers, a bearded man named Kale, stopped Garrett, pulling out a coarse bandage for his shoulder. Garrett stood still while Kale wrapped the cloth over the tatters of his coat sleeve. As he tucked the ends of the bandage in, Garrett glanced at the corpse on the floor beside them.

One of its bony fingers twitched.

"Let's go," Garrett said quickly, pulling away and turning for the tower stairwell.

The tower was windowless and so black that Garrett could scarcely see Kale in front of him, carrying a gear-bulb lantern. In the narrow stairwell, the yellow bulb pulsated with heat. After ten minutes of climbing, the sweat dampening Garrett's brow began to trickle down his face.

A nervous thrill raced down Garrett's spine. He would never have predicted they'd come across walking corpses on this venture, though he had hoped for some entertainment. Of course, what he called *entertainment*, other men called danger—searching for sea monsters in the Hyperic Ocean, chasing down bandits from the Desert Kingdom. Most people probably thought his thirst for danger bordered on insanity. He knew Demetri did, though the prince was too polite and too good a friend to say so.

Sometimes, Garrett thought he was a little insane himself. Certainly something had broken inside him when Snow died.

Truthfully, this venture hit too close to home for Garrett. These days, he liked a dangerous quest because he could lose himself in it and forget his ghosts for a time. He could dull the ache inside him in a rush of adrenaline. But this particular quest—to wake a *sleeping princess*—brought a different kind of rush. A rush of memories Garrett could not escape.

Halfway up the stairwell, they stopped. The air inside the tower was still and stale, but now Garrett could feel a draft. He peered over Kale's shoulder and saw Demetri bend his face close to the wall.

"There's a door here, I think," Demetri mumbled. He pushed at the wall. "It's hard to see—"

The wall opened abruptly, and Demetri fell through.

They all followed. As Garrett passed through the opening, he saw it *was* a door, built into the wall, only discernible by its iron-rimmed edges. Through the door, a wide corridor stretched before them, a burgundy paneled floor lined with marble pillars.

The corridor opened into a vast hall. Though it stood in darkness and disrepair, Garrett perceived it had once been quite lavish. The walls were intricately etched and covered with murals in an array of silvery blue and deep crimson. In the muted glow of their lanterns, the figures in the murals were cast in a sinister light—twisted fairies, black-eyed and waif-like, menacing kings, grim and monstrous. Demetri slowed as they passed through the room, and Garrett wondered if he was lost. But then he saw the wistful glint in Demetri's eyes, and Garrett knew he remembered this hall very well.

Demetri opened a set of oak-wood doors on the left. "This opens into the ballroom. From here, we can get to the throne—" He broke off.

When Garrett joined him, he saw why.

The ballroom was filled with corpses, like those in the courtyard. Drooping in gilded chairs and draped across benches, their skeletal arms dangling by their sides. Women in gossamer gowns frothy with lace, and men with old-fashioned cravats tied at their necks. Silent and still, rotting in their moth-eaten dress.

"All right," Kale said. "This is getting creepy."

Spencer cast him a dubious look. "Only just now? All the other corpses, not to mention the one that attacked us—that wasn't creepy enough?"

"Stones," Demetri mumbled. "The ball..."

"What ball?" Garrett asked.

"The night Briar fell to the sleeping curse. There was a ball. For her birthday—we met up before, and that's when she—" Demetri broke off, his face wan in the light of his lantern.

"So whatever happened to these people," Garrett said. "You're saying it happened the night your princess fell to her curse?"

"The same night, I think. Maybe *when* she fell to her curse."

Foreboding prickled at the back of Garrett's neck like a spider. "They weren't part of the curse, were they? I mean, it was just your princess who was cursed and not the whole castle?"

"So far as I know." There was a helpless note in Demetri's voice. "No, so far as any of them knew. If it was more than just Briar who was cursed, no one knew."

Garrett scratched his chin. "And if all these people were struck down like this, the same night of the curse—then who put your princess in this tower?"

"Begging your pardon, Highness," Jones said, "but maybe we should keep going. If any of these corpses come to life like that one downstairs..."

Most of the corpses lined the sides of the room, but many were sprawled across the floor, as though they had died while they were dancing. With Demetri leading them, Garrett and his soldiers picked their way through the ballroom the same way they might on a battlefield filled with fallen warriors.

The throne room occupied the third and fourth floor, stretching out below them. Two white, marble stairwells curved down into the throne room on each side. They had just reached the top of the stairs when Jones let out a terrible scream.

Garrett whirled around. At first, he could not see what had gone wrong. Young Jones stood frozen, as though she'd been petrified. Then she jerked, and that's when Garrett saw the white hand wrapped around her ankle.

One of the fallen dancers had grabbed Jones by the leg.

Jones, gibbering, tugged her leg, trying to free herself. Garrett stepped forward to help, but the corpse lurched, a blur in the darkness. Before Garrett could reach for his gun, it was on its feet and on Jones, ripping into her with hands and teeth like a rabid dog. Bits of flesh flew into the air as the corpse, clad in a spotted pink gown, bore Jones to the floor beneath its weight. Jones's screams devolved into breathless gurgles, her limbs twitching on the floor.

"*No!*" Garrett's repeater was in his hands before he knew it, but it was too late. Jones was gone. Garrett fought past a wave of shocked grief as he raised his rifle. He didn't care how bad his aim was; it didn't matter, anyway. There was no saving Jones, but he would be damned if he let that corpse savage her further.

Before he could start shooting, another shout cut through the air. Garrett turned and saw another of his soldiers wrestling with two corpses on either side of him. The soldier bellowed as one of the corpses sank its teeth into his neck.

"Garrett, look out!" Demetri yelled. Garrett turned a third time to see a corpse charging at him. Without a thought, he pointed his rifle and pulled back on the trigger. Like clockwork, the gears in the rifle spun and clicked, and bullets shot from the barrel in rapid succession. The *tack-a-tack-a-tack-a-tack* of the gun filled his ears, the force of it jarring him to the bone. But he didn't stop shooting, not even when the corpse fell to the floor. Through a haze of caustic smoke, Garrett watched as more corpses rose, lunging upright, peeling themselves off the walls.

It was a bizarre scene, like something out of a nightmare. Garrett kept his finger on the rifle's trigger and half-ran, half-leapt backwards. He nearly tripped over a mangled body that might have been one of his guards, and then he tumbled into Spencer, who held pistols in both hands.

Garrett stopped shooting long enough to shout, "Down the stairs!" and he and Spencer retreated to the third floor. He didn't see anyone else. Demetri needed to get to his princess so they could get out of this place. "Demetri!" Garrett shouted. "Where's Demetri?"

Spencer stumbled down the last few steps, looking blankly at his prince. The soldier was probably deaf from the gunfire. Garrett could hardly hear himself speak. "Demetri!" he yelled. "Where is—"

Then Spencer hollered—Garrett thought he said something like, "*Look out, sire!*" Spencer pushed past him and took aim with his pistol, firing off more rounds. He only got three shots off before the crack of bullets went silent; he was out of ammunition. Garrett raised his rifle at the oncoming gaggle of corpses, but when he pulled the trigger, nothing happened. He was out too.

"Stones," he cursed.

"Have we got a plan, sire?" Spencer asked.

"Erm." Garrett eyed the approaching horde. "Yes. We do. Run!"

They sprinted across the throne room, their boots beating an echo against the mosaic floor. Garrett ejected the spent case from his rifle as they ran, but he couldn't load it at full speed like this.

At the back of the throne room, they ducked behind a couple of pillars. Garrett bent to reload his rifle. "What happened to Demetri?"

"Don't know." Spencer teetered from one foot to the other as he watched the advancing corpses. He must have been out of bullets entirely, because he didn't reload his pistols. "I thought I saw him going down the stairs before us, but after that—I don't know, sire."

Garrett cursed. "Go." He jerked a thumb over his shoulder. "The tower should be that way. See if you can find that blasted princess, and—"

"Pardon, sire, but it's you who should go," Spencer interrupted. "I'll hold off these monsters. I won't leave you here, and if you can't wake that princess, you'll carry her better than I."

True enough. Spencer was quite scrawny, and though Garrett hated to leave him behind, there wasn't time to argue. "Here." Garrett handed his repeater to Spencer, and the last of his ammunition. Then he tore down the corridor behind him, hoping it would lead to the tower.

He slowed his pace as the darkness entombed him. He had no lantern and there were no windows this way. He jogged down the corridor, arm half-raised, grasping into the open air to keep from running into anything. His eyes began to adjust enough to glimpse his surroundings. Empty sconces built into the wall jutted over him like claws.

By some mercy, the corridor ended at a tower with a winding stairwell. Garrett looked left and right. Then he dashed up the stairs.

He couldn't run the whole way. His sides ached, his throat began to burn, and his shoulder throbbed beneath its bandage, in time with his racing heartbeat. He stopped to take several gulps of air before starting again. His legs quivered, threatening to give out, but he had to keep going. His life and all his soldiers' lives depended on it.

The stairs finally came to an end at the top of the tower, where there was a stout oak door. Pausing to catch his breath, he leaned against the door, listening for pursuit. But with his ears buzzing from the gunfire, all he could hear was his own panting.

Praying to all the stars that nothing was coming after him, he straightened, tugged on the iron door latch, and burst into the tower.

A dank cold struck him as soon as he entered the room, and it was such a harsh cold that a shiver spasmed through him. He found himself in a round room with a rough-cut, flagstone floor. The ceiling tapered overhead, and narrow windows lined the walls. Garrett suspected the room had once been a watchtower. The long windows allowed shafts of moonlight to pierce the dark, and it was by that light that Garrett saw the girl in the center of the room, sleeping upon a marble dais.

That was it. There was nothing else in the room. The dais the girl lay upon was like a bier for burial, and Garrett approached it with one hand on his pistol, half-expecting the girl to come alive and attack him like the others. But she remained still, and when Garrett stopped at her side, he was relieved to see she did not look corpse-like or rotted like the others had.

Someone had definitely placed her here. She was like a beam of moonlight, white arms crossed over the bodice of her diaphanous, cream gown. Her hair was pale, too pale to be called yellow or blond, and her face was pale too, her pointed chin and her hollowed cheeks and her upturned nose. The only color in her face was a purplish bruising beneath her eyes, like dark circles on the face of someone who hadn't slept enough. Which was ironic, not to mention weird. A hysterical urge to laugh rose in Garrett, but it withered quickly.

Garrett gazed at her. He listened to the wind as it blustered through the windows, the seconds ticking by. He hadn't the slightest idea how to wake this girl. Demetri had been told he would just *know* how to wake her, but Garrett had never met or seen her before. He had no idea what to do.

He dropped his hand from his pistol and curled his fingers into a fist. That wasn't entirely true. If he was honest with himself...if he allowed himself to think on his past.... He sucked in a breath. He felt jittery, and it wasn't because he'd just run up a flight of stairs.

It was because he did have an idea—an inkling—of what might wake this princess. But it hadn't worked for him before—he'd been told it would, and it hadn't, and his life had been dark and cold ever since. And besides, he was not the prince to wake this girl. He was not her true love. He didn't even know her.

He would just have to carry her out. The thought made Garrett's tired legs tremble and his bandaged shoulder ache, but he saw no other way. As he leaned down to scoop her up, a gunshot rang out below, reverberating up through the tower.

Garrett spun, darting to the door. He peered into the darkness, straining to hear something —another shot, a scream, footsteps, anything—but there was only quiet. If there were corpses coming—he couldn't fight them off and carry the princess, he couldn't do both—

"Curse me," Garrett swore. He had no choice. He had to try to wake her.

He crossed the room to her in five strides. Without stopping to think—if he thought about it, he couldn't do it—he leaned over her and pressed his lips against hers.

He kissed her.

Her lips were cold and unmoving. It was a quick kiss, but in those few seconds, memories flooded through Garrett, a tide he could not hold back. Memories of another princess, memories of his Snow. Black curls framing her laughing face. The touch of her hand upon his cheek. And worse memories—Snow sleeping upon a bier, just like Princess Briar. Her lips cold and still beneath his. Cold and still like death.

Then, he had pulled back from his sleeping princess, from Snow, and seen no change in her. Then, she had slumbered on like the dead, no matter how many times he kissed her. Then, he had failed to wake her. He had failed to wake Snow, his fierce, kind, radiant Snow.

He pulled back from Princess Briar now, his face inches from hers. The second that followed seemed to last an eon, time suspended in the air between his lips and hers.

And then, Briar opened her eyes.

3
RETURNED

BRIAR DANCED. SHE DANCED alone in a bright, empty hall. Candles burned in wooden chandeliers above her, but she was cold. She had been cold for the longest time. She knew what warmth was, but she could not recall what it felt like.

Her feet ached. Bruised, battered, bleeding. She had been dancing for such a long time. Her body felt like lead, weighted down, but she had to keep dancing.

Then everything...*flickered.*

Briar stopped dancing. That was a marvel—she couldn't remember a time when she had not danced. She spoke to people sometimes, here in this hall, but she never stopped dancing. She always, always danced.

And now she stopped.

She felt strange—light, as though a load had been lifted from her. And in that second when everything *flickered*—there was the faintest touch. A ghost of a whisper. A warm breath upon her lips.

Warm. Warmth.

Her surroundings fell away in a swoop, and then she was awake.

She knew instantly that she was awake. She knew she had been asleep. She didn't know anything else. She had been dancing (dancing?—she hated to dance), and now she was here. Awake.

Also, there was a man leaning over her, his face inches from her own.

Only for a second, and then he wrenched back. Briar flinched. Not really a man, she thought, her eyes sweeping over him. At the cusp of becoming a man, maybe a year older than herself. How old was she? Fifteen. No, not anymore—sixteen. She was sixteen.

Sixteen.

"By the gift." The words tore from her throat in a raspy voice. "The curse."

She sat upright, and every joint in her body creaked in protest. Keen pains woke all over her, as though she'd been trampled by a horse and carriage. She closed her eyes and breathed in through her teeth.

"Princess Briar?"

Briar opened her eyes. For a moment, her vision swam, everything blurry. That no-longer-a-boy-not-quite-a-man was still there. Briar blinked several times, allowing her eyes to clear. The stranger before her had a bloodstained bandage wrapped around his shoulder, over the sleeve of his gray coat. The coat was fine wool, but the style and cut were unfamiliar to her, buttoned at the top and cutaway down the front, revealing a navy blue waistcoat beneath it. He looked like a wraith, or like he'd seen a wraith. The only color in his face was two red spots on his cheeks, as though he was cold, or like he'd been running. He had pine green eyes—a little wild-looking—and blond hair, curls cut so short they could hardly be called curls.

Briar frowned at him. He *was* a stranger, wasn't he? Only, her mind felt muddied, her thoughts tangling together, and—there was just something familiar about this young man. She couldn't recall seeing him before; she didn't know his name, and yet.... When she looked at him, a sense of *rightness* came over her.

Briar swept another glance at him, and that was when she spotted the pistol in his hand. That sense of familiarity and comfort vanished, and she eyed the weapon cautiously, twisting her fingers in the folds of her skirt.

But the boy-man followed her gaze and holstered the pistol. "You are Princess Briar?" He didn't quite meet her eyes. "I didn't wake the wrong sleeping princess, did I?"

Briar tried to clear her throat. She was a little appeased by him putting his weapon away—a little. "How many sleeping princesses could there be?"

"You'd be surprised," the boy-man said. His voice was a smooth, deep timbre that she found oddly calming. Her wariness began to fade.

"I'm Briar," she said. "Who are you?"

"My name is Garrett." He raked a hand through his hair. "Are you—can you stand? Can you walk?"

Briar swung her legs over the dais. The movement woke dull aches and sharp pains all over her body. Her joints screamed in protest, her back throbbed. Everything was sore, and she didn't know if it was from sleeping on such a hard surface, or if there was more to it—if there was something *wrong* with her. Still, it wasn't so bad that she couldn't move, so she slipped onto her feet. She stood, waiting to see if she would fall over. She tottered a bit—*stones*, her feet ached—but she felt stable enough.

"I can walk," she said.

"Right. Well." Garrett still looked a little shell-shocked. He ran a hand over his mouth. "Look, I know this must be confusing, and you don't know who I am, and you probably have a million questions. But we're in a bit of a bind here, so if you could just follow me, then—"

"Follow you?" Briar surveyed him, pinpricks of curiosity mingling with suspicion inside her. No matter how nice his voice was—and his face, come to that—she had no idea if she could trust this Garrett. And something about what he'd said disquieted her. *A million questions.* Questions about what? Her thoughts were still confused and muddled, her memories dancing just out of reach. "Look, I *don't* know you and—where are we?" She looked around the sparse room. "Am I home?" The drab walls didn't look like home.

Briar tilted her head and gazed up at the dark ceiling. It seemed to go on and on, tapering to a point so high she couldn't see it. "This must be the castle. I was asleep, the curse..." She darted a glance at Garrett. His strange clothes... *The curse, the curse.* That had come to her the moment she'd opened her eyes, but the details had eluded her memory until now. Pieces suddenly fell into place. "Has it—did a hundred years pass? That's why I'm awake, isn't it? Stars and stones—" If it had been a hundred years, then— "Demetri," she breathed. *No.* If it had been a hundred years, then Demetri—he was *gone*—

A terrible force pressed down upon her. Grief. She felt like she was being crushed beneath it. But then, miraculously—

"Demetri's fine," Garrett said. "At least, I hope he is."

Briar's head snapped up. "He's *alive?* He's *here?*"

Garrett nodded.

Relief coursed through Briar. She felt like she was spinning, her whole body swinging through the pendulum of her emotions. "But the curse—"

"I broke it. Early."

"How?"

"And anyway," Garrett went on, "Demetri was kept alive these past eighty years by some spell. He hasn't aged a day. Look, princess—" The word *princess* did not sound like a title from him, but something more casual, like a nickname "—I know you have a lot of questions. But we're not alone here. There are dangerous...people...in the castle, and we need to get out of here. All right?"

Briar stared at him without really seeing him. Her mind whirred like a wind-up clock, all this new information bumping about in her head. Eighty years? Demetri kept alive by a spell? Dangerous people? She shook her head. It was too much, too fast. She felt like there was a bell between her ears, shutting out everything else—

"...Princess?"

The tolling stopped, broken apart by Garrett's deep voice. Briar shook her head one last time and looked at him.

"I don't mean to be insensitive," Garrett said, tossing a look at the door behind him, "but we *really* need to move."

Briar ran her gaze over him one last time. Her eyes alighted on a second pistol at his waist. "Can I have a pistol?" she asked. She'd feel much better with a pistol in hand.

He removed both pistols from their holsters and handed her one. Briar took it, impressed. It was a rare man, or boy-man, that did not object to a girl asking for arms. Then again, maybe times had changed in the past eighty years. She could hope.

Eighty years. The thought still made her dizzy. She knew there were other questions to ask, implications she had not considered yet. But her mind shied away from it all. She could only focus on what was in front of her. Pushing everything else to the back of her mind, Briar said, "All right. Lead the way."

Garrett hesitated, giving her a look she could not comprehend. Then he started down the stairwell.

She followed, using the wall to steady herself. The stone was like pebbled ice beneath her hand. Briar wondered what time of year it was. She could hear the wind gusting in through the tower top above them, but even in her flimsy gown, she didn't feel cold.

She kept her gaze fixed on Garrett's broad back as they made their way down the stairs, although even in the dark, she could see quite well—even better than she had back in the tower. Her eyes must still be adjusted to being asleep, she supposed. She wondered who these dangerous people in the castle were. Invaders? But who? There was something weird about the way Garrett had said *dangerous people.* Maybe not people at all. Fairies? But fairies were sworn not to kill humans, so how dangerous could they be?

A frantic laugh bubbled up in Briar's throat, and she swallowed it back. She knew better than anyone how dangerous a fairy could be.

"I heard a shot earlier, before you woke," Garrett said. His voice was a little loud, Briar thought, considering there were dangerous people about. "It must have been either Demetri or one of my guards, but no one ran up here, so..."

"How do you know it was one of them? What about everyone else in the castle?"

Garrett didn't answer. Perhaps he hadn't heard her. Briar raised her voice and repeated the question, and this time, Garrett turned around. A muscle worked in his jaw. "Princess," he said, "everyone in the castle—they're—"

Briar reached out a hand to silence him. She thought she'd heard something below, a noise resounding up the stairs. A sort of shuffling, like shoes scraping against the floor.

"What is it?" Garrett whispered.

"Something below," she said. "Can't you hear that? I think...maybe footsteps?"

Garrett tapped his ear. "I can't hear too well right now. Too much gunfire." He paused. "Do they sound friendly?"

"How can I tell if footsteps sound friendly?"

"Fair point." Garrett shifted the pistol in his hand. "I suppose we'll just have to go see."

He continued down the stairs. Briar inched along behind him, staying as close as she could. She did not know him, she reminded herself. She needed to be careful. But she couldn't banish the inexplicable sense of trust he instilled in her. She felt safer hovering behind him, close enough that she could have reached out and laid a hand upon his broad back.

But she didn't. She kept one hand on the wall and the other clutching her pistol. The gun's metal trigger was cold against the crook of her finger. She was not a very good shot, she remembered, though at close range, surely she could hit *something*.

They reached the bottom of the stairs and came out into a dark corridor. Briar realized she was holding her breath and blew it out, slow and silent, through her nostrils. She cast her gaze around, noting the walls, caked over in gray grunge. They used to be white, she realized, white limestone. For the first time, she recognized her surroundings. "The western tower? They put me in the *western tower*? That place is a dungeon. Why would my parents put me in there?"

Garrett started down the corridor. "I don't think they did."

Briar followed him. Apprehension created knots in her stomach. Her parents. Garrett said Demetri had been kept alive by a spell these past eighty years. "My parents. Are they—are they dead?"

Garrett went still. He turned around, his face drawn in solemn lines.

"Are they? They must be." He'd said Demetri had been kept alive by a spell—not *everyone* was kept alive by a spell. Briar waited for that force to sweep over her, that awful crushing she'd felt in the split-second when she'd thought Demetri was dead.

But it didn't come. The thought that her parents were dead—that *everyone* in the castle might be—wasn't a good one, but Briar mostly felt empty. There was a feeble ache in her chest.

She should feel terrible about that, she supposed, but then, she'd never really known her parents. They'd cut themselves off from her.

"Princess." Garrett drew a breath. "The thing is, your parents—and everyone in the castle—" He hesitated.

"It's all right," Briar said, though her voice did not sound reassuring. It sounded as hollow as she felt. "You can tell me—that is, I was never—"

She broke off, her gaze catching on something up ahead, beyond Garrett. A shadow. A darkness. She couldn't quite make it out, but something about the shape of it seemed wrong somehow, sending a sinister chill down Briar's spine. Lifting an arm to point, she said, "Sorry, but—what is that?"

Garrett turned, and then he stiffened. Briar stepped abreast of him. A lump of...*something*...lay on the floor. The two of them edged forward for a closer look, Briar's heart hammering in her chest. Then Garrett cursed.

It was a body. A dead man in a military uniform, Briar thought, judging by the brass buttons on the remains of his dark blue coat. She couldn't say much about the man himself, because he'd been...*shredded*. Leaving nothing but a viscous mass of flesh and sinew among tattered clothes. Briar watched the blood as it trickled down the corridor like spilled wine. She could not look away.

"*Damn* it." Garrett crouched down, his gaze intent upon what was left of the man's face. "Rigg." Pain rippled through his expression. "One of my soldiers. I bet it was him I heard earlier, the shot I heard."

"But—" Alarm shot through Briar like a bullet. She tore her gaze from the body. "What was he shoot—"

Before she could finish, something gripped the hem of her dress and *tugged*.

A hoarse cry escaped her throat as she toppled backwards. Her shoulder slammed into the floor, and her head *banged* against the flagstones. Dazed, she struggled to right herself, but her vision swam in a haze of shadows. Garrett shouted nearby—he had to be nearby, she thought, but he sounded faraway.

Then something was on her, squashing her against the floor, clutching her by the shoulders, and a hot, fetid breath assaulted her senses. She remembered her pistol too late; she had dropped it somewhere. She flailed beneath the weight of the...*thing*, hoping to close her fingers around the gun, but her hands scrabbled uselessly against the floor. The creature had her clavicle in a breaking grip; she expected the bone to shatter any minute. Then she was yanked to her feet, a cold arm closing across her chest. Fear tore through Briar, threatening to crush her as surely as the creature's grip. There was Garrett, fighting two...people?...twisted people, corpses come alive. As he kicked one back from him, he turned and—for a second—he met her gaze. His green eyes were desperate, and something about them *tugged* at Briar.

Then she was dragged backwards down an intersecting corridor, and Garrett vanished from her line of sight. Briar struggled, but the arm across her chest was so heavy that her breath stuttered, trapped in her chest. A door slammed in the darkness, and Briar was thrown to the floor.

She scrambled into a seated position, stifling a sneeze as dust-laden air filled her nostrils. Her heart was racing so fast, Briar thought it would burst right out of her chest. She was in a small, windowless room—a closet, maybe?—but she could still see in the dark. Half a wooden shelf, layered with mold, stood against the wall on her left, and ragged bits of linen covered the floor. Then her eyes fell on the...person...standing before her, and her breath stuck in her throat.

It *was* a person, but a person gone wrong. A girl her own age, or a bit younger, and a bit smaller. That didn't seem possible; whatever had grabbed her had constrained her with ease, but Briar should have had no problem fighting off this pinprick of a girl. But this was no normal girl. Her skin bore a bluish tinge, like she'd been soaked in dye, and bruises marred her neck and face. The dress she wore hung in scraps over her gaunt frame, and one of the sleeves had been ripped off, exposing an arm purpled with veins. Her limp hair was lined with gray, and her face ...that face...

Briar swallowed. The girl's face was sallow, her cheeks sunken in. The skin there looked thin and waxy, barely clinging to the bone beneath it, and her eyes bulged as though their place in their sockets was tenuous.

"Hello, Briar."

Briar recoiled. The girl—the corpse—*spoke.*

"Who—who are you?" Briar demanded. "What do you want?"

The girl's gaping mouth twisted. "You don't remember me, do you? To think. Your closest cousin, and you don't even remember me."

"Well, to be fair, I've been asleep for eighty years." Briar knew she was babbling, but her mind wasn't on her words. It was on her hand, casting behind her, hoping to find something she could use to defend herself. "So my memory is bound to be a little—" She sucked in a sharp breath. "*Stones.*" Her eyes traveled over the girl's face a second time. She *did* know her. "Laurel?"

"So you do remember." Laurel's voice was a sibilant whisper. "Remembrance. Memory. Sometimes, I can...remember. I remember *you*, Briar. I think every corpse in this castle remembers you."

"Every corpse?" Briar winced as her hand came down on something sharp behind her, breaking her skin open. She glanced down and saw a shard of glazed china beneath her palm. Her blood lay slickly over the white porcelain, staining it crimson. "What do you mean?"

"We're all corpses, Briar. Or hadn't you noticed?" Laurel's eyes gleamed with a manic light. "And do you know *why?* Do you know what happened to us?"

"No." And though Briar wanted to know, her desire to escape took precedence. She shoved down the fear inside her and shuddered away, half in pretense. As she dropped her gaze, she ran her eyes along the floor. Most of the china had been crushed to a fine grit, but there was a vase behind her, intact. "Although, I imagine most people would be corpse-like after eighty years."

She looked up to see Laurel lumber towards her. She closed the distance between them quickly, considering her awkward gait. "Look at you," the monster that had been Laurel said. She snatched a strand of Briar's hair and pinched it between her fingers. "All pretty and warm and alive. Well..." She ran a clammy finger down Briar's face. "Not warm. And not *so* pretty. But alive. Tell me, Briar—" She seized a fistful of Briar's hair "—why is it that you're alive, when all the rest of us are dead?"

Briar's heart seemed to trip over itself. "Dead?"

"We all rotted away," the Laurel monster whispered. Air whistled through her chipped teeth. "At first, we slept, like you. But then the hunger drove us awake. We couldn't move. Couldn't rise. Couldn't walk, couldn't talk, couldn't eat. Only our minds were awake. Awake and aware as we slowly died, year by year. As we starved and rotted."

"I don't understand." Briar scuttled back, her hand knocking into the vase behind her. "Why were you asleep like me? What happened to you? How can you be...dead?"

"Shall I show you?" Laurel cocked her head. "What it means to be dead?"

Before Briar could respond, Laurel's hands were around her throat. She squeezed so tightly that Briar's head should have popped off. But in that second, Briar moved too. Her hand closed around the slender base of the vase behind her, and she swung it forward into Laurel's face.

Briar had only hoped that it would be enough to knock Laurel off balance. But an odd thing happened as she swung her arm. Strength...flowed...through her limb. She felt it like an electric charge, jolting her muscles awake. And when the vase *crunched* into the side of Laurel's face, it sent the monster girl flying across the closet. Her rotted body smacked against the back corner so hard that the wall cracked, flecks of stony grit puffing into the air. Laurel collapsed on the floor, motionless.

Briar gaped, shock coursing through her. What had she done? *How* had she done it? She stared at her hand, where she still clutched a few shards of the broken vase. The china had sliced through her palm, and blood ran through her clenched fingers in dark rivulets.

A groan drew her attention. Laurel was stirring. Briar didn't wait for her to rise. She darted through the door, slamming it shut behind her.

She didn't stop running out in the corridor, though her muscles, aching even worse after struggling with the Laurel monster, protested every step. She ran until she nearly tripped over the body they'd found earlier, the soldier. This was where she'd left Garrett.

But he wasn't there. The corridor was empty. Save for her and the dead man.

Briar heaved in a breath, trying to get air to her burning lungs. But the panic she'd fought down before was rising to the surface, flooding her chest and leaving no room for air. Everything that had happened began to sink in. *The curse. Eighty years. Demetri, alive, put in a spell. Garrett. Garrett?*

Her parents. Laurel, a corpse. Everyone in the castle.

Had they all become these walking dead? *Why?*

"Garrett?" Her voice resounded in the dark. Clenching her lips together, Briar looked down at the dead man. She wondered if he had a gun on him. Or maybe her pistol was nearby, she had dropped it here—

"Briar?"

Briar choked on a scream as she spun around, but it was only Garrett, emerging from the dark corridor. She felt her pulse, drumming in her throat, begin to slow, and for the first time since she'd run from Laurel, she took in a full breath.

"What happened to you?" Garrett's eyes lit on her dress. "Are you hurt?"

"I—no." Briar followed his gaze and realized she had wiped her bloody hand on her waist, smearing the pearl white skirt with scarlet streaks. Belatedly, she remembered that her hand was bloody because she *was* hurt, but that didn't seem important right now. "I'm fine. Where were you?"

Garrett grimaced. "One of the corpses chased me back there—what happened to you?"

In a quaking voice, Briar told him. When she mentioned that she hadn't left Laurel entirely unconscious, Garrett took her by the arm and steered her down the corridor, towards the throne room.

Briar was still processing what Laurel had said. "She said they were all like her." Her words came out stilted. "Everyone in the castle. She said they...fell asleep. When I did. But that wasn't part of the curse, that shouldn't have happened—"

"Princess—"

"—and if they all slept, if they're all—like her—everyone, they're all dead, they're all *monsters*—"

"Briar." Garrett rounded on her. He seemed massive in the narrow corridor, crowding in on her. He placed his hands on her shoulders, exerting a pressure that seemed to ground her. The weight of his grip was soothing. "I know," he said. "I mean, I don't know, I'm still figuring this out like you are, but—" He inhaled "—I know. All right?"

She gazed up at him. His eyes bore a raw affinity for...what? For what she was feeling? For what she was going through, waking to this madness? She didn't know, but she felt it too, deep in the crevices of her soul.

The *click* of a gun being cocked sounded into the stillness. Briar and Garrett spun around. Two figures stood in shadow at the end of the corridor, where it opened into the throne room. Garrett began to raise his pistol, but Briar stepped in front of him. "It's okay," she said. "I know who it is." She would have recognized that gangly frame and tousled head of hair anywhere.

Demetri.

4

DISPLACED

D EMETRI WOULD HAVE BEEN dead if it wasn't for Spencer. When the corpses attacked in the ballroom, Demetri had descended into the throne room with two soldiers at his side, doing his best to fend off the monsters with his rapier. He and Kale had hidden beneath the grand staircase, but they were discovered, and then they would have been dead—if not for Spencer. The soldier had gotten hold of Garrett's repeater and charged in amidst the monsters, clearing the way for Demetri and Kale. Then he led the bulk of them out the eastern entrance, while Demetri and Kale headed towards Briar's tower.

Except Briar was here. Just outside the throne room, with Garrett, awake and alive and unhurt.

"Briar?" Demetri croaked. "Is that—that *is* you?"

The two figures, one pale and one tall, hurried towards them. The tall one was Garrett, looking disheveled and lost. And the other...was Briar.

She was really here. Demetri couldn't speak, but neither could he take his eyes off her. His emotions ran roughshod over him, so intensely that he almost felt like he would be sick. For years, he'd kept Briar alive in his memory. And as he'd searched for her in this castle, he'd imagined her as she had been that night in his quarters. Dressed in her cream muslin gown, her shining hair piled atop her head, her gray eyes fierce and storm-like.

In the past eighty-two years, that memory had weighed on him so heavily that he'd thought he might break beneath it. But now, as she stood here before him, his heavy heart vanished. He felt so light, he thought he might pass out. Briar was alive. She was awake.

She was...awake?

"Demetri!" Briar reached him and closed her hands around his arms. "You *are* alive—you're *you*—Garrett said you'd been put under a spell, he said eighty years passed, but you—"

"Eighty-two years," Demetri said, his voice as hoarse as hers. Her hands were so cold, he could feel it all the way through his coat and shirt. It lent an oddly unfamiliar cast to her touch, and Demetri had the urge to flinch away. It was just unsettling, he told himself. Her icy grip did not much ease his fears that she was a ghost.

He looked at her closely, but she seemed all right. Well, she seemed unhurt. But she was paler than he remembered, with dark circles beneath her eyes. Her hair was pale too, no longer yellow, but almost white.

"You're awake." Demetri struggled to dispel this glazed, surreal feeling, like he'd been knocked over the head. "Are you all right? How do you feel?"

"Like a herd of wild horses trampled me," she said, "and my throat's a bit dry, but otherwise, Demetri, I'm all right. I can't believe it—I can't believe you broke the curse—well, Garrett broke it, but—"

"Yes." Demetri tore his eyes from Briar long enough to look at Garrett. "How did you do that, by the way?"

Garrett cleared his throat. The prince seemed to avoid his gaze. "That's kind of a long story."

"Can't be that long," Demetri reasoned. He tried to sound lighthearted, but he could hear the shakiness in his voice. This all felt so *strange*. Like a dream. "You weren't gone long. I don't think. I suppose I lost track of time fighting off those—"

"—walking corpses?" Briar supplied.

"You've seen them?" Startled, Demetri turned back to her.

"Demetri, I saw—my cousin Laurel. She was younger than me, you remember her, don't you?" Briar's face was grim. "It was her, but...it wasn't her. She was *dead*, rotted, but she was impossibly strong and she talked to me—"

"She *spoke* to you? Incredible. I haven't heard any of them speak."

"Well, Laurel certainly had a lot to say," Briar said wryly. "Though little of it made sense." Quite suddenly, she threw her arms around him. "I'm so glad you're all right, Demetri. I thought you'd be dead, or, well—"

"Very old and wrinkly?" Demetri wrapped his arms around her in return. The touch of her skin was still clammy, but he didn't care. That urge to flinch away from her was gone.

A moment later, Briar dropped her hands to his elbows. "I don't understand any of this though. These corpses, what happened to everyone—it doesn't make any sense. Laurel said they all slept like I did, at first, but it should have just been *me*. I was the one cursed."

"Supposedly," Demetri said, his thoughts turning dark. "But this all feels very curse-like to me." In fact, he could think of no other explanation. How did they know that fairy—*the dark fairy*—hadn't cast another curse? A curse on everyone in the castle?

"Pardon." Garrett stepped out of the shadows to join them, breaking through Demetri's morbid thoughts. "I'd like to get to the bottom of this as well, and I realize you two have a lot of catching up to do, but I'd also like to get out of here, and we can have a nice discussion about everything later. Yes?"

"Sounds good to me, sire," Kale agreed.

Briar cocked an eyebrow at Garrett. "Sire?"

He bent his head in an appropriation of a bow. "*Prince* Garrett, at your service. Or didn't I say that before?"

"No. You didn't."

"Apologies. Demetri, have you seen Spencer? I left him here—"

Demetri's heart gave a nasty tug. *Spencer.* He related what the soldier had done, leading the corpses off alone. Garrett's shadowed gaze turned even more grave. "Spencer. And Jones, and—"

"Your Highness," Kale said, "under these circumstances, Spencer wouldn't want you risking your life or theirs—" He indicated Demetri and Briar "—to look for him. He understood the risk when he came on this mission—we all did. Spencer could be anywhere in this castle, and, well..."

"I know." Garrett rubbed a hand over his face. He looked at Briar. "Well, princess, do you happen to know the quickest way out of here? Because I'd rather not go back the way we came."

Demetri thought of the corpses in the ballroom, and a fearful tremor shuddered through him. "Me neither."

Briar looked surprised and pleased at being asked for her advice. Although she was a princess, Demetri knew that precious few people at court had cared much for her opinion. Most people, he'd gathered, didn't bother with a girl who was going to fall into a cursed sleep for a hundred years, even if she was the daughter of the king. "We can go this way, for now."

They crept along the edge of the throne hall, weaving through russet marble pillars. The hall was empty of corpses now, waking or sleeping. The rustle of their clothing and every breath they took seemed to resound from wall to wall. Twice, Demetri half-jumped at a shadow, only to realize it was his own. He cast repeated glances over his shoulder at Briar, half-afraid she might disappear, until she noticed and slipped her hand into his.

He still couldn't believe this was happening. That this was real, that *Briar* was real, that she was here and awake and with him. He remembered feeling the same way the first time he'd met Briar, a few months before her sixteenth birthday. They'd been betrothed as infants—before Briar was cursed—but he had not met her until he came to the Mountain Kingdom, seeking her. It had been strange then, to meet this girl he had only known on paper for so many years. And it was even stranger now, to find again the same girl, nearly a century later. And for both of them to look so unchanged, after all that had happened.

Demetri was not unchanged. The thought made his stomach give an uncertain lurch.

At the ballroom stairs, Briar drew to a halt. "Right, if we go this way—" She pointed left towards the western wing of the palace "—we can get into my quarters."

"And we want to do that because...?" Garrett asked.

"Of course. She's got a passage in her rooms." Demetri couldn't believe he'd forgotten, given the number of times they'd used it. "It leads into the servants' quarters downstairs, near a side exit."

"And it has a lift," Briar said gamely. "I installed it."

"Er." Garrett sounded confused. "*You* installed it? You mean you had it installed."

"No," Demetri said. "*She* installed it."

"But, erm—" Garrett coughed. "That is to say, it—works?"

Briar shot him a narrow-eyed look as she turned, leading them into the western wing.

"Garrett," Demetri said, "you know that repeater you had? The one that works on gears?"

"A repeater?" Briar's voice rose with interest. "A repeating firearm?"

"What about it?"

"When was it invented?" Demetri asked.

"Just a few years ago. The model I have is the second proto-type, actually."

"Well, if Briar hadn't fallen asleep for eighty-two years, it would've been invented a lot sooner. Say, about eighty years ago."

"I wouldn't go that far," Briar said modestly.

"Briar, you had a sketch for a repeating firearm," Demetri said, and he couldn't keep a touch of admiration out of his voice. "I saw it."

"That's all it was," Briar said, "a sketch. And it was more of a repeating cannon."

"My point is," Demetri concluded, "her lift is safe enough. Trust me."

When they reached Briar's quarters, Kale and Garrett entered the rooms first, pistols in hand. Briar and Demetri followed. Like the rest of the castle, Briar's rooms were in darkness, but that was soon remedied when Briar located an old-fashioned lamp on a stained table inside. The acrid smell of burning oil flared to life as they lit the lamp, and for a moment, Demetri felt warm, at home, as though he'd been transported back in time. The present felt cold in comparison, even with Briar by his side.

"Well, it's no gear-bulb," Garrett said, taking the oil lamp from Briar, "but it'll do."

"A gear what?" Briar's eyes brightened.

"You'll see." Garrett glanced around the sitting room in the orange glow of the lamp. "I don't fancy being shut in a passage or locked in a lift with those monsters coming after us. Maybe we should scout the surrounding rooms before we go."

"I want to grab a few things, anyway," Briar said.

"Kale and I will have a lookout then." Garrett glanced at Demetri. "Shouldn't take long. If we're not back in ten minutes..."

"We'll...go on," Demetri said reluctantly.

"I was going to say come and find us," Garrett said in a hurt tone, "but if you'd rather we do the noble thing..."

They set out, disappearing into the adjoining parlor. "Come on, then." Briar turned the handle into her bedchamber.

Demetri tensed as the door squeaked open, but nothing jumped out at them. They stood in the doorway, side by side, blinking in the dark and the dust. Then Briar ventured in, found another oil lamp, and lit it.

Briar's room was a mess, and at first, Demetri feared another encounter with the corpses, thinking they had wrecked the place. But Briar wore a rueful smile. "Just like I left you."

Demetri lifted an amused eyebrow. "Bit of a slob, aren't you?" He had forgotten that. Stacks of books stood in tumbling piles in every corner of the room, and a model air machine sat near the foot of the large, four-poster bed. A mahogany vanity table was littered with jeweled necklaces, gold and silver rings, and many, many ribbons. All different colors—deep mauve, pale blush, peacock blue, butterscotch yellow—though they had long since faded, and some had been chewed through by insects or mice.

"I was in a hurry, getting ready for that stupid ball." Briar's gaze fixed on the vanity. "I wanted a lilac ribbon, and I couldn't find one."

"I can't believe you remember that. After all this time." Briar had not been wild about the ball, he remembered. As much as Demetri loved to dance, he hadn't been either. It had seemed such a farce, throwing a birthday ball for Briar on the eve of her curse. As though nothing bad was going to happen. But then, that had been Briar's parents' solution to everything about the curse—to pretend it never existed.

Even to pretend that Briar had not existed.

"All this time," Briar echoed. Her troubled gaze traveled around the room. "Eighty years."

"Eighty-two," Demetri murmured, a lump forming in his throat. He could never forget that. Not a single second of it. He felt like he did remember every second. He was sure he had been awake the entire time, though one of the doctors who had tended to him—after he'd escaped—had said that was unlikely. The doctor seemed to think Demetri would have been thoroughly mad, had that been the case.

Demetri wasn't sure he wasn't a little mad anyway. After all those years.

"Eighty-two." Briar took a few steps into the room, her fingers trailing along the wooden walls, tracing the carvings, pausing over the parts that had chipped away. "It doesn't feel like it's been that long. It doesn't feel like *any* time has passed, Demetri. Not to me. It feels like it was just yesterday. I can remember it so clearly, everything about that day—riding out into the woods with you, hoping to find a way to stop it. But all for nothing..."

Demetri heard the same frustration in her voice that he remembered feeling back then, that he *still* felt, undimmed by the past eighty-two years. No, after all this time, it had grown into something bigger, darker. A helpless rage. That Briar's life had been ruined by the dark fairy, though she'd done nothing to earn such vengeance. That she had been taken from him, Demetri, just when he had begun to feel for her—

The lump in his throat grew, until he thought it would block out all the air. He felt shaky again. Cold and shaky.

"I remember feeling so defeated." Briar's voice was full of woe. Demetri tried to focus on her, but her voice sounded like it was coming from very far away. "Do you remember what I said? That I just wished everyone would sleep for a hundred years along with me? Even though my parents never cared about me, even though I had no one else. I was just so afraid of what it would be like, to wake and find everything I knew was gone."

"I remember." Demetri's heart ached with remembering. He hadn't been willing to give up. He'd told Briar so, when she came to meet him before the ball. It didn't feel like yesterday to him, but that memory was clear and unbroken. For the first and only time, she'd shown him how afraid she was. And he'd stepped in close to her and whispered reassurances—her lips had been so close to his, so close they could have shared a breath, shared a kiss—

But they hadn't. Because the curse had come earlier than they ever expected.

"It's weird, though," Briar said.

Demetri looked up, blinking. He'd been so lost in that memory. It felt more real to him than this present moment did. "What?"

"Well—I remember everything like it was yesterday, but...it feels like there *should* be other memories. Memories in between then and now." She laughed, but there was an edge to her laughter. "I suppose I must have dreamed, while I was asleep. When I first woke, Demetri—I had the weirdest feeling I had been dancing."

Demetri tried to smile. "Dancing? You?"

"I know." Briar wrinkled her nose. "But it's true. It almost feels like I lived this other life. While I was asleep. I don't remember it, but I have a...sense of it." She pulled a face. "A sense. It makes *no* sense. Memories I can't remember. It's a paradox. Memories you can't remember don't exist. No sense can come of them."

"Always so methodical." Demetri felt a rush of affection for her. "You haven't changed, Briar."

The gleam in her eyes heightened. "But you have." She stepped forward, closing the distance between them. Just as she had that night. The last night they'd been together. "Haven't you?"

"Me? I can't have." Demetri's smile began to feel fixed, dark thoughts swirling in his head. "I spent the past eighty-two years in exactly the same place, doing exactly the same thing."

"And what was that?"

Demetri faltered. His smile failed him. It was a tide he couldn't hold back, those dark, swirling thoughts, and in an instant, he was there again. A captive, imprisoned. His surroundings fell away, Briar fell away, and he was engulfed in unending darkness. He could feel the weight of packed dirt over his head, and he knew that the fusty stench clogging up his nostrils was the stench of death—

Desperately, he pushed clear of those memories. Somehow, he surfaced through the darkness. But he could still feel it hovering close by, ready to drown him in an instant.

He said, without much thought, "I was thinking of you."

Whatever Briar expected him to say, that must not have been it, judging by the pleased look of surprise on her face. "Thinking of me?"

Demetri gazed at her, but it was becoming painful. As happy as he was to be near her, he could not look at her without remembering those eighty-two years. What he had been through. Every tortuous second. And he had the sudden, strange, awful thought that she was part of that darkness waiting to smother him. That she was some kind of foe.

He banished that dreadful idea, shaking himself. "All I wanted was to get back here." His voice came out hoarse. "To save you."

"To save me." Briar's gauzy gown brushed his arm, and the silk fabric against his skin was like a balm. She was real. She was not some shadowy foe, she was *Briar,* and she was real, and she was here. And everything would be all right again. "Normally—" She took his hand in hers "—I'd go off telling you I don't *need* saving from anyone, thank you very much—"

"I know." Demetri gripped her hand, though it was still startlingly cold.

"—but I really did need saving this time." She leaned forward until her lips were inches from his. The tip of her nose brushed his.

Demetri felt dizzy. His breath hitched in his throat. "Well, technically Garrett saved you. Not me."

"You're spoiling the moment, Demetri."

"Sorry," he said, the word little more than a low noise in the back of his throat.

Then she kissed him.

Her lips were cold too, so cold she might have sucked all the warmth from him, but Demetri didn't care. Briar kissed him vehemently, so full of everything they hadn't had a chance to have. Demetri brought her hand up between them, curling it against his chest, and his other arm wrapped around her. He never wanted it to end, this moment, this kiss, the kiss he'd nearly had eighty-two years ago.

But then Briar wrenched away from him with a gasp. It was so abrupt that it was almost painful, like ripping a sticky bandage off a raw wound.

"Briar?" Demetri felt dazed, addled by her kiss and her startling retreat. "What's wrong?"

She didn't answer. Her face was blank. She yanked out of his grip. As he watched, the blankness in her eyes gave way to fear.

"Briar?" he ventured. His chest felt tight, as though someone had built a clockwork contraption between his heart and his ribs, and the gear was being wound taut. "Are you all right? I'm sorry,

I—did I—" He shouldn't have kissed her like that, it wasn't proper—only she had kissed him, hadn't she— "I didn't mean to—"

"Where..." Briar's gaze traveled around her room. When she looked at him again, her eyes were wild. "Who are you?"

For a moment, Demetri forgot how to speak. Then, "I—what? Briar, it's me. It's Demetri."

She took a step back, shaking her head.

"Briar?" Demetri didn't want to scare her, but she was scaring him. He reached out and closed his hands around her arms. "Briar, it's me. It's Demetri. You know me...don't you?"

5

ECHOES

"BRIAR, IT'S ME. IT'S Demetri. You know me...don't you?"

Demetri. *Demetri*. He'd said that twice now, and it still didn't sound familiar to Briar. This boy was mad, she didn't know him, she was sure she didn't...but she didn't know where she was either. She didn't recognize him, didn't recognize this room...

She ran her tongue over her teeth as the rank tang of fear grew in her mouth. She didn't recognize anything. She didn't know why she was here. As the foreignness of her surroundings intensified, they seemed to grow bigger—the walls looming around her, the ceiling stretching high into the unknown.

And then, everything shifted. Like a fog rolling out, a fog Briar hadn't realized was there, blanketing her brain. Now that it was gone, everything became familiar again—the real world returned, bright, crisp, and full of color.

And with it, her memory.

A quiver shook through Briar. "Demetri?"

"Yes." The tension in Demetri's face vanished. "It's me. Are you all right?"

"I'm—fine." Demetri's hands rested on her arms, and the heat from his touch was somehow oppressive. "I—I'm sorry. I don't know what happened."

"You didn't know who I was." The corners of Demetri's eyes pinched in a frown.

"I'm sorry." Briar eased out of his grasp—not pulling away, just steadying herself. "I just...went blank." She felt cold as she realized what had happened. For a moment—just those few seconds—she hadn't remembered, or recognized, Demetri.

What was wrong with her?

"It's all right." Demetri sounded relieved, but Briar was having trouble feeling the same. "Look, you've just woken from eighty-two years of sleep. You're bound to be a bit out of it, right?"

"Yes—yes." That's probably all it was. Her brain was still muddled. "That must be it. I'm sorry, Demetri."

"Don't be." He waved a hasty arm. "It wasn't your fault."

"Ready to go?"

Briar and Demetri jumped and spun around. Prince Garrett stood in the doorway, and his soldier, the bearded Kale, stood behind him.

"Stones," Demetri breathed, "you scared the hair off my head!"

"Sorry," Garrett said, with a grin that was decidedly not sorry. "Well, everything looks clear, and we didn't need you to come save us after all."

"Good." Briar swung her gaze around the room. "I just need to grab a few things—"

"I thought that's what you were doing." Garrett arched an eyebrow at Demetri.

Briar grabbed a sorry-looking satchel out of a corner, the thin leather crinkling in her grip. She stuffed several papers from her desk into it—most of her sketches, she hoped—before rooting out some of the clockwork creatures from her trunk. Lastly, she snatched up a brown wool spencer from an iron stand in the corner. She held the dusty jacket out and eyed it—it was a bit threadbare where moths had gotten at it, but it would do. She shrugged it on, then turned to the rest of them. "All right," she said, aiming for a brisk tone. "Into the passage we go."

A marble-top mantle ran along the wall with a finished edge that was actually a lever. Briar pulled down on the lever, and a large panel in the wall *clicked* open. A thrilled tremor ran through her when she realized she was really leaving, leaving behind the castle that had been her prison for sixteen years—for nearly a hundred years, really.

Demetri climbed through first. Briar evaded his gaze as she gathered her gossamer skirt to step after him. Some of her elation faded. For a full minute, she hadn't had the slightest idea who Demetri was, or where she was. Perhaps it *was* just the curse. It did make sense that eighty-some odd years of sleep would fog her brain up. But even if that was right, what if it happened again?

The thought terrified her more than any monster in this castle.

They had a ways to walk before they reached the lift. Briar held the lamp in front of her, but its tiny, flickering flame provided scant light in the black. Her mouth felt dry at the thought of corpses in these tunnels, waiting just ahead, beyond the stretch of her lamp's light. Somewhere in the bowels of the castle, a steady *plink-plink* echoed out, water from the damp dripping off stone.

The lift was set against that stone, though a narrow set of stairs had been cut into the rock, probably hundreds of years ago when the castle was first built. When they reached the lift, Briar stood before the brass grille door and stared into it. "I foresee a small problem."

Prince Garrett coughed. "That your lift is eighty years old and looks more than a bit unstable?"

"No." Briar shot him a frown. Old or not, her lift would run, and it would run well. "But as you can see, it's rather small. I didn't have much space to work with."

"Only two people can fit inside." Demetri slid open the grate with a grinding squeal. "Yes, I remember."

"Well, also," Briar added, "it will only hold so much weight."

"How much weight?" Garrett asked mildly.

"Up to about twenty-five stone, I should think."

"You *think?*"

"Perhaps you and I should ride together," Briar said. "You're the largest of us, and I'm the smallest. Demetri, you and Kale ride down together, and Prince Garrett and I will follow."

Demetri's eyebrows drew together. "All right. Let's get moving then." He and Kale stepped inside the lift.

The lift operated on its own, powered by clockwork gears that ran a counterweight system up the back side of the shaft. All Briar had to do was crank the start-up lever around to get it going. She turned the lever and stepped back, and Demetri and Kale disappeared down the shaft. The spinning gears emitted a continuous thrum as the lift descended, a sound which delighted Briar.

She watched it go for a minute or so. The gears continued to whir steadily, but the clanking of the lift grew softer and softer as it descended. Briar became very aware of Garrett's tall, solid presence, and of the fact that she was alone with him for the first time since they'd escaped the tower. He was a prince, it would seem. From what kingdom, she still didn't know. That ignited her curiosity, but what was even more curious was that he was from *this time*—this new world she'd awoken in.

It was hard to reconcile that. To accept that eighty years had passed when she was still in the same castle she'd lived in all her life. But as she swept a sideways glance at Garrett, she found it easier to believe. She eyed the pistols holstered at his waist. These were not unfamiliar to her, but they had small differences—a more complex firing mechanism, for one. Her gaze traveled upwards as she took in the strange cut of his coat—shorter than what she was used to on a man, but less form-fitting. And the collar was not so high—rather, it lay flat over his collarbone. And his *neck*—cravats must have fallen out of fashion, for she had never seen so much bare skin on a man's neck. She found herself staring until she realized how weird it was to stare at his neck.

But she couldn't help it. She was fascinated by him. By what he represented. Before she fell to her curse, Briar had been a little frightened of the idea that she would wake to a changed world, that she would find herself marooned in a time she didn't know. But now that she was here—taking it all in—she was more excited than afraid.

Her eyes continued to travel up Garrett and finally came to rest on his face. She half-opened her mouth to ask him a question but then saw his expression. He, too, was watching the whirring gears operating the lift, but with none of the enthusiasm that she felt. Actually, his face had gone a little green.

Briar suppressed a surge of irritation. "You know," she said, "my lift *does* work just fine."

Garrett cleared his throat. "I have no doubts in your mechanical abilities, princess. It's just, ah...well, nothing." He peered down into the shaft, and the pitch of his voice rose a little. "It's awfully far down, is all."

Suddenly, Briar understood. Her irritation vanished. "You're afraid of heights."

"I'm what?" Garrett looked around at her. "No. No, I'm not."

"You don't have to be embarrassed about it."

"I'm not embarrassed about it," Garrett said, though the way he evaded her gaze told a different story. "I mean, there's nothing to be embarrassed about. Because I'm not afraid of heights. So...I'm not embarrassed. About it. About anything, I mean."

Briar's lips twitched as she tried to contain a smile.

Garrett looked at her. "Let's just pretend I didn't say any of that."

"All right." Briar barely suppressed her smile as she turned back to watch the lift.

After another minute, the gears slowed and went still as the lift clanked to a halt. It was too far down to see Demetri and Kale exit. But they must have done so, for a minute later, the lift began its ascent up the narrow shaft.

"There's a start-up lever below as well?" Garrett's words were politely strained.

"Yes. Otherwise, it wouldn't do much good. We'd be able to go down but not up." Briar glanced at him. "Would you like me to explain how it works? Maybe—"

"No." Garrett's tone was resigned. "*You* understand how it works, don't you?"

"Of course. I built it."

"Then that's fine with me," he said. His expression, however, didn't look fine.

"I suppose you must have more advanced lifts nowadays," Briar said, voicing the question she'd wanted to ask before. As she spoke, the lift clattered into view. Once it came to a halt, she pushed aside the grate. She was a little surprised when Garrett stepped in without hesitation. Though he did keep his arms close at his sides and fixed his gaze straight ahead. Briar stepped in behind him, latched the lift shut, and reached through the slats to wind the lever up.

The lift barely jerked at all as it began its smooth ride down. Briar was rather proud of that. She looked at Prince Garrett, who had his eyes shut. "Well, do you?"

"What?" he asked, not opening his eyes.

"Have more advanced lifts nowadays."

"Oh. Yes." Garrett folded his arms over his chest. "Actually, most lifts run on steam nowadays."

"*Steam*-powered lifts?" Briar marveled, trying to imagine how that might work.

"Steam-powered engineering is becoming more and more common, because gear mechanisms don't work on everything. Like trains, for instance. They'll run for a short time on gears, but they run out of power after a small distance, no matter how much they wind them—it's a bit odd, actually, no one has really figured out why—"

"What are *trains?*" Briar interrupted.

Garrett's eyes popped open, and his gaze slanted towards her. "You've never seen a train. Of course you haven't. All right. Well, a train is a bit like a self-propelled carriage, only it's built in several cars—box-like compartments, and they're all connected..."

Briar listened with rapt fascination as he spoke about these *trains*, his voice a pleasant hum over the *tock-a-tock-a-tock* of the gears. He described what the trains looked like and explained how they worked. She interrupted him with multiple questions, some which he had no answer for besides, "Well, I'm not sure. I never really thought about that." Briar couldn't see how he could ride in one of these trains and *not* think about such things, but she kept that to herself.

When the lift reached the bottom and came to a halt, Garrett looked up, blinking. "That didn't take much time."

"Well, no, it doesn't. Only a couple of minutes."

"I just meant—" He shook his head. "Well, let's join Demetri and Kale, then." He slid the grate open.

But when they stepped out of the lift, Demetri and Kale were nowhere to be seen.

"Demetri?" Briar glanced around. The dark, empty tunnel before them was all bare stone, a passage not meant for public use. "Demetri!"

"Perhaps they went on ahead?" Garrett drew his pistol from its holster.

"If they did, it was really stupid of them," Briar said, with more calm than she felt. She reached back to take the lamp from the lift.

"Can't argue with that," Garrett murmured. He took a few wary steps down the tunnel, and Briar followed half a step behind. She caught a scent on the air as a draft flitted by—something fresh and earthy. Outside air.

"The tunnel ends up here," she said. It was close enough that she could see it a few paces ahead. "It comes out into—wait!" She grabbed at Garrett's sleeve.

"What?"

She shushed him with a hand, straining her ears. There was an odd noise coming from beyond the end of the tunnel. A slow, sluggish scraping, as though someone was being dragged—or dragging itself—

Briar held her breath for so long that her throat felt like it was closing up. She didn't think Garrett was breathing either, he'd gone so silent. The scraping grew louder until Briar was sure it was right around the corner. Her grip tightened on Garrett's sleeve to draw him back, but then a large shadow appeared, cast against the wall across from the exit. Briar tensed, and Garrett raised his pistol, cocking the trigger back—

A figure rounded the corner. Half a second later, two more figures appeared behind it, one of them crouched and bent, like some twisted ghoul.

But Briar could see that it wasn't a ghoul. Nor a rotting corpse creature.

Garrett fired a shot.

"No, wait!" Briar exclaimed. The shot smothered her cry, blasting so closely to Briar that she flinched and turned her head. There was a yelp and a sharp *crack* as the bullet hit the wall.

"Hey!" came a voice. "It's us!"

"Demetri." Briar's eyes watered, stinging at the caustic smoke from Garrett's gun. "Are you all right?"

"Demetri?" Garrett bit off a curse. "Stars and stones! Identify yourself next time!"

"I'll try to remember that," was Demetri's shaken reply. As Briar and Garrett approached in the near-darkness, Briar saw that Kale was with Demetri. The bearded soldier had some sort of rifle slung over his arm. He was also supporting something—no, some*one* with his other arm.

"Spencer!" A broad smile spread across Garrett's face. "We thought you were lost! Are you all right?"

"Mostly, sire," the straggling soldier replied. He coughed and spit, and Briar saw blood trickling down his chin. He looked like he could barely walk, hunched over, with Kale taking most of his weight.

"Well, hang in a bit longer." Garrett's voice was light, but his smile lost its mirth. Worried for his soldier, Briar thought, and she didn't blame him. The young man—Spencer—didn't look as though he could make it very far on foot. But if Garrett was thinking the same, he didn't say so. He merely stepped forward to take the rifle from Kale, unburdening him a bit.

"Where did you two go off to, then?" Briar asked Demetri.

Demetri looked penitent. "We thought we heard something and thought it best not to split up. When we went outside, we found Spencer."

"I...lost the corpses," Spencer grunted. "Somewhere—in the castle."

"Good," Garrett said. "Then let's get—"

"Hang on." Briar spun around, holding up a hand for silence. They all went still as she listened. Her left ear was ringing from Garrett's shot—maybe that's all she was hearing, or *not* hearing, as it were. An echo. She gazed down the dark tunnel where the lift stood open, just as they'd left it.

Briar was about to turn back, sure she was hearing things, when the lift *trembled*. The spasm resounded from wall to wall and traveled beneath Briar's feet, a vibration she could feel, as though the earth was shifting.

"What was that?" Garrett asked in a low voice.

They all stood still a second longer. Again the lift rattled, as though someone had grabbed hold of it and given it a good shake.

"Stones," Briar whispered. "I think something is—"

Before she could finish, a rotted corpse leapt down the shaft, bounded off the lift, and lunged down the tunnel at them.

Garrett let off four shots in a row, each one cracking like a whip. Before he could fire a fifth, his pistol clicked fruitlessly; it was empty. The bullets ripped through the corpse, bits of faded clothes and putrid flesh flying as they took the monster in the arm, the throat, and twice in the chest. The creature slowed, pushed back by the force of each hit—but it didn't go down. As it advanced, Briar stared at it, trying to identify the corpse as someone she might have known. A cousin or some lord she'd never liked. A servant or a guard.

But it was no one, not anymore. Just a monster.

Kale and Demetri pushed past Briar, raising their guns, as Garrett stepped back to load his firearm. The corpse fell to two bullets in the head, his skull bursting apart, but then a second corpse emerged from the lift shaft and ran at them.

"Well." Spencer, slumped against the wall, coughed. "I *thought* I lost them in the castle."

"I think these came after us." Briar glanced sidelong at Garrett. "Though I thought *some*one had scouted the area behind us."

"All right, all right." Garrett loaded his last bullet and spun the chamber back in place. He looked up as Kale took the second corpse down. "Those monsters are going to keep coming. There could be a hundred of them coming down that shaft."

"We should run, sire," Kale said, pausing to reload.

Briar glanced at the wounded Spencer.

"You have to—go," Spencer managed to get out. "Leave me, Your Highness. Give me a...pistol—I'll hold them off."

"You've already done that once tonight." Garrett clapped him on the shoulder. "I have a different idea. Princess, come with me. Demetri, Kale, cover us." Before Briar could object, he grabbed her by the arm, and they ran down the tunnel towards the lift.

"What are we doing?" Briar asked, raising her voice to be heard over the gunfire.

Before Garrett could answer, two more corpses fell from the shaft. Briar ducked down and to the side as one lunged at her; when she rolled back to her feet, it was coming down under a thundering rain of bullets. The other grabbed Garrett by the arm. He let out a pained grunt but threw the monster off as it took gunfire in its back. Briar pressed herself against the wall as she inched towards the lift, the rough stone digging betwixt her shoulder blades.

"Quickly!" Garrett called. He had reached the lift. He peered up into the empty shaft, dread darkening his eyes. "Wind up the lift!"

"Why?"

"Just do it!" Garrett shoved the lift grate back and took a small box of matches from his pocket.

Mystified, Briar wound the lever round. The air was filled with smoke laden with oily powder residue, making it difficult to see as she glanced up. Even through the smoke, she glimpsed pale figures half-falling, half-leaping down the back of the shaft, using the pulley cables to steady themselves. One in particular was getting very close—she looked to the lift as it began its slow ascent—

"Garrett—" Briar began.

"Hang on." Garrett lit a match and reached into his pocket, drawing forth a small, iron ball. "Wait for it..."

Briar's gaze darted at the descending corpse creatures. As the lift passed above Briar's head, Garrett lit a fuse on the iron ball. At once, the tip of the fuse flared into a sputtering, blinding white light that fizzled and hissed. Squinting, Garrett took aim and threw the ball up into the lift.

"Now what?" Briar asked, watching the ball's graceful arc through the air.

"*Now what?*" Garrett goggled at her as though she was crazy. "Now, run!" Without waiting for her, he sprinted down the tunnel with his arms half-raised over his head.

Run, of course. Her heart hiccupping in her chest, Briar tossed one last glance up the shaft. The closest corpse threw itself towards her, but it smacked against the top of the lift. Briar looked away, squeezed her eyes shut, and ran as fast as she could, expecting any moment to feel the corpse latch onto her—

As she reached the exit, an explosion roared into life behind her, flooding the tunnel with a heat so intense, it permeated even Briar's cold skin.

Briar threw herself around the corner, into the dark corridor beyond. Everyone else was there ahead of her. Garrett and

Kale lurched down the corridor, Spencer slung between them; Demetri stood just outside. As soon as she appeared, he grabbed her by the hand and they ran for the door, out into the bracing, open air, outside the castle, out into the night.

6

ATONEMENT

GARRETT FEARED THAT SPENCER would not make it down the mountain, not without medical care. His shirt was blackened with blood from the gash in his chest, and the night outside was cold and raw. They were out in the open now, but still too close to the castle's walls, overgrown with ivy and streaked with muck. A vast lawn sloped down the mountain before them, the grass made a soft gray in the approaching dawn.

Garrett glanced sideways at Spencer. He would not leave him behind, no matter how cold it was or how far they had to go. He did not consider that an option.

Demetri and Briar came up beside him. They were a ghostly pair beneath the violet sky, like something out of an old gothic tale. Briar's white hair was tangled, her ridiculously sheer gown ripped at the hem, while Demetri, his rapier in hand, looked drawn and dejected, like an orphan boy. He *was* an orphan boy, Garrett reminded himself.

Demetri caught his gaze. "The village isn't far—less than half a mile down the mountain. If it was daylight, we'd see it from here. We could...stop there?"

Briar chewed her lip. "I take it there aren't any corpses there? They were just in the castle."

"We don't know," Demetri admitted. "We went around the village up the backside of the mountain. The more direct route. The last people we passed were on some farmsteads, a good thirty miles from here."

Garrett shivered as the wind blew, cutting through his fine wool coat. The thought of facing more of those monsters exhausted him—and he was sure everyone else felt the same—but it was a good idea for a number of reasons, and he said so. "Not only can we see to Spencer, but if there *are* people there—people, not monsters—we should warn them. And if there are corpses there, well...it would be good to know that too."

"Yes." Briar's voice was glum. "I agree."

They started down the lawn, the dewy grass squelching beneath their shoes. With Spencer supported between Garrett and Kale, it took them a half hour to reach the village wall. It was a small village, a settlement just large enough to subsidize the castle, and its tan, thatched walls were not terribly tall. They approached the village at a measured pace, but like the castle, they found no one standing watch. Kale broke open a latch on the gates and slipped inside, and returned a few minutes later with little to report.

"The village looks abandoned, Highness," he said in a low voice. "No sign of people or corpses, unless they're hiding very well. I think it's safe."

Inside the walls, the village was empty and silent. It appeared to have been abandoned. Rows of coppery brown roofs over beechwood houses lay before them, with doors ajar, board-and-batten shutters left open, and wares from merchant stalls strewn across the paved dirt streets.

All in all, Garrett found the quiet rather eerie.

Demetri recalled a physician's house close by and led them to it. The door hung open, and the house was in disarray, chiffonier drawers torn open, dark rags and clothes littered everywhere, beds unmade, and a fine dust of glass where some bottles had shattered upon the floor. But it was as empty as the rest of the village, no corpses or anyone else.

They laid Spencer on a bed with a thick quilt, and while Demetri poked at the medical supplies, Kale peeled off Spencer's uniform coat. Garrett slumped against the doorframe. His wounded shoulder was stiff and sore from the bitter cold. He glanced at Briar, who limped over to a short stool to sit and inspect the torn soles of her shoes. She wore thin silk slippers, and they were worn through.

"I'm no expert on women's footwear," Garrett said, "but I'd say you need new shoes, princess."

"I need pattens," she grumbled. Her eyes brightened. "Or new shoes. Hang on, I'll be back." She hopped off the stool and left the room.

Demetri looked around, squinting at two jars in his hands, one long-necked and blood red, the other squat and midnight blue. "Where is she going?"

"I think to get new shoes." Garrett went to take over the medical supplies, since Demetri didn't seem to know what to do. "From somewhere."

"I'm going to see if I can get any heat going in this place, sire." Kale rose from Spencer's bedside. "Get some water boiling to sterilize everything." When he left the room, Demetri took his place beside Spencer, who had passed out.

"Well." Garrett began to lay out the medical supplies, taking out anything they might need: scissors, a needle, clean bandages. He tried to make his voice hearty so as to lift the tired, sorry mood. "Hopefully, we've made it through the worst of it. And we succeeded! You've got Briar back." He cast Demetri a quick glance over his shoulder. "What was it like, seeing her again? After all this time?"

"It was..." Demetri's voice sounded heavy "...weird."

Garrett snorted. "Not what I expected."

"No, it was—of course, I was happy. I am happy. It just doesn't feel quite real, I suppose. I keep expecting to...I don't know, wake up. Find this was all in my head, something I dreamed up to..." He trailed off. When he spoke again, his voice was soft and pained. "To get through the next minute. The next minute of captivity."

Garrett felt a *pang* of understanding. What Demetri had endured was beyond imagining—he couldn't blame the prince if he was still struggling with it all. "It's real, Demetri. Trust me." Garrett injected some lightness into his tone. "After all, why would you dream up monstrous corpses coming to life and attacking us?"

"Good point," Demetri said. He was quiet for a moment. The only sounds between them was Spencer's shallow breaths and the clinking of medical supplies as Garrett laid everything out.

Then Demetri said, "So, you never did explain how you managed to wake Briar from her sleep."

Garrett froze. He felt like something the size of an apple had lodged in his throat. "I didn't?"

"No," Demetri said mildly. A quick glance showed Garrett that his fellow prince was leaning over Spencer, inspecting his wound. "You just said it was a long story. And I said it couldn't be that long because it didn't take you much time to wake her."

Garrett brought a small bottle close to his eyes to read the faded label, his nose wrinkling at its acetic odor. The truth was, when Briar opened her eyes, the first thing he'd felt was a crushing weight he'd since realized was disappointment. That realization had soured inside him like rancid milk, because it was the height of selfishness to feel disappointed that Demetri had gotten his princess back when he, Garrett, had not.

Also, he couldn't stop marveling that the kiss had worked to begin with.

When Garrett said nothing, Demetri leaned back from Spencer and prompted, "Garrett?"

Garrett went to the bed and bent his head over Spencer's wound. He picked at the shredded bits of his shirt, wispy wool stuck in the dried blood on his chest.

"It is a long story," he said, because Demetri seemed willing to wait an eternity for a response. He supposed it made sense that Demetri was such a patient person. Enduring eighty years of captivity would do that to anyone, he thought, if it didn't drive them insane first.

"How so? What happened?"

"Before I tell you that..." Garrett glanced back for the short stool Briar had left. He dragged it over to Spencer's side and lowered himself onto it. "You know that I—lost someone. I told you that."

"Princess Snow," Demetri said. Garrett managed not to flinch at her name. "From the Mariner Kingdom. Yes, you told me."

"I didn't tell you how." Garrett rubbed his thumb over the ring on his finger. "She was also put in an enchanted sleep."

"She was? She was cursed too?"

"Not cursed. It wasn't a fairy that did it. It was a hex."

"A hex." Demetri sat upright in his chair. "A witch?"

"Yes." Garrett twisted his shoulder back, trying to ignore where his coat rubbed against the lip of his bandage. "A witch. Snow's stepmother, as it happened. She'd forced Snow into exile when Snow's father died. She was a cruel, selfish woman. She wanted the throne for herself, so she wanted Snow dead, and Snow's little sister too. We never knew what happened to her—she disappeared before Snow fled the Mariner Kingdom."

"I suppose I should be shocked that she would harm her own stepdaughters," Demetri said, "but if she was a witch—well, I've never heard of a good witch before."

Garrett hadn't either, and he had more experience with witches than the average person. Witches weren't heard of much these days. But everyone agreed that a witch, a human using magic, was unnatural. Magic was the province of fairies.

"So she hexed Snow?" Demetri said.

"Yes." Garrett bit the inside of his cheek. "And I discovered—or I thought I did—that I could wake her. Only, what I was told would do it—I—" He exhaled a breath. "It didn't work."

Demetri said nothing. The only sound in the dim room was the *putt-putt* of Spencer's clipped breaths.

"And the sleep didn't last." Garrett stretched his legs out in front of him and adjusted the holster at his waist. "She died a few months later."

"I'm sorry, Garrett."

"It was a long time ago. Nearly two years past." Not that the passage of time had helped. If anything, he felt he shriveled more and more with each day.

"But what was it, then?" Demetri asked. "The cure you were told would work for the sleep?"

Garrett clasped his hands in his lap to keep them steady. And because Demetri was his friend, he forced himself to look the prince full in the face. "True love's kiss."

"A kiss?"

"A kiss."

Demetri seemed to mull this over. "Not what I was expecting."

"Well, expected or not, it didn't work."

"That's what I hate about magic," Demetri grumbled. "It never makes sense. True love's kiss—what exactly does that mean? Someone *she* truly loved, or someone who truly loved her? But I suppose it didn't matter in your case, as you loved each other—"

"It didn't matter in my case because it didn't work." Garrett's tone was a little sharper than he intended. "My kiss didn't wake her. True love or not."

Demetri's forehead creased. "So...you must have been thinking about all this. This whole time. What with Briar being in an enchanted sleep as well." He looked at Garrett, his gaze questioning.

Garrett bit back another sigh. "Yes. I have been. But I hadn't thought much on how you were going to wake Briar since the fairy that freed you said you would *know* what to do. And she was cursed by a fairy, not hexed by a witch, so the two things are completely different."

"And," Demetri said, his voice rising with incredulity, "you are not her true love. Given that you just met her."

Garrett looked at Demetri. Realization lit his face.

"You...kissed her?" Demetri looked unsteady, as though someone had swung a hammer into his head. "*That's* how she woke up? That's why? Because you kissed her?"

"I only did it because, well—" Garrett scrambled, trying to remember *what*, exactly, he had been thinking when he'd done it. "I ended up there without you. And I thought I'd carry her out, but then I heard a noise, and I thought it might be more corpses, and I couldn't fight them *and* carry her, and, well..." He took a breath. "That was the only thing I had ever heard of. To break a sleeping spell. And even though it hadn't worked before, and even though, *of course*, I'm not her true love, I don't love her at all—I mean, she seems perfectly nice, I'm not saying that, I just meant—"

"Garrett," Demetri interrupted. "I know what you mean." He didn't sound angry. He seemed sort of shell-shocked, as though he was still processing this news. "Look, if you think I would hold this against you—please, don't. Of course I don't. I'm *glad* you woke her, and I don't really care how you did it...only..."

"Only, why did it work?" Garrett twisted his mouth. "Why did it work, when I don't even know her and she doesn't know me? And why did it work when it *didn't* work for me and Snow, the girl I actually loved?"

"Well...yes. Yes, that. All that."

The two princes sat in silence, mulling it over. Garrett clenched his hands together so tightly that his knuckle bones ached. This whole thing unnerved him more than he thought possible—not just for the walking corpses, but for *this*. Another sleeping princess, and this one woken by his kiss. The kiss of a perfect stranger.

"It must have something to do with the nature of the sleep," Demetri mused, "because Briar was cursed, and Snow was hexed."

"Which sort of makes sense, except it's meant to be true love's kiss. That's what I can't get around. Listen, Demetri." Garrett sat up straight and rubbed at his neck. "Given that she was, er, asleep when it happened, I'm fairly certain Briar doesn't realize that I...kissed her."

"And you don't want to tell her?"

"Do we have to? Does it matter? You said it doesn't matter anyway. Why bother her about it?"

"Why are you worried about it?"

"Well...it's a bit weird, isn't it?"

"I suppose," Demetri admitted. "Still, when you consider everything that's happened in the last twenty-four hours...corpses come back to life. That's weirder, isn't it?"

"I'm not sure it is."

Kale appeared in the doorway then and came into the room with a small pot of hot water. He set to sterilizing the scissors while Demetri began to sort the medical supplies again.

"I think I'll go look for Briar." Garrett rose to his feet. "Abandoned or not, it's probably not a good idea for any of us to go off alone for too long."

"True," Demetri murmured. "Though if there's anyone I've met who can take care of herself, it's Briar."

Maybe she could, Garrett thought, as he left the physician's house, but she didn't even have a weapon on her. He was beginning to worry that they'd let their guard down too much in this derelict village.

Garrett wandered down the street, calling Briar's name, peering through glazed windows. The sky had paled to steel blue as the sun edged the night away. The difference in the light heightened Garrett's concern as he realized just how much time had passed since Briar left the physician's house. He'd begun to worry that she was gone somehow—this village wasn't all that big—when a scuffle and a loud *crash* sounded out from a house across the street.

"Briar?" Garrett dashed into the beechwood house, taking his pistol from its holster. He found himself in a small room with nothing except a rickety table and two wooden chairs, both toppled over onto their sides. Jots of dust filled the air around him, brought to life by the daylight shining in through the open door. He thought maybe the chairs had caused the crash he heard, but then a rasp-like noise came from another part of the house.

Garrett cocked his pistol as he strode down a corridor on the right, his boots pounding against the boarded floor. At the end of the corridor, he rounded the corner into another room. This room was bare, save for a layered brick fireplace set into the far wall. And except for Briar and a small, gray figure, huddled against the fireplace.

One of them. A corpse.

Briar looked around. "Wait. Don't," she said in a hushed voice. "Don't shoot."

Garrett eased forward. Without lowering his firearm, he looked between Briar and the corpse. It was only a child, a girl, no more than twelve or so. She was emaciated, her ankles like crow legs. She *was* a corpse, like the ones at the castle, only…she didn't seem so *rotted* as the others. Her skin was pasty, but Garrett only saw the telltale mottling in a few places, around her skeletal wrists and at her hairline. She didn't look dead so much as ill. Very ill.

"I heard a crash." Garrett didn't take his eyes off the corpse girl.

"She surprised me," Briar said. "I was outside, I saw something move in here—I came in and found her. I knocked over a chair in the other room, and she ran in here. Or she tried to, anyway. She didn't move very fast."

Which didn't mean she couldn't, Garrett thought.

"Princess," the corpse girl croaked. "Princess Briar."

Garrett gawked, stunned to hear one of them speak.

"You know me?" Briar asked.

"No." The girl gave them a baleful stare. "*He* just said your name." She pointed at Garrett, and he saw that she was missing three fingers on her hand.

"But you know of me, or you wouldn't know I was a princess."

"Only princesses have silly names like Briar."

Briar's lips twitched in a near-smile. "True."

"What happened here?" Garrett asked. "In the village? Where has everyone gone?"

"All gone," the girl whispered. "All dead. Like me."

Garrett said in a taut voice, "But you're not like the others. The ones at the castle, I mean."

"No." The girl ran her pinky finger through the white ash in the fireplace. "We weren't so lucky. All the ones in the castle slept. My mother told me. She'd just left the castle for the day. The guards there, they all went to sleep. They went rigid, she said, like they were dying."

Garrett edged forward, shooting a glance at Briar. Her gaze was fixed on the corpse girl, her lips drawn in a tight line.

"She ran out, my mother," the girl said. "Shut the gates behind her. She thought they were sick, maybe. She came back here and told us what happened."

The corpse girl shifted. With an eerie grace, she lifted her hand, her remaining fingers stiff and bent. But she moved her hair from her face with practiced ease.

"Then...we got cold and sick and tired. And finally, we did sleep. For years and years. And then people came here. They came, and we woke, and we were *hungry*. Hungry and hungry, and no matter what we ate, *still hungry*." The girl's gaze crept over them, and her eyes gleamed. "Everyone began to kill the people who came. Everyone began to *eat* them. Then, when they were gone, everyone began to kill and eat each other. Others ran off. But I stayed here. Alone."

Beside Garrett, Briar took a step back.

"Until now," the corpse girl whispered.

When she lunged at them, Garrett was ready. He fired three shots off and she fell at their feet, her head bursting apart in a shower of pink mist.

Briar nearly ran out of the house. Garrett was right behind her, following as soon as he'd shaken off his grim stupor. He paused before exiting the front room, snatching up a threadbare coat hanging off a hook on the wall. He figured they might need it to wipe away any…viscera…that landed on them. Though he didn't want to stop and look himself over until he was outside.

When Garrett stepped out into the street, he found Briar leaning against the house's exterior, shaking visibly. Her pale face was clammy, covered in a sickly sheen. When she saw Garrett, she shot him a quick, startled look and pushed herself away from the wall, but then her knees buckled, and Garrett snapped an arm out to grasp her by the elbow, steadying her.

"I'm all right," she said jerkily. She tugged free of him, turned away, took several steps, and promptly leaned over and heaved.

Garrett gave her a few minutes as she emptied her stomach—or not, since he couldn't imagine she had anything in her stomach after sleeping for eighty years. He let his mind wander along that fruitless line. Wondering how Briar had survived without eating all that time was better than thinking about what had just happened in that house.

Then Briar straightened. Garrett held out the threadbare coat. "Here," he said, and half-turned aside while she used the fabric to wipe her face and gauzy skirt.

When she was done, she handed the coat back to him, letting out a long, shaky breath. "I'm sorry," she said, her voice little more than a croak.

"Don't be." Garrett dropped the coat to the ground. "It's not my coat."

"No, I meant—" She gestured vaguely. "I'm not normally…" She shrugged, flicking a glance his way. "Don't tell Demetri."

Garrett managed a small smile. "I don't think he'd judge you, if that's what you're thinking."

She returned the smile, though hers was rather tepid. "I don't want him to worry." She gulped in another breath. "I promise I'm not usually this helpless."

"I never thought you were." Garrett crossed his arms over his chest. "Honestly, I'm surprised it's taken you this long to be sick. Given everything we saw in your castle."

She cast him a wry look. "*You* were never sick. Or were you?"

"No. But I definitely considered it when we were riding in your lift."

This prompted a startled laugh from her. She had a nice laugh. Clear and melodious, like a bell. He wanted more of that from her—more laughter, less trembling—so he added, "What sort of princess builds lifts, anyway? And repeating firearms and who knows what else?"

The look she shot him from beneath her lashes was rueful. "A bored one. A—" She paused, as though considering what she was about to say. "A strange one."

He was quite sure she had meant to say something else and could not help but wonder what—*a cursed one? A doomed one?* He was distracted enough by his own curiosity that he said without thinking, "Well, that's all right. I like the strange ones."

She did not laugh this time, but the look she gave him was amused—and even a little pleased. "*Do* you?" she asked with interest.

Garrett suddenly felt hot. *Stones,* his cheeks were probably bright red. Why, by the gift, had he said that? What sort of fool was he? Even if it was just the plain truth, for Snow had been an unconventional princess too. She'd liked a good adventure as much as he did, if not more. Really, *she* was the one who had gotten him into such things.

He cleared his throat. Snow was the last thing he wanted to think about here, with this other sleeping princess he had kissed. He gave Briar an appraising look and was relieved to see she looked steadier and less sickly. "We should probably head back," he said, "if you're up to it."

"Of course." She followed him down the street, but as they left behind the house the young corpse girl had been in, she frowned.

"What is it?" Garrett asked.

"That—girl," Briar answered. "She said people came here. Who do you think she meant? People coming to investigate the castle? I mean, people must have wondered what happened to everyone there, right?"

But Garrett shook his head. "From what I understand, Demetri's parents closed the border separating your kingdoms when you fell to your curse. I don't think they knew exactly what had happened here, but *some* stories got out, stories that worried them. The border has been closed all this time. We...well, I suppose you could say we had special permission for this quest." Briar's frown deepened, and Garrett went on, "I'm guessing whoever came here was just trespassing. Looters, perhaps. There is a whole castle up here, full of riches. That's enough to entice some people, no matter what terrible stories are told."

"I suppose." Briar still sounded troubled. "Whoever they were—they're all dead now anyway. Killed by the villagers."

"Yes." The implications dawned on Garrett in a way they hadn't before. "Because the villagers also became these living corpses."

"It wasn't just the people in the castle, Garrett." Briar's voice was grave. "The villagers were affected too, by this—disease, curse, whatever it is. The question is...how far does it go?"

How far does it go. Garrett suddenly felt cold.

"What if it's everyone?" Briar whispered. "What if it's the whole kingdom?"

7

RETREAT

BRIAR FELT SICK AS she limped down the mountain, her stomach like a stone beneath her ribs. Prince Garrett led their sorry little group. Behind him was Kale, who supported Spencer, and Demetri, who trudged at Briar's side. No one spoke as they picked their way through mounds of rock, preferring to preserve their waning energy. The descent was steep, and Briar knew there must have been a real path once, but that path was long gone, overgrown with juniper shrubs and strewn with eroded gravel. They all could have used a good rest, Briar thought. But they couldn't stop. They had to reach Garrett's soldiers at the bottom of the mountain.

Briar's feet ached. She had replaced her tatty slippers with a pair of slender brown boots that she'd found in the village, but even so, she could feel every stone through the leather soles, every rock poking out from the ground. And she would have killed for a breeze. The driving wind had died as the sun climbed higher and higher into the sky. Every time she glanced back to make sure no one was following them, the glare of the sun scorched her eyes.

She should have been thrilled to be out of the castle, but sober thoughts intruded upon her elation. She thought of the dead girl back in the village, the one Garrett had killed. She knew there had been no choice, but she couldn't stop seeing the small, twisted body and the red, viscid mush on the floor—what was left of her brain.

That girl had become a monster, but she'd once been a person. She'd once been *Briar's* person, a subject. Briar had never thought of the people in the kingdom as *hers*. She'd been so removed from them her entire life, shut away in the castle.

Her parents had done their best to remove themselves from Briar, to protect themselves from losing her. And yet she'd never been allowed to leave the castle, ostensibly for her own safety. They had sought to protect her, but at the same time had resigned themselves to her fate. And presumably, everyone else in the castle had known about the curse too, because they'd all kept their distance from Briar. So she'd never had any friends, no one she was close to. Only Demetri.

But those people in the castle, in this kingdom, *were* hers—and they were as good as dead. And she had no idea why.

Well. That wasn't entirely true. Deep down, some part of her suspected this had something to do with her own curse. And with the fairy who'd cast it.

The dark fairy.

Briar shuddered. As they'd fled the castle late last night—or perhaps very early this morning—Briar had thought she'd *seen* her. The dark fairy. As they'd scurried down the hillside, Briar had cast one last glance at the looming castle, and she could have sworn she'd seen a dark figure, crouched atop one of the towers. She might not have seen it at all, were it not for the massive, bat-like wings unfurling against the dark, cloudy sky. But then Briar had nearly tripped and looked away, and when she'd glanced back again, the shadow was gone.

Perhaps she had imagined it. But for a second, she had been sure it was the dark fairy. Watching Briar escape.

It was near noon when they reached their destination. Briar glimpsed the camp as they came around a rocky knoll near the bottom of the mountain. From the distance, the camp was a teeming, shifting mass of indigo bodies. As they came nearer, soldiers swarmed forward to meet them, some flocking to Garrett and others rushing to help Spencer. Briar's vision blurred as her tired eyes gave out, and a cloud of faceless voices billowed over her, twittering, murmuring, shouting. Then Demetri put a hand on her arm, and his touch snapped her back into focus.

Garrett stopped only long enough to order his men to pack up camp so they could head out. "We can't stay here," he told them. "There could be trouble coming down the mountain after us."

"What kind of trouble?" asked a gruff, older soldier.

"The walking dead kind," Garrett said.

It was telling, Briar thought, that none of the soldiers questioned this. Either they had a large amount of respect for their prince, or they were just used to this sort of madness from him.

As most of the soldiers moved to pack up, and others still stayed to get more answers from Garrett, Briar turned away. She could feel them staring at her, and it was unnerving. Being a princess, she was used to being gawked at, but these stares reminded her what a bizarre experience she'd been through, sleeping for eighty years and waking in a castle full of rotting corpse monsters.

"Are you all right?" Demetri asked.

Briar turned to answer him and then stopped. She gaped over Demetri's shoulder. "What is *that?*"

Demetri looked around, but Briar moved past him, approaching two soldiers working at the back of a lightwood, three-wheeled cart. The cart had a deep bed for storage but no driver's seat, and the reason for that became apparent when Briar leaned in for a look.

In the back of the cart, a few inches below the storage bed, the soldiers had removed a wooden slat to reveal a complex system of gears and springs. One of the soldiers was arranging wooden cams around the gears, much like the smaller cams Briar used to direct her clockwork creatures.

"Is this a self-propelled cart?" she asked.

The soldier who had been tending the cams jumped when she spoke, and the cart shifted beneath the loss of his weight, the little cams rattling in place. He was a young man, perhaps in his mid-twenties, with dark skin and a round face. He looked up at her, his expression distracted. "I'm sorry...Your Highness?" he added, as he seemed to realize who she was.

The other soldier grinned. "She asked if this was a self-propelled cart, Finn. And yes, Your Highness, it is."

"It's powered by springs?" Briar peered down at the gears. Their oiled, coppery odor was like sweet perfume to her. "And you use cams for direction, I see."

The round-faced soldier, Finn, answered. He had a soft, gentle voice. "Yes, Your Highness. That's what I was doing, setting the cams."

"There's a second one here," a voice from behind said, "which we will ride in for the moment."

Briar looked around. Garrett had come up behind her. "Still having some trouble with the power?" he asked his soldiers.

"Some, sire," Finn said. "We still have to wind up the cart too often to keep it going. Luckily, it's at fairly regular intervals, so as long as someone stays on top of it, we can keep them going."

Briar looked at him curiously. "Why would you have to keep winding it? The gears—"

"—don't work well over long distances, as I told you earlier," Garrett said. Before she could protest, he took her by the shoulders and turned her in the opposite direction. "You can interrogate my soldiers about it later. Right now, I want to get as far away from your corpse-filled kingdom as possible. No offense."

The second cart was already whirring to life, and when Briar stepped into it, she saw why—Demetri was inside, winding the cart up. The cart was about ten feet in length and six feet wide, though as there were some supplies loaded in as well, it seemed cramped once Garrett crowded in behind Briar.

"We usually use the carts just for supplies," Garrett explained, "but given that all of us are dead on our feet, my soldiers insisted we ride inside for a bit. Catch some sleep." He slumped to the cart floor.

"Spencer and Kale?" Briar asked.

"In the other cart," Garrett said.

Demetri stepped back from the wind-up lever, and the cart lurched forward at a measured pace. Briar glanced at the gear bed, but all her questions were going fuzzy as a heavy lassitude swept over her. With a long sigh, she leaned back upon a thick canvas laid over a board. It wasn't exactly comfortable, but the moving cart purred like a contented kitten beneath her, and Briar closed her eyes, the noise lulling her into a relaxed state. She twisted around to pull her jacket off and draped it over her head. The darkness was bliss.

Even still, Briar lay awake for an hour or more. She could hear Demetri's sound breathing whispering through him, and when she peeked out from beneath her jacket, she found Garrett asleep in the corner, his long legs sprawled out. The soldiers around them were quiet, no more than a low hum of voices, but even so, Briar could not sleep. Her body felt weighted down and unyielding.

When she did manage to fall asleep—with the sun low in a red-washed sky—she fell into a nightmare. She dreamt that she was dead, a rotting corpse like those at the castle. Her skin was a mass of bruises. Her limbs bent at gawky angles, like they had been removed at the joint and screwed on wrong.

Then she dreamt that she was in that small closet in the castle with corpse-monster Laurel. As she swung her arm around, an inexplicable strength surged through her. Only this time, she held no vase in her hand. This time, her fist smashed through Laurel's throat, plunging through soft, rotted flesh, snapping cartilage and bone. And when she ripped her hand free, blood streamed from between the cracks in her fist like crushed grapes. And she couldn't stop it when the strong, corpse version of herself lifted her hand to her lips, inhaled the metallic aroma of blood, and opened her mouth to *taste*—

She wrenched awake, knocking over a metal pot with her flailing elbow. It toppled to the bed of the cart with a *clang*.

"Briar?"

Briar jerked straight up and looked around. Dark had fallen while she slept, and tall trees clustered on either side of the cart, gangly spruces and stout oaks. Demetri was still on the other side of the cart, sitting upright. His cropped, black riding coat was rumpled, and his floppy hair stuck up at the back of his head. Briar smiled.

"You're awake." Demetri returned her smile.

"Yes." Briar realized they were the only two in the cart, which still trundled forward. "Prince Garrett?"

"He went to look in on Spencer."

"Where are we going?" Briar frowned. "We can't just run, surely. There's nothing stopping those corpses coming after us; they won't stay in the castle for long." *And some of them may have never been in the castle to begin with.*

"I know." Demetri leaned his head back. "But we're only about forty people here, with limited firepower. Garrett wants to get back to the Glen Kingdom, tell his father what's happening here. He seems confident his father can help."

Briar nodded. She hated having no recourse but to flee, but she supposed Demetri was right. There wasn't much they could do with their limited numbers and resources—not only to contain her people, but to help them. Then she frowned. "Hang on." She arranged her ripped, white skirt around her, flicking off a dried speck of mud. "Why to the Glen Kingdom? That's *your* realm. Where is Garrett from?"

Demetri wore a sad smile. "It's not my realm, Briar. Not any-more."

The words washed over Briar with no meaning. "What? What do you mean? I know it's been eighty years, but your descendants, surely—only, you were an only child, weren't you—but you must have had relatives who hold the throne—"

"No." Demetri cast his gaze around. He leaned forward, rooting a lamp out of the supplies. He bent his head to wind the lamp up at the bottom, and Briar could not see his face as he spoke. "Did Garrett tell you anything about me? I mean, about what happened to me after you fell to your curse. How I survived all this time—"

Briar frowned, casting her mind back to what Garrett had said when she first woke in the tower. "He said you'd been put under a spell, one that kept you from aging...but that was all, really..."

"Yes." Demetri fiddled with the lamp. The bulb within it flickered to life as the gears zipped into motion, and Demetri looked up, his careworn face lit by the brilliant glare. He set the lamp before him. Its white glow encircled them, casting everything beyond the light into shadow. "That day of the ball...we were in my quarters, remember? And when you pricked your finger and fell to the curse, I sat there with you. I called for help. And then I heard someone coming, I thought it was a servant..."

The shadows beyond them suddenly seemed deeper, encroaching on their little circle of light. "Who was it?"

"I don't know." There was a helpless catch to Demetri's voice. "Whoever it was, they were cloaked and hooded. And after they came into the room...I don't remember anything else, Briar. The next thing I knew, I woke up in total darkness. I couldn't move, except to breathe. I couldn't speak. And no one spoke to me. No one ever came. Not until a couple of months ago, when someone freed me."

Briar felt like she had tar in her brain, keeping her from making sense of what he was saying. Because what he was saying was unfathomable. "You were in total darkness, alone, all this time?"

Demetri nodded. A black moth swooped towards his face, but he batted it away.

"And you were awake? I mean, you were aware? Of where you were, of what…" Briar wanted to take his hand, but something held her back. She wasn't good at this sort of thing. She didn't know how to comfort someone, certainly not for something this huge. What had happened to him was *far* worse than being cursed to sleep for a hundred years. "Who freed you?"

"I don't know that either," Demetri admitted. "I couldn't see who it was, but I thought it might have been a fairy…. Whoever it was, they told me where you were in the castle. Then I lost consciousness, and when I came to, I was outside at the base of the western mountains. West of the Glen Kingdom." He shrugged. "I found my way to the castle, and that's where I met Garrett."

"Garrett," Briar echoed. She watched a second moth flitter around their lamp. "In the Glen Kingdom. Where he's the prince…but he's not related to you? Not descended from your family?"

Demetri shook his head. "No. You see, when I disappeared all those years ago, after your curse…well, I was presumed dead." His voice became strained. "My parents—there aren't many accurate accounts left, but it sounds like they didn't take it well. There were all sorts of horrid stories out of the Mountain Kingdom, and they had no idea what had happened to me. My mother died shortly after, and my father fell ill."

It was as though the light had dimmed, as though a hundred moths had landed on the lamp's glass and blotted out its gleam. Briar knew Demetri had been much closer to his parents than she had been to hers. For him to lose them like that, without ever getting the chance to say goodbye...

"It was a ripe time for an invasion," he went on. "Garrett's people are from the Black Forest. His ancestors were the remnants of the fallen Forest Kingdom. His great-grandfather led those people out of the forest and invaded the Glen Kingdom. My father was killed—or perhaps he died of his illness, I don't know—my family was ousted from the throne. And ever since, Garrett's people have ruled there."

Briar had no idea what to say, but her heart wrenched for Demetri. All this time, she had not realized where Garrett was from, what realm his family ruled. There were plenty of kingdoms, after all. She had never thought *this* was the answer.

Demetri had lost everything. He had lost his parents, his family, his home. And he was no longer a prince. Or at least, he had no place to be prince *of*. Ruling a kingdom might not have meant much to Briar, but she knew that it had been everything to Demetri. Not for the power, but because it was what he'd been raised for. It was his duty, his life's purpose.

"But," she said, "you and Garrett are friends. It seemed like."

"Yes." Demetri's forehead pinched. "Oh. You think it's weird that I'm friends with someone who invaded my kingdom and overthrew my family? But he didn't. That all happened long before he was born. Even his father hadn't been born yet."

"That's true. Still—"

"Did I consider holding it against him when I first met him?" Demetri mused. "Maybe a little. I thought more of holding it against his father, who wasn't exactly welcoming. I think he thought I might try to contest him for the throne. But all I wanted was to find you, Briar." Demetri met her gaze. "And Garrett didn't hesitate to offer help."

The cart slowed to a halt. Briar looked around as the door swung open and Garrett poked his blond head inside.

Briar cleared her throat. "Are your ears burning?"

"No." Garrett looked puzzled. "Actually, they're quite cold. It's chilly out here. Why?"

"Never mind." Demetri climbed to his feet. "Are we stopping to camp?"

Garrett nodded. "I want to be up early. So I recommend you get some food, find a tent, and get some sleep while you can." He disappeared, presumably to take his own advice. Briar followed him, stepping down from the cart.

They had stopped in the thick of the woods. The air held a muggy, resinous scent. Briar shivered. The last time she'd been in the woods—the *only* time she'd been in the woods—was her last day, the day of her birthday ball, when she'd fallen to the curse. She and Demetri had snuck out into the woods in search of answers, a way out of the curse.

But there had been no help for her here. Now, in the black of night, the trees towered, disappearing into the darkness overhead. The silence of the wood was broken by a single cricket's *chirp-chirp*, as though it was the only living thing within. Briar knew that wasn't true though. She was all too aware of what lived in this wood.

The last thing she wanted was to run into one of *them*.

"Come on." Demetri took her hand. Their cart had stopped ahead of the bulk of the soldiers, and Demetri turned towards the distant light of starting cookfires. "Let's see if we can find..."

His voice was drowned out by a roaring swell, and an insidious fog stole over Briar's brain. In an instant, everything familiar disappeared.

Briar blinked, looking around. The first thing she noticed was that it was dark, too dark...though she could see well, considering. Her heart leapt into her throat, its erratic beats choking her. She was panicking and she didn't know why. It was the darkness, it was...she had no idea where she was. Her eyes traveled around her surroundings. Tall, gruesome trees—the way they closed in around her made her feel trapped. Tiny. Insignificant. Like she was utterly alone. The only person in the world.

"Briar? Are you all right?"

Briar looked around. There was someone else here. A boy, a young man. He had a fair face and serious brown eyes, and he was not too tall, barely taller than her.

There was nothing familiar about him.

Briar took in his clothes: breeches tucked into boots, a short jacket over a waistcoat, and a shirt with a high, stiff collar. Briar searched his face, but it was no use. She didn't *know* him.

A vast isolation stretched before Briar, and she felt lost in it. Not only that, but she felt she had lost *something*. A part of her had fallen away.

The boy was speaking. "Briar?" His eyes lit with alarm. "Briar, it's me. Demetri. Are you—"

"I don't know you," Briar said, her voice coarse. The boy reached a hand towards her, but she reeled back.

"Briar." The boy's voice was pleading. "Briar, please, you *do* know me, I'm—"

"No." Briar was sure of this. She knew herself, she knew her own mind...she did *not* know this boy. Her heart began to beat so fast that she felt dizzy and hot. There were other things she didn't know, she realized, things she should know...where she was, how she'd gotten here....

What had happened to her?

When the boy took another step towards her, all rational thought crumbled.

She ran into the darkness.

She could hear the boy yelling after her, but Briar ran into the woods, darting around thick trees. Her feet tripped over upturned roots like traps left to catch her, and her muscles felt stiff and heavy. She could run faster—she was sure she could. But she felt like she was moving through molasses.

Briar ran for a long time. She couldn't hear the boy calling her anymore, and the woods were pitch black. She slipped to a halt, her chest heaving, and wrapped an arm around a tree for support. The bark was rough and sticky against her palm.

Something *snapped* through the bramble behind her. Briar whirled around, but there was no one there. The tree branches grasped for her like spindly fingers. She stepped back, turning to run again, but she was so, *so* tired.

The wind rushed past, slapping her hair into her face. Briar looked around, terribly lost. She felt stupid now. Running into the woods alone at night, that was stupid. She should go back, but...she had no idea how far she'd run, what direction she'd come from. The woods all looked the same.

She turned in a complete circle, and when she completed the turn, a creature stood before her.

The creature was tiny, but in this shadowy forest, she seemed like a giant. Her hair was burnished red and her skin tinted pale green, like a ripe pear. There was a delicateness to her features—small lips, sharp cheekbones, pointed ears. But she was also wild-looking. Her dress was layered rags in shades of brown, a skirt cut above her knees, sleeves barely there, baring her arms. Her knotted hair was matted with leaves and feathers. Weirdest of all, her eyes were completely black, as though they'd been filled with ink from brim to brim.

Then Briar noticed something stranger. Great, feathery wings, the same color as her hair, sprouted from the creature's back. They stretched high above her head, fluttering back and forth in time with Briar's shallow breath.

A sense of familiarity struck Briar. "I know you," she said, gawking at the fairy.

Then it all came flooding back.

8

SHADOWS

DEMETRI TRAMPED THROUGH THE dark forest, damp pine needles crunching beneath his boots. He held a gear-bulb lantern in one hand, and the other hand strayed close to the hilt of his rapier. He felt tense, as though his muscles might burst apart beneath his skin. There was a tautness inside him too, growing in his chest and climbing up his throat.

He could not stop seeing Briar just before she ran from him. The way she'd looked at him. The uncomprehending in her eyes had been shattering. He'd almost torn off after Briar alone, but Garrett had stopped him, and now he, Demetri, and ten soldiers were searching the woods.

It was full dark now, darker than ever beneath the lofty trees, for they allowed no hint of starlight through their branches. The only light was their own, provided by the gear-bulb lanterns. Their white, gleaming orbs dotted the forest's inky darkness, but they only lit a few feet in front of them. It was a dangerous time to roam the woods.

Demetri supposed it was best that Garrett had prevented him from running after Briar—it would have been beyond stupid to run into the woods alone. But he couldn't stop thinking they had wasted time assembling soldiers, and there was no telling how far Briar had gone into the forest. "I should've stopped her." He flexed his fingers, stiff in the cold. "I should have realized what was wrong—"

"How could you have done?" Garrett asked. His deep, reasonable voice only heightened Demetri's unease. "How could you predict she would—you know—go blank and forget who you were?"

"It wasn't the first time. I told you."

"We'll find her, Demetri."

They had been walking for over ten minutes. Demetri tugged at his stiff collar. It felt like it was choking him. He swung his lamp from one side to the other, peering into the foliage on his left.

A pair of black eyes ogled him from the dark greenery.

Demetri yelped and tripped. Garrett jerked to a halt, and most of the soldiers as well, everyone reaching for their firearms.

"What is it?" Garrett demanded.

With a trembling finger, Demetri pointed.

Garrett peered over his shoulder and grunted in surprise. Demetri was sure that surprise was nothing compared to what followed when the black eyes emerged from behind a scraggly dogwood shrub, revealing their owner. She was petite—a good head and more shorter than Demetri. She had a pointed chin and pointed ears, and her skin was washed with a pale, mint green, as though she'd been stained by the foliage. And of course, she bore the telltale, unnerving black eyes. This one had hair the color of chestnuts, and she wore a tattered, basil-green tunic. Leaves stuck to her clothes and hair like she was producing sap, and Demetri knew the feathers woven in her hair grew there naturally.

As naturally as the feathers coating the sweeping wings that spread out from her shoulder blades. She looked like an overgrown moth. The gentle beat of her wings put Demetri on guard, as though it was a warning, a predator scenting its prey before it attacked.

"It took you a long time to notice me," the fairy said. Her low, gravelly voice seemed at odds with her slight frame.

Garrett recovered first. "It's quite dark out. And generally, when one wants to be noticed, they don't hide in the bushes."

"I didn't *want* to be noticed." The fairy surveyed them. "You are Briar's friends?"

Hope surged within Demetri. "Yes. Have you seen her?"

"Of course." The fairy gave a haughty toss of her head. "Otherwise, why would I speak to you? Come." She turned and drifted into the darkness on light feet, like a ballet dancer.

Garrett swung his rifle over his shoulder. "Snobby little thing, isn't she?"

"They all are," Demetri said sourly. "Come on. I guess she'll take us to Briar."

They followed the fairy, who slowed long enough for Demetri and Garrett to join her. She looked at Demetri and said, "Are you the one who came here before? With Princess Briar."

Demetri's mouth went dry. *The one who came before*. He had been trying not to think about that time—the morning of Briar's sixteenth birthday. When the two of them had ventured into these woods, seeking help from the fairies here. He didn't want to remember how useless the whole attempt had been, how hopeless he'd felt afterwards.

Demetri swallowed. "Yes."

"Curious," the fairy said, though she didn't sound all that interested. "I do not remember you well."

A spark of anger flared within Demetri, emboldening him. As though it was so easily forgotten. But then, *he* had forgotten—he had forgotten what these fairies were like. They walked like humans and talked like humans, but they were *not* human. Briar's curse was a testament to their vindictive natures. So, of course this fairy was so unconcerned, totally oblivious to the tragedy and ruin that had followed that morning. For Briar, for Demetri. For the whole kingdom.

"I don't remember you either," Demetri retorted. When they had last been here, the fairies had treated Demetri as though he was little more than the mud on their feet. They had regarded Briar with slightly more warmth, but even so, they were far from friendly. "But then, if there is one thing I've tried to forget these past eighty-two years, it's how incredibly unhelpful you lot were."

The fairy stopped and rounded on Demetri. Her pulsating wings stilled. Demetri's heart stilled too, but he stood his ground. Beside him, Garrett tensed, half-reaching for his pistol.

"As we told you then—" the fairy sniffed "—there was nothing we could do. No fairy can alter a curse. We *certainly* cannot alter another's curse. We cannot even alter our own curses."

"Well, that's a bit backward," Garrett said affably. "What if you change your mind about a curse you cast?"

The fairy looked him over with an imperious gaze, as though she was the royal, and he less than a serf. "We don't." She turned and continued through the forest. "One *can* cast a second curse, but it's not the same thing. And it is only possible to do to your own curse."

Demetri stood for another second, watching the fairy go. He waited until some of the anger had drained out of him, though the loss of it left him feeling shaky. Then he stepped forward, following as the fairy picked up speed. Her mud-stained feet flitted a few inches off the ground. Demetri raised his lantern, squinting through its glow.

They were approaching an ominous copse of squat, gnarled trees. The trees twisted around each other, forming a cave of groping branches and dangling ivy.

"Here we are," the fairy said, and she disappeared into the thicket.

Garrett and Demetri ducked after her. They came out into a small, dirt grove enclosed from the rest of the woods. It was even darker than the forest around it, and at first, Demetri couldn't see anything. He lifted his lantern and peered at his surroundings.

Briar sat on the packed earth across the grove. With her pale hair and pearly white gown, she was a beacon in the darkness. She sat with her knees pulled up to her chest, and she looked cross. She held a hand up to her eyes when the lanterns fell over her, but then she saw Demetri and she stood.

Demetri crossed to her, shakier than ever. His bones felt like they'd turned to jelly. There had been clear recognition in Briar's gaze; she knew him. Her memory had returned just like last time. Still, his relief was tempered with anxiety. The first time, it had been easy to dismiss; she had just woken from eighty-two years of sleep. But for it to happen a second time...now, he was worried.

When would it happen again?

When Demetri reached her, Briar held out a hand to him. "Demetri, I'm so sorry."

"It's all right," he said, though a part of him felt that it was not all right. It wasn't her fault— he would never think that. She certainly didn't need to apologize. But it was not all right. Not when he didn't know why this was happening or if she was going to be okay. Still, he tried to shove away his distress.

"Are you the human who came last time with Briar?"

Demetri looked around. The fairy that had brought them here stood back, but there was a second one now, her figure bleeding into the backdrop of deformed trees.

"Of course he is." Briar's words crackled like a blazing fire. Her hand slipped out of Demetri's.

The fairy stepped out of the shadows. She was identical to the first fairy, except she wore a brown tunic instead of a green one, and her hair and wings were copper-colored. She clucked her tongue at Briar. "All humans look the same to me."

Briar turned to face the fairy, planting her feet. "You recognized *me* easily enough."

The fairy lifted her shoulder in a graceful shrug. "You're different. You're a princess. Descended from one of the five original families. The five royal bloodlines."

"I'm descended from one of them, too," Demetri said through gritted teeth.

The fairy frowned. "But you're not a *princess*."

"Well, obviously," he retorted. "Well-spotted."

Garrett—who was *not* descended from one of those original bloodlines—stepped forward, dropping his lantern to keep from blinding everyone. "What does that have to do with anything, anyway?"

The brunette fairy rounded on him. Her wings swept forward with the force of a blustering wind. "Do not ask questions about things you cannot understand."

"Don't tell him what he can understand." Briar didn't flinch into the gust of the fairy's wings. "We *will* ask questions, and you're going to answer them."

The fairy's wings stilled. Even though Demetri had done so himself a few minutes earlier, he wished Briar wouldn't provoke the fairies. He felt suddenly exhausted. All the anger and worry had sapped his energy. He was keen to leave this forest, and the fairies, as soon as they could. He was certain they would be of no more help now than they had been before. There was no point trying to get answers out of them.

"Most humans know better than to anger a fairy, Briar," the brunette fairy said.

"You can't hurt me," Briar scoffed. "By the Gift, the pact you made, no fairy can harm a human."

"By the Gift, no fairy can *kill* a human." The fairy raised her guttural voice into a falsetto pitch, mocking Briar. "I would think you, of all people, would well know how a fairy can harm a human."

"I suppose I do." Briar leaned forward, casting half her face in shadow. "Given what your *dark fairy* did to me. But then, she never agreed to the Gift, did she?"

"She isn't *our* dark fairy." A visible shiver spasmed through the red-haired fairy. "She just...is. And it doesn't matter if she agreed with the pact—she is fairy-kind. She is bound by the Gift like any other fairy, whether she likes it or not."

For all the good that was, Demetri thought grimly. If the dark fairy *had* cast a curse over Briar's kingdom and caused this...*rotting* malady...then she had as good as killed all those people.

The brunette fairy cast a swift glare at her counterpart. "You should leave now," she said to Briar. "Prence will lead you back to your road." She indicated the other fairy.

But Garrett spoke up. "But you haven't told us what you know about these corpses." The prince stood at ease, slouching a little, but Demetri knew he wasn't as relaxed as he looked. "The ones at the castle."

Both fairies blinked at Garrett. "Why should we tell you anything?"

"So you do know something about them," he deduced with an innocent smile.

The brown-haired fairy flexed her fingers, like a cat flashing its claws. "We know nothing. We keep to our own kind."

Demetri couldn't help himself. As weary as he was, as desperate to get out of this forest, some small part of him piqued with interest. "Why did a fairy help me, then?" he asked.

The entire grove rippled with movement as everyone—human and fairy—turned to look at him.

"What do you mean?" the red-haired fairy, the one called Prence, asked.

Demetri fidgeted with the cuff of his sleeve, feeling ill at ease with all those eyes on him. Especially the fairies' eyes. He regretted that he'd said anything. "There was a fairy who helped me." He waved a hand like it was nothing important. "I was held prisoner for the past eighty-two years. I couldn't move or speak or anything. Then someone freed me and told me how to find Briar. It was a fairy, I think. A blue fairy."

The fairies looked scornful. "There is no blue fairy," Prence said.

Demetri frowned. "I remember a blue...glow. That's why I thought it was a blue fairy."

At once, the wings of both fairies went still. There was no hostility in their eyes exactly, but suddenly, Demetri remembered how feral these creatures were. They had the air of a pair of deer caught in the crosshairs of a hunter's rifle. Made dangerous by desperation.

"A blue glow?" Prence said after a long silence.

"Yes." Demetri eyed her with suspicion. "Why? Does that mean something to you?"

"There is no blue fairy." The brunette fairy glared at him. "Fairies are creatures of the wood. There is no *blue* fairy."

"If it wasn't a fairy," Garrett said, "then what—or who—could it have been?"

"How should we know?" Prence snapped. "We do not know who helped you, or why. And we do not know by what curse these corpses sprang from. If it was a curse at all."

If not a curse, then what could have caused it? Demetri's shoulders slumped. Anger grew inside him again, but this time, it was a simmering rage. He had no energy for anything else. He wondered if the fairies were telling the truth, and there really was no blue fairy. It was possible he had imagined that blue glow, he supposed—but then, it could have been anyone, even just a regular person. Only, why wouldn't a regular person identify themselves? Explain who they were, how they knew about Briar, why they were helping him?

And yet, the fairies were clearly hiding something. They knew more than they were saying. Stymied with frustration, Demetri allowed himself to be led out of the grove with Briar and the others. As the twisted trees loomed over them, Demetri felt a swift, devastating stab of *déjà vu*. He nearly staggered beneath it. He felt more helpless now than when they had entered this forest, and it so mirrored the way he'd felt all those years ago, in these same woods, that for a moment, he was *there* again, transported back to that day.

He blinked several times, squeezing his eyes shut, and forcibly reminded himself that it was all in the past—Briar's curse was broken, she was here, and she was all right. His eyes sought her out, a ways ahead of him, but the sight of her did not help shake him back to the present.

Demetri struggled to draw a breath. He felt as though the trees were closing in on him, burying him in darkness. His eyes darted beyond Briar, latching onto one of the soldiers in blue uniform—and then onto Garrett, just in front of the soldier. Somehow, the sight of the prince helped, grounding Demetri in the here and now.

He was not stuck in the past, Demetri assured himself. He managed to suck in a deep breath, drawing it in and letting it out. The curse lay behind them, not before them. Briar was all right.

She had to be.

9
GROUNDED

BRIAR WALKED NEAR THE front of their little troupe as they followed their fairy guide through the woods. Demetri was somewhere behind her, though where exactly, Briar didn't know. Logically, she knew what was happening to her was not her fault, but she couldn't help but feel guilty when she looked at Demetri. There had been something *off* about him when they'd been reunited in the grove. He hadn't quite met her gaze, and she'd felt a distance growing between them, one she didn't know how to breach. She didn't think he blamed her for what had transpired, and yet...something was different. Something was wrong.

The fairy leading them was the one called Prence, though Briar whispered to Garrett that "Prence" wasn't her full name. "Her full name is Prencitisitalialala or something stupid like that," she grumbled. "All fairies have ridiculous names like that."

Garrett chuckled and made some joke, but Briar didn't quite catch it. She glanced over her shoulder, looking for Demetri. It had grown so dark that all she could see was a clump of people weaving through the murky trees, one indistinguishable from the rest. But—there. Her eyes snagged on a familiar silhouette near the rear of the group, and she knew it was Demetri. There was just something about the way he walked, the set of his narrow shoulders, that told her it was him.

When she turned back, she found Garrett looking at her curiously. He walked beside her, only a single guard separating them from the fairy in the lead. "Everything all right?" he prompted.

Briar nodded. "Just looking for Demetri."

Garrett cast a quick glance over his shoulder. "I'm sure he's back there somewhere."

"He is. I saw him."

Garrett's lips twitched in a near-smile. For some reason, Briar felt self-conscious. "What?"

He shook his head. "Nothing. You have good eyesight, is all."

"I suppose." Briar hesitated. "I'm sorry about this, by the way. That you all had to come out here in the dark." She *was* sorry, but she found she didn't feel the same shame as she had facing Demetri. It should have been embarrassing, she thought, but she didn't feel embarrassed with Garrett. Maybe because he'd already seen her puke her guts out.

"That's all right," Garrett said bracingly, and he didn't sound like he was just saying it to be polite. There was a genuine quality to him that made Briar feel even more at ease. "It wasn't your fault. Anyway, now I can say I've met a fairy."

"You've never met one before?"

"No." A smile flitted over his face. It was there and gone in an instant, but an imprint of joviality remained. There was just something appealing about Garrett's face—a pleasantry that was always there, even if he was not smiling outright. "I know.

Shameful for an adventurer like myself." He shook his head. "I know they were common in the Glen Kingdom once, but they've more or less all retreated here to the mountains. From what I've heard."

"Of course," said Prence, and Briar and Garrett both gave a start at realizing the fairy was listening to them.

Prence continued, her voice almost sad. "There is no more of our blood left in the south. Well, perhaps in the far south. But there are very few trees there, and we don't like to be without trees."

Briar and Garrett exchanged a mystified look. "In the far south," Garrett echoed. "You mean, the Desert Kingdom?"

"Yes. Far south."

"What do you mean you have no blood left?" Briar asked.

"I mean the royal bloodlines," Prence said haughtily. "The original five bloodlines established by the Gift." The fairy spun around to face them, floating backwards, her toes scraping over dead leaves. "The Glen and Forest bloodlines still exist, of course, but they no longer hold any power over the land. The Mariner bloodline is extinct. That leaves you, Briar, here in the Mountain Kingdom. And the Desert Kingdom far in the south."

"With no trees," Garrett echoed faintly. Briar glanced at him. She couldn't be sure in the dark, but he looked white, as though all the blood had drained from his face.

Something the fairy said had upset him. But what?

"With no trees." Prence nodded.

"Wait a minute." Briar held up a hand. "You said the royal bloodlines, *established* by the Gift. What does that mean?"

Prence blinked at her. "It was the Gift that granted the first royals their power."

"Because the fairies made peace with them?"

"No, because of the fairies' *gift* to them." Prence sounded quite impatient.

Garrett shook his head. His face had regained some of its color. "I thought the peace *was* the Gift."

"The Gift was a *gift*," Prence said haughtily. "A gift of fairy blood."

Briar and Garrett exchanged looks of stupefaction. "Come again?" Garrett said.

"Fairies gave the royals—including my ancestors—their *blood?*" Briar shook her head. "Did they...drink it or something?"

Prence looked at her like she was some kind of savage. "No. Of course not. There was a ritual—it's complicated to explain. But the royals bore fairy blood in their veins from then on, as do all their descendants. That's why fairies will always recognize you, Briar. Because you carry the gift of blood."

"So does Demetri," Garrett pointed out, "and none of you recognized *him*."

Prence shrugged. "The blood is stronger in females."

Briar was still digesting this. She wasn't sure how she felt about having fairy blood in her veins, given what a fairy had done to her. She didn't like the idea of a connection between them. Still, this was interesting to consider. "So, do I have any special abilities? Because of this fairy gift?"

Prence looked confused. "Like what?"

"I don't know..." Briar cast a glance at Garrett. "Enhanced eyesight, maybe?"

Garrett flashed her a grin.

But Prence said, "Don't be silly. You are still human, Briar. The gift of blood means you are connected to the land. In a way other humans aren't." She shrugged. "I do not know how else to explain it."

Briar resisted the urge to roll her eyes. "Of course you don't." She kicked up a flake of dirt with her boot. "Perhaps you'll explain something else then. You say you know nothing about what happened to my kingdom. But *could* the dark fairy be responsible? Is she powerful enough to curse an entire kingdom?" *Certainly she is vile enough*, Briar thought darkly, *pernicious enough.*

A draft whistled through the trees, and Prence fluttered her wings against the wind. The movement was distracting enough that Briar almost missed the look that passed over Prence's face. It was difficult to identify through those liquid black eyes. "Certainly she *could* do it." The fairy's voice grew somber. "She is one of the oldest of our kind. You humans grow frail in your old age. You lose your health and strength. But fairies only grow stronger as they get older." Prence shuddered. "And Tenalabralilah—the one you call *dark fairy*—is over a thousand years old. Closer to two thousand."

It was fear, Briar realized. The look on Prence's face was fear. She was *afraid* of the dark fairy.

"*Two thousand?*" Garrett echoed. "I had no idea there were fairies that old."

"There are not many," said Prence. "Most of the old ones live in seclusion. They do not stray far from their trees."

"But not the dark fairy?"

"She has never been like us." Prence's voice was so hushed, it was almost a whisper. Another breeze blustered past them, and Briar shivered. "She doesn't even *look* like a proper fairy. Her wings are black as night and her flesh pale like a human's. As though she has none of the earth in her, none of the woods. As though she is not bonded to the land." The fairy shook her head. "But she must be, or she would not have the power to curse."

Well, she certainly had that. Briar could attest to it. A rush of ire flooded through her. "She might not have lived so long," said Briar, "if you all had just dealt with her when she first started causing trouble."

Prence frowned, but before the fairy could respond, Garrett asked, "When was that?"

Briar blinked. "When was what?"

"When did she start causing trouble?"

Briar looked from Garrett to Prence, but the fairy gave no answer. "Oh, I don't know," Briar said, vexed by Prence. "Probably when she refused to agree to the Gift, for one thing." She was surprised to see the blank look on Garrett's face. "You don't know the story?"

"I don't really know anything about the dark fairy except that she cursed you," Garrett admitted. "Come to think of it, I don't even know why she did that." At Briar's incredulous look, he spared her a small smile. "Like I said, we don't have much to do with fairies in the Glen Kingdom. I don't know much about them. Nor do most people."

Prence seemed to take exception to this. She eyed Garrett with an affronted gaze. "Tenalabralilah—the dark fairy—was one of the most powerful fairies over a thousand years ago, when humans and fairies still warred." In light of Garrett's ignorance, she seemed to forget her pledge to stay silent. "She is credited with slaughtering the most humans in the wars, felling thousands of them by her own hand."

"*Credited*," Briar muttered. As though it was a high honor, slaughtering as many humans as possible.

"She hated humans." Prence cast a glance over her shoulder, as though to make sure she was going in the right direction. "When fairies and humans decided to make peace, she was against it. She would have used force to keep the Gift from happening if her own brethren had not stopped her."

"Stopped her," Briar echoed. "Imprisoned her, you mean. They should have killed her. That would have really stopped her. Permanently."

Prence's black eyes blinked, shock evident on her face. "Fairies do not *kill* each other. That is barbaric."

This time, Briar did roll her eyes. She didn't condone killing, of course, but in the case of a creature like the dark fairy....

"Well, she must have escaped this prison?" Garrett asked. "Given that she was free to curse Briar?"

Prence said stiffly, "Her prison stood for over a thousand years."

"So she broke free when?" Garrett looked as though he was calculating in his head.

"Just over a hundred years ago," Briar replied. "Shortly before I was born." It was a chilling thought. This story suddenly felt real. This was the part she had lived, after all. She looked bleakly at Prence. "I don't suppose you want to explain that? Just how *did* the dark fairy escape such a powerful prison?"

But Prence gave her a disdainful look and swept around, turning her back on them. Apparently, she was done telling stories.

"Well." Briar lowered her voice, pitching her words for Garrett alone. "The dark fairy escaped somehow. And the first thing she tried to do was kill more humans. She wanted to start another human-fairy war, I think." Briar tried to keep her tone light, but this was difficult to talk about. Especially here, in the dark of the woods, where fairies dwelled.

Unthinkingly, Briar drifted closer to Garrett. "But of course," she continued, "she couldn't wage war on humans anymore. Like Prence said, the dark fairy is as bound by the Gift as the rest of her kind. She can't kill a human." Briar clenched her hands. "Not directly, anyway."

Garrett leaned towards her, either because her voice was so low, or because he, too, felt the dread inherent in this story. "Directly?"

"Instead of starting a war with humans," Briar said, "she tried to start one *between* humans. Between my father—the king of the Mountain Kingdom—and Demetri's parents. The rulers of the Glen Kingdom."

"How did she think to manage that?"

"I don't know." Briar alternated her gaze between Prence, drifting ahead of them, and Garrett, his face lit by the white lantern he carried. "She's quite clever. From what I understand, she nearly succeeded in starting a war. But then—" Briar smiled grimly "—my father found out about the dark fairy and her plot. I'm not sure how. Someone discovered it and told him, I suppose."

"A fairy," said Prence, and Briar nearly clutched Garrett's arm, she was so startled. Once again, she hadn't realized the fairy was listening. She hadn't realized she could *hear* that well. Briar had practically been whispering. "A fairy told your father. One from Tenalabralilah's inner circle."

"Really? Someone betrayed her?"

Prence nodded. "Oh, yes." Her voice was grave. "And he paid for it. Dearly."

Briar was about to ask how exactly, but Garrett spoke first, asking her, "So is that why you and Demetri were betrothed? To ensure your kingdoms remained at peace?"

Briar nodded. "Yes. Unfortunately, it was only days after the betrothal was announced that the dark fairy enacted her revenge—by cursing me. I think she thought to hurt my father and spoil the alliance all in one go. But my parents kept the curse a secret from Demetri and his parents, so the alliance remained intact. And," she added, her voice turning sour, "if my father was hurt by what she did to me, I wouldn't know."

Garrett frowned at her, but before he could say anything—Briar was not sure she wanted him to—Prence stilled, coming to a halt in front of them.

Garrett's eyes flew from Briar to the fairy, immediately alert. "What's wrong?" he asked in a low voice.

The fairy did not answer right away. Slowly, she sank back to the ground, her dirty little feet landing soundlessly on the forest floor. Her wings were still beating, but barely, a whisper in the silent woods. "Something," she said softly, "is out there."

Briar realized she was holding her breath, her chest tightening. The entire group behind them, the soldiers and Demetri, had gone still and quiet. Briar hardly dared cast her eyes beyond the light of their lanterns, but she did, her gaze questing into the darkness. She looked for any unnatural shape, any sign of movement.

But there was nothing. Only darkness.

Then Prence let out a long, audible breath. "I know who it is." She called in a hushed voice, "Jas? Is that you?"

Without a glance for her human companions, the fairy darted into the trees, vanishing into the gloom.

A tense silence lay over the group, left in the fairy's wake. Briar and Garrett exchanged uncertain looks. "Er—are we supposed to follow her?" Garrett asked.

"I am," said Briar, and she plunged into the woods after the fairy.

Garrett followed as well, as did two of his soldiers. Luckily, Prence had not gone far, but neither was the path they took an easy one. They struggled through a dense cluster of tangled sweetbrier shrubs, the prickly branches ripping through Briar's gauzy gown. Once through the thorny patch, they found Prence standing before a monstrous, rotting mountain oak. It was so thick that even Garrett could not have reached halfway around the tree, Briar thought, with his arms spread wide. But a gaping hole had hollowed through the tree from the ground up, leaving a black, ominous cavity where the wood had been.

Prence looked at them soberly. "It's only Jas. We scared him, I think."

"Are you going to tell us," Briar said irritably, "who this Jas is?" She approached the tree hesitantly. Even a few paces away, she could smell the air within the hollow, stale and ripe. She started to breathe more shallowly, trying not to take too much of the stench in. She was beginning to think they should turn back when Prence spoke.

"He is the one you wanted to know about," the fairy said. "The one who betrayed Tenalabralilah. The one who told your father of her plans."

Briar stopped short. She didn't know what showed on her face, but beside her, Garrett laid a hand on her shoulder, as though he was concerned. He dropped it a second later, but Briar could still feel its warm imprint through the sleeve of her jacket.

"The one who betrayed the dark fairy?" Briar whispered. "He's here?"

Prence gestured towards the hollow in the oak tree. Briar stared intently into the black crevice, and as her eyes adjusted beyond the glare of Garrett's lantern, she could just make out a small, hunched shape inside the tree. Leaving the light behind, Briar stepped forward and laid a tentative hand on the tree, leaning to peer into the hollow.

The creature inside was small and frail, its face hidden from Briar. Its matted hair was the color of squash, though it was so streaked with mud, it almost looked brown. His green-tinged skin and the pointed ears poking through his hair marked him a fairy, but there was something wrong about him. He was slender, but not in that willowy way, like the other fairies. Instead, he was gaunt, like a homeless child.

"I told you fairies do not kill each other," Prence whispered, "but Tena is different. *Evil*." She shivered in the dark. "She as good as killed him. She made him mortal. She *grounded* him."

That was when Briar realized. There was something else different about this fairy.

He had no wings. Crouched as he was, with his back turned towards her, Briar could see where his wings should have been. But there were no wings. Only two, short stubs.

Briar's breath tangled in her throat. "I don't understand." Well, she did. She just couldn't comprehend it. How gruesome it was. "What did she do—cut them off?"

"Cut them, ripped them." Prence's voice went numb. "What does it matter? She made him mortal."

A gust of wind blew past them, whisking Briar's unbound hair across her face. She pushed it away.

"He might know," Prence said. "About your kingdom. If it was the dark fairy's doing, he might know. They were close once. Before he betrayed her. Before she—"

The wingless fairy, Jas, suddenly snapped his head around, drawing Briar's gaze. His black eyes latched onto Briar's face. "*She*," he rasped.

Briar swallowed. He was so wild-looking, it was almost strange to hear him speak. "The dark fairy," she said. "You knew her."

Jas quivered from head to toe. "Yes. I knew her."

"Do you…" Briar hesitated. This damaged little creature looked as though one wrong word could set him off, but she had to ask. She had to know. Choosing her words carefully, she said, "My kingdom…something has happened. To all the people. They're sick, or cursed, I don't know—they're *rotting*. Like they've become corpses." Briar was picking up speed, her words tumbling from her mouth. "I don't know what happened. What caused it. Do you know? Was it her? Did the dark fairy curse my kingdom?"

Jas bared his teeth like a wild animal. "She took my wings."

"I know." Briar cast Prence an uncertain look, but the red-haired fairy was watching Jas with an expression that was half-horrified, half-fascinated. "But—"

"She took my wings," Jas repeated. "I hid from her. After I told the king what she was planning. For many years, I hid." He closed his black eyes. "Until the curse fell."

"The curse," Briar echoed. "My curse?"

Jas began to rock back and forth. "She was so angry," he whispered. "She was so angry, because it wasn't enough. That was what she told me when she found me. It wasn't enough, so she cast another curse." He opened his eyes and looked at Briar. "She cast a second curse. A *rotting* curse. A curse to make monsters."

10

ACHING

GARRETT WINCED AS HIS medic, Thatcher, wrapped a clean bandage around his newly-stitched shoulder. Most of the bleeding from the bite had stopped, but the skin was still raw and bruised. "What do you think, Thatcher?"

"Well, sire." Thatcher was near forty, one of the older soldiers in Garrett's company. A scrub of iron gray hair covered his head, and his dark skin was beginning to look stretched over his wiry frame. "In future, I recommend you avoid bites from rotting corpses."

"I'll try to remember that."

Two nights had passed since their run-in with the fairies. They'd spent the previous day traveling south through the woods before stopping to sleep for the night. Now it was morning, the soft light of daybreak filtering through the canvas walls of Thatcher's tent.

"Let me know if the pain worsens," Thatcher advised him. "Given that we don't know exactly what's happening to those rotting people—physiologically speaking—we don't know if you've been infected with anything. I want to know of anything strange about that wound, Highness. Understand?"

"Thatcher." Garrett summoned his most winning smile. "When have I ever concealed anything from you regarding my health?"

"Do you really want me to answer that, sire?"

When the medic was done wrapping his shoulder, Garrett stood, pulling his white shirt and black waistcoat on. He didn't intend to deceive Thatcher, but he didn't want to worry the medic—or any of his soldiers—for no reason. He'd collected all sorts of injuries and scars over the past couple years, and he always turned out all right in the end.

He pulled on his cutaway coat as he stepped out of the medic's tent. Their camp here in this wild, tangled woodland was packing up for the morning. A thin, brisk fog hung in the air, as though the night was lingering, stealing more of the day as autumn arrived. Garrett squinted in the marigold light of the dawning sun, savoring the crisp air. On such a bright, brilliant morning as this, it was easy to forget the horrors of Briar's castle and their subsequent venture into the fairy woods.

But Garrett had not forgotten. Though it was hardly surprising to learn that the dark fairy was responsible for these corpse monsters, it brought them no closer to finding a solution to the curse. Which was why they traveled south now, retreating to the Glen Kingdom—where they could consult with Garrett's father the king.

They were still three days from the ford crossing, and the depot where their train waited was two days beyond that. Another five days. Garrett wasn't only concerned about everyone's physical safety, but about the overall mood of his soldiers as well. The danger in this particular venture had been a little more significant than anticipated, and they'd lost three soldiers in the castle. He didn't want anyone getting bogged down in fear and grief.

He picked through the remains of the camp. The hubbub of pots clanging and soldiers nattering filled the air. He came across Demetri directing several soldiers who were packing supplies into the carts. Garrett smiled, passing on without comment. It was a dreadful shame, really, that Garrett was going to be the next king of the Glen Kingdom and not Demetri. Demetri was far more suited to the task.

Garrett didn't realize he was looking for Briar until he spotted her beside her tent, and a light, airy feeling descended upon him. The princess had discarded her sheer white gown in favor of more practical clothing. She wore a pair of stiff, dark brown breeches tucked into her boots—probably borrowed from one of his female soldiers—and a cotton shirt beneath her short, tatty jacket. Her pale hair was pulled back into a tight braid, giving her face a sharp cast. On someone else, the look might have been too severe, but on Briar, it only made her more striking.

"Morning," Garrett greeted her. "I like this new look. Much less cursed princess, more...clockwork inventor."

Briar pulled on the ends of her jacket. "One of the soldiers you set for me—Kinsley—he said it looked all right."

"That settles it, then. Kinsley is always up to date on the latest fashions. And he's my best sharpshooter. Two good reasons to have him as your guard."

They walked together through a small copse of beech trees where their horses were tied. Garrett greeted all the soldiers they passed, pausing for a few seconds to banter with some of them.

"You seem very close with your soldiers," Briar noted.

"My father would probably say I'm too informal with them," Garrett confessed.

"I don't think so," Briar mused. "I think it's good you know them so well."

"It's just weird for me to be too much of the prince with them, I suppose." It weighed on Garrett sometimes, the authority he wielded. Even after all these years—eight years already—it did not feel quite natural to him. "Most of them have accompanied me into far too much danger—and seen me at my worst," he added with a laugh, "to be so formal with them. None of that comes easily to me anyway. I wasn't raised as a prince until I was ten years old."

"What do you mean? Why not?"

"I was born a commoner." Garrett often felt awkward discussing his parentage with other nobles, certainly with other royals—but he thought Briar probably wouldn't care. "My mother was a peasant woman; she lived and worked in town. My father met her after his first wife died, they carried on an affair, and, well, the usual thing happened. I was born. I lived in town with my mother until she died when I was ten. Then my father took me in at the castle."

"Really." True to Garrett's assessment, Briar did not sound scandalized by this. She only looked at him, sweeping a stray strand of hair back from her face. "I'm sorry about your mother. You must have been close."

"Of course," Garrett said, the reply deep in his throat. He did not like to think much on his mother. Sometimes he worried he did her a disservice, locking away his memories of her, but sometimes it was the only way to cope. "But my father wasn't a total stranger to me. He visited often when I was a boy. And he didn't hesitate to take me in when my mother died."

"So he made you his heir, then?" Briar asked.

"Not right away." They had strayed into some rather personal territory for him, and yet, Garrett didn't hesitate as he spilled out his life story. For some reason, talking to Briar felt like talking to an old friend, even though they had only known each other for two days. "My father had an heir, his son by his late wife—my elder brother. But he was...exiled...several years ago. That was when I was made heir."

"Oh," was all Briar said. Garrett kept his eyes fixed on the forest floor, listening to the leaves crunch beneath his boots as he waited for the inevitable questions about his brother. Questions he did not want to answer. Not only because he didn't *have* all the answers, but because he preferred not to dwell on the few memories he had of Gryphon. They hadn't exactly been close.

But Briar did not ask any more after his family. Maybe she sensed he didn't want to discuss it. Or more likely, because they'd just passed his soldier Read with his handheld box camera, which diverted Briar's attention.

Garrett couldn't contain a grin as he watched Briar exclaim over the camera, asking Read to open it so she could examine the gear mechanizations inside. She delighted in so many things that, to her, were new inventions, and Garrett was impressed by her detailed understanding of them. Many of these things were old hat to Garrett, things he couldn't imagine living without, like gear-bulb lamps, firearms with revolving barrels, and the combination lock he used on his traveling trunk. Other items were newer—Read's camera, for one, and the repeater rifles. But still, these things were of little consequence to Garrett. And aside from understanding how to operate them, he never put much thought into how they worked, the *science* behind them. But Briar was fascinated by these things; she wanted to study them, she took notes, and she asked a million questions.

As intrigued as the princess was by these things, Garrett was more and more intrigued by *her*. By her curiosity and resilience. If it had been him, he thought—if he had been the one transplanted into a completely new century—he would have been lost. But not Briar. She was oddly, wonderfully fearless.

Her enthusiasm for the camera and the other gadgets they'd encountered was nothing compared to her reaction when they reached the train depot a few days later. As Garrett had requested earlier, the train was there waiting for them. Black smoke wound up from the train's chimney, looping into the air as the engine purred beneath it. As the soldiers and train workers began to unload their supplies from the carts—which they'd borrowed from the depot—Briar inspected every inch of the train, from the wheels, rails, and the funnels to the interlocking carriages and the tender. Then she disappeared into the cab up front, and Garrett found her there some twenty minutes later when they were ready to depart.

"It's weird, though," she was saying as he poked his head in. "Prince Garrett told me that, though he didn't know why."

"Know what why?" Garrett hoisted himself up into the cab. He leaned against the back corner as the conductor, Miles, swept him a low bow.

"Why trains won't operate on gears," Briar said.

"No one really knows why, Your Highness," Miles said, his voice a pleasant tenor. He was an older, fair-skinned man, with very little hair under his cap. "Though scientists are doing all sorts of research on it, I hear. It's not only trains, though that's what everyone's talking about. The gears just don't last long on a train."

"Maybe it's to do with some fault in the elarium," Briar murmured.

"The what?" Garrett asked.

"The elarium," Briar repeated. Garrett, unfamiliar with the word, shook his head. To which, of course, Briar turned an incredulous eye. She said, "You know, the ore used to manufacture gears."

Garrett frowned. "I thought gears could be manufactured from a variety of materials. Iron, copper, brass—"

"Well, technically they can be." Briar rocked forward on her heels as she raised her hands to illustrate her point. "And those will do for some things—small things mostly, though it's not really to do with the size so much as what the mechanism does. Your self-propelled carts, for instance—they could be powered by springs alone, but they wouldn't go far without winding. It's that specific ore—the elarium keeps them going longer. I thought maybe your carts weren't built with elarium, though I don't know why you'd build them with something else—but I thought maybe that's why they had to be wound so often. But I checked, and they were elarium-forged, though they were painted to look brass. Which people do with a lot of things, though that's just an aesthetic consideration. Like your gear-bulb lanterns—most of them are painted over silver or brass." Briar stopped short, huffing out a breath.

"Right." Garrett stared at her.

"You really didn't know that?" Briar asked. He could tell she was striving for a polite tone, but disbelief edged her words. "About the elarium?"

"I might have heard something," Garrett said flippantly. "Or something about elarium being such a high commodity, anyway. I *am* prince of the realm, after all."

Briar's lips twitched as though she was trying not to smile. "I'd almost forgotten."

They left the cab, ready to be off. Garrett led her into a middle carriage, where the sleeper compartments and dining car were. As he showed her to her compartment, he twisted around in the tight corridor to look at her. He had asked her once before—sort of obliquely, he supposed—how she'd become interested in building things, but she hadn't given him a real answer. "How did you become so interested in all this...scientific stuff?" he asked now. "Or was it always a hobby?"

"I suppose so," Briar mused. "I was forbidden to leave the castle grounds, so there wasn't much to do. I did learn all the things noble ladies were supposed to—dancing, piano, drawing, painting. I was never much good at any of those except for drawing. Only instead of sketching portraits or bowls of fruit, I'd sketch inventions."

It sounded a lonely life, Garrett thought. And stifling, especially for someone like Briar, who was so full of questions about the world. He thought of her lift and suddenly understood why she would build such a thing—a secret way out beyond the castle walls.

They reached Briar's sleeper compartment and Garrett opened the door for her. She ducked beneath his arm to enter and looked around with intent eyes. Yellow sunlight poured into the compartment through a glass window, framing Briar with a hazy gleam. "I think it first started when I was about seven," she continued. "I was meant to be practicing piano, but instead I opened the piano up and looked inside to see how the keys worked. I sketched them out and took notes—"

"—the way you do." Garrett smiled as he leaned against the doorframe. He had seen her sketching many times over the last few days—in the mornings before they set out, during traveling breaks, and even in the saddle, once or twice. He found this dedication endearing, especially in light of everything she'd been through this last week.

"After that I started sketching lots of things." Briar drifted forward. "Like an old sextant I found, and safety locks and thermometers and clocks—lots and lots of clocks. My father was a bit of a collector, so he had lots of them, just for decorative purposes, you know. Though he was very angry one time when I—" She broke off, an abstracted expression coming over her face.

"When you what?" Garrett prompted, leaning in a little.

Briar's brow furrowed. "I—uh—nothing. Never mind."

The train lurched to a start, the floor tremoring beneath their feet. Garrett remained steady thanks to his grip on the compartment doorframe, but Briar staggered a little, placing a hand flat against Garrett's chest to keep from falling into him. She dropped her hand almost as soon as she'd touched him, but Garrett felt a tug in his chest as her fingers fell away. As though she'd taken something from him. It was an unsettling feeling, but gone too fast for Garrett to think about it.

He hadn't realized how close to her he'd been standing, leaning in from his vantage point against the doorframe. He cleared his throat and stepped back. "I'm going to see about lunch in the dining car. Coming?"

"Maybe in a bit." Briar dropped her gaze as the floor began to sway to the rhythmic beat of the chugging train. "Do you know where Demetri is?"

"I haven't seen him. I'm surprised he hasn't come looking for you."

"I'm sure he's just tired, or—or hungry." Briar's offhand tone was not quite convincing. "I'll look for him later."

Garrett left her and headed for the dining car. He saw Demetri there and told him Briar had asked after him. Demetri nodded, and Garrett couldn't help but notice that his friend didn't quite meet his gaze, his eyes wandering from wall to wall. Garrett wasn't sure why.

Demetri had been quiet the past few days, which was weird. Well, it wasn't weird that he had been quiet, but moreover, he had kept to himself a lot. That was the weird part. Not only did Demetri enjoy conversing with people, but Garrett thought that the prince's eighty years of isolation drove him to seek out company more often than not. Yet over the last several days of travel, Garrett realized he could not recall seeing Demetri much. Garrett himself had spent much of that time talking with Briar. Yet now that he thought about it, Demetri had never once joined them in their conversations.

Several hours later, as darkness crept over the horizon outside, Garrett headed back into the passenger carriage. He'd spent some time checking on Spencer, who was well on the mend, a week after he'd been wounded in the castle. Garrett was looking for some of the other soldiers when he passed an empty compartment—or at least, he thought it was empty. The varnished cherry-wood door stood open, and the compartment inside was thrown in shadow. But upon a second glance, Garrett glimpsed a form inside, something—or some*one*—curled up in the corner. He half-reached for a pistol before he recognized the person.

Garrett leaned into the compartment. "Briar? Why are you sitting in the dark?"

"What?" Tucked in the shadows, Briar's words seemed to float out of nothing, a disembodied voice. "Oh. I don't mind the dark."

Garrett stepped inside and wound up the bulb latched into the wall, set within an etched glass shade. It never occurred to him that she might not want company—he had spent enough time with her by now to know she was a fairly direct person. She would tell him if she didn't want his company—though she never had so far.

Garrett was glad for it. He really liked talking with Briar, spending time with her. She was a strange girl, and yet he found it so easy to be around her. Garrett was not a person who ever had trouble conversing with anyone, but that didn't mean he thoroughly *enjoyed* talking with just anyone. But with Briar, he did.

Really, it had been a long time since he had enjoyed talking with someone as much as Briar. A very long time.

Cross-legged on the cushioned seat, Briar squinted as the white light of the bulb eased to life, brightening as its gears tumbled and ticked. She lifted a paper from her lap and gestured towards her satchel and notebook beside her. "I was looking at these."

Garrett didn't understand how she could look at anything in the dark, but he didn't press the issue. Instead, he lowered himself into the seat across from her, relaxing against the upholstered backing. His muscles, heavy with fatigue from days on horseback, seemed to sigh as he stretched his legs out. "More inventions?"

"Actually—" Briar set her wrinkled paper upon her knee and smoothed it with a gentle hand "—this one is a letter. From Demetri."

"Ah, he wrote you love letters, did he? What a romantic."

"No." Briar eyed him with a suspicious slant to her gaze, as though wondering if he was making fun of her. Which he was, a little, but all in good humor. "He didn't write me love letters. He wrote me this letter when he was nine."

"What?" Garrett snorted.

"We were engaged when we were infants, remember?" she said. "Before I was cursed."

Garrett slumped more comfortably in his seat. "That's right. You said your parents kept the curse a secret from Demetri and his parents." He frowned. "If you don't mind me asking...why did they do that? Just to make sure the alliance would remain intact?"

Briar eyed him from beneath her lashes, her expression almost furtive. "I think so. That was the whole point of it, after all. But also..." She dropped her gaze to her lap. "My parents were always in a weird sort of denial about my curse. Partly. On the one hand, I was never allowed to leave the castle, for my own safety. And my parents always kept their distance from me—I think they even told others in the castle to do the same. But they often acted as though everything was fine, as though the curse was never going to happen. Like the ball they threw for my sixteenth birthday... it was like they were pretending I wasn't going to fall to the curse that very same night."

She said all of this in a quick, hushed voice. As though she wasn't sure how he would react.

Mostly, Garrett just felt stunned. "What do you mean, they kept their distance from you?" he asked, his voice slightly strangled. "What...why?" He recalled that, earlier, she had said something about her father not feeling sad when she was cursed. Which made as little sense now as it did then.

Briar shrugged. It was an obvious attempt at apathy, so obvious it made Garrett ache for her. "To protect themselves, I think. After all, if they didn't love me, then it wouldn't hurt so much when they lost me." She managed to keep an even tone until she said the word *lost*. Her voice cracked—just a little—on that word.

"That's mad," said Garrett, and then he winced at his bluntness. "That is...I'm sorry, Briar. That's awful. I can't imagine..." Garrett had always had a parent who loved him, even before he knew his father well, and even after his mother died. And while his father wasn't the warmest person, he certainly cared for Garrett and never hid that from him. But Briar....

Garrett couldn't imagine the loneliness. No wonder she never told him to go away, he thought. She probably welcomed any company, no matter who it was. That thought deepened the ache in his chest.

But Briar smiled a tiny smile, flitting her gaze in his direction. She lay her palm flat over the curling end of the letter. "Anyway. They kept the engagement, for whatever reason. And Demetri and I, we wrote each other over the years. Though I didn't meet him in person until he came to the kingdom when I was fifteen. Almost sixteen."

Garrett canted his head back against his seat. "Where is Demetri, anyway?"

"He's asleep," Briar said quickly. A little too quickly. "I looked in on him a short while ago—I thought maybe—but he was already asleep." She tucked the letter between the pages of her worn leather notebook.

Garrett watched her, noting how her gaze lingered on the letter, noting her pale hands as she folded them before her. His chest felt funny. He rubbed it absently, digging his fingers between his ribcage, trying to make the strange ache go away. He realized it was the same spot where Briar had laid her hand upon him earlier, when the train departed.

A deep disquiet woke inside Garrett. For the first time since he had met Briar, he felt shaken, disconcerted in her presence. Not *because* of her, not because of anything she'd said or done. No, it was him. It was this feeling...this strangely familiar, strangely troubling feeling.

Garrett swallowed. It was quiet in the compartment. Briar gazed at her letter, and Garrett gazed at her. At the slant of her gaunt cheekbone. At her slender fingers, spread out over her crinkled letter.

It was so quiet. So still. Garrett was struck by how alone they were here, just the two of them. Ensconced within the bright glow of the gear-bulb, so little space separating them from each other. Beneath them, the train grumbled as it sped down the tracks, but the noise of the world outside was shut out by the thick, glass windows, making the woods and its inhabitants silent for once.

"I should go," Garrett said. He ran a hand over his eyes. "I mean. It's getting late. I'm exhausted. See you in the morning?"

"Sure." Briar spared him a small smile. "Goodnight, Garrett."

He left the compartment, breathing deeply, trying to disperse that feeling in his chest. Every second bulb along the corridor had been turned off, dimming the train for the night. Garrett passed into the sleeper carriage, but when he reached his compartment, he paused. Demetri's compartment was just a bit further down. Given his withdrawn behavior earlier—and recalling Briar's reserve about him just now—he wondered if he should check on his friend.

Garrett started for Demetri's compartment. The train rattled on the tracks as it chugged along, like the even breathing of someone asleep.

Garrett was five steps from Demetri's compartment when something *thudded* onto the ceiling overhead.

He spun around, his gaze snapping up. Something had fallen onto the train top outside. Whatever it was sounded heavy. A tree branch, maybe? They were still in the woods. He stood still, eyes lifted, fixed on the train ceiling. Several seconds passed, and he heard nothing.

He turned back towards Demetri's compartment.

Bam. Bam. Bam.

He whirled around, looking up. The train rooftop had been dented in. As though someone had pounded it down—pounded down several inches of solid steel.

He reached for his pistol, only to realize it wasn't there.

Then the windows crashed in, and corpses spilled into the train.

11

STRANDED

BRIAR WAS STILL IN the empty train compartment when she heard the bashing against the roof, even though it was a whole carriage down. A second later, the windows crashed in, and *that* was loud enough to draw everyone's attention.

A large group of soldiers were gathered in a compartment nearby. Briar heard them piling into the corridor, readying weapons and shouting at each other, but by that point, she was already running, her feet flying down the carpeted corridor. Time seemed to slow as she ran, the seconds ticking by more slowly than usual. She noted everything around her, all the details—the sound of her boots smacking against the floor, *thwop-thwop-thwop*, and the scattered beat of her pulse in her throat. And yet she realized—like she was outside of it all, watching herself—that she was moving very fast. Her stiff joints and sore muscles vanished in an instant, and she raced down the corridor with abnormal speed.

She ran so fast that she slammed into the door between car-riages before she could get it open, her shoulder thudding against the hard glass window. She slipped through the door into the sleeper carriage, where a scene of horrific chaos met her.

Most of the high windows along the corridor had been smashed in, including the window on Briar's right. Shards of glass littered the floor; a few pieces crumbled beneath her boot when she stepped inside. As the train raced down the tracks, wintry air *whooshed* in through the gaping windows. A few ten-drils of hair escaped Briar's braid and lashed across her face, and she flinched, struggling to see through the roaring wind as it beat at her.

Several of the gear-bulb lights had shattered like the windows, and the few left intact flickered, providing an intermittent gleam to see by. But Briar didn't need to see well to identify the three corpse monsters in the corridor. One was down on the ground, half of its ribcage crushed in, and it struggled to rise, its limbs jerking like a clockwork creature whose gears had wound down. Another corpse, a huge man, wrestled with Garrett, who either wasn't armed or couldn't get a hand on his gun. The corpse had him in a headlock, but before Briar could move to help, Garrett elbowed the monster *hard* in the gut. The corpse loosened its hold enough for the prince to escape, and he turned, punching the monster across its sagging face.

A third corpse was further down, battering against a com-partment door, trying to break through. Briar's eyes widened. Demetri's compartment. She started down the corridor, clinging to the wall to keep steady against the wind.

She didn't make it halfway there. Something wrapped around her ankle and she tripped, her arms windmilling in an effort to stay upright. But she pitched forward and fell, landing half on the floor, half on top of the corpse that had grabbed her. The one with the crushed ribcage.

For a moment, she lay there, her hip bone smarting where it had banged against the floor. The *clank-clank* of the train clattering down the tracks screeched in her ear. She was completely disoriented, enveloped in flashing darkness, unable to hear, too pained to move.

Her hand burned. She turned her head and stared at the large shard of glass jutting out of her palm. Dark blood oozed around the glass. Before she could process this, a hand grabbed her by her braid and *tugged*.

Briar choked on a scream as she was yanked around, her neck straining until she thought it would snap. Still on the floor, she came face to face with the corpse that had grabbed her ankle. He was an older man, or had been, a few scraggly bits of hair on his head. He glared at her with bloodshot eyes and a mouth that was little more than a gash in his face. Briar felt frozen. It was not his ghastly appearance that gave her pause, but that this had been a live man once, a man from her kingdom.

But she couldn't help him now. All she could do was stay alive.

Briar yanked the shard of glass from her hand and shoved it through the corpse's bulging eye.

The corpse's gash of a mouth fell open in a moan, and he let go of her. She scrambled to her feet, slipping over the slick patch of blood she'd left on the floor. More blood seeped from the gash in her palm, but she didn't feel it. She kicked the corpse on the floor, hard, in the face, mashing in part of his head. He went down, though probably not for long. But long enough to get to Demetri.

A shot rang out, splintering through the noise of the speeding train and howling wind. Briar wheeled around. The corpse at Demetri's door fell back beneath a blitz of bullets, and a cloud of smoke engulfed the spot where he'd been. A moment later, Demetri emerged through the haze of powder smoke with a pistol in one hand and two more in the other. "Garrett!" he called, tossing a pistol to the other prince.

Briar didn't get the chance to see Garrett before the carriage door burst open behind her, *whumping* against the wall as soldiers spilled inside. At the same time, more corpses tumbled in through the windows, one, two, three, four, five, Briar counted. Two lunged for Demetri, who began shooting, while others went for the soldiers bottlenecked in the carriage door. One lunged at Briar and grabbed her round the throat in a crushing grip, hoisting her off the ground. Her feet dangled in the air. She lashed out, trying to hit the thing, but she couldn't reach him. Then the hand around her throat tightened, and breathing became much more important than hitting the corpse. A dull, heavy pressure began to build in her face, along the ridge of her nose, as she fought for wisps of air that weren't enough. Her hands went for the fingers at her neck, trying to pry them free. She managed to get one, and the icy, slimy finger broke off in her hands. But the others weren't coming off.

She could hear someone calling her name. Someone darted into view, someone with dark, curly hair. Read. The soldier with the camera. He didn't have a gun, but he charged at the corpse strangling Briar. Before he could reach her, another corpse leapt at him. Briar watched, eyes wide, hands scrabbling at her own neck, as the corpse seized the soldier by his curly mop of hair and ripped Read's head right off. The rent pieces of Read—his soundless head and his limp body—fell to the floor, blood leaking from their gunky, gaping ends. Two corpses threw themselves on the body, chunks of flesh and viscera spurting into the air as they tore him apart with hands and teeth.

They were *eating* him.

Briar's reaction was instant and powerful; her stomach heaved even as she struggled to breathe, to draw in a smidge of air. The rushing wind seemed to swell, filling Briar's head, and her blood flared with heat. Black spots appeared before her eyes, but it didn't matter. This *thing* was choking the life out of her, people were dying around her, good people, maybe Garrett, maybe Demetri—

Briar reached out with her injured hand and seized the wrist encircling her throat. The pain in her palm became something else. Not pain, but *strength.* She was steel.

With a swift flick of her wrist, Briar bent the monster's hand back until it *snapped,* freeing herself. She dropped, her feet thudding into the ground, sending a jolt up her wobbly legs. It took a second for the shadows clouding the corners of her eyes to flee. She still held the monster's wrist, but it snarled at her, and its other arm hammered into her chest. The hit sent her reeling, and she barely caught herself on hands and knees.

Briar tried to rise. Somewhere in the back of her mind, she knew that a hit like that should've knocked her out. But that mysterious strength fueled her, coursing through her like a drug, numbing her pain and encasing her in iron.

Before she could stand, the corpse snatched a handful of her hair and yanked her up in a lurching, tripping movement. The monster was going to rip her hair out, maybe rip her head off, but when it spun Briar around to face it, she was ready. She couldn't control her body's momentum as she swung around, but she used it, bringing her arm back as she spun. And when her fist connected with the monster's throat, it broke through its mottled skin, crunching through cartilage and bone.

The monster lost its hold on her. As it fell to its knees, Briar pulled her arm free. Her fist came away covered in dark, sticky blood. She kicked at the monster's head, and so little remained to hold it to its body that it rolled off. The headless thing slumped to the floor, unmoving.

Briar gaped at the corpse, a true corpse now. She felt numb. Her gaze traveled from the corpse to her hand, coated in clumpy gore. As though she'd stuck her hand in a jar of grape jam and pulled out a glob of it. It was her nightmare come true. She couldn't comprehend the sight of the blood-like substance running down her arm in thick rivulets. She couldn't comprehend how *warm* the blood felt, given how cold the monster's skin had been. She couldn't comprehend the flesh caught between her fingers. She tried to process it all, reconcile it with what she'd just done. But the two wouldn't connect.

She used her other hand to pat at her hair, half of it hanging loose from her braid, and looked down the corridor. Most of the corpses had been vanquished by the soldiers, though quarters were so tight that many of the soldiers had never made it into the carriage, and fewer still could use their firearms to shoot the corpses down. On her left, Demetri stood with a pistol in one hand and his drawn rapier in the other, the blade slick with violet blood. One corpse lay at his feet and, as Briar watched, he finished a second, taking its head. His high-collared waistcoat bore a long rent down the front, but there was no blood that she could see.

Briar didn't see Garrett anywhere. "Where's Garrett?" she called to Demetri.

"On the roof!" Demetri pointed with his rapier. "He thought there were more up there, so he went to knock them off."

"What? Is he mad?"

Demetri looked at her. "Well, yes. You hadn't realized that by now?"

As though in response to his name, something large and heavy smacked against a window, one that hadn't broken in. It was a person, visible through the glass, hanging over the edge of the roof. Briar couldn't see a face, but she recognized the dark waistcoat. It was Garrett.

"Stones!" Briar swore. She half-turned to Demetri, but another corpse dove through a window beside him. As Demetri hacked at the corpse, Briar climbed on top of an upholstered seat to reach through a broken window.

As she hoisted her body out the window, she went deaf. The gunshots had already muted her hearing, but out here, with the wind screaming and the train grinding down the tracks, she couldn't hear a thing. It was pitch black too, but Briar could make out what lay before her. She reached for the edge of the train and kicked herself out the window, scrambling stomach first onto the cold, steel roof. She didn't think she could stand without flying off the top, but she got to her knees, even with the train jolting beneath her. From there she could see that the train was fast approaching a long, high bridge over a wide body of water—the river.

Much closer, Garrett hung off the edge of the roof. A corpse creature, with yellow hair dangling down her back in twisted tendrils, stood over him, poised to kick him off. Still on her knees, hunched over against the biting wind, Briar crawled, praying the monster wouldn't turn and see her. As she came up behind it, she stood and threw herself at the corpse. She was moving against the wind, but her hands connected with the creature's back and her momentum knocked her forward. The corpse tumbled off the roof, straight over Garrett.

Her momentum, and the train's momentum, also knocked Briar flat on her stomach, her head and arms dangling over the edge of the train. For a terrifying second, her arms were out of control, whirling about in the wind, as though they were going to fly right off her body. But then she grabbed at the roof edge, steadying herself. Below her, Garrett still hung, his feet flailing to get a foothold. He looked up at her and yelled something—she was pretty sure she heard the word *mad*—but most of it was swallowed by the wind.

As the train began its way across the high bridge, dark river water appeared below them. Holding on with one hand, Briar stretched the other towards Garrett. He grabbed onto her, his huge hand engulfing hers, but no matter how she pulled, she couldn't hoist him up. It was like trying to lift a sack filled with bricks. Stars and stones, where had her inhuman strength gone?

Her grip on the roof began to slip. Her hand was numb with cold and the edge of the roof bit into her fleshy palm. She adjusted her hold on Garrett, wrapping her hand around his forearm. She'd be in a better position to pull him up if she was on her feet, but if she stood, she'd fly off the train. Garrett managed to get his other arm on top of the roof. Maybe if she kept steadying him, he'd pull himself up—

The train stuttered like it ran over a groove in the tracks. All at once, Briar lurched forward, losing her grip on the train. Before she could stop herself, she pitched over the edge, off the roof. Garrett's arm still clutched hers, and she pulled him off after her, his heavy weight driving them down fast, tumbling into the black below—

Then Briar came to a breakneck halt. One moment, she'd been weightless, falling, air rushing past her—and then she stopped. It took her another second to realize Garrett must have caught hold of something. As they jerked to a stop, her entire body swung back without any control.

Her temple connected with something sharp and hard, and everything went black.

Briar came awake to darkness. The first thing she noticed was the pounding in her head, especially behind her eye. Her back and arms ached, the muscles strained and taut. And her ears rang with an incessant buzz, as though there was a fly zipping around her. Then sound came rushing back to her, muffled but breaking through the buzz.

"Briar? Briar!"

Briar groaned, reaching a hand to her head. The skin felt tender at her temple. It took her eyes a few seconds to adjust to the dark, and then she saw Garrett—beside her, right in front of her. For a moment, she was forcibly reminded of waking like this before, in the near-dark, with Garrett's face hovering over her. But this was not the tower. This was not her castle.

This was...where was she?

"Briar?" Garrett's voice was near and anxious.

"I'm fine," Briar croaked. "I'm here. What...happened? Where are we?"

"Thank the stars," Garrett said. "We fell off the train, remember?"

The train. Oh. Oh, yes, now she did remember. She couldn't hear the speeding wind anymore, or the chug of the train careening down the tracks. She blinked, leaning to her right—

"Whoa!" Garrett's arm shot out and gripped her by the shoulder, righting her. "Don't—don't *do* that."

Briar heard the edge in Garrett's voice. She looked out again, this time without leaning. Even in the dark, she could make out the landscape before them. Thick fir trees ahead and towering redwoods behind—not around her, but in the distance, row upon row of them. The woods, on either side of—

"The river." Briar's eyes widened as she gazed at the long, dark body of water, stretching out *beneath* her. The water reflected the light of the stars above, and it glittered like a great, scaly serpent, slithering into the distance. She looked at Garrett, who sat close beside her, his shoulder pressed against hers, her knee resting against his. Subtly moving her leg to break the contact, she looked around at the russet metal beneath them, and the steel latticework above them.

They were on the bridge. Seated in a groove of one of the supporting arches below the bridge, though still very, very high above the river.

"I grabbed onto the edge before we could fall further." Garrett's voice sounded hoarse. "But—"

"The train." Briar felt like a heavy stone had settled inside her. "It's gone?"

"It went straight by," Garrett confirmed. "It was gone before I got us in here. And you hit your head, you were unconscious and—are you all right?"

"Fine," Briar said, though she took a moment to inventory for injuries. Her muscles ached more than usual—probably from trying to lift Garrett from the train's roof, all while fighting against the wind. She'd hit her head—that explained the pounding. And she'd sliced her hand open back inside the train, on a piece of glass.

Briar raised her left hand, palm flat, and looked at it. The blood on her hand was dry, bits of it flaking off as she looked more closely. Even deep *in* the gash, the blood had gone dry, caked within her skin like old icing peeling off a pastry. She flexed her fingers, but it didn't hurt, not even a little. "Weird," she whispered.

"What?" Garrett asked.

"Nothing," said Briar, but her voice sounded hollow in her ears. Something was unspooling inside her, deep in her gut. An unwelcome, sickly feeling. "I'm fine." Briar shifted, pulling away from him.

"What are you doing?" Garrett's words came quick and sharp.

"I'm going to try to stand." She got her knee under her. "See if we can climb out of—"

"No!" Garrett's hand closed around her arm, his fingers digging into her skin through the sleeve of her spencer. "Don't. That's mad, if you fall—"

Briar tugged at his grip. "I'll be careful—"

"No, Briar, please don't." Garrett's fingers tightened even more. "Please. If you fall, I—just don't. All right?"

Briar looked at him. She didn't know how well he could see her face in the darkness, but she could see his plain as day, save for where the arch above them cast a shadow. The set of his jaw was tense, and his eyes were fearful.

Of course. She'd forgotten. He was afraid of heights. She couldn't imagine what it had taken for him to pull her up here, to climb into the groove. Now that they were here, he didn't want to move.

"We have to get out of here somehow," Briar said. "Sometime."

"We can just wait." Garrett's words tumbled over each other. He still hadn't let go of her arm. "It's too dark, we can't see what we're doing—it's too dangerous. Let's just wait until it gets light, I—it might be hours, I don't know, and I know it's cold and this is mad, sitting here, but Briar—"

"All right." Briar relaxed, settling down. She leaned back against the metal arch, though it was impossible to do so without resting her shoulder against Garrett. Garrett dropped his hand from her arm, though she could still feel his fingertips near her elbow. He was shaking, she realized, his whole body vibrating. She didn't know how to calm him; she didn't know if she should reach out to him, maybe take his hand. She desperately wanted to, she realized. But she didn't, and after a few minutes, she felt his trembling cease and his breathing even out.

She didn't relish the idea of staying here several more hours, and she was sure Garrett really didn't either, but he wasn't wrong about it being dangerous to climb out in the dark. Although, given how weirdly well she could see in the dark, a part of her was curious to see if she could make it anyway. But she doubted she could convince Garrett to move.

The wind soughed through the trees across the bank, whispering as it rippled over the water below. Briar didn't feel cold, but beside her, Garrett shivered. He didn't have his coat, only his linen shirt and waistcoat. She wondered how cold it really was. She couldn't tell.

She clasped her hands together, feeling her fingertips. They were cold as ice to the touch, but she didn't *feel* cold. She ran her fingers over the wound on her palm, over the dried blood. It didn't hurt at all.

Briar clenched her teeth, trying to keep her chin from quivering. She remembered how impossibly fast she'd run down the corridor. Now that it was behind her, it began to dawn on her how insane that was, that she'd moved so fast. And she thought of the corpse she'd destroyed. She didn't want to look at her other hand, also encrusted with blood, but not hers. Dark, taupe blood. She remembered breaking through the monster's neck.

"What's happening to me?" she whispered.

Garrett shifted. "What?"

"I'm—I'm not right." None of it made *sense*, and she couldn't ignore that. "Garrett, back on the train, I—I did something impossible, something crazy—"

"You mean when you tore out that corpse's throat?"

Briar whipped her head around. "You saw that?"

"Just before I went onto the roof. I was going to help you, but since you had it handled, I headed out."

She searched his face. "*And?*"

"I was a little jealous. I wish I could rip someone's throat out with my bare hands."

"You're not even joking about that, are you?"

Garrett sighed, his broad chest moving up and down. "Briar, I was just glad you were okay. But—"

"But it's not normal." The words came tripping out of her, fueled by a rush of anxiety. That sickly feeling inside her was growing, pushing *out*, consuming her from the inside. "Garrett, it's not just that. I'm—I never sleep anymore, I'm cold all the time, my whole body aches and I *look* different—"

"Briar," Garrett interrupted her. His voice had regained its deep, smooth timbre. "You were cursed. You slept for *eighty years*. I know it's weird, what's going on with you, but there are bound to be side effects, don't you think? I'm sure things will return to normal in time."

She heard him, but she was thinking about something else. She remembered the dream she had that first day out of the castle, in the cart. The nightmare where she'd been one of *them*, and she tore out a corpse's throat—

Part of that nightmare had come true. What did that mean?

The answers were there, dancing just out of reach—but reaching for her. Grasping towards her. Briar shied away from them.

"Briar?" Garrett prompted.

"And my memory." Briar's words were deep in her throat, almost stuck there. "Garrett, you should have seen the look on Demetri's face. When I—went blank. I couldn't remember him then, but I remember *now* how he looked.... That *can't keep happening*. And what if..."

"What if what?" Garrett asked. She could feel the vibration of his voice rumbling through his chest.

"Earlier." Briar squeezed her eyes shut. She couldn't keep her fears at bay any longer. "When we were talking in the train—I was telling you about my father's clocks. I was going to say—something about—" She cast her mind back, desperate to remember. "I was telling you a story, something to do with one of his clocks and—I forgot."

"Forgot what?"

"What I was going to tell you." The fear felt like thick, black oil, pooling inside her. "It's like, as I was talking to you, *right then*, it slipped away from me. The memory. And I know I was going to tell you something, and I know it had something to do with my father and that clock, but *I can't remember.*"

"Briar, people forget things all the time."

"No, Garrett, it wasn't like that, it was like—when I began to tell you about it, I knew what I was going to say, but—the memory dissolved right before my eyes, right *then*—and now it's just gone." Like something had gone out inside her, a flame snuffed out. "It's gone and I don't think it's ever coming back."

Garrett was silent. She wondered if he was putting the pieces together like she was, the fullness of these implications washing over him as they washed over her.

If she lost her memories, then who was she? What could she do, what use was she to anyone?

"I'm losing it," Briar choked. She clasped her bloodstained hands before her, but she couldn't stop their shaking. "I'm losing me." Her chest felt tight. A terrible surge welled up in her throat, but she wasn't going to be sick, she realized. That welling in her throat was a sob. But her eyes were dry. She couldn't summon a single tear.

Something warm touched the back of her arm. Garrett. His fingers wrapped around her elbow, a comforting pressure. He reached across with his other hand and laid it over both of hers, dried blood and all. The warmth from his hands seemed to seep out of him, spreading through her body. Chasing away the fear.

"You're not losing you," he said, his voice an anchor in the darkness. "You're right here."

12

BLOODSTAINED

GARRETT DREAMED OF SNOW.

It began as a memory, hazy but bright, warm but distant. They ran through a dense, green landscape. The marshy woodlands west of Snow's castle, close enough to the sea that Garrett could taste its briny scent on the air.

Snow's hand enveloped his own. She was laughing, tugging at him, and he followed, helpless to her whims. Happily helpless. Her dark hair shone beneath the dappled light piercing the trees, her fair skin so lustrous, it nearly vanished in the sun's glare.

"Where are we going?" he asked. His voice sounded strange, muffled, as though he was underwater. Talking underwater.

Snow didn't answer. She only laughed and ran. Suddenly, she was running too fast. Garrett's hand slipped from hers.

"Snow!" he called. But she didn't stop. Didn't come back.

The woodland was growing darker, vibrant greens fading into muddied blues. The deep blue of twilight. Snow's distant form grew hazier in the distance, until she vanished completely. The sunlight was gone. The treetops closed in over him.

Garrett felt cold. He felt lost. He shivered, alone in the woods. Stranded, desolate. Everything dark and unfamiliar.

"Snow!" he called, his voice pitiful and broken. "Snow!"

He turned around. There was something behind him. A long, low shape, half-covered in vines and moss. Garrett's heart hardened when he saw it, as though it had turned to ice.

He didn't want to look, didn't want to draw closer. But some inexorable force pushed him forward, until he stood beside the thing.

It was a stone bier. And atop it lay Snow. Her eyes were closed, her skin whiter than ever. Her lips were red, bright red, like blood.

She looked dead.

But she couldn't be. She just couldn't. Desperate, disbelieving, Garrett dropped to his knees beside the stone bier. The moss beneath him was cold and damp.

Garrett leaned over Snow and kissed her cold, unmoving lips.

He drew back.

But it was no longer Snow lying there, cold and dead on the bier.

It was Briar.

Something blared in his head, and Garrett jerked awake.

For a moment, he didn't know where he was. Blazing daylight blinded him, and a strong breeze blew past, cold and disorienting. There was something soft but solid on top of him, and he reached for it unthinkingly.

"Uh—you're awake."

Garrett blinked, his vision clearing.

Briar's face slowly came into focus, inches from him. She was leaning over him, practically stretched across his lap. They stared at each other for a moment, and then, belatedly, Garrett realized he was holding onto her shoulder.

His other hand was on her waist.

Hastily, Garrett released her. He blinked again, just as another loud *bleating* sounded in the distance.

"It's a boat coming down the river." Briar turned her head but did not climb off him or back away. It was a moment before Garrett realized why.

The river. The bridge. The *train*. It all came flooding back. Nearly plummeting to their deaths and climbing into this groove in the bridge, where they still sat precariously. He'd fallen asleep. He couldn't believe he'd fallen asleep, with nothing between him and the river below but the steel latticework of the bridge and a lot of open air.

Now it was morning. And Briar was leaning across him, waving her jacket to flag down the steamboat bearing down the river, its bleating horn sounding again as it neared the bridge.

Garrett rubbed a hand over his eyes. He felt clammy and flushed at the same time. The dreadful cold and despairing darkness of his dream lingered, clinging to him, and it was difficult to shake off those emotions, to convince himself it was not real.

He squeezed his eyes shut and tried to focus on physical sensations, rooting himself to the waking world. The daylight, a little too bright. His shoulder, sore and aching—both from his bite wound and from nearly dislocating it last night, when he'd caught onto the bridge and stopped their fall. His knees, cramped and stiff from sleeping here all night.

The open air beneath him, giving way to the river far, far below.

That sensation was a little too terrifying. Garrett gulped and sought for something else to distract him.

Briar's knee, pressed against his hip.

Garrett let out his breath, slow and shaky. That was terrifying too, though for other reasons. Reasons he didn't want to think about.

"I think they've seen us!" Briar said. "Yes—they're waving back!"

Garrett had never been more relieved in his life.

He was also relieved that their escape off the bridge did not, in the end, involve climbing up onto it. He was incredibly disappointed, though, that it did involve climbing *down* a narrow, rickety ladder onto the steamboat.

The ensuing half hour was pretty much the worst half hour of Garrett's existence. It didn't matter that Briar insisted the ladder was not rickety, given it was built from steel, or how much the steamboat crew padded the deck below in case he *did* fall. It was still the most terrifying thing he had ever done, climbing down that ladder, and given the kind of danger Garrett faced on a weekly basis, that was saying something.

The crew of the steamboat deposited them on the riverbank as they requested, but Garrett had a harder time convincing them to leave them there. After insisting they would just follow the railroad tracks to find their people, the crew assented to leave and carried on their way down the river.

"Good thing they didn't realize who we are." Garrett turned from the sloping, muddy riverbank to face the woods. "Or they'd never have let us go on by ourselves."

Briar nodded. She'd made it down from the bridge just fine, and she'd seemed all right on the steamship. Now, though, as Garrett peered at her, he thought she looked dreadfully pale. Paler than usual. He wondered if his terrible dream had colored his vision, making him see Briar worse than she was, but he didn't think so. The dark circles beneath her eyes were more pronounced than ever, giving her a sallow look. And she shivered, though she wore her jacket and the morning was not especially cold.

"All right?" Garrett asked her uncertainly.

Briar nodded again. "Yes. Let's get going."

They started into the woods, following the railroad as it wove through the giant Glen redwoods that grew in abundance on this side of the river. The air was balmier than it had been, the sun out in full force, but the further they got into the woods, the less they saw of it. When Garrett glanced back and saw Briar walking with her arms clutched around herself, he turned to face her head-on. "Are you sure you're all right?"

Briar stuttered to a halt, looking like she'd forgotten he was there. "What? Of course." Her voice was scratchy. "I'm fine."

"Yes, but—" Garrett gestured towards her. "Just look at you."

"I can't look at me." Briar shivered as a burst of wind blew by. "How do I look?"

Garrett ran his gaze over her, taking in her tangled hair, her hunched posture. She'd gone so pale he could see the purple veins running up her neck. Or maybe that was just bruising from the fight last night. Either way, she did not look good. She looked— "Terrible," he said.

"Well, thanks." Briar's voice was flat. "That's nice to know."

"Look." Garrett scraped his boot over a gnarled root. "You didn't get any sleep last night. And it was cold out on the bridge—maybe you took a chill—"

"Garrett," Briar interrupted. "Yes, I'm tired. Of course I'm tired. But what else can we do except keep going? There's no telling if there are more corpses around, and we'll be safer with the rest of the group. You said yourself that they probably didn't get far before noticing we were gone, so I'm sure we don't have more than a few miles to go. I can make it a few miles."

Garrett drummed his thumb against his thigh. It was true he had told the steamboat captain that their train probably hadn't gone far, but he'd exaggerated a bit. The fact was, if the train was only a few miles downriver, then they would have run into Garrett's people by now. He knew they would've stopped once they realized he and Briar were gone, but given that they were fighting corpses at the time, it was possible the train had gone five or ten miles down the tracks before coming to a halt.

Still, Briar had a point. He really, really didn't want to risk stopping in the woods for too long.

"All right." Garrett fiddled with the empty holster on his left side. "We'll keep going. But if you start feeling worse and need to rest, tell me, all right? I do have a pistol." He patted the gun on his right hip, the only weapon he'd taken from the train. "We're not completely defenseless out here."

They continued for a half hour, stopping twice to stretch a little. Their hike was doing wonders for Garrett's muscles, cramped and sore after the night in the bridge. The wind died down into an occasional soft breeze, carrying the dank scent of the river as it blew south.

He estimated the time at about mid-morning when they stopped for a longer break to eat some of the provisions the boat crew had provided for them. They discovered a small brook a short ways from the railroad, winding a crooked path through a grove of pine trees. Briar sat on the ground beside the gurgling brook, taking no heed of the mud as she munched on an apple. As Garrett crouched by the stream to splash some water onto his face, Briar said, "How did you break my curse, Garrett?"

The question was so unexpected that Garrett spluttered, spraying water everywhere. "How did I—what?" He wiped a hasty hand over his face and straightened.

"The curse." Briar's gray eyes were unblinking. "You woke me. How did you do it? You never said. I actually forgot about it—there was so much going on, what with the corpses trying to kill us or eat us, or in my case, reminisce about old times—anyway. But when I ran into the fairies in the woods, they asked how I woke from the curse early. And I realized I didn't know."

"That was a full week ago," Garrett said, his voice strangled. His dream felt suddenly fresh in his mind—Snow, Briar, the both of them, lying on the mossy bier in the dark woods.

"I know." Briar folded one leg beneath her. "But I wondered why you wouldn't have told me. Honestly, I wanted to see if you would. Since we've talked about—well, just about everything else over the last few days. But you haven't, so I thought there was probably a reason. Why you didn't want to, I mean." She took another bite of her apple.

"*Or* I just hadn't thought of it." Garrett tried not to fidget beneath her gaze, but his cheeks felt warm.

Briar swallowed a bite of her apple and said, "Well, if that's the only reason, then tell me now. How you did it."

Garrett didn't answer right away. He stepped back to perch atop a boulder. The stone seat was cold and damp with moss, and again, Garrett was forcibly, distressingly reminded of his dream. He said, "I shook you by the shoulders. Then you woke up."

"You did not shake me by the shoulders."

"Yes, I did." Garrett forced himself to meet her gaze.

"I don't remember that."

"If you remembered it—" Garrett threw an arm into the air "—then you wouldn't be asking, would you?"

Briar only looked at him, but her eyes tightened. A crow cawed balefully overhead before taking flight, the flurry of its wings breaking through the silence.

"What do you remember?" Garrett fiddled with the ring on his finger, slipping it round and round. His palm felt sweaty. "I mean...did you dream while you were asleep? What's the last thing you remember before waking?"

Briar pursed her lips as she set her apple aside, half-eaten. "I think I dreamed. Before you woke me—" He wished she wouldn't keep reiterating that *he* woke her "—I thought I was dancing. I must have been dreaming it, I think. And then, every-thing shifted. Like the dream broke around me. And I was so cold, or I had been, but then there was this...warmth...like..." She reached up and placed a white hand over her lips.

Garrett tensed so much, it felt like his ribs were pressing into his skin.

Briar dropped her hand. "I don't know. Then I woke up. And you were there. I remember thinking your clothes were very weird and you looked...unnerved. Like you'd seen a ghost." She leaned back on her arms. "You *did* do something to wake me, didn't you? Only you looked so stunned, like you weren't expecting me to wake and—"

"I loved this girl once," Garrett interrupted. "Her name was Snow. And she was cursed—hexed, actually—into unwaking sleep. Like you." He closed his eyes. His neck and jaw felt tight, like his head was too heavy to hold up. "I couldn't wake her, though. I never did. And she died."

When he opened his eyes, Briar was staring at him. Garrett could not read her expression, but he felt naked beneath her gaze. But then, that was only natural, he supposed, since he'd just blurted out the one thing he never talked about.

But he didn't stop there. He told her the whole story, like he'd told Demetri. Only it felt different than telling Demetri. Telling Demetri had felt freeing. It had been a relief. Telling Briar.... It was freeing, yes, but much more painful. It was like sloughing a pitted rock over an open wound. It was painful, and yet he *wanted* to tell her. All of it. This wasn't just getting it off his chest, it was *confiding* in someone in a way he had not since...well, since Snow.

He told Briar how he'd met Snow when he was sent by his father to court her, how they'd fallen in love in a matter of weeks, as though they'd been waiting all their lives to meet. How her stepmother had tried to kill her after he left, and how Snow fled to live in the woods that separated her kingdom from his.

How she fell into an enchanted sleep when her stepmother hexed her.

He did not tell Briar how he'd tried to wake Snow. When he reached that part of the story, he only said that he'd tried and failed. The rest of the story had poured out of him like a flood, a river overspilling its boundaries, but when he got to the part about true love's kiss...the words got lost somewhere.

Briar remained silent through his whole telling, shifting only a little when he didn't specify the manner of his attempt to wake Snow. But when he was done, she didn't ask about that. She only said, "I'm sorry, Garrett." And he could tell it was true by the softness in her eyes. "I'm so sorry you lost her."

"So am I." His voice had gone hoarse. "You would have liked her. I think. Well. She was a lot like me, actually." He rubbed a hand over his eyes. "We were both impulsive, and fearless. I never thought—I think we thought we were invincible. That nothing could ever happen to..." The words lodged in his throat.

"It's easy to feel that way," Briar said, and her tone was not unkind, "when you have no reason to think otherwise. I used to think that too, before I found out about the curse with Demetri." She looked up at the leafy branches above them. "I wish I could get it back. That certainty that nothing so bad could ever happen to me, or anyone I care about."

Garrett looked at her. His heart thudded in his chest so violently, he felt it echo into his head. It wasn't a good feeling and yet.... With her words, a kind of peace settled over him. With that simple statement, she had expressed a struggle he'd been fighting since Snow died.

It felt a bit like closure, maybe.

Garrett got to his feet. "We should probably get going before—"

"Garrett," Briar cut in, her voice pitched low. Her gaze sharpened. With a minuscule nod, she indicated something beyond him.

Garrett froze. "Corpse?" he mouthed.

"Don't know," Briar whispered. She hadn't moved from the ground. "But I saw...something move."

With slow movements, Garrett put one hand on his pistol and motioned for Briar to stand. She winced, climbing to her feet with much effort.

"Where is it?" he asked, his eyes on her.

"About ten paces." Briar's eyes darted right to left as she took a careful step towards him. "Maybe more. A little to my left."

Trying to look natural—not that a corpse would notice if he looked natural—Garrett turned and scanned the woods before him.

At first, he saw nothing. Just the trees, a smattering of scrubby grass, and a squirrel scampering by. Then the wind picked up, and as it *swished* through the trees, he caught a snatch of movement behind a massive redwood—like the edge of a cloak blowing in the breeze. Would a corpse wear a cloak? Most of the ones he'd seen wore little more than rags.

Garrett turned, keeping the area in question in the corner of his eye. "Walk with me," he muttered to Briar. "But slowly."

They resumed their trek with vigilance. Garrett kept his gaze fixed on the place where he thought he'd seen something, but as they came abreast of the spot...as they eased past it...he saw nothing. Nothing except a squat boxwood shrub, its chartreuse leaves stirring in the wind.

Garrett relaxed. That was probably all they'd seen, the leaves in the wind. "I think it's all right," he murmured. When Briar didn't respond, he turned to look at her. "Briar?"

"Hmm?" Briar stood back. She had her arms around herself again and squeezed her elbow as another breeze gusted by. "Oh. Yes. I guess it was nothing."

Garrett opened his mouth to respond, but before he could, a piercing *snap* behind him cut through the silence. Frowning, Garrett turned his head—just as something heavy plowed into him.

Garrett pitched forward and knocked into Briar, who fell back and hit the ground hard. Garrett nearly crashed into her, but he managed to get his hands up at the last second to keep from landing on top of her. His palms stung, scraped by broken twigs and roots, and his knees creaked as he got up onto them. Struggling to regain his breath—it felt like all the air in his lungs had *whooshed* out of him—Garrett looked around for who, what, had barreled into him.

He knew before he saw it, standing a few paces away. Slouching over, arms dangling, with a bug-eyed, hungry gaze. It wore tatty farmer's coveralls like a person, only it wasn't quite a person.

It was a corpse monster.

Ignoring the ache in his knees, Garrett scrambled to his feet, fumbling for his pistol. He leveled it at the corpse and squeezed the trigger, the *crack* of the bullet like thunder in the woods. The bullet took the monster in its throat, and it swayed, dark blood spurting from the wound. Stepping over Briar, Garrett took another shot, then another, and another. All three took the corpse in the head, ripping through rotted flesh, splintering bone and spongy brain. The monster fell motionless to the ground.

Garrett watched the corpse—no more than a tangle of gaunt limbs now—to make sure no part of it twitched. The forest was still and silent, no birds singing or squirrels darting through the brush. Once Garrett felt sure the corpse was dead, he let out a long, low breath. Turning his back on the slain creature, he looked for Briar—but when he spotted her, his relief guttered and died.

At first, he couldn't comprehend what he saw. Briar, sprawled across a bedding of dead leaves and patchy grass. Her head tilted to the left, hair strewn across her face. Her right shoulder twisted at an odd angle, away from her body. Bright, stark blood staining her white shirt. And the jagged tip of a branch jutting up from her chest.

Garrett stood still. For a second, the world rocked and he felt weightless, untethered to the earth. He couldn't see Briar's face, covered by her hair. All he could see was the blood. It wasn't even a lot of blood, just coating the tip of the branch. But she lay so still.

He lunged forward and fell to his knees, lifting the top half of her up. She stirred a little—*not dead*, he thought, the words skittering across his mind, *she's not dead*, and he couldn't stop his brain from adding a *yet* to that. Cringing, he touched the bloodied tip of the branch—just brushing its rough, peeling surface. He didn't dare pull it out. It wasn't that big—less than an inch around and short enough that it had barely gone all the way through her. He kept thinking that as long as he didn't pull it out, she would be all right.

But she was so still. So limp. So cold.

"Briar?" Garrett whispered. He got a hand beneath her head and cupped her neck. Tangled though it was, her hair felt like silk against his palm. He turned her face towards him.

Her gray eyes moved. Sliding from one corner to the other. As they passed over his face, he imagined, for a moment, that her gaze met his. And maybe it did—for a moment.

But then her gaze slid to the side, and her eyes grew glassy and unseeing, and she went heavy in his arms, a dead weight.

Dead. Now, she was dead.

13
REPOSE

DEMETRI PACED BEFORE THE cab of the train. The sun rose higher overhead with every passing minute, though its light was dampened by a thin, wispy layer of clouds. "Maybe it's something to do with the fuel," he suggested. Not for the first time.

"No, we've double-checked that, Your Highness," Miles said politely.

"Triple-checked, even," Alec added. At least, Demetri thought he was Alec. He couldn't tell him apart from his twin Aden, but he thought Alec was the one with some mechanical abilities. And the one who grinned all the time, even in inappropriate situations like this one.

Demetri raked his hand through his hair. Also not for the first time. He probably looked a mess. The bandage around the splint over his wrist was unraveling, he had picked at it so much. His shirt, sticky with sweat, clung to his back, and he could feel a line of perspiration along his forehead. The thought of removing his coat crossed his mind, but he dismissed it. Walking around without his coat on would be even more inappropriate than Alec's grinning.

Demetri squinted up at the sky as a light smattering of rain began to fall, drizzling over the field. The sun had vanished behind gray clouds, but Demetri knew it must be near noon. The party that had gone in search of Garrett and Briar had left several hours ago, around dawn. The corpse attack and subsequent breaking down of the train took place hours before that, but one of the soldiers, Iain—a gruff, older man, who seemed to be in charge without Garrett around—had insisted they stay inside the train until the sun rose, as it was likely there were still corpses nearby, and they were vulnerable in the dark.

Those hours waiting inside the train had been agony to Demetri, and not only because he'd sprained his wrist in the attack. But because all the while, he knew Briar and Garrett were out there somewhere. But it would have been near-suicide to venture out in the dark, especially with all their wounds.

Demetri understood that. But it had been agony all the same. And it was little better now, waiting for the search party to return. Helping with the repairs—even if he was not really helping—was as good a distraction as any.

Demetri wiped a hand across his forehead. He ignored the slight tremble of his fingers, a sign of how little he'd slept. "Well," he said to Miles, "what about—"

"Your Highness!" Demetri turned and saw Alec's twin, Aden, running towards him. The young man picked his way over the mess of the camp, darting around half-pitched tents and leaping over packs, pots, and bedrolls. He was slim like his brother, and had the same brown skin and sleek, dark hair. "Prince

Demetri—they've returned, the search party, Gemma and Kelley and Kinsley and—"

Demetri interrupted him before he could go on; he knew who made up the search party. What he wanted to know was who they'd *found*. "And Garrett? Briar?"

"I—well—yes." It was an odd answer, because in spite of the happy news, Aden's face fell. "Yes, they found them, Your Highness...but, well—you should come and see."

His stomach in knots, Demetri followed, the two of them winding their way to the other end of the grassy clearing. As they neared the line of pine trees at the edge of camp, Demetri saw the search party dismounting their horses. There was a dispirited air to them—a slump to their shoulders, a weariness in their faces. And the quiet, a dead quiet, among them.

He spotted Garrett first, as he was a good head taller than the others, even taller than his soldier Kelley, a burly man. Four others had gone with Kelley and Demetri spotted them all—Garrett's best tracker Gemma, red-haired, freckly Evans, Dom, dark-eyed and mischievous, though he wore no smile now. And—

Briar. He had yet to see Briar or her guard Kinsley. As he and Aden stumbled over a pile of cooking pots, Demetri called, "Garrett!"

Garrett's back was to him, but Demetri saw the way he stiffened when he heard his name. Something black and terrible surged through Demetri, a whisper of foreboding wrapping around his heart. He tried to tamp the feeling down, but it was impossible to ignore.

Garrett turned to him. His face was white and unsmiling, his eyes bloodshot, and the knees of his trousers were ripped open.

Demetri stepped towards the group. He couldn't understand why he felt so sick. The waiting was over; they were back. Only he didn't see Briar, and Garrett looked weird and grim, and everyone was staring at him, all the search party, with pity in their eyes—

He forced himself to turn to Garrett, who stood at hand now. "Garrett," he said, wondering why it was so hard to look his friend in the eye, "what happened? Where is—" He glanced aside as Gemma and Dom dismounted and the last horse behind them came into view—Kinsley, the pale-skinned, black-haired soldier that Garrett had assigned to guard Briar. He was the only person still sitting his horse, but he didn't sit it alone. He had...something...on the saddle in front of him, wrapped in a large, dark cloak. Whatever it was bore a strange, knobby shape and was so long that Kinsley was having an awkward time with it.

That was when Demetri realized it must be a person.

But why would Kinsley have a person wrapped up like that, covered from head to toe and so limp in the saddle...

The air seemed to crystallize, dropping several degrees in a second, even though the rain had stopped and the sun was peeking out. It came to him in a way without words. It was not a coherent thought, because he refused to put words to it, even only in his mind. But he knew. He couldn't stop the knowing. "Garrett." Demetri stared at Kinsley and the shrouded figure. "Where is Briar?"

"Demetri—"

"Where is she?"

Garrett—Garrett, who always laughed and smiled and reassured, even when things were darkest, even in the worst dangers—looked at Demetri with no light in his eyes. Then he looked at Kinsley and nodded.

"No." Demetri shook his head. He could not look at the shrouded figure again. "That's not Briar."

"Demetri—"

"That can't be—that's not—why would you wrap her like that, that's mad, she can't *breathe*—"

"Demetri," Garrett said, and his voice seemed loud. The prince bent his head and put a hand on Demetri's shoulder. The words he spoke next were gentle but clear. "She isn't breathing anymore."

Garrett's hand felt too heavy on his shoulder, a weight boring him into the ground. Demetri ran the words over and over in his head, but they didn't make sense. He understood their meaning, but what didn't make sense was how they could pertain to Briar. How could Briar not be breathing? How could Briar not be—?

He shoved past Garrett, past the startled horses, who reared and whinnied as he dashed through them. He stopped beside Kinsley's horse. The guard's blue eyes were crinkled as he handed the shrouded figure down to Demetri, and to Garrett and Dom, who stepped forward to help. Everyone had gone silent, but Demetri felt like the silence was screaming. Desperation warred with dread inside him as Garrett and Dom lay the swathed figure on the ground and unwrapped the shroud. He was desperate to see her, to see that maybe he was wrong, maybe he had misunderstood—but dreading that he hadn't misunderstood, dreading to see—

Briar.

A strangled sound escaped Demetri's lips, halfway between a cry and a whimper, and he fell to his knees beside her. She was sallow and cold, but she was still *Briar*. Her lips were blue, her shoulder bent and twisted, her shirt stained with crimson blood, her eyes closed, as though she was only sleeping—

An image flashed through his mind, a memory from eighty-two years ago. Briar, her eyes falling shut as she pricked her finger, collapsing against his chest. With gentle hands, he'd laid her down on the floor, peaceful in sleep.

She didn't look so different now, he told himself. It was just the same; she was only sleeping. But when he put a hand to her neck, he could feel no pulse beneath his fingers, and she lay so still, her chest unmoving without breath.

"I—don't—" He didn't know what he was trying to say. He looked at Garrett and it came to him in a flash of clarity. "*What happened?*"

Garrett opened and closed his hand, forming a fist over and over. "We were on our way here, following the railroad tracks. A corpse attacked—it knocked us over, and Briar—she fell on this—"

He held up a short, slender branch. It was coated in dried blood, like a quill dipped in ink. Demetri tried to comprehend that this little stick had taken Briar's life.

"I thought she was okay." Garrett looked baffled, as though he still couldn't understand that she was *not* okay. "At first. I thought maybe—the branch was plugging the wound—I thought if I could just bring her here, Thatcher could do something, he could've..."

Demetri sat back and ran a shaking hand over his eyes. Every word hit him in the gut. He couldn't bear to hear these stark terms, these violent words applied to Briar. He peeked through two fingers to look at her, spread out before him.

Still immobile. Still dead.

Something black and heavy rose inside Demetri, filling his chest. He kept hearing that word in his head, over and over again. *Dead. Dead. Dead.* After everything, after *everything*—everything they had done to get here, everything Demetri had endured over the last eighty-two years, everything Briar had done to fight against her curse and now—

"But I guess—I think—" Garrett sounded like he was speaking through gritted teeth. "The damage…was too much."

Demetri dropped his hand to his mouth. There was a scream buried deep inside him, striving to tear free. But it was stuck somewhere between his chest and his lips, and instead he felt it balloon inside him, threatening to devour him. He tried to focus on Garrett's words, but they didn't matter. None of it mattered.

Briar was dead.

⸻◆⸻

Demetri stood within the near-empty train compartment, watching as Garrett's soldiers lay Briar flat upon a large steel crate. *Briar's body. Not Briar.* His eyes followed their movements, but it was like looking out a speeding train's window, the scenery vanishing as soon as it appeared. He didn't really *see* her until they had gone—all except Garrett—leaving him in the storage compartment, alone with Briar.

Briar's body. Not Briar.

Demetri stepped up to the black crate and stood by her side. With quivering fingers, he laid a hand over her shoulder, the one that was twisted at an unnatural angle. Like a mishandled doll, or a bird with a broken wing.

180

Behind him, Garrett said, "Thatcher said he could fix her shoulder—make it right."

Something wet fell upon his hand. It was a moment before Demetri realized it came from him. His eyes stung with tears, and he realized he'd been crying since they first unwrapped her body. "Why?" he said in response to Garrett. "She doesn't need it anymore."

Garrett made no reply at first. Then he said, "I'm sorry, Demetri."

It was such a heartfelt apology that Demetri turned to him. For the first time since they'd returned, he saw Garrett—really saw him. The prince was a wreck. Demetri was used to Garrett smiling, Garrett laughing, Garrett joking. Even Garrett comforting or Garrett taking charge.

He had never seen this Garrett. He looked awful, broken. Even when Garrett had told him about his princess, about Snow, he had not looked so awful. His shoulders were hunched in a defeated slump. His eyes were red, though whether from his own tears or just exhaustion, Demetri didn't know. And there was a distinct lack of—of *something* in his gaze. A deadness.

"It isn't your fault," Demetri said. He meant that, yet the words sounded hollow. He knew how useless it was to tell a person not to blame themselves sometimes. "What happened. It wasn't your fault."

Now something came into Garrett's eyes. A bitter gleam. For a moment, Demetri thought the prince was going to argue with him. But then he shrugged. "I spoke to Thatcher and told him...how it happened—well, he said he wasn't sure that he could have done anything, even if—if I brought her back here before—" He broke off. "I'm sorry, Demetri. You don't want to hear this."

Demetri felt like his throat was stuffed full of wet wool, expanding as it dried, cutting off his airway. Then the words came out of him in a rush, the thought that had been consuming him all this time. "It's my fault."

"What? Demetri, of course it isn't."

But it was. Demetri *knew* it was. He couldn't explain it, not really, but he tried anyway. If only so Garrett would tell him he was right. Damn it, he *wanted* someone to tell him it was his fault. "I didn't see her go up on the train roof." Demetri's voice was choked. "Or I would've stopped the train at once—I mean, I meant to as soon as *you* went up, but there were too many of the cursed corpses and—"

"It was utter chaos, Demetri," Garrett cut in. "We were all fighting for our lives, yourself included—there's no use second-guessing every action you took—"

Demetri tried another tack. "Then it's my fault because I—because I w-was—pushing her away. I *was*, don't pretend you didn't notice," he added when Garrett tried to interrupt him. "I know you did—I could see it on your face yesterday on the train, when you told me she was looking for me—" He had been avoiding her these past several days, ever since the incident in the forest with the fairies.

But this was harder to explain. "I just—I didn't think any of this would happen, you know."

"Of course not. How could you?"

Demetri clasped his hands in front of him, squeezing them together. "I just meant...well, it sounds stupid now. But I thought the worst of it was behind us. I thought I'd wake Briar, break the curse. And we would be together again, and everything would be all right. Everything would be like it was." He shook his head. "I mean, I'm not *that* stupid. It's a different world, things are different—I'm not a prince anymore, for one thing—but I don't care about any of that, none of that matters. I told myself, so long as we were both all right, so long as we were together—that was all that mattered—"

Everything he said felt like ashes in his mouth. And he was more than stupid. He was awful, ungrateful, expecting everything would just be perfect. Because of course it wasn't.

At first, he'd thought he was avoiding her because of what had happened. Because she'd lost her memory again. And that *was* part of it. Maybe it made him a coward, but he was so terrified that it might happen again, terrified to see that look in her eyes, that utter lack of recognition—and to know he was helpless to do anything for her, to bring her back—

Twice it had happened. Twice, she had eventually regained her memories.

He had been terrified it might happen again...and that she wouldn't remember. That she would just be lost.

He was terrified that he would have failed her, in the end. No matter all his efforts to get back here, to wake her, to rescue her from that castle—he would have failed.

But it had been more than that too. That hadn't been the only thing Demetri was terrified of. He was also terrified of what lay before them—the dark fairy, another curse to contend with, and he was afraid it was too big, too much—

He was afraid—after all he had been through—that he wasn't enough. That he couldn't *be* enough. For Briar. For her kingdom. For anyone.

"Demetri," Garrett said now, his voice quiet. Gentle. More gentle than Demetri deserved. "Whatever was going on between you—even if you were pushing her away—that doesn't mean this is your fault. Whether you'd spent the whole last week together or not, the corpses still would have attacked the train. It wouldn't have been any different."

"It's just—" Demetri swallowed and forced himself to look at Briar again, where she lay upon the crate. *Briar's body. Not Briar.* His eyes traveled over her face, taking in her shuttered eyes, her matted hair. "I could have spent every second of the last week with her. But I didn't. And now—" He reached out to lay his hand at Briar's forehead and found he couldn't do it. "Now I regret it. Every second I didn't spend with her."

"I'm sorry, Demetri. I can—if you want me to stay—"

"No," Demetri said hoarsely. "You need to see to your people, and I—I'd like a minute alone with her."

Garrett murmured his assent and took his leave.

Demetri stood with her for more than a minute. He stood there for hours. He was vaguely aware of the day passing outside, loud voices fading into murmurs as the bustling soldiers settled down in the twilight. The time passed in the blink of an eye. Demetri stood there and gazed at Briar, and not a thought passed through his head.

It was the dark that jolted him out of this trance, the orange glow of campfires twinkling outside. Because he knew someone would come to fetch him, to bring him away from her. The thought of leaving her was too much to bear. Demetri's chest ached as though all the air had been sucked out of the compartment. Leaving her would mean it was real. It would mean she was really gone. So long as he stayed here with her, maybe he could fix it—

He turned and paced to the other end of the compartment, folding his hands behind his head. Could he fix this? There had to be a way. He had to do *something*.

It came to him in a flash.

A kiss.

A part of him—the part that operated on reason—shut this theory down at once. That could not work; she was not enchanted. This was a more permanent sleep, and there was no breaking it. But Demetri pushed those thoughts to the back of his mind and clung to the mystical hope that this could work.

"It will work," he muttered. "It *will* work, it has to—"

He turned back to Briar just in time to see her sit up.

Demetri stopped dead.

At first, he thought he must be seeing things. The compartment was dark, cloaked in the shadows of dusk. He thought something or someone else must have moved. But no, that was the crate *she* was lying on, and that was *her* tousled hair, streaming down her sides as she sat up straight—

Briar, eyes open and alert, reached for her twisted shoulder, and with a shocking *snap*, wrenched it back into place. "Whoa. That felt weird." Her gaze traveled over the compartment and then settled on Demetri. "What did I miss?"

14

REPAIRS

BRIAR SAT IN THE shadows and tried to remember the last thing that had happened to her. She had memories—they were there—but coming in bits and pieces, out of order. She remembered meeting the fairies in the woods, she remembered talking with Garrett about his mother, she remembered kissing Demetri at the castle. She remembered the corpses leaping down the lift shaft, the wingless fairy Jas, waking from the curse, Garrett shooting the little corpse girl, seeing Demetri for the first time since waking, talking to Garrett on the train—

The train. She remembered the train. Casting her gaze around, she realized that's where she was. Not in her sleeper compartment or a passenger carriage. But in a dark, sparse place, filled with wooden barrels and scrap metal. A storage compartment. And it was dark outside—the compartment door was pulled back—though she caught a glimpse of flickering light. Campfires, maybe.

She couldn't remember how she got here. She remembered the corpses attacking the train, and how she'd gone up onto the roof after Garrett, into the screaming wind and bracing cold—and they fell off—and then...

And then what?

Briar rolled her shoulder, wincing at the painful twinge in her joint. She tried to remember what had happened next. Just then, though, her memory reel was interrupted by Demetri's scream.

Briar gave a violent start. He didn't just scream—he really *screamed*. A high-pitched scream that bounced from wall to wall in the small compartment. Her gaze darted left and right for the source of his panic—more corpses?—but there was nothing.

She looked at Demetri. And that's when she realized that he was gaping, wild-eyed and white-faced, at *her*.

"Demetri?" Briar spoke in an even tone, like she might if addressing a skittish horse. "Are you all right?"

"Am I—am *I*—h-how did—what are—you just—" Demetri ran both hands over his face. "What—"

Briar curved her palms over the edge of her seat and slid off the crate. "Demetri—"

"No—!" Demetri took a hasty step back, still looking at her like she'd sprouted horns and a tail. He thrust a hand out in front of him. "Don't!"

"Demetri. *What is wrong?*"

"You're dead!" Demetri burst out.

Briar gawked at him. *Dead*. Her brain rejected this at once. She wasn't dead, she was standing right here, talking to him. "What are you talking about? That's mad, Demetri, I'm clearly not dead."

"No—no." Demetri's words ran over each other, his voice strained. "You were dead. You were definitely dead. You had no *pulse*, Briar. You weren't breathing—you haven't been breathing for the past several hours!" He let out a hysterical sound that was almost like a laugh. "I didn't imagine that!"

Briar began to wish this was a dream she would wake from any second. Because he was scaring her. She took a step towards him, but when he backed away, she stopped. "I am not dead."

"Are you breathing?"

What a ridiculous question. Briar held a hand to her mouth and blew two, audible breaths onto it. "Yes."

"Do you have a pulse?"

Briar put two fingers to her neck. It took a moment to find it, but then she nodded, raising her eyebrows at the absurdity of it.

And just like that, his entire face changed. His panic melted into the most vulnerable expression she had ever seen on him. "Are you really not dead?" he whispered.

"Demetri." Briar didn't understand—maybe *he'd* been dreaming. Otherwise, she didn't know why he would think her dead when she very much wasn't.

But you don't remember anything, a voice whispered inside her head. *You can't remember what happened*. Her pulse picked up a little, but Briar took a breath and said, "I'm really not dead. I'm right here."

A small, tentative smile formed on Demetri's face.

Then someone shouted, "Demetri!" and in an instant, Garrett and three soldiers spilled through the compartment door—all with firearms raised.

"Stop!" Demetri sprang forward. "Don't shoot!"

Briar turned towards them, squinting in the glare of the camp-fires. It was a moment before she realized their guns were pointed at *her*. Confused, she waited for them to lower their weapons, but no one did. Instead, they all gaped at her like Demetri had.

Briar almost raised a hand to wave, then thought better of making any sudden movements with four guns trained on her. "Erm—hello."

"What is—" Garrett's face was bloodless. "Briar..."

Briar looked at him. And as she returned his stare, gazing into his shocked green eyes, a rush of mixed emotions flooded through her. Jumbled, overwhelming, and so rapid, she could not pick out one emotion from the next.

But then came a second rush—a rush of memories. They'd fallen off the train—and then— "We were stuck on the bridge," Briar said slowly. "Overnight. You didn't want to—" He'd been terrified, she remembered, too terrified to try and climb off the bridge in the dark. But then the morning came... "And then the boat came—and we got off the bridge...and then..."

A burst of distant laughter from outside broke through her thoughts, and she shook herself.

"And then what?" Demetri prompted, an urgent catch to his voice.

"I'm not sure," Briar admitted. "We were walking through the woods...I wasn't feeling well..." She could practically feel it all over again—the chill seeping into her bones, the fog of exhaustion tugging at her, dragging her down into a darkness she couldn't escape. *Not feeling well* was rather an understatement.

Garrett must have thought so too, for he made an incredulous noise deep in his throat. He still pointed his pistol at her, Briar was not pleased to see, as did the others. She flexed her hands, clenching them into fists. "What is going on?"

Garrett returned her a grim gaze. "I'm not sure I know. Demetri?"

"She's a ghost," one of the soldiers whispered.

"She's a corpse!" exclaimed another.

"She's not." Demetri came and stood beside Briar, putting himself in the line of fire. "Garrett, please put the guns down. It's all right."

Garrett's eyes flashed in his direction and then returned to Briar. He held her gaze for a long time. In that gaze, Briar saw a torrent of emotions not unlike her own—a swirling torrent too heavy and complex to untangle. Briar hardly dared draw a breath as he looked at her.

Then—slowly—Garrett lowered his pistol. The soldiers followed suit.

"What happened?" Garrett demanded. He stepped up into the compartment. "Demetri, what did you *do?*"

"I don't think he—" Briar began, but then Demetri flung his arms around her and crushed her against his chest.

"I can't believe it," he murmured. "I can't believe you're alive."

"Yes," came Garrett's voice, "and *how* is that exactly?"

Briar wanted to know the same thing—or rather, she wanted to know why they thought her dead to begin with. But she had never seen Demetri so shaken, not even on her sixteenth birthday with the curse looming over her. So she let him hold her. It was reassuring, being closed up in his arms. Resting her head against his neck, she inhaled a deep breath.

The scent of him. The heady scent of his skin. The savory scent of his blood pumping *beneath* his skin, blood and muscle and sinew and bone...

He smelled so...*appetizing.*

Choking on a breath, Briar wrenched out of Demetri's arms and shoved him away.

"What?" Demetri tottered, his eyes wide. "What's wrong?"

"Nothing." Briar ran a shaky hand through her knotted hair. What was wrong with her? Had she really just thought Demetri smelled *appetizing?* As though he was a seasoned side of beef? It had only been for a second...she must have imagined it.... Forcing a smile, she hastened to add, "I'm fine, Demetri. I just *really* need someone to tell me what happened."

"Do you remember the corpse?" Garrett asked. "In the woods?"

Briar shook her head, but then it came back to her. "No—wait, yes. Sort of. I remember I saw something moving...I thought it *might* be a corpse..." That really was all she remembered. She'd been so tired...

It had been more than that, though. Briar repressed a shudder. It had been like...well, it had felt a bit like when she forgot Demetri and forgot who she was. A fog stealing over her brain...only this time it had come on slower, creeping in instead of happening in an instant.

"I don't remember after that." She spoke with a deliberate calm, careful not to let any trembling through. "Nothing. So...what happened?"

Garrett and Demetri exchanged uneasy glances. Demetri said, "You had best tell her. You're the one who was there."

Garrett did not look pleased, but he didn't argue. After dismissing his soldiers—Briar supposed he was convinced she was not a ghost or a corpse—he seated himself atop a wooden barrel. He began to speak in a slow, fixed tone, though Briar caught a shaky word here and there. He told Briar how a lone corpse had attacked them and how he'd killed the creature—but that she had fallen onto a small branch that impaled her through the chest.

Briar couldn't believe she didn't remember that. That couldn't be right. She felt fine...

She cast a glance at herself. That was when she noticed the dark red stain down her front. She ran a light hand over it, feeling its gritty thickness. She fingered the tear in her shirt near her breastbone. Where she had been...*impaled*. But then she should have some wound, some pain, and she didn't feel anything...

As Garrett went on, telling how his soldiers had found them, Briar tugged her shirt out from the waist of her breeches and reached up beneath it. Her fingers ghosted along her torso, grazing her skin—

—and slid across the ragged edges of a gaping hole in her flesh.

"Agh!" Briar yanked her hand out as though her skin had burned her.

Looking like he didn't really want to know, Demetri asked, "What's wrong?"

"Look—" Briar grasped the bottom of her shirt and began to roll it up.

"Uh—" Garrett, his cheeks reddening, spun around so he couldn't see her. "This really isn't appropriate."

Demetri flushed pink. "It really isn't."

"Oh I don't care, just—look." Briar dropped the front of her shirt to grasp the back instead, lifting it up. Demetri and Garrett stepped behind her, both of them blushing. After a quick look, Demetri whirled around to face her, his face rather green.

"Did you see it?" Briar's bare skin, exposed to the cold, began to prickle. "The wound?"

"It's weird-looking." Garrett seemed not as squeamish as Demetri, because he inspected the wound at length. "Not healed, exactly—"

"Of course it isn't healed!" Demetri threw a hand in the air. "She has a hole in her!"

"Not straight through, though." Garrett sounded fascinated. "I mean, it looks nearly healed. Like her body knit itself back together, just not all the way through. And it looks—well, like an old wound. Like you took it weeks ago."

"None of this makes sense." Briar dropped her shirt and Garrett came around to face her. "I mean...if I was really *dead*—"

"Briar, none of us were mistaken about that." Garrett looked grave. "Even Thatcher declared you dead. And he doesn't make mistakes about dead people."

Briar flinched. No matter how many times they said it, she couldn't absorb it. She ran her hand over her shirt, fingers skating against the dried blood. Even the hole in her chest wasn't real enough for her. How could she have been dead?

A sliver of fear rippled through her. Briar tried to focus on what she knew. It was just that what she knew added up to something she didn't want to consider.

Everything she'd felt since waking from her curse—everything she'd said to Garrett on the bridge. Her pale skin, the bruises beneath her eyes, the growing fatigue and—right before she died—the extreme cold that had taken her. It all fit.

"It's kind of," she said, and her voice sounded far away, like someone else was saying it, "like I was rotting."

She looked at the boys and found them gawping at her.

"That's mad," Garrett said.

"Rotting?" Demetri's voice squeaked. "You mean—like those—like your kingdom? But that's impossible."

Briar stifled an aggravated sigh. Their responses might have comforted another person, but this habitual denial of logic didn't help her. It only made it worse. "Why is it mad?" She forced a patient tone, the kind of tone adults took with children. "Why is it impossible?"

"Because—we—" Demetri stumbled.

"Briar, you're not like those corpse creatures at all," Garrett objected. "They're *monsters*. We've met precious few who seem to know who they are—"

"And I've been forgetting who I am, remember?"

"But that's different!" Demetri spluttered.

"They eat people." Garrett countered. "Do you want to eat people?"

Briar dithered. "Well...not exactly. But I haven't wanted to eat anything normal either."

"Look, you just woke from eighty-two years of sleep!" Demetri burst out.

"And we have no precedent that tells us that returning from death, clotted wounds, no appetite, and lost memories are typical symptoms of someone who's been in a cursed sleep!" Briar shot back. "But we *do* have evidence that those symptoms are exhibited by these rotting creatures!"

"So say this is true then," Garrett said.

"I am saying that."

"Right." Garrett looked at her, working his jaw, like he was trying to remember how to speak. Then he said, "How can you be so calm about this?"

Briar blew out a breath. "I'm not." She bent her head low and ran her hands through her hair. "*Stones*, I'm not, I just—" She dropped her arms to her sides. "It makes sense." And things that made sense were comforting to her. Usually.

"It doesn't entirely make sense." Demetri sounded more composed than he had a minute ago. "What's happened to you isn't like what happened to the rest of the kingdom, Briar. So far as we know, they all rotted while they slept. That's why they're so far gone. But if *you're* rotting, then it's happening much more slowly. Why would that be?"

Briar shrugged, awakening another twinge in her sore shoulder. "Well—I don't know. Maybe—"

"Maybe that isn't what's happening to you at all," Demetri said firmly. "At any rate, there's no use speculating. We ought to have Thatcher check you out and see what he thinks. He is the medic, after all."

Thatcher took Briar's rise from the dead with more calm than Briar expected; she was rather impressed by his composure. She already liked the man; he had a low, rumbling voice that she found soothing, and she appreciated his no-nonsense way of viewing things. He had first inspected Briar when they returned from their run-in with the fairies over a week ago. Now, by the white light of four, pitched gear-bulb lamps spaced around his tent, Thatcher inspected Briar again. Whether or not she was rotting, though, he couldn't say.

"I think it's too early to tell," he said. "Do you still feel unwell, Princess?"

"Not really." Briar scooted back on the stool she sat upon. "A little tired, maybe."

"Well, I think the best thing is to monitor you over the next several days, Your Highness. See if you exhibit any further symptoms similar to this rotting disease. And until you do, I would advise you try and not worry about it. No use worrying over something that may not be."

"That's what I said." The crease in Demetri's forehead smoothed out.

Garrett nodded.

Briar tried to conceal her vexation. Thatcher was right that there was no use worrying. Even if there *was* cause to worry, Briar wouldn't have seen the point. Worrying wouldn't help her.

But neither could she let it go and that was why. Worrying wouldn't help her. What would help was figuring out what was wrong with her, so they could then figure out how to deal with it. And she didn't much relish Thatcher's "wait-and-see" approach. She didn't much relish sitting about and doing nothing for the next several days.

At any rate, they had plenty else to worry them. Miles and his crew weren't any closer to fixing the train. The conductor suspected there must be damage somewhere from the corpse attack, but they hadn't located it yet. On top of that, Garrett had lost a number of men in the attack, and more were injured. Given all this, it seemed prudent they take a few days' rest in whatever shelter they could find.

"Where are we, exactly?" Garrett asked, after visiting with his wounded soldiers. He, Demetri, and Briar sat beneath a large canopy the soldiers had erected for them. It was late, and many soldiers were retiring for the night at Garrett's instruction. Demetri looked like he would have liked to do the same, but Briar felt wide awake. She had, she supposed, spent the day resting. While she was dead.

One of the soldiers brought Garrett a map, and, after studying it for a bit, Garrett said, "I know where we can go."

"Where?" Demetri asked, leaning over to frown at the map. "There's not much in the area but more forest. That town Ledbury is sixty miles southeast of here and Eastwood is even further. Unless you know of a lodger's settlement—"

"Not lodgers," Garrett said. "I know someone who lives out here. Usually. And if she's not there, the house will be. We can leave in the morning and be there in two hours."

They were up early and on their way by the time the sun began to show its face. Miles and his crew remained behind to work on the train, along with fifteen soldiers in able condition. The rest of them set out through the woods.

Briar looked up as they left the clearing, watching the last of the azure sky before it vanished, blocked out by green-and-gold leaves and the stout, knotted branches of oak trees. As they ambled through the wood, early birds chittering around them, Briar slumped in her saddle. She found she had to concentrate on not falling *out* of the saddle. She had only ridden a horse once before she fell to her curse, and she was tired, given that she hadn't slept well. None of them had, camped by the broken train, exposed and weakened by the last attack.

"Where do you think they came from?" Demetri posed this question to Briar and Garrett as they rode. Unlike Briar, he sat straight in his saddle despite the heavy bags under his eyes. But he was an excellent rider, and he sat his saddle like he was molded to it. "The corpses that attacked the train, I mean. There were a dozen of them, maybe more. Could a number like that have followed us all this way? They can't move very fast."

That was true, Briar realized, hooking onto this statement. They possessed impossible strength, but none of the corpses she'd seen had moved very fast. But she had—when the corpses had attacked the train, she ran quite fast to get to the besieged compartment. Was that a point against the theory that she was rotting? Or maybe it meant nothing. It wasn't until the next morning, after all, that she'd grown fatigued and sluggish.

"...that little corpse girl," Garrett was saying. "The one Briar and I encountered in the village. She said something like—that when they all woke, some of them ran off. Well, after they ate a bunch of people, anyway."

"So you mean, there could be corpses all over these woods." Now Demetri did slump, his face glum. "And the ones that attacked us didn't follow us from the castle, but were already there—before we arrived?"

"Maybe." Garrett rolled his shoulder back, pulling a face. He sat stiff in his saddle, as though he wasn't a good rider either, but Briar knew that wasn't true. She supposed he'd been rather banged up in the attack.

"It's not just the people from the village." Briar ducked as her horse meandered beneath a low-hanging branch, laden with tufts of dead pine needles. "The dark fairy cursed the whole kingdom. That includes people who lived in the woods or nearby farms."

"Well," Demetri said bleakly, "that's a happy thought."

"Isn't it, though?" Garrett agreed.

"Why have they never attacked a train before, though?" Demetri wondered. "I mean, I think you would have heard about such a thing," he added to Garrett.

"But the corpses haven't been running around all this time," Briar objected. When Demetri turned a confused look on her, she returned it with a surprised one of her own. "I thought that was obvious. If they had been, they surely would have ventured south of the mountains by now. They probably would have reached the Glen Kingdom."

"But then—"

"That little girl," Briar explained, "in the village. She said they woke when 'people' came. And the corpses in the castle woke when you all came. The little girl said their hunger drove them awake." Briar remembered—fleetingly—the thought that had crossed her mind when she'd hugged Demetri last night. *No, she told herself, you imagined that.* "I think it was the arrival of people that roused the corpses."

"Also," Garrett pitched in, "the train doesn't usually run up this far. With the border closed, there was never any reason to. Any trade through the mountains typically travels by road or river."

Demetri shook his head. "Why even build a train track and depot this far north, then?"

Garrett pulled a wry face. "Knowing my grandfather, he probably hoped to expand into these lands one day. But I suppose he never got around to investigating up here. And my father has always been more concerned with things closer to home. He prefers to build alliances rather than take what he wants." Garrett flashed a smile. "His grandfather would be appalled. We've grown civilized."

The sun was high in the sky when they reached their destination. It was a sprawling manor set in a clearing in the woods, an overgrown shrub line around it. In spite of its medieval, thatched roof, Briar judged it a newish construction—or it would have been new in her day, before the curse. It was built from white limestone and boasted four colonnades, typical of a style that had been popular eighty years ago. Two white chimneys rose on either side of the roof, and long, paned windows lined the front of the building.

"This is it." Garrett nudged his horse forward. "Isabelle's house."

15

SANCTUARY

DEMETRI GLANCED BACK AT Briar as he accompanied Garrett and three soldiers up the stone steps to the manor in the woods. She remained behind with the rest of the soldiers, waiting for the "all-clear" from them first.

He still could not quite process that Briar had been...dead...and now she was here, alive, beside him. Everything that had happened in the last twelve hours felt surreal. People did not die and come back to life. On top of that, Briar hadn't been dead for a terribly long time, so it was easy to feel like it had never happened. Like he'd dreamed the whole thing.

Only, he could still remember what it felt like—brief as it had been—to lose her. To mourn her. The feelings were too fresh to brush aside as a bad dream, and even now he couldn't quite let them go. Given that he could still lose her all the same, if she was afflicted by the rotting curse.

"You said she may not be home," Demetri said as they reached the dark front door. What had once been varnished wood was chipping now, and the black walnut shutters over the windows had seen better days.

"Only one way to find out." Garrett grasped the heavy brass knocker and knocked three times.

A couple of minutes passed as they waited. Demetri squinted up at the sky as a gray swathe of clouds passed overhead, blotting out the sun. A shiver wormed down his spine.

Garrett knocked again.

"Isn't there a bell?" Demetri frowned.

"No. She doesn't like to be disturbed."

"So why are we here again?"

"She won't mind *me* stopping by," Garrett said. "Anyway, seems she may not be in. Let's take a look, shall we?" He opened a pouch at his belt and removed two pins, one slightly thicker than the other.

"And why exactly does a crown prince know how to pick a lock?"

"I'm an adventurer first, Demetri," Garrett said, "crown prince second."

Demetri looked around at the soldiers. One of them, Falcon, grinned, but gruff Iain, his eyebrows drawn low, only shook his head.

Garrett had the door open within a minute. Demetri stepped inside, eyes darting left and right. The air in the house was thick and stale—not quite moldy, but like the house needed airing out.

A muted, rosy light shone from somewhere down the corridor. Garrett led the way, turning left into a lit room. It was a parlor with a large bay window. A fireplace was built into a gilded, ebony mantle on the far wall, and though some ashes lay heaped within it, they were long cold. But a tall grandfather clock stood in the corner, and it still whirled and clicked out the seconds behind its brass, enameled face, which meant someone had wound it up not too long ago.

Then a heavy *thump* sounded over their heads.

"What was that?" Demetri asked. He began to wonder if coming to this manor was such a good idea. They were alone out here, and stranded. If they ran into more of those corpses...

Garrett removed his pistol from his holster. "Let's go find out."

They started up the narrow staircase in the corner. One of the peeling, hardwood steps gave a baleful *cr-e-e-eak* beneath Demetri's boot, and he cringed, throwing a glance into the darkness above.

The top of the staircase opened into a shadowy corridor. The air was not so stuffy up here, and quite a bit colder, which was odd. There were glazed glass gear-bulb lamps built along the wall, but none of them were lit, and all were covered with a sheen of dust. They crept down the dim corridor, gray daylight coming in through the half-moon windows, until they reached a door on the left. It was partway open, emitting a faint glow—not daylight, but the white, steady gleam of a lamp. Garrett paused, attempting to peer inside. Then he kicked the door in, and as it rebounded off the wall with a *bang*, he and his guards spilled into the room.

Demetri heard a strangled yelp. "By the stones of—! *Garrett!* What are you *doing?*"

Demetri filed in with the others, just as Garrett dropped his pistol and said, "Oh. You are home."

The room was some kind of study. The girl they had almost accosted sat behind the desk. She was around Garrett's age, eighteen perhaps. Her skin was dusky and her long hair, tightly curled, was tied in a loose knot at the nape of her neck. A small pair of spectacles perched on her nose. She looked rather lost, blinking at them all in astonishment.

"Yes, I'm home." She tucked a stray curl behind her ear. There were a number of open books spread out on her mahogany desk, six or seven, some laid atop one another. "You might have knocked!"

Garrett beamed a most pleasant smile. "We did. A few times."

"Well—oh." The girl—Demetri presumed her to be Isabelle—scrambled to her feet. "I'm sorry, I was going through a few comparative texts on the early settlements in the Mariner Kingdom—"

"A few?" Garrett eyed the tomes on the desk.

"—because I came across a reference in Clemens' *Early History of Shipwrights' Working Unions* about settlers from a string of islands in the Hyperic Ocean that didn't sound—"

"You know," Garrett interrupted, "you really should get a bell."

Isabelle came around the desk. She wore a deep blue dress in the current fashion—a high-necked collar and a narrow skirt, draped to create much volume in the back.

"I don't like most visitors." Isabelle's eyes strayed back to her desk. "And a bell would only interrupt my concentration."

"You live in the middle of nowhere thick in the woods," Garrett pointed out. "It's not like solicitors are going to ring the bell every hour." He flashed a smile. "It's good to see you, Isabelle."

Isabelle returned the smile. "And you, Your Highness." She removed her spectacles, depositing them in her dress pocket.

Introductions were made all around, and when Garrett informed Isabelle that fifteen more people waited outside, her eyes popped open wide and she hurried to let them in. In spite of her declaration against visitors, she made a point of greeting each soldier by name, as well as Briar. She arranged rooms for everyone and assured them they could help themselves to anything in the kitchen.

"Although I'm not sure how much *food* is in the kitchen," she added, "given it's just me here."

"Yes, why is that?" Demetri asked. "I understand you like your solitude, but I'm surprised a lady such as yourself doesn't have a few servants on hand."

"Well, I'm no lady, for one thing." Isabelle watched him with a fixed gaze, like an owl. Garrett had informed her of Demetri and Briar's origins—that they were born nearly a century ago—and Isabelle seemed to be restraining herself from pestering him with questions. "Also, this isn't really my house. I'm squatting."

"But with the permission of the crown prince," Garrett added, "so it's practically legal. And I'm pretty sure the former owners of this place are dead."

Demetri raised an eyebrow. "You're pretty sure?"

"I may not have looked into it as thoroughly as I should have."

Once Briar was informed that a room was ready for her, she opted to skip out on food and went to rest instead. Demetri went with her, just to make sure she was all right.

Briar's room was on the second floor in the western wing, with a long window facing the sparse garden behind the house. Demetri helped Briar pull the heavy, plum curtains shut and watched her out of the corner of his eye. He was a little concerned that she hadn't wanted to eat—they'd only had a hasty breakfast of bread and pears before leaving and hadn't stopped once to eat anything on the way. When he brought this up, however, a strange expression flickered across Briar's face. "That's all right, Demetri." She crossed the room and rearranged the fat, satin-covered pillows on the bed to her liking. "I'm not very hungry. Just tired."

"Right." Demetri slipped his hands into his pockets, trying to appear casual. He must have failed, because as Briar climbed onto the bed, she shot him a knowing look.

"I'm fine, Demetri," she assured him. "I don't feel ill. But it was..." She yawned "...kind of a long night. I just want some sleep."

Demetri was also exhausted, but too wired to sleep. He knew he should leave Briar to her rest, but he didn't move and Briar didn't ask him to go. She kicked off her boots and laid against her pillows. They spent a quiet moment together, punctuated by the low voices of soldiers passing outside.

Briar lowered the shade on the lamp at her bedside, dimming its white glare to a gentler glow, casting shadows that turned the bare, beige walls a soft gray. She said, "Demetri, I'm sorry."

"About what?"

Briar rolled onto her side, resting her cheek against her pillow. "For what's been happening to me. After everything *you've* been through, you shouldn't have to worry about me—"

"I'm not worried." Demetri said it with such resolve that he almost assured himself. Almost. "No need to worry, remember? That's what Thatcher said. And Briar, you don't have to apologize. None of this is your fault."

At first, Demetri thought she was going to protest, but then she stilled. He tensed, but she only shook her head, pale hair pooling around her face. "I know it's not."

"We'll figure it out, Briar." Demetri tried to inject some confidence into his voice. "We'll save your kingdom, undo what the dark fairy did. I know we will."

Briar smiled, but it seemed forced, like he hadn't quite convinced her.

Demetri wasn't sure he'd convinced himself. When Briar had returned from the dead, he'd been, momentarily, so flooded with happiness and relief that he'd forgotten his previous fears and reservations. It had felt like a second chance to be there for Briar. And he was determined to do just that.

But it was hard to fully shake the darkness weighing upon him, the worries that he couldn't measure up. With every complication thrown at them, he began to fear that nothing was normal anymore, and that things might never be all right. That the happily ever after he'd envisioned would never come. Maybe he had been an idiot to think things could be that easy, but they had been, once upon a time. Why couldn't things go back to the way they were? Or was this all life was, getting harder and harder?

Briar yawned again, pulling a paisley quilt across her. "I was thinking," she said, "when Isabelle showed us the kitchen. Remember that time we snuck down to the kitchen in the castle? It was past midnight, and we were meant to be asleep, but I sent you that note to meet me—"

"I remember." Demetri leaned against the side of the bed. "I was really tired—"

"You were not," Briar protested. "You were as ridiculously pleased as I was—"

"Well, we ate a whole loaf of currant bread. And it was warm and perfect—how could I not be pleased about that?"

"And you made me dance with you." Briar gave a dramatic sigh to convey her suffering. "Even though you *know* I hate dancing."

"Except with me," Demetri teased. "You don't hate dancing with me."

"No," she said softly. "I don't hate anything with you."

Demetri took her hand, enclosing it in his. Her skin was as cold as ever, but the way her hand slipped inside his, like it was meant to be there, gave Demetri some peace.

If only he could hold onto that feeling. If only it could keep him afloat.

He looked at Briar and saw her smile had gone, as though her thoughts had turned similarly somber. The look in her eyes was haunted.

"I remember that," she murmured. "That night in the kitchen."

"Yes," Demetri said, but there was a lump in his throat. "Me too."

He left her to rest and sought out Garrett. He was so exhausted that he was having trouble focusing, but he knew if he slept now, he'd be up all night. So he forced himself, on wavering legs, to find Garrett, who was in the library.

Isabelle was there too, having seen to everyone's rooms. The library was an enormous, five-walled room built into an alcove in the eastern wing, and it bore the nutty fragrance of old books. The far wall was lined with three large windows looking into a stretch of thin cedar trees outside. It was the only wall not covered in bookshelves. Demetri did not think the room used to be a library when the manor belonged to someone else, because the bookshelves were of different woods and styles—unvarnished redwood, dark chestnut, black walnut, and a few that were not wood at all, but brass metal. They were pushed against the walls in a haphazard fashion, books stacked in side by side, on top of each other, double-shelved, and crammed in wherever they fit. The disorder would have driven Demetri mad, but he suspected it wasn't disordered to Isabelle. She seemed too sensible a person not to have a system.

"Demetri." Garrett waved him over. He sat in a cushy scarlet armchair, feet propped up on an upholstered footrest, muddy boots and all. His gray sack coat hung over the back of the chair, and the bottom button of his waistcoat was undone.

If Isabelle minded mud on her furniture, she didn't say so, or perhaps she hadn't noticed, given her fixation with a large tome she had open on a stained gray-wood table. She stood over it, her dark eyes preoccupied.

"I asked Isabelle what she might know about these corpses," Garrett explained. "Or how to break the curse on them, anyway."

Demetri looked at Isabelle. "Are you some expert in magic? Or diseases, maybe?"

"Neither." Isabelle flipped a page in her book. It was a thick, leather-bound book with sheaf-like parchment for pages. Very old, Demetri guessed. "I don't put much stock in magic. But I'm a big reader."

"Oh?" Demetri leaned against the table. He was afraid if he sat down, he would fall asleep and start snoring.

"History, mostly," said Isabelle. "I read a lot of history—a *lot* of history. Any history, for that matter, I don't take particular interest in a single period or event like some scholars do. I find that a very limited way of learning about the world. But I read other things as well, philosophy and theologies and theoretical science—"

"Which sometimes strays into magic," Garrett broke in. "Or so she tells me."

"Yes, so, well, I do have a lot of works on magic. What little has been recorded anyway. There isn't much, especially in the past two hundred years."

"I just want to get a handle on this." Garrett swung his feet off the footstool and leaned forward. "Now that we know what's caused these monsters, that it's a curse—"

"Cast by the dark fairy," Demetri muttered.

"—we just need to know how to put a stop to them. How to break the curse, if that can be done."

"Oh, it can be done," Isabelle assured him. "From what I've read, every curse cast by a fairy has a loophole built into it. It's required. The problem is, a fairy isn't required to make that loophole known, so it can be difficult to figure out how to break a curse. Especially this one, given that it was cast eighty years ago."

"Eighty-two years," Demetri said tensely. Everyone waved those two years off for convenience's sake. Demetri couldn't do that. He couldn't wave off a single second of his imprisonment.

"In which case, we may just have to a find a way to neutralize these corpses." Garrett tapped a restless foot against the hardwood floor. "If there are as many as we think there are, and not confined to the castle, then we're going to need a lot more manpower and a lot more firepower."

Demetri shifted his weight from one aching foot to the other. "But you've sent word to your father, haven't you?"

"Sure." Garrett drummed his fingers against the arm of his chair. "I sent him a telegram at the train station. But he only replied that we would discuss it at home. Of course, we should have been home by tomorrow—but I'm concerned he isn't taking me seriously. I've faced a lot of things in the past few years, but rotting corpse people sounds a little absurd even for me."

"Well," Isabelle said, "seeing as he's never been on a quest to find a magic sword or gone hunting trolls—"

"Don't be silly. There's no such thing as a troll," Garrett said with a straight face. "But you're right. My father was never the adventurous type. He believes in what he can see."

"Anyway, if this threat is as widespread as you think, you may not get the backup you need in time," Isabelle pointed out.

"Thanks, Isabelle."

"You're welcome. Oh, here's the passage I was thinking of." She smoothed both hands over the pages and adjusted her spectacles.

"You don't actually need spectacles, do you?" Garrett asked. "You're only seventeen."

"Oh, I don't need them. I just like to look scholarly. So far, I haven't come across anything that speaks specifically to breaking curses, but I think this passage might be helpful. It discusses the origin of magic in our land. Only, the conclusion is that no one really knows the origin of magic."

"That's helpful," Demetri said glumly.

"It goes on to say that magic is the province of fairies." Isabelle swept her finger along the passage. "There's a bunch of jabber here about fairies having the only natural access to magic because fairies are 'tied to the land.' Whatever that means. It's not very clear. There's also a bit about the Gift here, when the fairies made their pact of peace with humans and the Five Kingdoms were established—Mountain, Glen, Mariner, Forest, and Desert." Isabelle pushed a stray curl back from her face. "It talks about a gift of "magic" but then goes on to clarify that they *didn't* gift the humans with magic. So I'm not sure what that's about."

"That fairy said something about that." A frown marred Garrett's face. "She said they gifted the royal families their blood, but then she said that didn't mean the royals had any magic or power themselves." His frown deepened. "The thing is, humans *can* do magic too. Isn't that what a witch is, after all?"

"Well, yes, that's what I'm getting at. Fairies have the only *natural* access to magic," Isabelle explained. "Humans using magic is unnatural."

"Evil," Garrett murmured.

"I don't think it's inherently evil for humans to use magic," Isabelle said, the pages of her book *swish-swishing* as she flipped through them. "You and I have had negative experiences with witches, yes—"

Demetri shot Isabelle an interested glance. So she'd had a bad run-in with a witch as well?

"—but there *can* be good witches. It just doesn't happen often because—here we are." She stopped on a new page. "This is where it talks about humans using magic. Whatever means fairies use to access magic, humans can't use. Their only option is to go through a fairy. Ideally—this is how a good witch would operate, I suppose—a fairy would serve as a sort of familiar for the human witch."

"Good chance getting a fairy to help a human," Demetri said.

"That's exactly the problem, Your Highness." Isabelle glanced up. "Most fairies would never agree to such a thing. Witches have come up with some way to force a fairy to aid them. What that way is, I don't know." She closed the book firmly and a waft of dust flew into the air. Isabelle sneezed.

"So that's it?" Demetri said. "But how does that help us break the curse?"

"Well, it doesn't, not directly." Isabelle turned and leaned her hip against the table. "But this could be a lead. Witches obviously have some kind of power over fairies, and they're only human like us. I'll continue to look into ways to break curses, but this is something else to look into as well." She glanced at Garrett, who had gone quite still, his fingers made into a steeple beneath his chin. "Garrett?"

"Hmm?"

"What are you thinking?"

Garrett didn't answer right away. Then he said, "Well. I'm thinking that maybe, the best way to find out what power witches have over fairies would be to talk to one."

"But what witch would help us?" Demetri asked. "I certainly don't know any."

Garrett met his gaze with a grim look. "I do."

Isabelle's wide eyes went even larger. "Garrett, no. You can't be serious."

"I am very serious."

"Why would she help? She has no reason to. Unless you're planning to give her something in return, and I do *not* recommend such a thing."

Demetri looked between the two of them, puzzled. Then he realized. There was one witch that Garrett was acquainted with—more than acquainted with. "Hang on," Demetri said, "you don't mean—"

"Yes." Garrett's voice was calm and distant. "The former queen of the Mariner Kingdom. Snow's stepmother. The woman who killed her."

16

ULTIMATUM

Garrett thought neither Isabelle nor Demetri understood how much he did not want to pay a visit to the witch responsible for Snow's death, given all the ways they tried to talk him out of it. But he saw no other solution, nowhere else they could turn for answers, so in the end, it was decided they would do just that. The train was still broken, and they all agreed it would be best if Briar had a few days to rest, per Thatcher's instructions. And it just so happened that the queen's prison was only a hundred miles south of Isabelle's manor.

"It doesn't bother you?" Demetri asked Isabelle. "Living so close to her prison?"

Isabelle glowered at Garrett. "I didn't *know* I lived so close to her prison."

Garrett looked unrepentant. "I thought best not to mention it. We can find you a manor in the Black Forest, if you prefer."

"What a choice." Isabelle rolled her eyes. "A witch, or ghouls and beasts?"

"There's no such thing as ghouls," Garrett said. "And if there are, then someone find me some for my next quest."

He joked, but inside, Garrett felt like his stomach was shriveling. He hadn't laid eyes on the queen since she was tried a year and a half ago. He had no desire to see her again. He feared what memories and feelings she might drudge up. And then he felt annoyed with himself for fearing his own feelings.

"It should be a two-day ride on horseback then," Demetri mused.

"Forget horseback," Isabelle said. "There's an old self-propelled carriage in the garage. I'm not sure it works, but you can try it?"

The black, four-wheeled carriage was old, a model that was used in the earlier half of the century before trains became the common mode. As a result, the carriage was not quite in working condition, but with Alec's help, they got it up and running in time to leave first thing the next morning.

Before setting out, Garrett made a stop by the kitchen to pack some provisions. One of the soldiers had already seen to that, of course, but Garrett liked to have an extra snack or two on him.

He rounded the entrance into the kitchen and ran straight into Briar.

"Oh." Before he could stop himself, Garrett reached up and grasped Briar's arm, half to steady her and half to keep himself from toppling forward. Briar backed up a step, into the kitchen counter, and Garrett dropped his hand in a flash, as though he'd burned it. "Sorry."

"It's all right." A brief smile touched Briar's face. "My fault."

"No, it wasn't," said Garrett, and then he cursed himself, wondering why on earth he was being so stupid and arguing with her. He stumbled back a step and bumped into the doorframe behind him. Quickly, he crossed his arms over his chest, trying to make it look as though he'd done it on purpose. He leaned against the doorframe, adopting a casual pose.

Another smile tugged at Briar's lips, and Garrett couldn't help but wonder if she'd seen through his pose. If so, she didn't say so. She only said, rather too politely, "About to set off, then?"

Garrett nodded. "Yes. Just about." He cleared his throat. "You're sure you'll be all right without us?"

"Given that I'll have Isabelle, Thatcher, and about fifteen guards here, yes, I think I'll be fine," Briar said. She didn't sound annoyed. On the contrary, if he was not mistaken, she had just done a rather accurate imitation of his own pleasant tone. The one he used to make sure he did *not* sound annoyed.

Now it was Garrett's turn to smile. Which helped him relax a little. "You want to come with us, don't you?"

"Well, it would be better than sitting around for four days," she said, "but given we still don't know what's going on with me, I can see Thatcher's logic in wanting me to stay put. I suppose," she added in a grumble.

Garrett was still smiling. He didn't think he could stop if he tried. His amusement was spreading, blossoming into something warm and pleasant—something very like affection. "And logic is probably the only thing keeping you from insisting on coming with us, isn't it?"

"How well you know me," Briar said dryly.

Garrett's smile faltered. That warm feeling inside him dissipated, and in its place was a deep unease—a much *less* pleasant feeling. One that made him feel like his chest was caving in. It took him a second to sort out what was wrong, why he felt so unsettled.

How well you know me. She'd said it in jest, judging by her tone, but she was not wrong, thought Garrett. He felt he did know her, very well, even though they'd just met...what, ten days ago? But they'd spent so much of their traveling time together, talking, getting to know each other, and they'd been through so much—more than most people experienced together in a lifetime, when it came to harrowing experiences—

Maybe it wasn't so strange to feel he knew her so well. But it was still unsettling. Because he couldn't remember the last time he'd felt so close to someone so quickly.

No. He could remember. And that was why this was unsettling.

"Garrett?"

Garrett started and realized Briar was staring at him—or rather, he was staring at her. And he must have had a peculiar look on his face, because Briar asked, "Are you all right?"

Garrett didn't trust himself to answer right away. His throat felt tight. He forced himself to take a breath and then managed a shaky smile. "Fine." He hoped his voice didn't sound weird. "I was just thinking about something."

Briar's brow was furrowed. She stepped away from the counter and stood less than a pace from him. "Something upsetting, by the look on your face," she said, and before he could do anything to stop it, she reached out and laid a hand on his arm.

He didn't pull away. Part of him wanted to. Part of him knew he needed to make his excuses and walk away, before his self-command crumbled, before he said something stupid. (Well, more stupid than the things he'd already said.) But he was trying to act normal, damn it, and...and...

And he just didn't want to pull away. It was all he could do to keep from laying his own hand over hers.

"Garrett?" Briar repeated. Her fingers squeezed his arm gently.

Garrett drew in a ragged breath. "I was just thinking," he said, pulling the words at random from somewhere, "that—I'm really glad you're not dead."

And there it was. Something stupid(er).

Briar's eyebrow hitched. "Erm...me too?"

Garrett let out a short laugh, and she laughed too. For a moment, some of the tension dissipated. But then he found himself dwelling on her laugh, how genuine and melodious it was. And then, when she dropped her hand from his arm, he felt the loss keenly, his whole body going bizarrely cold.

His throat tightened even more. What was wrong with him?

"It wasn't your fault, you know," Briar said suddenly. "What happened in the woods. Me...dying."

"I know," said Garrett. Even though he was not sure he did know that. But she wasn't dead; she was here, and he supposed that was what mattered. "It was just—when I thought you were gone—when you *were* gone—"

He broke off. He had no idea what he was about to say, but he was very sure he shouldn't say it. Briar was watching him with the oddest look on her face, one he couldn't decipher.

"I'm just glad you're not dead." He straightened, easing around the doorframe, and took a step back. "Anyway. Need to get going. I'll see you in four days, I suppose."

"Yes," she said, "I suppose," but Garrett had already turned away, leaving the kitchen, and Briar, behind.

He was all the way outside and halfway to the garage before he realized he hadn't gotten any snacks.

<hr />

The self-propelled carriage wasn't any faster than a horse, but it was more comfortable—though it took a great deal of manual steering on Alec's part, given there was no road to the prison. The seats inside, though a bit lumpy and moth-eaten, were cushioned and upholstered, and the small windows in the side doors were open, allowing a cool stream of air in as they rode.

Garrett sat in the bumpy carriage and scratched at the edge of his bandage through his coat sleeve. Thatcher had looked at it last night—as had Garrett himself, and he rather wished he hadn't. The wound looked like a dark bruise, and the surrounding flesh was an angry red, oozing a yellowish fluid that gave off a noxious odor once exposed to the air. Thatcher had gotten quiet and not said much to Garrett, mumbling to himself instead.

Garrett knew his medic well enough to take this as a bad sign, but he didn't have time to worry about it. So he told Thatcher to wrap the shoulder, and with pinched eyes, Thatcher had done so. Now, sitting in the carriage and gazing out at the forest, Garrett tried to ignore the pulsating twinges of pain that came and went. He rested his head against the window ledge, breathing in deep. The dry, smoky perfume of North Glen cedars scented the air. This part of the wood was thick with cedar trees—some thin and rickety, stretching into the dreary sky with branches protruding like a porcupine's spines. Others were squat and knobby, filled with broad clusters of hunter green leaves.

Cedar trees grew thick in the south of the kingdom too, in the swampier woods that separated Garrett's kingdom from the Mariner Kingdom—where Snow had lived. He remembered many adventures with her in those woods, under the shade of the trees, where moss grew thick and hung off branches like draping curtains. Snow had taken refuge in those woods after her father was killed, when the queen accused her of the murder and sought her execution.

"By the way," Demetri said, "Briar told me what happened on the bridge that night."

Garrett looked around, startled. "What?"

"She told me she wanted to climb down in the dark." Demetri gave him a rueful smile. "But you insisted on waiting for daylight. I was just thinking it was a good thing you did, given how ill Briar became. You probably both would have ended up dead. You know, instead of just Briar," he added wryly.

"Oh." Garrett's voice creaked like a rusty hinge. He had not been thinking about his insistence that they stay on the bridge until morning. He had been thinking about the hours they'd spent there, huddled together in the darkness, Briar's cold hand in his and her head on his shoulder. Not that there was anything wrong with that. Such physical closeness might not have been strictly proper, but they couldn't have sat further apart without falling off the bridge, and besides, Briar had been upset and Garrett had been terrified. Which was more than enough reason for anything that might have happened, he felt. Not that anything untoward *had* happened.

He put the thought behind him and focused on the soothing sway of the carriage as it trundled through the forest, its mechanical wheels chomping through dead leaves and stray twigs. He needed to get himself together if he was going to face the queen and keep his composure.

They reached the prison in two days.

The queen had been overthrown when it was discovered she used black magic to kill Snow and her father. After some wrangling with the counts in the Mariner Kingdom, Garrett's father had arranged to take custody of the woman so she could be tried and sentenced in the Glen Kingdom. There was no precedent for it, but the Mariner Kingdom was superstitious about witches and magic. They were eager to be rid of her.

The queen was kept in her own private prison in the midst of the woods. It was a squat fortress, built from dark stone mined from the quarries in the far west—a very medieval structure with no embellishment or decoration, which Garrett thought fitting, considering who it housed.

A guard named Link led them inside to the queen's cell. There were no windows, not even in the stark entry hall, where the ceiling was so low that Garrett felt like it was closing down on them. They went down a winding stairwell which opened into a musty, hallowed-out cavern below. The unpaved dirt floor had merely been cleared and scattered with gravel. Four guards kept watch there with a single gear-bulb lantern.

A damp cold gripped Garrett as he descended into the cavern. He told himself it was a natural cold, given the bare stone and muddy ground, but it was such a sudden chill, sinking into his bones, that he couldn't help but wander to less rational thoughts.

The queen's jail cell lay twenty feet into the cavern. There was an outer cell with iron bars, which was empty at the moment. A couple of feet beyond it was the solid iron door which led to the inner cell. There were no windows within; day in and day out, the queen lived in darkness.

Garrett and Demetri approached the bars, their boots crunching over gravel. Their guard Link instructed another guard to open the inner cell. The guard wound up an iron lever at the base of the bars; it let out a long, whining squeal as it turned. The lever was connected to a set of gears above the iron door, and as the gears clicked and turned, the door rose up.

"Come out, witch," Link called. "You have visitors."

Garrett steeled himself in the moment that followed. Handing his lantern to Demetri, he clasped his hands in front of himself and planted his feet.

A dark figure unfolded in the shadowy doorway. She was forced to bend to come through the half-open door, and the posture gave her a tentative air. When she stepped out and straightened, however, there was nothing tentative about her.

She was Queen Delphine, regal and contemptuous as ever.

Her indigo eyes alighted on Garrett with a triumphant gleam. As though she considered his presence a personal victory, without even knowing why he had come.

"Well, well, well," she breathed. "Who should be my visitor but my darling stepdaughter's Prince *Gallant*."

Garrett felt like she'd burned him with a red hot poker. "Gallant" had been Snow's nickname for him, and to hear it from her murderer's lips made it difficult to maintain his stony expression.

The queen swept her gaze over Demetri. "And who is this? Another young princeling?"

"Hardly young," Demetri said. "I was born a century ago. I wonder which of us is older."

The queen's eyes flashed. Garrett would not have been surprised if she had used magic to maintain her youth. But all she said was, "A century ago? How have you kept your pretty face then?"

"A fairy."

"A fairy." The queen's lips curved in a semblance of a smile. "If you've dealt with fairies, then I imagine you don't find me all that frightening, do you?"

"No. Not really."

The queen's smile widened. "I eat fairies for breakfast. Boy."

Garrett eyed her by the light cast from their lantern. She looked unaffected by her eighteen months of bleak captivity. Her dark hair was neat and maintained, though it hung quite long, reaching her waist. Faint lines marred her face, lines that had not been there before. That was something at least. She was also thinner, though that did not diminish her much. She was already a small woman, much shorter than Garrett. Shorter than Demetri, even. And her dark wool dress hung unfitted over her, giving no shape to her frame.

Still, none of this changed her much. Not as much as Garrett would have liked.

The queen turned her smile on Garrett. "I like this little prince. How thoughtful of you to bring me such a gift, Your Highness."

"We didn't come to chat." Garrett bit his cheek, hating the next words out of his mouth. "We've come for information. About your magic."

One of her eyebrows shot up. "Have you? And what will you give me if I give *you* information?"

Garrett was a little unsettled by how to-the-point she was. He realized he was fidgeting with his sleeves and thrust his hands behind his back, locking them together. "Your life. I won't kill you."

Any trace of a smile vanished from her face. "Murder, Prince Gallant? I don't believe it. Not of you."

"Then you underestimate me, Delphine," he said. He wasn't going to waste titles on this evil witch. "Maybe you can't comprehend what you took from me. I wouldn't be surprised, given that you're incapable of compassion or remorse."

"I comprehend love and passion well enough, *Gallant.* More than you could possibly imagine." Her eyes glittered as though she knew some secret.

"Good." Garrett was pleased to hear how steely his voice came out. "Then believe me when I tell you I would have absolutely no compunction about killing you right now, right here. Given that I am prince of the realm, it's unlikely these guards would bother to report it to my father the king. So. Will you help us, or will you die?"

The queen's face melted into a hideous glower at his threat. "So you want information about magic. Do you have anything more specific? To educate you in the delicate and complicated art of magic would take more time than I care to waste, princeling. Not to mention, more capacity for complex systems than your mind can manage."

"All we want to know is how you *do* your magic." Garrett squared his shoulders. "We know you get your power from fairies, or through them or whatever."

The queen's eyes lit with interest. "What business do you have with fairies?"

"None of yours."

"I can hardly help if you aren't more specific. What is it that you're after and why?"

Garrett glanced at Demetri, who shrugged. Gritting his teeth, Garrett outlined the situation with the corpses and the dark fairy. To her credit, the queen listened and made no attempts to interrupt him. He made no mention of Briar, but the queen was too shrewd for that.

"The infamous dark fairy," the queen said when he was done explaining. "But if I remember correctly, she didn't curse the entire Mountain Kingdom." Her gaze veered in Demetri's direction, as though she knew the situation was sensitive to him. "The story *I've* heard is that she cursed a *princess* from the Mountain Kingdom."

Garrett placed his hands behind his back again, turning the ring on his right hand over and over until it felt like it would scald his finger. He wasn't sure why he was so loathe to mention Briar.

"I also remember," the queen went on, "that she cursed this princess to *sleep*."

Garrett repressed a flinch.

"Curious. Why would you avoid mentioning her? Because poor little Snow died the same way?"

"Briar isn't dead," Demetri retorted.

"Or is it something else? Are you trying to protect this new princess? Oh, Garrett." The queen startled him with the use of his real name. She let out a peal of booming laughter that echoed through the hollowed cavern, bouncing from wall to wall like a clanging in Garrett's head.

"How adorable you are." Delphine fixed Garrett with a know-ing look. "Standing here with such a scowl. As though you could hide your thoughts from me." She clutched the bars on either side of her, gripping them until her knuckles whitened. "I can read you like a book, little princeling. And I find it curious indeed. You so loved sweet, sickening Snow. Yet you replace her so easily with another sleeping princess? Well, I suppose I can see the attraction. Maybe you can actually wake this one."

Her words snapped at him like the jaws of a rabid dog. "She is awake," he managed to say, his voice grating. The idea that he could replace Snow with Briar, that he would even want to—it made his blood boil. Briar wasn't free to be his anyway. She was with Demetri.

Why that thought crossed his mind, he wasn't sure.

"And she doesn't need protecting," Demetri placed one hand over the gilded hilt of his rapier.

"We're not here to talk about her," Garrett added.

"No. You're here to talk about the fairy who cursed her." The queen shook her head. "You poor fools. Most humans know enough to avoid drawing the ire of *any* fairy. But you want to meddle with the dark fairy?"

"We just want to know how to break this curse she's cast," Garrett said.

"We know every curse has a loophole," Demetri noted, "but given that the dark fairy never bothered to tell us what that is, it's not very helpful."

"Well, there is another way to break a fairy's curse." The queen's eyes cut them with an eager gleam. "I don't think you'll like it though."

"What is it?"

The queen smiled. "I told you I eat fairies for breakfast. Did you think I was joking?" She gave a small chuckle at the incredulous looks they turned on her. "Well, I don't actually *eat* them. But their blood is instrumental. Fairies are attuned to the land and the land is magic. Humans, though, have no such link." The queen fixed her gaze on Garrett with a sudden intensity. "I wonder if you could hazard a guess at the number of fairies I've slaughtered in my time."

"You *kill* them?" Garrett recoiled, his boot scraping over muddy grit. Fairies were vicious creatures, but to kill one.... Killing a fairy was said to bring the worst doom upon yourself. And besides that, it was impossible. There was a reason the pact between fairies and humans included a clause forbidding fairies to kill humans, but not the other way around. No one knew how to kill them.

Except, maybe, a witch.

"Oh, yes." The queen's eyes burned. "Of course, one doesn't *have* to kill a fairy to garner magic from it. But I find spilling their blood is the easiest way." She leaned her forehead against the iron bars and combed her long-nailed fingers through her dark hair. She seemed to take a savage pleasure in their revulsion. "I told you that you wouldn't like it."

Garrett massaged his temple, trying to regain his focus. "So you're saying...*that's* how you can break a fairy's curse? By killing the fairy who cast it?"

"Yes. So you could call what I do a good deed, really. How many unjust curses do you think I've broken?"

"Probably not very many," Garrett said tightly, "since most fairies don't go around casting curses anymore."

"But how do you kill a fairy?" Demetri asked.

"That's not really important," Delphine demurred.

"I would think it is, if that's our only option."

"I doubt you'll consider it an option when you hear the rest. You see, it isn't possible to spill a fairy's blood and retain your soul."

Garrett frowned, mulling this over. "Explain."

"Killing a fairy is forbidden. It is a crime against nature. The...universe, shall we say?...won't allow it, not without consequences." Delphine pressed her whole body against the bars as she twisted her head to one side. An expression of delighted reminiscence stole over her face. "I once saw a man kill a fairy. The result was..." She inhaled, her voice turning languid. "A person can live without their soul, you see. In fact, a person without a soul looks like any other person. They walk, they talk, they eat, they sleep—but they aren't a person. Not anymore. They have no concept of right and wrong. They believe in nothing, care for nothing. They have nothing to tether them to the world, no meaning to their life."

"So you have no soul," Garrett said. "That explains a lot."

"I have a soul, you fool." Delphine leaned back. "I made a deal for it like most witches do. So long as I live, I can kill fairies and retain my soul."

"A deal? A deal with who?"

"That doesn't concern you."

"We need to know—" Demetri began.

"Why?" The queen laughed, and it was like a frigid draft gliding through Garrett. "Because you want to make the same deal? I may not know *you*, little princeling, but I know Prince Gallant here, and I imagine you are cut from the same cloth. Suffice it to say, I sold my soul to dark forces. *Old* forces, forces as old as the

fairies themselves. And when I die—whenever that may be—"
She turned her gaze on Garrett "—I will belong to those forces
forever. And be subject to whatever treatment they wish on me."

Garrett looked at her, his throat burning like he'd drunk
something caustic. He'd almost forgotten what a vile person this
woman was, and being here with her made him want to pound
his fists into a stone wall until they bled. In a weird way, he felt
more like the person he used to be, the boy who hadn't tried to
squash his emotions or dash into danger in an attempt to leave
them behind.

That should have made him feel better, really, to be more in
touch with himself. But instead he felt unstable, like dynamite
that had been stored for too long. He'd learned to repress such
volatile feelings, and he feared what might happen if he let them
out now.

"So now you see." Delphine's words were laced with smug
satisfaction. "Unless you're willing to give up your souls to kill
this fairy, you'd best find another way to reverse her curse. I don't
know a way to do that, but perhaps you'll get lucky."

Garrett didn't know if he believed her. The queen was a master
of manipulation, and she lived for it. Still, that didn't mean she
was lying now, and her words had the ring of truth to them. "If
you don't know anything more," he said, "then we have nothing
more to say."

Demetri interjected, "I have a question for her."

Garrett cast him a sidelong glance, trying to look like he'd
expected this.

"Ask away, princeling," Delphine purred.

Demetri adjusted his grip on the lantern pole. "When witches
do their magic, do they ever...glow blue?"

The queen's eyes narrowed to slits, as though she was trying to determine if this was a serious question. Garrett understood at once—the mysterious stranger who'd freed Demetri had emanated a blue glow. And since the fairies had denied that a fairy could do such a thing, then maybe...

"Glow blue," the queen repeated. "No. I've never heard of a *witch* glowing blue. Of course—" She flicked her fingers "—djinn, on the other hand, are known to emanate a blue glow from their faces."

"Djinn?" Garrett and Demetri echoed simultaneously.

"What's a djinn?" Demetri asked.

"The only living thing that can kill a fairy without losing its soul, without consequences. And you've seen one, haven't you?" The queen bared her teeth in a slow smile. "Oh, princeling. You've gotten yourself entangled in an ancient feud no human should be part of."

"What feud?"

"A feud between djinn and fairies, of course."

"You're making this up," Garrett scoffed. "I've never heard of djinn."

"They're all supposed to be confined to their shadow world." The queen waved a negligent hand. "Evidently one managed to slip free. If you've seen one."

Garrett and Demetri exchanged a troubled glance. If one of these djinn had freed Demetri and if they could kill fairies.... But even if that was true, they had no way of tracking down this creature. And Garrett wasn't sure he believed all this, anyway.

"We're done here," Garrett said, looking to Demetri. "Yes?"

Demetri nodded.

"I suppose we are." The queen's eyes glinted in the scant light, belying her dismissive tone. "Come and visit me again some time, Gallant. Sometime when you aren't busy fighting something. There are so many things we might discuss."

"I'll think about it." Garrett turned his back on her. If there was any luck in the world for him, he would never see this woman again.

17

DETACHED

BRIAR SAT SOAKING IN the porcelain tub in her washroom, running one hand over the other. The bath water was warm, and wax candles lined the ledge along the tub, their flickering flames evoking a soft light. It should have been relaxing, but Briar was struggling to relax for a number of reasons.

Garrett had been right; she hated staying behind while they went to get answers from this witch. Not because she was particularly interested in meeting a witch, but just because doing *anything* would have been better than sitting around, waiting to see if anything bad happened to her.

Waiting to see if she was really rotting like the rest of her kingdom.

And also, she was worried about Garrett. Briar had never been particularly good at reading people or tapping into their emotions. Whether because she'd had so little practice, given her lack of human connection growing up, or just because it wasn't something that came naturally to her—either way, it was not her strength.

But for some reason, Garrett was different. Maybe because she'd had more conversations with him than almost anyone else in her life, despite the short time she'd known him. Almost anyone, because there was Demetri, of course. But even Demetri she'd known for a good few months before she felt she'd known him so well that she could tap into what he was feeling and thinking.

With Garrett, it came much easier. There was just something about him—that feeling Briar had when she'd first met him. Like she'd known him all her life. And whatever that was, wherever that *came* from, it made him so easy to talk to. And so easy to read. Which was why it had been obvious, in the kitchen that morning before he left, that he was upset about something.

She could hardly blame him. Considering what he'd been about to do. Setting off to speak with the witch who had killed the princess he'd loved. Princess Snow. And not just *speak* with her, but ask for her help. Briar shook her head. She tried to imagine what it would be like to come face to face with the dark fairy. She had no idea what she would say, and she *certainly* couldn't imagine asking for help. Not that the fairy would ever give it.

Briar kicked her foot, splashing droplets over the edge of the tub. So here she was. Worrying about Garrett. Worrying about herself and what was happening to her. Thatcher had been monitoring her, and though she hadn't begun exhibiting any obvious symptoms of rotting, there were a few things that were cause for concern. For one thing, her pulse was slow—almost impossibly so. She also continued to feel tired all the time. A persistent, heavy lethargy that she couldn't shake.

Briar breathed in deeply, inhaling the ethereal scent of rose and jasmine bath oils. She wasn't sleeping well, so it was not so weird that she was tired. That might be nothing. But her cold skin was harder to dismiss. Briar didn't *feel* cold, but her skin, her fingers.... She submerged her hand in the warm bath water for so long that her fingers shriveled like prunes. And even so, they were cold to the touch, as though she had turned to glass.

With a sigh, she grasped the edge of the tub and pulled herself to her feet. She reached for the peacock blue towel on the counter and wrapped the smooth linen around herself, securing it over her chest. She made a point of not looking at the hole in her torso, which looked the same as it had three days ago—it wasn't showing any further signs of healing. Her palm was also the same, though Thatcher had stitched the gash together and bandaged it. Which was why, when Briar stepped out of the tub, she slipped.

She placed her wrapped hand on the marble countertop to steady herself, but the cloth bandage was damp and she lost her grip just as she lifted her leg over the edge of the tub. With a shriek, Briar pitched forward like a puppet with cut strings, her flailing hand slamming against the bath-side table. She crashed to the ground, cracking her knee against the tiled floor and sprawling out on her stomach.

For a moment, Briar lay on the washroom's cold, wet floor, struggling to regain her breath. She groaned, bending the knee that smacked into the floor. That was going to bruise. And if she was rotting, it was never going to *un*-bruise. "Ow," she mumbled, climbing to her hands and knees.

The door burst open before she got upright. "Princess Briar?" Briar recognized Kinsley's dulcet voice, sharper than usual. "Are you all right? What happened?"

Briar sat up straight, her sopping wet hair dripping onto the floor. She realized, to her mortification, that she was undressed, clad only in a towel before Kinsley. "I'm all right," Briar said, her eyes on the floor. "I just slipped getting out of the tub—"

"Uh—Princess," Kinsley began.

"I tried to grab onto the table—"

"Your Highness—"

"—but instead I knocked *into* it and then—"

"Briar!"

Briar snapped her head up, eyes wide. Not that she minded, but Kinsley never addressed her by her name. "What?"

Kinsley cleared his throat. He looked a little wild around the eyes. "Pardon the interruption, it's just...erm...well..."

"Yes?" Briar prodded. "Just what?"

"Where—" Kinsley bit his lip. "Where are your fingers?"

Briar stared at him. It was like he was speaking a different language. "Excuse me? What do you mean, where are my..." Her voice trailed off as she lifted both hands and looked at them.

Her left hand looked normal. Her right hand was missing every single finger except her thumb.

Briar gaped. She stared at the place where her fingers should have been. Her knuckles ended at the base of her palm in stubby, pink stumps. There was no pain and no blood—she couldn't feel anything. The lack of sensation, combined with the absurdity of the situation, made it impossible for her brain to reconcile what she was seeing.

"Stars and stones," she whispered.

"Princess—"

"Where—are—my—fingers?"

"That's what I said."

Briar looked at Kinsley. Panic welled inside her in a sudden, overwhelming onslaught. She could *feel* her heart thudding frantically in her chest. "*Where are my fingers?*" Her voice was a hoarse, hysterical gasp.

"Your Highness—"

"Help me." Briar's eyes darted left and right. "Help me find my fingers! Now!"

To his credit, Kinsley did just that. Briar spotted one—no, two—of her fingers first. Her *fingers*. Her slender pinky finger and what she thought was her ring finger lay on the floor in the groove between two tile pieces beside the small table.

They looked normal. There was no blood on them. They were just her fingers. Fallen off her hand.

"Oh, stars," Briar whimpered as Kinsley set the fingers on the table. Like they were earrings she'd dropped on the floor. Briar's stomach churned. She thought she was going to be sick.

"Hang on." Kinsley lowered himself to the floor. His long legs curled up against the bathtub as he sprawled on his stomach to reach beneath the table. "I think the other two rolled under here—"

"Rolled—rolled," Briar echoed. Her fingers had *rolled*. Under the table. She stifled a gag.

"Got them." Kinsley pulled his arm out from beneath the table and got to his knees, holding her two fingers in the palm of his hand.

Briar glared at him. "Why are you being so calm about this?" He was making her feel stupid for being so agitated, and it was definitely *not* stupid to be agitated about her fingers falling off. Her fingers. Falling. *Off.*

"Well, it seemed best that we both don't panic," Kinsley said.

Briar felt something bubbling up in her throat. Vomit, she thought. She *was* going to be sick.

No—it was laughter. A peal of hysterical laughter erupted from her lips. Kinsley had made her laugh.

She thought she might love him for that. In that moment. "Kinsley." Briar inhaled deeply. The laughter had calmed her. "I could kiss you. I really could. Have you ever been kissed by a princess?"

"No, Your Highness." Kinsley's brow was furrowed, as though he was concerned by her reaction. But he smiled a little. "Truthfully, I'd prefer a kiss from a prince."

"Oh, right." Briar had forgotten that. She inhaled another deep breath, her panic seeping out of her, and looked down at her hand.

There was no blood. No blood, and no pain. Her knuckles just ended. She could see bone and muscle and sinew within those stumps, but she couldn't feel a thing.

"My fingers fell off." Her voice sounded like it was coming from very far away. That was something she never thought she'd say. "When I hit them against the table."

"Does it hurt?" Kinsley asked.

"No. I didn't even feel it—they'd gone so cold they were numb." Numb, like her blood wasn't circulating through them.

Another hoarse laugh escaped Briar.

"Your Highness?" Kinsley shifted his weight.

"I'm sorry, it's just—" she said, taking another deep breath. "Thatcher—he said we should be on the lookout. For anything that might suggest I'm rotting." She tried to smile, but it didn't work. "This is a pretty good sign, don't you think?"

"I would say so, Your Highness."

Briar clenched her jaw to keep it from trembling, or worse, to prevent another bout of laughter. "What do we *do?*"

Kinsley seemed to consider the question. He looked at the fingers in his palm and then at the two on the table. "Well. I am rather good with a needle."

Briar goggled.

"We could sew your fingers back on," he suggested.

Fifteen minutes later, Briar, dressed in a cotton night shift and a blue dressing robe, sat in her iron-framed bed against a mountain of plushy pillows, holding her arm out for Kinsley. Three of her fingers sat in a silvered glass candy dish on the bedside table, all but the pointer finger. That one was halfway attached to her hand, as Kinsley bent his black-haired head over it, sewing it on by the light of a gear-bulb lamp.

"I can't believe this is happening." Briar gazed at the black grille foot of the bed. She was determined not to watch as Kinsley reattached her fingers. She didn't think she *could* watch. It was not that she was squeamish, exactly. It was more that, if she watched him do it, then...it would be real. All too real.

Panic was still roiling inside her, threatening to overtake her. She couldn't let that happen. And if she watched what he was doing, it *would* happen.

Kinsley made a small noise in the back of his throat. "The, ah, possibility hadn't occurred to you before now?"

"Well, yes, that's why Thatcher—hang on." Briar swung her gaze towards him. Towards his face, not his hands. "Had it occurred to *you?* Or did Garrett say something? I didn't think—"

"Prince Garrett didn't say anything to me about this. Nor to any of the soldiers, so far as I know. But I knew something was going on." Kinsley glanced up. "Are you sure this doesn't hurt?"

"I told you, I can't feel a thing," Briar said numbly. "What do you mean you knew something was going on?"

"Well, you were dead, after all," Kinsley explained. "I was the one who carried you—or your body, rather—back to the train site. So I *knew* you were dead. I knew Prince Garrett hadn't been mistaken about that. And then you came back. After something like that, rotting corpse creature starts to make sense."

"Why didn't you say anything?"

"Well, I didn't know for sure, and I didn't want to scare you if it wasn't true. And if you had already realized it—which, apparently, you had—it just would've been rude to ask if you were becoming a corpse creature."

Briar let her head sink back into the pillows. "Does anyone else know?"

"I didn't say anything to anyone, if that's what you mean. I didn't want to cause a panic." He sat back, letting go as he finished with the first finger. "One down, three to go."

"It *would* cause a panic, wouldn't it?" Briar's stomach churned. "I mean, the soldiers—"

"Actually, we've all seen some fairly weird things with Prince Garrett—man-eating beasts, sea monsters, fire-breathing necromancers—"

"*Fire-breathing necromancers?*" Briar muttered.

"—so this isn't so bad, really. I don't think anyone will mind much."

"Good," Briar said dryly. "I'd hate to inconvenience anyone."

Kinsley spared her a brief smile, then fell silent. He remained quiet as he attached the rest of her fingers. Briar was too, listening to the wind as it whispered through the stiff leaves of the elm trees outside.

Even though *she* was the one who had suggested she might be rotting, she couldn't quite bring herself to accept it was happening. Until now, everything else could be explained as something normal. Even coming back from the dead might have been some kind of mistake, for all that Garrett insisted Thatcher didn't make mistakes. Without realizing it, she'd clung to that—that beneath all this, there was a rational explanation. But now...

Well, there was a rational explanation. She was becoming a rotting corpse creature.

The implications flooded through her. So did her memories, flashes of the monsters she'd seen. Corpses leaping down the lift shaft. Laurel dragging her down a dark corridor. The little girl in the village, her brains splattered across the floor. The corpse snapping Read's head clean off in the train—

"Are you all right, Princess?" Kinsley asked. He was nearly done with the last finger.

"Fine." Briar's tone was mechanical. But now she could hear Laurel's words skittering across her brain. *Remembrance. Memory. Sometimes I can...remember.*

Briar clutched at her pillow. That was the part she had really tried not to think about. Laurel had remembered enough, been enough of *herself,* to talk to Briar. But she hadn't been anything like the cousin Briar remembered. Maybe Laurel had just really, really resented Briar for what had happened to her. Maybe she blamed Briar. But even still, Briar could not reconcile that violent creature with the memory of her cousin, the only family member who had bothered to get to know her.

Was she, Briar, going to become like that? Forget more and more, until she wasn't herself any longer? Would she lose herself to violence and bloodlust? That was far more terrifying than any physical symptoms. That was as good as dying.

She'd rather be dead, she thought, than lose her mind.

Once Kinsley tied off the thread on her last finger, he stood to clear away the needle and thread. "Your Highness."

"Hmm?"

"Are you really all right?"

Briar lifted her head. Something must have shown on her face because Kinsley smiled ruefully. "I'm sorry," he said. "I know that must sound an amazingly stupid question."

"No. No, it's not." Briar scraped a hand through her damp hair. "Look, would you—would you keep this to yourself for now? Not tell anyone what happened here, I mean."

Kinsley's brow furrowed. "Not even Thatcher?"

"I'll talk to him first thing in the morning," Briar promised. "Just right now...I'd just like to sleep. If possible."

"All right. Would you like me to bring you something to eat first? You missed dinner."

Briar's stomach twisted. "No, I'm not hungry. But thank you."

Kinsley sketched her a bow and left the room. Briar switched off the lamp at her bedside, plunging the room into darkness.

If only I could shut off my mind so easily. The thought flashed through Briar's brain, and she regretted it at once. It could be all too soon, she realized, before her mind did shut down, and she would be reduced to a raving monster. The fear of that rose inside her, a monster of its own. She fought to push it away, to smother it before it could smother her. But she could not banish it completely.

Stones, she would never get to sleep with that fear and dread looming over her. And she wanted to sleep. She wanted one night where she didn't have to contemplate becoming a monster.

She thought of Garrett and Demetri and felt a little soothed. The fear trickled away. Just a little. But it was enough.

She slept a bit. But her sleep was riddled with nightmares of rotted corpses gorging on human flesh. The dreams were so vivid that she tore awake in the middle of the night, bound up in twisted sheets like a caterpillar in a cocoon. She woke so frantic that she felt she should be drenched in sweat, but her skin was dry and cold.

She tried to go back to sleep, but her stomach felt queasy. She was so tired that her eyes stung, but the longer she lay there, the more impossible sleep seemed. The roiling in her stomach grew worse, until it felt like acid burning a hole through her. Briar dug her fingers into the folds of her quilt. It became so *huge*, this discomfort, this agony, that she couldn't think beyond it.

No, not agony. *Hunger.*

That was the last thought in her brain before the fog stole over and shut her out.

She didn't sleep. Her brain just shut down. She couldn't string two thoughts together. She didn't know or care who she was. Her body, stiff and heavy, moved of its own accord, tripping out of bed, dragging knotted sheets behind her. She staggered into a long corridor outside.

She lurched down the corridor, cold wood beneath her bare feet. A white, glaring light on the wall flickered, casting bumbling shadows across the floor. She didn't know where she was going, driven by some base instinct, some feral gnawing that urged her on.

She passed several closed doors and rounded a corner, rough stone scraping against her palm as she grabbed at the wall to steady herself. She turned another corner. She kept going—she didn't know for how long—until she passed another door. It looked like all the others, but something was different here. Something caught her attention.

Something inside. Something that clawed at the hole in her gut.

Her fingers fumbled with the latch on the door, yanking it down. It drifted open with a *squeak*.

The room was dark like the room she'd left behind, save for a beam of moonlight coming in through a large window. She could see the redwood bed against the far wall, and she could see the long, slender shape beneath its sheets, and the head of a person resting against the pillows. A shaft of light from the corridor spilled into the room, and as she stepped inside, the person in the bed stirred and opened her eyes.

The person was a girl. She had dark skin and dark, curly hair. She was thin, almost bony.

But there was something about her. A savory aroma, radiating off her in waves. An aroma that made the gnawing pain inside her *twist*.

The girl spoke to her, words she didn't understand. It was just noise, squawking, maddening noise. She moved forward, forcing her leaden muscles to work, towards the bed, towards the girl.

She moved like a sloth, feet dragging against the floor. She moved until she stood at the foot of the bed.

Then she lunged for the girl.

Everything that came next happened in a blur. The girl screamed, the sound cutting through the dark, and she threw herself off the bed. Briar wobbled, tangling in the sheets. She struggled to get free, but it was so difficult to make her limbs work. The hunger drove her. When she got free and stood clear of the bed, she saw the girl disappearing out the door, running too fast to catch. But Briar staggered after her, a wordless growl escaping her lips.

She *needed* to eat.

When she lurched into the corridor outside, the girl was nowhere to be seen. Instead, a man stood there, a young man with white skin and black hair. He held something in his hands. A rifle.

"I'm sorry, Princess," he said.

He brought the rifle up and smashed the butt of it against her skull.

Everything went black.

18

FADING

B RIAR SLOWLY OPENED HER eyes. A small light across the room was the first thing she noticed—too bright, burning. She recoiled from the glare, trying to back away.

Only, she couldn't move.

She glanced down. She lay in a bed. Her bed.

And she was strapped into it. Manacles, biting into her skin despite the pads over them, strapped her wrists and ankles to the bed. She tugged at one, but it wouldn't budge.

Trying not to panic, Briar lay her head back, the ends of her hair tickling her collarbone. She had been shackled to her bed in Isabelle's house. Why had they—

It came back to her in a rush.

"Stones," Briar whispered. She shrank back, pressing her body into the mattress.

Isabelle.

She had tried to eat Isabelle.

She remembered it all. She remembered how the hunger took over, deadening her mind. She remembered Isabelle in her room in the dark of night, sleeping in her bed. She remembered all this, even though, at the time, she had been so mindless with hunger that she hadn't been able to recall who anybody was—herself, Isabelle, Kinsley.

Oh, stones and stars, *Isabelle.*

Kinsley knocked her out. That was the last thing she remembered. It didn't add up though. The maddening hunger was gone. She didn't feel so listless—in fact, for the first time in days, she felt awake and alert. And not only could she move her muscles with ease, but they felt strong, buzzing with energy. For the first time since she'd woken from her curse, she felt...normal. She'd forgotten what that felt like.

What did that mean?

She should have realized. They'd seen the corpses feed on people. She should have realized this would happen.

The door creaked open. Briar lifted her head.

"You're awake."

"Kinsley?" Briar's voice came out hoarse. "Is that you?"

"Yes." He shut the door and came to her bedside. Briar ran her eyes over him, looking for any sign that she'd hurt him, but he looked the same as always. "How are you feeling?"

"How am I *feeling?*" Briar croaked out something like a laugh. Now that she had seen him, now that she was sure he was not hurt, hot shame rushed through her. "I tried to eat our host and would have killed you to get to her, and you ask how I'm *feeling?*" She could hardly stand to look at him, but she forced herself to.

Kinsley's cordial expression did not alter. "Well, you didn't eat her and you didn't kill me. Also, you seem to remember me, and you sound like yourself again. Do you feel hungry at all?"

"Not really." Briar's stomach tightened. "Why is that?"

"I'll let someone else explain that." He bent down to unlock the manacles around her wrists and ankles. "How are your fingers, by the way? Holding up?"

"Yes." Briar lifted her freed hand and flexed those fingers. "I can even move them."

"Good." Finished with her shackles, Kinsley straightened. "So, Prince Demetri and Prince Garrett just returned. And one of them would like to see you."

"What?" Briar scrambled into a seated position, backing against the headboard. "They're *here?* Oh, please, no, I can't see Demetri right now, not like—"

"Actually, I think Demetri is downstairs talking to Thatcher. Prince Garrett is out in the corridor though."

Garrett. "Is that any better?" Briar asked warily.

"I don't know. You tell me." Kinsley paused. "Look, he is my prince, but you're my charge. If you want me to tell him to go away, I will."

Briar swallowed. On the one hand, the thought of seeing Garrett right now was mortifying. Stars and stones, what would she even *say?* What would he say?

On the other hand...she ached to talk to him. Because she remembered how afraid she'd been last night, when she'd tried to sleep, and she remembered how the thought of Garrett and Demetri had soothed her. And she needed that. More than she needed to preserve her dignity.

"It's all right," she told Kinsley. "You can let him in."

Garrett came in wearing his gray cutaway coat with a pistol holstered at his waist, and his blond hair was a little disheveled, so he and Demetri must have just arrived, Briar deduced. She forced herself to look him in the face, even though she was afraid of what she might see there.

But all she saw was relief. He looked at her, and his expression flooded with relief.

"Briar," he said, and his voice was heavy with it too. "You're all right? Kinsley said you were, but I wasn't sure I believed him."

Briar choked a little. "You're asking if *I'm* all right? They did tell you what happened, didn't they?"

"Yes." Garrett dragged a chair over to her bedside and flipped it, seating himself in it backwards. "They did."

"They told you I—I—" Briar struggled to put it into words. "Lost my mind? Tried to eat Isabelle? Almost attacked Kinsley? They told you all that?"

Garrett nodded, his brow furrowed. "Hence...the concern?"

"You should be concerned about Kinsley!" Briar said, exasperated. "And Isabelle! I could have hurt them."

"But they aren't hurt," Garrett said calmly. "They're both perfectly fine."

"I find that hard to believe."

"You just saw Kinsley for yourself. And Isabelle—"

"That's not what I meant." Briar glared. She knew she was being overly hostile, but she couldn't help it. It was a defense mechanism, she supposed. She didn't *want* Garrett to be angry with her—she had wanted his comfort, in fact. But now, in the face of it, she couldn't stand it. She couldn't *bear* it. It made her feel vulnerable, and she was not sure she wanted to be so vulnerable in front of him. She had been before, but this was different.

This was...deeply personal.

Briar leaned back against the bed. The headboard's iron grille bars were cold against her flesh, which made her realize she was only wearing her night shift with its thin strap sleeves. Perhaps that was why Garrett did not quite look at her, but more at the floor between him and the bed. Hastily, Briar snatched a wool blanket from the foot of the bed and draped it around her shoulders.

"What I meant was," she continued, trying for a more level tone, "I find it hard to believe they could be all right after...*seeing* me that way. I mean, all right, Kinsley is a trained professional, and judging by what he's told me, he's seen a lot worse in service to you. But Isabelle must be terrified! I wouldn't be surprised if she never wanted to see me again."

"Oh, please." To Briar's astonishment, Garrett rolled his eyes. He propped his elbow up on the back of his chair and laid his chin in his hand. "Trust me, Isabelle has experienced far worse than a rotting princess trying to eat her. *Far* worse."

Briar blinked. "*Really?*"

"Yes."

"Like what?"

"You really don't want to know." Garrett eyed her over his chair. "So? Does that make you feel better?"

"Well..." Briar said dubiously. "I don't know if 'better' is the right word. It makes me feel better about myself, I suppose. But sort of wary about Isabelle now."

"Yes," Garrett agreed. "She's made of hardier stuff than she looks."

Briar fisted her hands in her blanket, balling them in her lap. "In all seriousness, Garrett..." She hesitated.

"Yes?" She heard him shift in his chair, scooting it closer.

Briar sucked in a breath. Lifting her head, she looked at Garrett. His pine green eyes were somber, a small wrinkle in his forehead the only visible sign of concern. He was worried about her, just like she had been worried about him. Perhaps that should not have been so surprising, given everything that was going on. But it was. It surprised her. And it unnerved her.

It unnerved her because she desperately wanted that comfort now. She didn't care what she'd done, how *embarrassing* it was—that she'd lost her mind, forgotten who she was, attacked Garrett's friends. She wanted him to tell her everything was going to be okay. She wanted...*stones*, it was terribly improper. But she wanted him to hold her. Or to take her hand, at least, like he had that night on the bridge. To take her hand, and let her rest her head on his shoulder...

But she couldn't do any of that. Couldn't allow it. For so, so many reasons. Because she was afraid of how he would react, afraid he might flinch away. Because she couldn't bear to hear him say everything would be all right, when she knew it was just a lie.

So instead, she drew in another breath and said, "Kinsley said you would explain why I wasn't hungry anymore. You said I didn't hurt anyone. So what happened?"

"You didn't hurt anyone." Garrett crossed his arms over the top of his chair. "But you *did* eat something."

Briar stared. "I what? What are you talking about? The last thing I remember is Kinsley knocking me out—"

Garrett nodded. "According to him, you didn't stay unconscious long. You came awake and they had to restrain you. But Thatcher and Isabelle came up with an idea. You were desperate to eat, obviously."

"And they fed me?" Briar's voice was little more than a whisper. "Fed me what?" Her imagination drummed up all manner of horrors, eating fingers or bits of brains—

"Raw rabbit." Garrett's tone was matter-of-fact, as though they were discussing eating scones at tea. "Isabelle's idea, of course. She thought it might suffice as well as—well, er, as well as human flesh, I suppose. So Gemma went out and caught a couple, and they skinned one and fed it to you. Raw. I think you ate the whole thing."

"The whole thing," Briar repeated stupidly.

"Mm-hmm."

"I don't even remember this," Briar said. The whole thing should have made her nauseous—eating *raw* rabbit—but it didn't feel real. Because she *couldn't remember* it. That was horrifying. She felt like she was sinking into thick, sludgy mud, grasping for something to hold onto as her head went under. She didn't remember being fed raw rabbit. She'd been so out of her mind that she hadn't been herself.

Garrett looked unruffled. "Well, maybe Kinsley knocked you on the head too hard." He narrowed his eyes. "Your forehead is a little dented in."

Briar's eyes widened. "*Dented in?*" She clapped a hand to her forehead in mortification.

"Anyway, Kinsley said you calmed down after you ate the rabbit," Garrett went on. "You went to sleep and slept all day."

"I can't believe this." It *did* make sense, sort of. Briar tried to focus on that. *Things that make sense are comforting.* If flesh was what the corpses fed on, then it made sense it refueled them, made them more themselves. Though given the degree of the other corpses' mindlessness, eating flesh couldn't help much in the long run—though perhaps most of the corpses hadn't had a chance to eat much flesh yet. "There are too many variables," she grumbled. "I can't provide a logical conclusion."

"What I don't understand—" Garrett leaned back "—is why you aren't decaying like the rest of them. I mean, sure, you bruise easily, but that's nothing compared to what those people in the castle look like."

"I think it's just happening more slowly. Though I don't know why."

"I think maybe you just bruise easily," Garrett repeated.

Briar held up her right hand.

Garrett stared at her, nonplussed. "What am I looking at?"

"My fingers fell off," she said. "Kinsley sewed them back on. How's that for decaying?"

Garrett's jaw dropped open. Then he clapped a hand over his mouth, but not before Briar saw the start of a grin.

"Don't—don't laugh!" she exclaimed.

"I'm not laughing," Garrett protested. "I mean—okay, I am laughing, but—it's not that they fell off that's funny. But Kinsley sewed them back on?" he chortled.

"Well, what would you have done?" Briar glowered, even though his laughter warmed her, inappropriate as it was. So long as they were laughing about it, it didn't seem so bad.

"No, no," Garrett agreed, getting his laugher under control. "That's a very sensible solution. And Kinsley is nothing if not sensible." He drew in a deep breath. "So. You *are* decaying, though at a slow pace."

"Give it time," Briar said quietly.

"Briar." Garrett's tone was suddenly sober. The lamp's glimmer cast light over his face, but its luster seemed faint without his smile. "Look, I'm sorry—making jokes and all. I know it must be a mad thing for you to deal with. It's just, that's how *I* deal with mad things. I laugh." He stood briefly, just long enough to spin his chair around to face her. "I'm just too emotional for my own good. I laugh so I don't cry."

Briar smiled. "Really."

"Really. I'm a big crier. I'll cry over anything."

"Well, that makes one of us." Briar slumped back. "Now that I'm dead, I don't seem capable of producing tears anymore."

Garrett's face was grave. "You're not dead, Briar."

"I may as well be."

"You may have, you know, died, technically. But you came back and now—"

"Now what, Garrett?" Her words came out harsh, but she didn't try to moderate her tone. She couldn't. She gazed into the lamp's bright gleam until she saw spots. "Maybe I did come back. But I'm still rotting and not just physically. Those corpse monsters—their minds have gone. Who they used to *be* is gone. And that's going to happen to me too." She said it in a rush, her fear slipping out before she could stop it. "It's *already* happening. When my memory lapsed with Demetri—"

"Those lapses weren't more than a few minutes," Garrett argued, leaning forward in his chair. "Right? Most of the time, you're...*you*."

"For now. But I told you. Sometimes a memory slips away. And it doesn't come back." She lifted her gaze to his face. His eyebrows were drawn, his jaw tense. She shouldn't be so maudlin, she thought. She'd upset him, and she didn't like seeing him upset. "Can I be who I am, be Briar, without the memories that made me...me? Won't I be dead, really, if those memories go?"

That was the root of it. She wondered if he understood. To lose her mind...to lose who she was. She couldn't live like that, not knowing her own self. Even worse, she couldn't help her people if she became one of them. It was ironic, really, that finally finding herself so much like them would mean the end. For them all.

Garrett took her hand.

Briar looked at him, startled. She hadn't seen him reach for her. But there it was. His hand enclosing hers. The warmth of his touch radiated up her icy arm, and she marveled at that. That he was enough to chase away the cold inside her.

"We're going to fix this," Garrett said. "You aren't going to die. You aren't going to forget who you are. You aren't going anywhere. All right?"

"I—" Briar looked into his eyes. She felt caught by his gaze, ensnared. "I don't know—"

"I promise," he swore, squeezing her hand. "All right?"

Briar held his gaze a moment longer. She hadn't wanted him to lie to her. But when he said it...looking her in the eye with such fierceness...it didn't feel like a lie. It wasn't comfort for the sake of comfort.

He meant it. He believed it. And he made her believe it.

"All right." She squeezed his hand back, and he didn't flinch away. "All right."

<hr>

Briar didn't see Demetri until later. Garrett left her to rest, but having slept all day, she found herself wide awake. She was also craving something. Not flesh—something sweet. A biscuit or some sweet bread. It was a relief to realize she still wanted to eat normal things.

Her muscles were more responsive now. She discarded the blanket, rooted out her wool dressing robe, and pulled on a pair of soft leather boots before slipping into the corridor.

When Kinsley heard she was after a snack, he offered to accompany her. There was a narrow staircase at the end of the hallway, which led down into the kitchens. When they reached the bottom and turned the corner, however, they found the kitchen was not empty. Demetri was there.

"Briar." Demetri held a cup of something steaming in his hand. He put the cup down on the counter with a soft *clink*. "I thought you were asleep."

"No. I slept all day." Briar wavered, studying his expression for some sign that he didn't want her there. But if he was alarmed by her, he didn't show it.

With Demetri in the kitchen, Kinsley made a small bow and headed back upstairs.

"Want some tea?" Demetri gestured to his cup.

Briar inched into the kitchen. Her booted footsteps seemed too loud against the floor. It was a large, square kitchen with rustic birch wood cabinets, and a huge iron stove centered against the back wall. "Actually," Briar said, "I was looking for something sweet—some biscuits maybe, or—"

"Oh, there's this bread. Isabelle made it with apples, I think—it's really good." He cut a couple of slices, bringing them to the center counter. Briar approached the counter as though she was walking on glass and stood across from Demetri.

"It's no currant bread," he said with a reminiscent smile, "but it's pretty good."

Briar helped herself to a slice, returning his smile. "Cook's currant bread was the best." She took a bite of the apple bread, and the taste was a burst of sweetness in her mouth. She didn't think she'd ever appreciated food this much in her whole life. "But this is pretty good too." She cleared her throat. "So. You know what happened. Don't you?"

"Yes," Demetri said. "How are you doing, Briar?"

A gale of warmth streamed through Briar. Because this was his first question—his first concern was for her. Most of the time, she abhorred anything resembling pity—because, she supposed, of the implication that she was lacking in some way. It was why she'd found it so hard to face Garrett just now.

But this was Demetri. He had always helped her, and that was all right. "I'm fine." She took another bite of bread, chewed, and swallowed. "What...do you think about it?"

"What do I think?" Demetri folded his arms atop the counter. "I think we'll find a way to stop it. Barring that, a way to manage it."

"That's it?"

He said, "What else is there? Briar, I just want to help you. I want you to be okay. So. If you're *not* really fine, please tell me. You can, you know. I'm not going anywhere."

Briar didn't think he knew what it meant to her to hear those words. But she also worried. She worried that *he* wasn't as fine with this as he said. Demetri always looked for solutions, even when he didn't know what to do. He had been that way when he first discovered she was cursed. But she also thought he'd put his own feelings away then, and she didn't want him to do that now. Not if he wasn't really all right.

He'd spent eighty years locked up and alone. How all right could he be?

She remembered the fear on his face the first time her memory had lapsed and it pained her. Demetri had been through more and worse than she had. Briar had slept, and if her sleep was tormented, she didn't remember that. But Demetri endured eighty-two years of forced solitude, paralyzed in the darkness, paralyzed in time.

She hated to see him suffer any more. Not Demetri, the only person who had ever been there for her.

So she put down her bread and put on a mischievous smile. "Before you left, we talked about that time in the castle when we snuck into the kitchen. Remember?"

"Yes, I remember. Why?"

"You made me dance with you. Remember?"

"Yes," he said, the words deep in his throat. "Yes, I remember."

She reached across the counter and took his hand, wrapping her fingers around his. "Dance with me again, Demetri."

"Princess Briar," he said, his tone teasing, "are you asking me to dance with you? Princess Briar, who never, ever dances?"

"No, I'm not asking you. I'm telling you."

He came around the counter to join her. He took her hand in his, interlacing his fingers through her sewn-on ones, and placed his other hand at the small of her back. She placed her hand on his shoulder, his wool waistcoat soft beneath her palm. The kitchen was swathed in shadows. The glow of two gear-bulbs set over the stove was the only light in the room, and the near-darkness intensified Briar's senses. She felt hyperaware of the closeness between them, of Demetri's soft breath, of his woodsy scent.

Demetri glanced down. "You're wearing boots. I don't think that's fair. We both know you'll step on my toes."

"I will not!" Briar said, her words a low, breathy protest.

"It's all right." He pulled her closer. The warmth of his hand on her back intensified, heat blazing through her dressing gown. "I'm willing to take the risk. For you."

As he began to move, right, then left, forward, and back, leading her in the age-old steps, Briar slid her hand behind his head, the downy hairs at the nape of his neck tickling her palm. They danced slowly, carelessly, though Briar was sure Demetri had not forgotten a single step.

It wasn't like her to be so sentimental. Thinking wistfully on old memories, asking Demetri to do something so silly as dance with her. But it felt like it had been so long since she'd spent any real time with Demetri. And she found herself desperate to hold onto this. Now that she knew it might fade away.

A smile tugged at Demetri's lips. She couldn't say why until he dropped his hand from her back and spun her from him. She stumbled a little, but she didn't care. She even laughed as he pulled her back, and she laughed again when she stepped on his foot.

"Ouch," he said, still smiling. "See, I told you it would happen."

"That was entirely your fault. You have only yourself to blame."

Then he twirled her. She spun beneath his arm, and in that instant, she lost sight of him.

It was only for a second, but in that second, a thick, insidious fog stole over her brain.

She gasped as she swayed, throwing up a hand to steady herself. That hand landed upon someone's chest. Briar found herself in someone's arms with no idea how she got there. She tensed, looking up at the boy who held her.

He was a stranger, a boy with brown hair and brown eyes. There was nothing imposing or frightening about him, but she didn't know him, and she had no idea what he was doing, holding her so close.

"Briar?" he said. His voice was strained, spiking a surge of panic within her. "Briar, what's wrong?"

She wrenched out of his grip. Stranger he might have been, but her hand felt cold without his, and that only made her feel worse. A sense of isolation expanded within her. "Who are you? Where am I, why..." She glanced around, finding herself in a dark kitchen. "What's going on?"

The boy wrung his hands together. "Briar, it's me." His voice was laden with misery. "It's me, Demetri, you know me—"

"No." Briar backed away, tripping over her own feet. "No, I don't know you, I don't—" She turned and ran, nearly crashing into the garnet brick wall behind her. She scampered to her right, out of the room.

She didn't get far. She ran into a dark corridor, but only took two steps before a tall figure rounded the corner ahead. Briar smacked into him. She would have fallen if this figure had not reached out to steady her.

"Briar?" the person said, and something in his smooth, deep voice pricked at her. "What's going on?"

Briar looked up into his face. The torrent of recognition that rushed through her was staggering.

"Garrett," she gasped, as it all came back to her. "It's you."

19

CONFESSION

DEMETRI DASHED OUT OF the kitchen after Briar. His boots squeaked against the floor as he tottered into the corridor. He reached out to steady himself and looked up to see Briar smack into a tall shadow—Garrett, distinguishable by his blond hair in the darkness.

"Briar?" Garrett took her by the elbows.

Demetri lifted a hand to keep Briar from fleeing again. But Briar looked up at Garrett, and even in the dim light, Demetri could see the change in her as the tension left her body.

"Garrett," she gasped. "It's you."

Demetri could not have predicted what a crushing blow it was to hear those words. He felt like all the air had been knocked out of him, the words resounding in his head. There was relief too—he *was* relieved Briar had regained her memory. But there was something in the way she said Garrett's name, a catch in her voice, like he had saved her. Like he'd saved her from Demetri, the stranger she'd run from.

Briar stepped out of Garrett's grip and turned towards Demetri. Her face was crumpled and pasty. "Demetri?" she ventured. "I—we—oh, stars—*not again*—"Her voice wrenched.

Demetri's heart faltered. He should say something, assure her it was not her fault. But the words wouldn't come. They were stuck somewhere down his throat. So was all his air; his breaths were beginning to feel shallow. He couldn't reconcile what had happened from one moment to the next; they had been dancing, content, in a scene so reminiscent of their past. And then it was gone, snatched away. And this time, Demetri felt like those memories had been taken from him too.

"Demetri." Briar stepped forward. "Demetri, I'm *sorry*—" She reached for him, but he took a step back.

"Don't," Demetri said. His voice sounded far away in his ears, strangely muffled. "Don't—be sorry." He was not convincing; he could hear it in his words. But he felt bereft, like a man lost at sea.

She'd regained her memory when she saw Garrett. That didn't mean anything, he knew it didn't. But he could not stop hearing it. *Garrett.*

Garrett had helped her when he couldn't. Just like Demetri had feared, he himself wasn't enough.

Of course you're not, a nasty voice in his head said. *You're too cowardly. You're too broken.*

"What happened?" Garrett looked between them. "Are you both all right?"

Or maybe—Demetri closed his eyes, gulping in another shallow breath—maybe it *was* him. His stomach eddied at the thought. Every time Briar's memory lapsed, it was with him. Not just when he was around, but *with him*. When he kissed her in the castle. When they were alone in the woods. And now in the kitchen, dancing, trying to recapture a moment from their past.

It's me. Demetri felt boneless, his body collapsing beneath its own weight. *It's me. It's all me.*

Demetri croaked, "I can't do this anymore."

"What?" Briar looked like she'd been punched, her body caving in as she recoiled.

"It's me." Demetri drew back. He still couldn't draw a proper breath. The corridor was starting to feel too small, too narrow, tightening around him—

The weight of packed dirt, pressing down on him. Trapped in unending darkness. The stench of death clogging up his nostrils—

Demetri shook himself. "It's me." Now the corridor was spinning, the shadowy darkness blurring around him. "I—I can't be with you—"

He heard Briar answer, and she sounded far away too. "You can't mean that." Her voice was strangled. "Demetri, I'm *sorry*. I can't stop this, the forgetting—"

"No, don't you see?" Demetri pleaded. She didn't understand. It wasn't *her*. It wasn't anything she'd done. He was the one who was wrong, who was deficient, broken, *stars*, he was draining all the life out of her, all the memories— "It's *me*. I'm making it worse."

He saw Briar reach out to him, but he stumbled back. He had to get out of here, he needed space, he needed *air*, he needed to get someplace *open*, where the walls weren't closing in on him—

He turned and fled the kitchen.

If Briar called after him, Demetri didn't hear. His mind was flooded with misery and memories, and the two were intertwined, his memories and his misery. It was all wrong, all of this.

Things would never go back to the way they were. He had been stupid to think they could. And if that had been all, he could have made peace with it. He could forge a new life with Briar, no matter the difficulties.

But *he* was the difficulty. *He* was the problem.

Demetri found himself outside the back of the manor. The night was black and frigid, and Demetri had never felt either so fully—the cold air reaching inside him like icy fingers, the darkness like staring into an abyss. But at least the sky was open above him, stretching out in an unending universe. Demetri huffed a breath, his lungs finally filling with air. There was a small ache in his chest he hadn't noticed before, but as he stood on the white porch and breathed, he felt it begin to dissipate, slowly fading away.

But was he fooling himself? *Was* he the problem or was that just a convenient excuse? Demetri felt sick with it, but he knew he couldn't get a handle on the way everything had changed. So much had happened. *Too* much had happened.

Demetri had spent eighty-two years locked in darkness, and he couldn't see his way out. He'd thought he *was* out of it; he'd escaped, after all. But he realized now he was still trapped there. Or some part of him was. He'd left some part of himself in that prison, some vital part of himself. And he couldn't see a way forward with Briar, not without dragging her down into the dark with him. To be smothered as surely as he was.

He wouldn't do that to her. Couldn't do that to her.

He slipped off the porch and stumbled around the house, where he pressed his back against the wall. The limestone was damp with cold against his waistcoat, and he let out a long exhale, watching his breath mist in front of him.

And Briar—if Demetri was honest with himself—he loved Briar. He ached with loving her, but when he looked at her, he didn't only see *her*. He saw those eighty-two years, everything he had suffered. He saw the loss of his parents, the loss of his home, the loss of his title. He saw the dread of her looming curse, a fate neither of them could avoid. He saw his failing hope. He saw his captivity.

He saw the darkness.

It wasn't that he blamed her for any of it. She was just as much a victim as he was.

But nevertheless, he could not look at her without seeing it all.

How could he have a future with her if he admitted that?

"You don't look well, Your Highness."

Demetri looked around, his shoulder blades twitching. He relaxed when he saw a figure approaching him in the navy blue uniform of Garrett's soldiers. "I'm all right." He peered at the man but could not make out his face. "I just needed some air."

"Ah," the figure said. His voice was a silken tenor. "I would ask what upset you, but after all you have been through, Demetri, I would be a fool to ask."

Demetri jerked his head around. "What are you—"

He broke off. In place of the man's face, something came to light.

An unearthly, blue glow.

"You!" Demetri cried, lunging forward. He grabbed the man—if it *was* a man—by the cuff of his coat and thrust him against the wall. The creature did not fight him, and close up, his face was visible.

It was a man, or nearly so. He had brown skin and al-mond-shaped eyes. The ears that peeked through his sleek black hair were pointed like a fairy's ears, though not quite so pronounced. And along the sides of his face, from his jaw to his temples, were dyed symbols, markings. And from them emanated a faint, azure glow.

"You." Demetri's voice was raw. "You're the one that rescued me from that prison. Why? Who are you? *Why?*"

If the creature was affected by Demetri's belligerence, he didn't show it. His eyes sparkled and he spoke with aplomb. "I wouldn't say I rescued you so much as let you go."

Demetri tightened his grip. "What do you mean?"

"Well, seeing as I was the one who took you prisoner in the first place," the creature said, "you couldn't really say I *rescued* you, could you?"

"Demetri? What's going on?"

Demetri strode into the sitting room, dragging the marked creature with him. Behind him, the porch doors clanged shut, one of them rebounding off the wooden frame. Briar and Garrett were both there, Briar curled up in a cream-colored armchair. She jumped up when Demetri barged in, looking from him to the creature.

Garrett stood across from Briar, on his feet before the empty fireplace. He, too, looked to the creature. "Who is that? And why is he wearing one of my soldier's uniforms? What—" He stopped mid-sentence as he faced the creature head-on, taking in his pointed ears and marked face. The markings weren't glowing anymore, but they were there, inked in black.

"This—" Demetri thrust the creature from him "—is the creature who freed me from my prison. Only, he was *also* the one who took me captive to begin with."

"*What?*" Garrett said.

"*He* did?" Briar's eyes flicked towards the creature. "But what is he? What are you?" she addressed the creature. "You're not a fairy."

"Not a fairy." The creature's voice was like a slick layer of oil. "Though similar, I'm grieved to admit. We're something like...distant cousins."

"You're a djinn," Garrett said. "Aren't you?"

The djinn bent at the waist, flourishing a bow. "At your service, my prince. The name is Dev. Well, actually it's quite a bit more than that, but your human tongue wouldn't be able to pronounce it."

"Wait, a what?" Briar shot Garrett a vexed look. "What's a djinn?"

"The queen told us about them." Garrett clasped his hands behind his back, seemingly at ease, though Demetri noted his hawk-eyed gaze, mindful of the djinn. "She said a djinn is the only thing that can kill a fairy without consequences. And they're *supposed* to be confined somewhere. To some shadow realm." He turned to face the djinn. "Only you don't look very confined to me."

"The better question," Demetri said grimly, "is *why* did you take me captive all those years ago? What did I ever do to you?"

"It's not what you did, dear prince," the djinn called Dev said, "but rather what you might have done. You see, Demetri, *you* were the key to breaking the curse."

"You mean my curse?" Briar said.

The djinn turned his gaze on Briar, and when he looked at her, it was as though Garrett and Demetri had melted out of sight. His gaze was somehow...proprietary. "Briar, Briar," he said, his tone coated with fondness. "How *lovely* to see you again."

Briar's eyes crinkled. "Do I know you?"

"Of course you do. Though never in the waking world." Dev ran a critical eye over her. "You don't look so well in this world, do you? Perhaps you should have stayed with me after all. It was my intervention that kept you alive and well all those years while you slept."

Every word from the djinn's mouth was like a cacophony in Demetri's head, a screeching bow on a violin string. But if Briar was disturbed by this creature, she did not show it. She marched towards the djinn and said, "Enough half-answers. What do you know about my curse? You say you didn't want me to wake from it, yet you claim you protected me while it lasted. Were you responsible for the curse?"

"Don't be silly. The dark fairy cursed you. Everyone knows that. It was only a happy coincidence that it happened to benefit me." Dev seemed unapologetic about this.

"How?" Briar asked. The word was like steel on her lips.

Dev gave an exaggerated sigh. He cast his dark-eyed gaze around the room and gestured towards an armchair. "May I?" he asked, with all the genteel of a courtier. Without waiting for an answer, he plopped down into the chair. "I know it's terribly rude to sit in the presence of royalty, but you, Demetri, no longer have a realm to call your own, and you, Prince Garrett, are a usurper. So I'm sure you won't mind. Now then." He turned back to Briar. "You asked how your curse benefited me. As Prince Garrett said, my kind were all confined to the shadow world over a thousand years ago. Long before you humans came to these shores."

"What *shadow world?*" Demetri resisted the urge to drag the djinn out of his comfy chair. "What does that even mean?"

"I won't bore you with the details." Dev buffed his nails against the arm of his coat. "It was fairies who confined us. Given that we're the only thing that can kill them—and that we're all too willing to do so—" A predatory smile stretched across his face "—they wanted us out of the picture. There is one thing we can use to free us, however. And keep us free."

"And what is that?" Briar said.

"The life force of a princess," Dev replied. "A princess descended from one of the *original* royal families."

Demetri asked, "What do you mean by life force?"

"And what's so special about these original royal families?" Garrett waved a dismissive hand. "The fairies made a big deal about them too. And about princesses in particular—" He broke off, understanding coming over his face. "This is about the blood, isn't it? The fairy blood? That fairy, Prence, she said it ran more strongly in women."

Dev eyed him appraisingly. "Well. You're more intelligent than you look, aren't you? Yes, it's all to do with the gift of blood. You see, it's really the life force of a fairy that works best. The fairies foolishly sealed us in the shadow realm with their own blood, and it is their blood—or the magical properties their blood possesses—that can free us. Unfortunately, fairies are, by and large, too powerful to gain access to, especially from within the shadow world. But *princesses*—" Dev turned a speculative gaze on Briar. "They carry a strong enough life force to free us.

Yet they don't possess the power of a fairy, a power which could otherwise protect them."

Briar said, "But how do you access this life force?"

"Didn't I say?" Dev's eyes went wide with innocence. "Through your dreams. While you sleep."

Rage flooded through Demetri. He took a deep breath and turned away, resting his head against the bay window's cool glass. His breathing was turning shallow again, but not because he was panicking, not because he was boxed-in. No, this time, it was pure anger pounding at him, filling him up from the inside.

"That's why you didn't want my curse broken." Briar spoke slowly, the way she did when she was putting together a puzzle. "Because you could use my—life force, or whatever, to be free." Her voice rose in intensity. "And yet you claim this was just a happy coincidence, my curse—"

"Well, it was," Dev said. "The dark fairy now—she really, *really* harbors a hatred for you, dear Briar. Or for your family, anyway. Why do you think she extended your curse?"

Demetri turned back to face the room. "You mean by casting the rotting curse? How do you even know about that?"

"I was there," Dev said. "At the castle, when it happened. I took you captive, remember? The dark fairy was there too. She didn't know about me, of course—she would have tried to lock me back into the shadow world. But I saw her, and I heard her curse Briar. *'I curse you to rot,'* she said, *'until you are no longer human, but a monster.'* Those were her exact words."

"And," Garrett deduced, "you were the one who put Briar in that tower, weren't you?"

"Guilty," Dev admitted. "It seemed better than leaving her on the floor."

"But *why* did the dark fairy cast a second curse?" Briar demanded. "And why extend it to the rest of the kingdom? Cursing just me wasn't enough?"

"Well," the djinn said, "that actually—"

"But everyone else rotted while they were sleeping," Garrett said. His tone bore a note of suspicion. "Briar didn't. She was fine until—"

"Until she woke," the djinn said smugly. "That's because she was in the shadow realm while she slept all those years. With me. Not physically, of course—when I say she was there, I mean her *consciousness* was there, while I fed off her life force—but that was enough. Her being there protected her from the effects of the second curse. Until she woke and returned to this realm."

"Wait a minute," Briar interrupted. "What does all this have to do with Demetri? Why take him captive? You said he was the key to breaking my curse."

"Of course. All fairy curses have a loophole built into them. A way to break them."

"And what was mine?" Briar thrust her arm out in exasperation. "How was Demetri a threat to the curse? He wasn't even the one who broke it, that was—"

"Uh," Garrett broke in. His cheeks were flushed. "I don't know that we really—"

"Yes, funny, that." Dev beamed, looking from Demetri to Garrett. "The key to breaking your curse, Briar, was a simple thing, though it's rarer than most people think. That's why it used to be all the rage, as a way to break curses."

"What was it?" Briar demanded.

"You mean you didn't tell her?" Dev blinked at Garrett. "As I say, it was a simple thing. True love's kiss."

20

DOWNFALL

GARRETT WISHED HE COULD sink through the cracks in the hardwood floor. Maybe it had been naïve of him, but he had really hoped he wouldn't ever have to explain to Briar that she was awake because he'd kissed her. But that hope was gone now. Thanks to this slimy, jumped-up djinn.

"True love's kiss?" Briar repeated. "What...do you mean?"

Garrett was still wondering that himself, even as he tried to pretend he'd gone invisible. Yes, a kiss woke Briar. But not true love's kiss. A kiss from a perfect stranger.

Inexplicably, Delphine's words played back in his mind. *I can read you like a book, little princeling. You so loved sweet, sickening Snow. Yet you replace her so easily with another sleeping princess? Well, I suppose I can see the attraction. Maybe you can actually wake this one.*

"True love's kiss." Dev spoke in a blithe tone. "That is why I took Demetri captive. I assumed he would be the one to wake you. Being your true love and all. Apparently, I was wrong about that."

Demetri closed his eyes and muttered under his breath. Garrett thought he knew what he must be thinking. All those years Demetri had been held captive and he'd never known why. Even if he *had* been the key to awakening Briar, he hadn't known it.

"A kiss." Briar's gaze was unfocused. "You're saying a *kiss* woke me?"

Slowly, like a mechanical dancer rotating in a jewelry box, she turned to Garrett.

"Well." Garrett tugged at his necktie. It was suddenly very hot in the room, even though there was a wintry draft coming in through the open door and there was no fire in the grate.

"A *kiss?*" Briar's tone was incredulous. She likely had an expression to match, but Garrett couldn't say, since he was staring at the silent grandfather clock in the corner. "*That's* what this was about, all this time? That's why you wouldn't say anything? Why didn't you just tell me? Garrett!"

Garrett sighed, forcing his gaze around until he met hers. "I didn't want to make things...weird."

"Oh, well, good on you." Briar's words were laden with sarcasm. "Because this isn't weird at all. If you had just told me from the start, it wouldn't have been weird!"

Garrett turned a dubious stare on her.

"Well, okay," she conceded. "It might have been a little awkward. Given that I didn't know you and—hang on." Briar rounded on Dev. "You said *true love's kiss*. But Garrett doesn't love me! He didn't even know me, for the Gift's sake! How does that qualify as true love's kiss?"

Dev tipped a nod in Garrett's direction. "Maybe you should ask him."

"How should I know?" Garrett protested. "She's right. I didn't even know her."

"But you knew a kiss would wake me." Briar was perplexed. "How could you have guessed that?"

Garrett's shoulders slumped. "It's how I was meant to wake Snow. I was told true love's kiss would break the spell. Only it didn't. It didn't work."

Briar let out a slow breath. "Of course. I thought it must have something to do with Snow. Because you started telling me about her when I asked you about *me*—oh, you know what I mean—and you never did say..."

She trailed off, her brow furrowed. When she lifted her gaze a moment later, she gave him the strangest look. Garrett couldn't put a name to the expression, but there was something familiar about it even so.

And something about it tugged at him. Tugged at his chest.

"Briar?" he said, his voice hoarse.

"You—" she began, but then she stopped, casting a glance in Demetri's direction. She dropped her gaze. "You should have just told me."

Garrett flashed back to the kitchen, four days ago. To his encounter with Briar before they'd left to see the queen. He had seen that same look on Briar's face. When he'd told her he was glad she wasn't dead, when he'd started to say something stupid about how it had felt, to think she was dead—

He had stopped himself then. And it had been difficult. He'd had so much he wanted to say to her, and it had been all he could do to shut up and get out of there. To keep his thoughts and feelings, complicated and unbelievable as they were, from spilling out.

Standing before her now, he had no idea what to say. His mind was utterly blank.

He managed a weak shrug. "But I didn't." It was ridiculous, Garrett knew. But he felt like he had betrayed her somehow. "I'm sorry," he hastened, struggling to explain himself better. "I just didn't want—I mean, it's really no big deal, is it? I was just trying to—it's not like it meant anything. Right?"

Briar half-opened her mouth to respond but then shut it, looking confused. Garrett did not think she could possibly be as confused as he was at that moment.

"No." Briar's voice sounded distant. "I guess not."

Garrett felt the cold now, the draft from outside creeping over him. He wished, for some reason, they were not having this conversation in front of two other people, especially Demetri. Though he'd nearly forgotten Demetri until the prince said, "I'm going to get some of the soldiers. We should put this wretch under guard." He quit the room, his boots ringing a swift pace against the floor.

Dev showed no alarm at the prospect of being put under guard. He made a steeple of his fingers beneath his chin, looking between Garrett and Briar. "Interesting," he murmured.

"You know, there's one thing you never explained, djinn," Briar snapped. "You're the one who took Demetri captive, but you also let him go. Eighteen years early. Why?"

Dev smiled. "Perhaps I've grown fond of you, little Briar."

Garrett resisted the urge to lunge for the creature's throat. "You've spent the past eighty years *using* her."

"You don't know me," Briar said to the djinn. There was no contempt for the creature in her voice. Just a sort of clinical detachment. "I don't care how many years I spent in your shadow world. It was little more than a dream to me. You can't *know* me."

"Oh, but I do." Dev leaned forward. "I know you better than any other princess I've used. I've known you *longer* than any other princess. You may not remember it, Briar, but I know you very well." A peculiar smile played at his lips. "Humans are much the same to me. But you're different. I think of you almost like my own little sister."

Demetri returned with the guards. It was for the best, Garrett supposed. He didn't want to hear another word out of the djinn's mouth.

⎯⎯◆◇◆⎯⎯

It was past midnight when Garrett got to bed. He entered his room to find it shuttered and dark. He left the lamp off and cracked open the frosted window by his bed, pausing to lean his head against the chilled glass.

He was exhausted—in more ways than one—and kicked off his boots with a grateful sigh, flexing his feet. But when he collapsed atop his quilted bed, he could not sleep. His shoulder ached worse than ever. And it had been a long, long day. Traveling back to Isabelle's, only to arrive and discover what Briar had been up to. And that cursed djinn turning up.

And all that business with Briar and the kiss.

Briar.

Garrett rolled onto his side, the quilt rumpling beneath him. *You so loved sweet, sickening Snow. Yet you replace her so easily with another sleeping princess?*

At first, he had dismissed the queen's words as a meaningless taunt. Yet it continued to nag at him more than anything else she'd said. Those words stirred something inside him, dredging up feelings that were both frightening and elating. Things he had not felt in a long time.

He could never replace Snow. He loved her. She had been gone almost two years, but he still missed her. He couldn't imagine the day he might wake and find he didn't love her anymore.

And if he still loved Snow, then he couldn't have feelings for someone else, could he?

People moved on, he knew that. It was possible. For other people, maybe. But Garrett had long been convinced it wasn't possible for him. He loved Snow too much to put her behind him. How could he?

But...Briar.

There was a lot he liked about Briar. A lot he *admired* about her. How resilient she was, how curious about the world. A lot of people could have lived the same childhood she had and turned out very differently. Being so neglected, so ignored her whole life—that was enough to turn anyone cynical. But not Briar. Briar wanted to know everything and everyone, and she wasn't afraid to laugh or make a fool of herself doing it. She was strange, but only in the most fascinating ways, and she was funny, even though sometimes she didn't mean to be.

As captivating as Briar seemed to find the world around her, Garrett was captivated by her.

In a way, Snow had been like that too. She had not been particularly interested in science or engineering like Briar, but she had been fearless. She had shied away from nothing. Anything new was a challenge, something to be conquered. Garrett had learned that spirit of adventure from her. He had never been shy, exactly, but he had kept to himself a lot before he met Snow. After his mother had died, he had learned to guard himself.

But Snow had broken down the walls he'd built. Made him see the world in new, vibrant, dazzling colors. Taught him how to embrace everything about life, even the parts that were frightening or unsettling.

Yes, in some ways, Briar reminded him of Snow. And maybe that explained how he felt about her. Not because he was replacing one with the other, but because it would take someone extraordinary, someone as fearless and tenacious and diverting as Snow, to make him feel that way again. And how he felt about Briar...well...

He cared about Briar. An awful lot. Which in itself didn't mean anything. Especially given everything they'd been through together, breaking her curse, escaping the castle, the attack on the train and the night on the bridge. After all that, of *course* he cared about her, and of course he trusted her. That was only natural.

But earlier tonight, when she spoke about losing herself, about dying—the dread in her eyes had touched him to the core; oh, how he *hated* seeing her so afraid. And when he'd thought she was dead after that corpse attacked them in the woods.... Well, it was what he'd wanted to say to her, wasn't it? What he'd stopped himself from saying.

That when she'd been dead, he hadn't just been sad for Demetri, losing the princess he loved. He hadn't just been sad for Briar, losing her life so soon after regaining it. No, the grief he'd felt had been more personal than that. It had struck him to the core.

And now, with her in danger of becoming a corpse creature, of slipping away—the thought of losing her like that—it scared him more than he thought possible.

He didn't want to live in a world without Briar.

"Oh, stones," he groaned, rolling onto his stomach. He buried his face in his satin pillow. He loved Snow. He couldn't fall in love with someone else if he still loved Snow.

Could he?

He didn't sleep well. His head was full of troubled thoughts and fuzzy dreams, and he never quite sank into sleep deep enough to forget the pain in his shoulder.

In the morning, he woke to the most annoying, high-pitched twittering songbird outside. He sat up with a grunt. He felt like he hadn't slept at all. With the window open, his room was icy cold, but his cotton shirt was soaked in sweat. He rose and changed clothes—he'd slept in the same clothes he wore yesterday—swapping out his shirt for a dry one and a clean, black waistcoat. Leaning over the porcelain sink in the washroom, he splashed water onto his face. The eyes that gazed back at him from the mirror were gaunt.

He should have been hungry for breakfast, but the aroma of sizzling bacon wafting up the stairs turned his stomach. He opened his door to go look for Demetri, but instead, as he stepped into the corridor, he ran into Briar.

"Oh." He stopped dead when he saw her. She looked well—much better, in fact, than Garrett had ever seen her. Her face was not so ashen; rather, her cheeks glimmered with health in the pale daylight shining through the high windows. "Um. Morning."

"Right." Briar looked him up and down. "You look terrible."

"Really." Garrett ran a hand over his unshaved chin, disguising a nervous swallow. "Erm. Listen. I'm glad I ran into you."

A slight hitch to her eyebrow was her only reaction. "You are?"

"Yes." Garrett leaned back against the doorframe. "Only, I realized we never filled you in on what we learned from Snow's stepmother."

"Oh." Briar's eyes widened. "That's right. With everything that—I forgot. You said she told you about the djinn." Her gaze darkened. "Does he have something to do with breaking the curse? I know he said he can kill a fairy—"

"Actually, the queen told us killing a fairy will break all curses they've cast. Though somehow I doubt the djinn will agree to kill her for us."

Briar glowered. "Might be worth a shot to ask him, though. The queen didn't have any other suggestions?"

"Well. She did tell us that it *is* technically possible for a human to kill a fairy. That's how most witches gain access to magic. By killing fairies and taking their blood."

Briar looked aghast. And she had more reason than most to want to kill a fairy. "Did she tell you *how* to do it?"

"No, because it comes with a price." He explained what the queen had said—that it wasn't possible to kill a fairy without losing one's soul or making a deal with dark forces. "Neither of which seems a viable option for us," he concluded with a sigh.

"No." Briar's voice sounded hollow. "I'd rather not lose my soul. Whatever that means."

Garrett looked at her. His chest hurt with all the things he wanted to say—not how he felt about her, but something to reassure her. Like the things he'd said last night when she talked about losing her mind. He just wanted to say...something like that. He wanted to let her know they would do this, that they would find a way to cure her, to cure everyone.

But for some reason, he couldn't find the words.

"Well," he said instead, "Isabelle is still looking into other means to break the curse."

"I'll think about talking to Dev." Briar chewed her lip. "Maybe if I ask him as a *friend*—" She rolled her eyes heavenward "—he'll consider getting rid of that fairy for us."

"Sure." Garrett tried to smile. "Maybe. Have you seen Demetri this morning?"

"Oh." Briar's face fell, and Garrett felt like kicking himself. Bringing up Demetri after last night, after what happened between the two of them, was beyond tactless. "No. I looked for him earlier, but—well, I'm not sure where he is." And with that, she slouched off. Leaving Garrett to feel like a thoughtless idiot.

He found Demetri in the corridor outside the room where they had put the djinn under guard. The prince sat in a cane-seat chair next to Gemma and Beckett, another one of his female guards. The three of them were centered around a small, splintering table, playing cards.

"Morning," Garrett said.

Demetri looked up from their game. "Hardly. It's nearly noon." A wave of concern washed over his face. "You don't look so well."

"Thanks," Garrett said. "Beckett, has there been any word about the train?"

"Yes, sire," Beckett said. "They figured out what was broken, but they're missing a part to fix it. The crew and the soldiers are headed back to the train station to get what they need."

"So another week or more." Garrett pulled a face. He looked at Demetri. "Can I have a word?"

"Sure." Demetri left his cards and stood, following Garrett into Isabelle's empty study.

"I spoke to him earlier this morning," Demetri said as they entered the room. "The djinn. I tried to get him to tell me why he let me go, but he wouldn't. He kept saying it was none of my business, which is just—" Demetri clenched his hands into fists.

Garrett eased the door shut. "I'm sorry."

"I always thought it was her." Demetri flopped into a dark armchair in the corner. He reached over to wind up the gear-bulb lamp beside him, though the gray light sifting in through the window provided some illumination. "The dark fairy. I assumed she took me captive, though I didn't know why."

"He told us he let you go because of Briar." Garrett ambled forward. "The djinn. Like he did it because they were such great friends. But I don't think he meant it. I think he probably had another reason."

"Great friends." Demetri's words rang with bitterness. "Right. Of course."

"Have you spoken to her this morning?" Garrett said, though he knew full well that he hadn't.

"Who? Briar?"

"No, Isabelle. Yes, of course, Briar." Garrett leaned back against the mahogany desk near the window. The window stood open, making the room as cold as his own had been, but Garrett liked the frigid air. His waistcoat felt uncomfortably tight and warm against his chest.

"Oh." Demetri's shoulders drooped. "No. I haven't seen her."

"Why?" Garrett asked bluntly.

"What do you mean, why?"

"It was a rather crazy night last night," Garrett pointed out. "A crazy twenty-four hours, actually. Briar tried to eat Isabelle, then her memory lapsed, then that cursed djinn turned up with all sorts of pleasant surprises. I just thought you might have checked in with her."

Demetri rolled his shoulder back. "Well. I suppose I should. But it's not that simple," he said glumly. "After last night..."

"Are you referring to when you ran out on her after her memory lapsed?" Garrett crossed his arms over his chest. "After you said, and I quote, '*I can't be with you.*'"

Demetri tilted his head. "Are you angry at me?"

"Why would I be? Answer the question."

"Well, yes, then. That's what I'm referring to." He slumped back in his chair. "I *can't* do this anymore, Garrett. I can't be with her."

"When you say *can't*," Garrett said, suppressing the urge to raise his voice, "do you mean can't, as in something is physically preventing you from being with her, or do you mean won't, as in you've decided to give up on her?"

"Give up on her?" Demetri echoed. "I'm not *giving up* on her. Stones, you *are* angry."

"No, I'm not."

"Except clearly you are. You'd think I was breaking things off with *you,* not her."

"Because she was upset, you idiot!" Garrett threw his arms in the air, then winced at the sharp pain in his shoulder. A part of him felt this conversation was not going the way he meant it to, but his brain was too fuzzy to think about the way words were coming out of his mouth. "I know she acts like an automaton and doesn't come right out and say it, but she's terrified, don't you get that? She's becoming one of those corpses, and she's losing her memories, and you're just going to leave her *now?*"

"First of all—" Demetri leaned forward in his chair "—no, I'm not just going to *leave her*. I intend to stay right here until we've figured out how to save Briar and her people. And secondly..." Demetri sighed. "Look, you don't understand. *I* barely understand." He slumped back. "I know what's happening to her is awful. That's why I have to keep my distance."

"That makes no sense. Why would you need to do that?"

"Because I'm making it worse!" Demetri jumped to his feet. "It's me, don't you see? *I'm* making it worse, I'm—I'm triggering her lapses, I'm bringing it on, me!"

"What?" Garrett scoffed. "Don't be stupid. How do you figure?"

"It only happens with me. Haven't you noticed? Garrett, it only happens around *me*. She loses her memory with *me*, she forgets *me*."

"She forgets everything."

"We don't know that," Demetri retorted. "When it happened last time, she regained her memories as soon as she saw *you*."

"So?" Garrett grasped the edge of the desk to steady himself. He was beginning to feel lightheaded. "What do I have to do with this? What are you saying?"

"I'm saying you kissed her!" Demetri burst out.

"I kissed her." Garrett rubbed a hand over his eyes. "You mean—no, that's absurd. My kissing her has nothing to do with her memory. Are you saying if *you* had kissed her and broken the curse, she wouldn't forget you?" There was a sort of ironic symmetry to that, but Garrett doubted that was how it worked. "Demetri, you're seeing connections that aren't there. You said the first time, she regained her memory almost right away. When she was still *with you*. And the second time, she regained her memory in the woods with the fairies. Who she doesn't even like. So..." He squeezed his eyes shut. He was losing the trail of this argument. "So what were you saying, again?"

"I don't know." Demetri collapsed into the chair, running a hand over his face. "I don't know what I'm saying. I'm sorry, Garrett. This isn't about you. I shouldn't have brought you into this."

"Right." Garrett coughed. "Except...you didn't actually. I came and found you. And started all this."

"Oh." Demetri blinked. "Right. Well, then..." He rose from his chair with some difficulty, as though he were in as much physical pain as Garrett was. "I suppose I should check in with her. Look, Garrett. I wouldn't give up on her, no matter what. But I *am* making it worse. Even if I'm not causing it—every time she lapses and then comes back—the way she looks at me, like it's her fault. And it's not her fault." He kneaded his hand at his neck. "If it's anyone's fault—if all this is anyone's fault—it's mine."

"How can you say that? This is that fairy's fault."

"I know, but—remember we told you Briar fell to her curse when she pricked her finger? That was the curse—that she would fall into sleep by pricking her finger."

"I remember. Bit random, isn't it."

"It was," Demetri said. "Very random. I told you she came to see me in my quarters. I was getting ready for the ball. I had a pin on my shirt collar." He reached up and dug his fingers into the base of his throat through his stiff, upturned collar. "The backing fell off right before she came in and..."

"She pricked her finger on your pin," Garrett said. "Is that what you're saying?"

"She had her hands on my shoulders." Demetri's voice sounded scratchy. "On my neck—she was—we—" He sucked in a breath. "If only she hadn't come to see me—if I'd just picked that cursed backing off the floor—"

"Demetri," Garrett interrupted, *this isn't your fault.* Briar was cursed. She would have pricked her finger no matter what you did. You can't keep going over the 'what-ifs.' They'll drive you mad. Believe me," he said wryly, "I know."

"That may be true, but it doesn't change anything. I can't be with her." Demetri looked desolate. "How can I be with her—how can I forge a new future for us—when the one time I tried to help, I only made it worse?"

Garrett didn't understand. Not entirely. Maybe, being in the position he was in, he should have been glad to hear this. He would have hated himself for it, but if Demetri really felt he couldn't be with Briar, then she was free. To be with...someone else.

But Garrett didn't feel glad, not even a small, shameful part of him. He sighed. He felt so tired, the ache in his shoulder weighing on him like an anvil. "Look, I don't know what your plans are." Garrett tried to focus on Demetri's face. "And maybe you don't either. But you can still help Briar."

"Yes, I—" Demetri's stricken expression melted into one of concern. "Garrett, are you all right?"

Garrett tried to answer him, but the words got stuck. It was too warm in here, and he was so tired, and his shoulder hurt *so much*. Demetri and the study gave a violent tilt around him.

When his legs crumpled beneath him, he couldn't keep from falling. But he never hit the floor. Everything went black first, his surroundings dissolving in a haze of pain and heat.

21

CULPABLE

BRIAR PACED ACROSS THE library, gingerly feeling the joints of her knuckles where Kinsley had sewn her fingers back on. For the first time since she'd arrived at this house, she was back in day clothes—snug trousers she'd borrowed from Isabelle, a cotton shirt, and her brown wool spencer. The clothes helped her feel normal again—unlike her breakfast of raw rabbit this morning, which was decidedly *not* normal. This time, she ate the raw flesh fully aware of what she was doing, and it was...weird. A little disgusting, at first. The rabbit did not taste *bad*. She didn't enjoy it like she enjoyed eating other things. But she couldn't deny she felt *better* afterwards. Not only were her achy joints and sore muscles gone, but her whole body thrummed with energy.

At least there was no harm in eating raw rabbit. Unlike eating people.

"...this text doesn't say anything about breaking curses," Isabelle said. "I thought it might, but it's only a record of different kinds of curses that fairies have wrought—oh, no, some of these are really horrible, like—" She broke off, glancing up. "Would you stop that?"

"I'm sorry," Briar said.

"Don't."

"But I *am* sorry!" Briar insisted. "I *really* am."

"And I told you, it's fine." Isabelle tucked a stray curl behind her ear. She sat on a rickety wooden stool with a thick book in her lap. "You've apologized about fifty times already."

"Well, how can you say it's fine?" Briar tossed a hand in the air. "I tried to eat you! Most people would not be okay with that."

Isabelle flipped a page, the thick parchment rustling. "Yes, yes, it was all very scary and frankly, very weird. But it's not like it was the first time someone tried to eat me."

"Huh?"

"Never mind," Isabelle said. "Look, I'm over it. It's not like you did it on purpose. Although." She closed her book, marking the page with her hand. "I've been wondering. You passed several other rooms with the soldiers in them before you got to my room. Why did you go for me? Or do you remember?"

"Uh. Not really," Briar muttered. "I think it might have had something to do with the way you smelled."

"The way I smelled? So I smelled...savory?"

"No," Briar shot back. "But you know, soldiers are usually quite sweaty and dirty and really don't bathe often enough, whereas you—oh, all right," she said, when she saw the smile creeping across Isabelle's face. "You're teasing me."

"A little," Isabelle admitted. Without rising from her stool, she turned to the brass bookcase beside her, fingers trailing across the spines. She selected a smaller book. "I forgot about this one.

I skimmed through this ages ago when I was looking for a reference on the history of the Gift, but I never did look through the whole book...hmm..."

As Isabelle thumbed through her book, Briar turned away. She was meant to be helping with researching fairy curses, but she couldn't focus. She stared out the large bay windows on the far side of the room. Dark storm clouds were rolling into tight clusters in the sky outside, dampening the afternoon light.

"Hmm. Interesting," Isabelle said.

"Did you find something about breaking the curse?"

"No. I was just reading something this text said about using true love's kiss as a way to break a curse. Apparently, it used to be all the rage."

"I don't know why." Briar flicked her finger against the window glass. "It doesn't seem all that reliable to me. Garrett managed to break my curse, and he doesn't love me."

"Well—no. Of course not." Isabelle coughed.

Briar turned from the window. "When Garrett kissed me, he and I had never met. He wasn't even thinking of me when he kissed me! He only did it because of Snow. Ergo, he must have been thinking of her."

"Well, that could be why it worked." Isabelle adjusted the spectacles on the tip of her nose. "He was thinking about the girl he loved, *ergo*.... I'm thinking there could be another reason though. The text here says something about the caster's intentions being an important part of the magic, whether they're aware of it or not. To be honest, it's all sort of muddled, but I just wondered—maybe the dark fairy couldn't really specify the loophole to her curse enough because of who she is."

"I don't follow."

"Well, she hardly seems like the kind of person who's capable of love, does she? So perhaps, because she can't comprehend love, she couldn't work it into her curse like she meant to. And that's why Garrett could wake you—possibly, *anyone* who kissed you might have."

"Maybe." Briar tapped her thumb against an ebony shelf, beating an incessant rhythm into the wood. "That could also explain why it *didn't* work for Garrett and Snow...." She shook her head. "But it's still very woolly, if you ask me."

"Well, of course it is." Isabelle licked her finger and flipped another page. "It's *magic*. It's all rather unreliable."

This was what Briar appreciated about Isabelle. She was, like Briar, a girl who enjoyed and relied on what was *rational*. "Which is why this is starting to feel like a waste of time," Briar said. "Not that I'm not *incredibly* grateful to you for doing all this research, because I am. But I'm starting to think that—distasteful as it is—killing that fairy would be the easiest way to solve this."

Isabelle looked up. "But didn't they tell you? The queen said that killing a fairy—"

"—destroys your soul, I know. But I wasn't thinking of doing it myself. I was thinking of persuading that djinn to do it."

"Oh. Yes. Much more reasonable."

Except that he would probably never do it, and even if he did, Briar didn't like the idea of being in his debt. "Would it really be the worst thing ever? Losing one's soul, I mean."

The words were out of her mouth before she considered them. But if there was one person she could actually talk to about this, it was Isabelle. She wouldn't overreact like the boys would.

"Well." True to Briar's estimation, Isabelle did not sound shocked. Which was a relief. She sounded as though she was seriously weighing the question. "I mean. Yes, I would think so."

"But what even *is* a soul? No one really knows."

"Well, that's true, but I think we can rely—" Isabelle grimaced "—sort of—on what the queen said. Which is that a person *can* live without a soul—they function like any other person. But it sounds a terrible life. The queen said a person without a soul has no moral compass." She pursed her lips. "Frankly, a person without a soul sounds a bit frightening. Not the kind of person you want loose in the world, I think."

"I suppose," Briar murmured. "But I'm not sure that life as a mindless, flesh-eating monster would be much better."

"It's not much of a choice," Isabelle agreed. Most unhelpfully.

Briar didn't press it. Instead, she said, "Look, I haven't been much help here. I'm going to try to get that djinn to talk to me."

Briar left the library but stopped in the corridor, slumping against the wall. She'd dressed smartly this morning, putting on her clothes like armor. She'd braided her hair back, choosing a style that was striking and severe. Now she wanted a task, something she could *do*—anything to distract her from how useless she felt. And how terribly alone.

It's not much of a choice. It really wasn't. But Briar almost didn't care. She knew it was silly. Petty, even. But after everything that had happened last night, she felt so very small—what did it matter if they could save her or not?

It was mad to think that just two nights ago, she'd chased away her fears with thoughts of Demetri and Garrett. The only two people in the world, she'd thought, who cared about her. But now, Demetri was leaving her, and Garrett—Garrett...

In a way, she was angrier with Garrett than Demetri. Maybe that wasn't fair. But the truth was, she knew there was something going on with Demetri. He'd said a million times that he was fine, but she knew he wasn't. She could see it in his eyes. It was why she had given him space while they were traveling, as he had clearly been avoiding her.

She just felt sad for him. She wished there was something she could do, some way to help him. All she had ever wanted was to help him, to pay him back for all the ways he had helped her. But she had never been good at that sort of thing, never known how to reach out to someone. She needed him to tell her what she could do. If only he would.

As for Garrett...Briar wilted at the thought of him. It wasn't that he had lied to her by omission. It wasn't that he hadn't told her about the kiss. She felt stupid about being in the dark for so long. But really, that wasn't it at all.

It was that she could still remember how she'd felt, in that moment, when he'd said, *"It's not like it meant anything. Right?"* It was that she could remember how her insides had shriveled, how some piece of her cracked in two. And the worst part of it was, she didn't entirely understand why.

She just knew it felt awful.

So today, she was doing what she could. Putting on her armor. Looking for tasks she could accomplish. While the two princes were off doing stars' knew what. Briar told herself she didn't even care.

The djinn's room was on the same floor as Briar's, but on the opposite side of the manor. There were guards posted in the corridor. According to Beckett, Demetri had just been there as well, but left with Garrett a few minutes ago.

It was a small room, probably one of the smallest in the grand house. The only window was shuttered tight, leaving the room lit by two gear-bulb lamps in the corners. The effect was a dark room, the shadows cut with swathes of white light.

The creature sat on the edge of his narrow, brass-framed bed, shackled hands on his knees. Briar disliked the gaze he turned on her. "I didn't expect a visit from you, Briar." His voice was a pleasant tenor, smooth as glass, and the sound of it made the hair on the back of her neck prickle. "But I'm glad you came."

"Whatever." Briar planted herself before him. "I want you to kill the dark fairy." She'd thought to play on Dev's liking of her to ask him this, but now that she stood before him, she was in no mood for games. Either he would do it or he wouldn't.

Briar didn't expect him to agree outright, but neither did she expect him to laugh in her face—which he did. "Why would I do that? She did me quite the favor, cursing you to sleep."

"But I'm awake now." Briar dug her nails into her palm. "So there's no harm in killing her."

"Yes, no harm at all." Dev examined an imaginary fleck of dust on his sleeve. "Except if I try to kill her and fail, she'll send me straight back to the shadow world."

"So don't fail."

Dev spared her half a smile and said nothing.

"It's not like she set out to do you a favor, you know." Briar's tone bore an irritable bite.

The djinn stood, his face cast in shadow, just out of the lamps' white glare. Briar had to remind herself that he was shackled. "Like I did for you?"

"You, do me a favor?" Now it was Briar's turn to laugh. "What, 'protecting' me from the rotting curse by *using* me, by *feeding* on my life force as I slept? Your protection was incidental, you said that yourself."

"There were other dangers I protected you from," said Dev. With his face shrouded in shadow, this remark sounded ominous. "Dangers in the shadow world."

"You said I was never really there," Briar scoffed. "What could I have been in danger from?"

"I said your physical body wasn't there," Dev corrected her. "Your consciousness was. And a consciousness can be harmed just as easily as a physical body. More so, even."

"That doesn't make sense."

"Can you die in a dream?" Dev asked. "As easily as in the physical world? Of course you can. Your mind can be injured, sometimes irrevocably so." Seeing Briar's confusion, Dev explained, "Being in the shadow world—for you, Briar—was like living in a dream. It's the easiest way I can explain it. It's why you don't remember it, aside from bits and pieces. The same way you likely don't remember most of your dreams."

Against her better judgment, Briar took a step forward. "Then how could you protect me? From a dream? Did you have control over it or something?"

"In a manner of speaking." The djinn's voice darkened. "Until I didn't. Hence the danger."

Briar shook her head. "You don't talk sense. And I don't see that you did me that big a favor, *protecting* me from the rotting curse. After all, if you could do that, you might have protected the rest of the kingdom too. In case you didn't notice, the dark fairy cursed them as well—"

"But she didn't," Dev interrupted. "She didn't curse the kingdom. Only you."

Briar frowned. "No. She cursed everyone—*you* told us, you heard the dark fairy cast the curse—"

"Yes," the djinn said. "On you, Briar. I tried to tell you last night, but your dear friend Garrett interrupted me. She cursed you to rot, not the whole kingdom."

"But that doesn't make sense. I'm not the only one affected. The entire kingdom is."

"Yes, but that is your doing, Briar." Dev stepped back, resuming his seat upon the bed. "Not the dark fairy's."

Briar jerked her head up. "My doing? What do you mean?"

The djinn said, "You made a wish. And I granted it."

"What are you *talking* about?"

Dev drummed his fingers against his knee. "It is the power of fairies to curse. We djinn have a similar power. Ours is the power of wishes." He smiled, but his eyes were cold. "And to think that we djinn get such a bad name over fairies. Theirs is a much more vindictive power, wouldn't you say?"

"Wishes," Briar repeated. "So you're saying I made a wish? For the kingdom to rot?" A horrid shiver ran through her. That wasn't right, she *knew* that wasn't right. She would never wish this on anyone. The djinn was lying, or confused, or just plain *wrong*. "That's not—"

"You didn't wish for the kingdom to rot," Dev said. "You wished for them to sleep. Like you."

Briar shook her head. "No, I never—"

Then she remembered.

I wish everyone would sleep for a hundred years with me. My parents, everyone in the castle—the whole kingdom. I wish they could all sleep and wake with me, all those years from now.

She had said that. To Demetri. On their way back from the woods, the day she fell to the curse. She'd been angry and despairing, thinking that even if she did wake from a hundred years of sleep, it would be too late—because the world she knew would be gone, and Demetri would be dead.

But they were just words. She hadn't meant it—of course she hadn't meant it—

That same horror-fueled thrill shook through her. This time, Briar couldn't fight it back. Everything in the room fell away. There was nothing but a black void, and her, and this djinn. The full implications of what he was saying sank into her every pore.

"No, I—" She wasn't sure where the words came from. They couldn't have come from her. Something was clogging her airway, stealing her breath. "I never meant—"

"Your Highness? Are you all right?"

A hand on her shoulder brought the room back into focus, dragging her out of the void. Briar recognized Kinsley's voice, though she never heard the door open, never heard him come into the room. And somehow, when Briar wrenched around to face Kinsley, it all became real.

"No," she whispered.

Kinsley's brow wrinkled. "No, you're not all right?"

Briar whirled around to face Dev. "That wasn't a wish." The words rasped out of her throat. "I never meant—and even if I did, I said I wanted them to *sleep*, not to rot, not to become these—these horrible—"

"You wished they could sleep like you." The djinn cocked his head to the side. "It seems reasonable to me. You didn't want to wake to find everyone you knew had gone. You wanted them to share in your curse—"

"No!" Briar burst out. "No, I didn't!"

"—so I linked them to you. To your curse. To your fate." He gave a careless shrug. "Which didn't turn out so well, since the dark fairy expanded your curse. But how was I to know—"

"I didn't mean it, you mad—you *vile*—" It was a moment before Briar realized she had tried to jump at the djinn, and only Kinsley's firm grip on her arms held her back. "People say stupid things they don't mean all the time, I never wanted—I never *asked* you to do this, I didn't—"

"I grant wishes." Despite her struggles to get at him, Dev leaned forward. "It's what I do. I heard your wish, and I granted it. Unfortunately, the wish linked all your people to you. When the dark fairy added on another curse, they shared in that curse."

With a surge of strength, Briar yanked out of Kinsley's grasp. She reeled free of him, stumbling into the djinn. Dev reached out his shackled hands as though to steady her, but Briar scrambled back. "*Don't.*" Her words were barely intelligible through her ragged breath. "Don't you touch me, don't...don't..."

She couldn't look at him any longer. She tripped in her haste as she pushed past Kinsley and fled down the corridor. She heard the soldiers calling after her, heard them burst into the room, probably thinking the djinn had done something to her.

But he hadn't. He had done something to her entire kingdom.

Briar didn't realize where she was running to until she nearly reached her room. As she rounded the corner, she smacked into someone, someone thin but solid. Briar bounced back and almost fell before she caught herself. Dazed, she looked up and saw it was Wilton, one of the guards. He was very young, around Briar's age, and quite shy. "I'm very sorry—Your Highness—I was just looking for you—Miss Isabelle sent me."

Briar stared at him. His words barely registered. She was just about to shove past him and run into her room when he blurted out, "It's Prince Garrett. He's not well. You should come. Quickly."

22

POISONED

DEMETRI COULD BARELY LOOK Briar in the face when she appeared in the corridor outside Garrett's room. The anxiety in her eyes was enough to tell him that Wilton had filled her in.

"We were just talking," Demetri told her. He was not the only one here—Isabelle stood beside him, her face chalky under the glare of the light fixtures, and a whole cluster of soldiers, waiting for word on their prince. "He didn't look very well, but I just thought—I didn't realize anything was seriously wrong. He mentioned several days ago his shoulder was still paining him, but—"

"His shoulder?" Briar interrupted.

His shoulder. Why hadn't Demetri realized it was still bothering him? "One of the corpses bit him, back in the castle. Before he woke you. I didn't think it was that bad—but Thatcher is worried it might be infected." Demetri was worried it could be a lot worse than that.

While Isabelle went to sit with Garrett, Briar and Demetri consulted with the medic in the antechamber to Garrett's bedroom. Thatcher's dark face was drawn, his wrinkles more pronounced than ever. "I've never seen anything like it," he said. "The corpse's bite had something like venom in it."

"Venom?" Briar echoed. She sounded calmer than Demetri felt, but then, she was good at that. "You mean its bite was poisonous?"

"Something like that. There are different remedies used to treat poisonous wounds, but most must be applied within a short time of the victim receiving a bite." Thatcher wiped at his eyes with a handkerchief. "There is something I've heard of—a process some scientists in the Desert Kingdom are working on. They've been creating an antidote to different venoms. But the process is still very experimental—" Thatcher raised a hand in a helpless gesture "—and I don't think we have the time. I would need to research how it's done, and I would need access to resources we don't have here."

Briar tugged at the ends of her jacket. Demetri watched her, and he knew how distressed she must be. He knew what Briar looked like when she was trying to seem composed, but despaired on the inside.

"And how long does Garrett have?" she asked.

"Unless I can find some way to cure him..." Thatcher's voice was hopelessly grim "...he'll be dead in a few days."

⋯⊰◦⊱⋯

Sometime much later, Demetri found himself outside Briar's room. He faltered, standing before the door. He wasn't sure what he was doing here. The last time he'd spoken to Briar—*really* spoken to her—he'd told her he couldn't be with her anymore. And he hadn't changed his mind, but now, with Garrett...

He wasn't sure if he was looking for comfort or thinking of comforting *her*. But he didn't know what else to do.

Slowly, as though in a dream, he rapped on the door three times.

The response was immediate. "Come in," Briar called.

Warily, Demetri pushed open the door and stepped inside.

The light was scarce in Briar's room. That was to be expected; it was nearly ten o'clock at night. She had only a single lamp lit, and she'd lowered a shade around it so only a faint glimmer shone. Briar, though, was not in bed. She sat on a cane-seat chair in the darkest corner of the room, so shrouded in shadows that he could not see her face. She was still mostly dressed, in trousers and a cotton shirt.

"I was afraid I would wake you," Demetri said. He half-reached to shut the door and then stopped. He still wasn't sure if he was welcome.

"I haven't been sleeping much anyway." Briar's voice was low and rough, and somehow made more so by the darkness "You can close the door, Demetri. What are you doing here?"

"I couldn't sleep either," he admitted. He didn't know what else to say, even though there was so, so much more.

Briar's chair *creaked* as she stood. She kept her distance but stepped forward to face him in the light. The muted look in her eyes and the tense set of her mouth spoke to her weariness.

"Is that all?" she asked.

Demetri dithered. He wondered if he should just apologize for bothering her and leave. But she had asked, and that was not all. Not all by far.

He said, "I feel so useless."

He half-thought she might tell him that, yes, he was quite useless. But instead, her shoulders slumped and she said, "I know. I do too. I hate this, Demetri. I hate not being able to help him." Her eyes flickered up to meet his. "He *can't* die."

Demetri's heart clenched. The desperation in her face made him think of last night, when she'd run into Garrett after losing her memory. How relieved she'd been to see him, how comforted by his presence. And it made him think of the two of them earlier, with the djinn, confronted by Garrett's lie—or concealed truth, as it were—about waking her.

He thought of the confusion in Briar's eyes, the misery on Garrett's face. He thought of how upset *Garrett* had been earlier, about Demetri's leaving Briar, about Demetri hurting Briar.

They cared for each other, he realized. They cared for each other a *lot*.

He didn't know how he was supposed to feel about that.

He pushed those thoughts away. They didn't matter. Not now, when Garrett was dying. "I hate it too," he said to Briar, "but I don't know what to do."

Briar looked stubborn. "He can't be another person that gets hurt because of me."

"Briar. He's not. Garrett came on this quest willingly." He tried to smile but didn't quite manage it. "He's quite the one for daring quests, from what I understand."

"Why?" she whispered. "Why is he so reckless with his life?"

Demetri rather thought it had to do with losing Snow, but he didn't voice this. "I don't know."

Briar was quiet. Then she said, "I do." Perhaps also thinking of Snow. She rubbed her hands over her face. "It doesn't matter now. All that matters is that he *is* hurt and it *is* because of me."

"Briar," Demetri protested, "none of this is your fault."

Briar laughed hollowly. "That's where you're wrong, Demetri." She cut him a sideways glance. Her eyes were sharp. "I talked to the djinn earlier." She swung away from him and began to pace. "He told me something. About the rotting curse. The fairy wasn't responsible for cursing my kingdom after all. Apparently, *I* did that."

"What—?" Demetri thought he must have heard her wrong. "Briar, you're not talking sense. What did the creature say to you?"

Briar stopped and gripped the back of her chair, leaning forward. "Do you remember, Demetri—" Her voice was cool and ghost-like in the shadows "—when we left the woods to return to the castle that day? On my birthday? Do you remember what I said to you?"

"You said a lot of things." Demetri's voice came out hoarse. She had told him he was the only person who'd ever cared about her. But somehow, he didn't think that was what she meant. The thought made him tense with foreboding.

"Do you remember I made a wish?"

"You said you wished everyone would sleep for a hundred years too," Demetri recalled. "Your parents, the kingdom. So that when you woke, it would be like nothing changed. But what—"

"It's part of a djinn's power, Demetri," Briar said. "Granting wishes. Fairies cast curses. Djinn grant wishes."

Demetri didn't understand at first. It took him a moment to connect these things—djinn granting wishes and what she'd said about the kingdom sleeping. That hadn't really been a wish—he'd never thought of it that way. It was only something she'd said in her despair, not a real wish—

"What are you saying?" he asked. He thought he knew, but he didn't want to know.

"It was me, Demetri." Briar's voice was terrible. "Me and the djinn. He granted my wish."

"But he wasn't even there—how could he—"

"He was. He'd probably been stalking me for days." The calm, detached way she said this was truly horrifying. "He was there when I fell to the curse, remember? He was just waiting for it to happen."

"But you weren't really making a wish—" The unjustness of this djinn, the *presumptuousness* of this "wish," ignited a hot surge of rage inside him.

"It's the way the magic works, evidently. He granted the wish by linking the kingdom to my curse. So when the fairy cast a second curse, it befell them too."

Demetri stepped towards her, out of the lamplight and into the darkness. As his eyes adjusted, more of her became visible, enough to see that her cool voice was a ruse. Her hands gripped the back of the chair so tightly, it was a wonder the wood hadn't snapped in two.

"Briar." Demetri wasn't sure where his voice came from. His rage for the djinn flared so brightly and so hot, it should have burned his voice out. "That's—that's—" Awful. It was awful. But. "It's not your fault though. You have to know that."

"I do." Briar let go of the chair and flexed her fingers. "I know it's not my fault, Demetri. But it happened because of me. Just like what happened to Garrett. And that's why I have to be the one to fix it."

"You can't do it all on your own, Briar."

"That's not what I mean." Briar stepped around the chair and away from him. Always away from him, but then, he supposed he was to blame for that. "I mean it's my responsibility. The kingdom, *they're* my responsibility. I never felt that before, you know? I was so separated from them. No one bothered to raise me to be their queen—it was never going to happen, not with the curse. But *this*, what's happened to them—that makes them my responsibility. I know it's not my fault, but it happened *because of me*."

"I don't understand the difference."

"The difference is, if I thought it was my fault, there would be lots of wallowing," she said dryly.

"Briar."

"I don't *blame* myself, Demetri." There was something terrifying and thrilling about the determination in her. She embodied it, so much that she didn't look like *Briar* anymore, but only that, that resolve. "But so what? I blame the dark fairy, I blame the djinn. Neither of them is going to fix this. Which means I have to. No matter the cost."

He didn't like those words. "We'll find a way, Briar. We'll find a way to fix it."

Briar looked at him. "I didn't think it was still 'we.'"

Demetri felt gutted. He could feel his words hovering between them, irrecoverable and weighted. *I can't do this anymore. I can't be with you.*

"It's still 'we,'" he said quietly, "when it comes to saving your kingdom."

He hated himself for needing to make the distinction.

Briar dropped her gaze. "I'm just worried it won't be enough."

He was worried about that too. If only she knew how much that worried him.

They were interrupted by a knock on the door. They both looked around, startled. It was so late and so dark that Demetri had forgotten they were in a house full of people. Briar called, "Come in," and it was Kinsley who entered, with good news.

"Thatcher has asked to see you both," he said. "He thinks he might know how to save Prince Garrett."

Demetri and Briar exchanged a quick, wordless glance. Then they followed Kinsley down the corridors to Garrett's room, where Thatcher waited for them in the antechamber.

"I don't know if it will work." This was the first thing Thatcher said, without greeting and without preamble.

"What is it?" Briar asked.

"Well." Thatcher crossed his arms and leaned back against a long, stained poplar table. "I've been thinking about what I said before, that the corpse's bite worked like a venom. You see, there are some species of snakes—not many, and it's subject to debate—that have shown to be immune to their own venom. I was thinking that might be true of these corpses. And if it *were* true, I could use some of their blood and transfuse it into Prince Garrett's bloodstream. Normally such a process wouldn't be possible—injecting a snake's blood into a human's—but since these corpses are technically human, it might work."

Briar said, her tone dubious, "There were a lot of 'mights' and 'ifs' in there, Thatcher."

Demetri silently agreed.

"It's all I've got." Thatcher's shoulders slumped.

Briar let out a long exhale. They were all of them quiet. Demetri didn't know enough about any of this to feel confident making a call. He didn't want to make things worse—but then, Garrett was certainly going to die if they didn't do *some*thing, so he supposed things couldn't get worse. But where would they even get corpse blood?

Briar said, "Would my blood work?"

Demetri looked from her to the medic, alarmed.

"It's possible." Thatcher said this in a tone that indicated it was *not* possible. "But, Princess...normally, a simple blood transfusion isn't fatal to the donor. But given that part of your condition involves your failing bloodstream—I would be extremely wary to take even a small amount of blood from you."

"So you're saying this blood transfusion might kill whoever you took the blood from. Permanently kill, I mean." Demetri shot Briar a pointed look, hoping she wasn't still entertaining the idea.

"It's very likely," Thatcher admitted, "and I don't want to risk it on you, Princess." He looked at Briar. "Nor would Prince Garrett, I think."

Briar's expression was mulish. Demetri was half-afraid she was going to insist they use her anyway. But then she said, "Well, if not me, then we'll just have to use someone else."

"Another corpse, you mean?" Demetri interjected. "But where would we possibly find one?"

Briar met his gaze. "I'm going to go out and get one, of course."

"This is a terrible idea," Demetri protested, as Briar strapped a low-slung belt over her trousers and shirt. They were gathered in her bedroom, along with Isabelle, who was helping Briar get ready. "Can we just take a minute? This is insane. We need to stop and think about this."

"We don't have time." Briar began weaving her hair into a braid. "This is the only hope Garrett has."

"I understand that, but Briar, this is too dangerous."

Isabelle took Briar's sheath of white hair in her hands, pulling it into a tighter braid. "Are you sure you'll be able to find one of these corpse creatures? Out in the woods?"

Briar replied, "It may not be easy, but I imagine some of them *are* out there. We were attacked on the train not twenty miles north of here."

"Wonderful," Isabelle muttered, yanking on Briar's hair. "An evil witch *and* the walking dead. I definitely need to find a new place to live."

Briar winced at Isabelle's forceful ministrations. "Anyway, that's why I need to go. I'll be the most useful. I've got good eyesight in the dark, and good hearing. Probably because I'm becoming one of them."

"It's still too dangerous," Demetri muttered, more to himself than anyone else. "I should come with you."

"*No.*" Briar stepped away from Isabelle. Demetri was struck by how *different* she looked, how unlike the girl he remembered from eighty-two years ago. He wasn't sure what it was—the clothes maybe, or the hard look on her face. But her expression softened when she looked at him. "Please, Demetri. Please stay here with Garrett." She hesitated. "You're his friend and—I don't—"

"All right." Demetri repressed a sigh. She didn't have to say it; he understood. She didn't like to leave Garrett. "All right. But Briar, please—be careful."

Briar nodded, pulled on her spencer, and left the room.

Demetri followed behind as Isabelle led Briar outside into the cool, stormy, precarious night. Five soldiers waited for her on the front steps—the twins Aden and Alec, Gemma the tracker, Kinsley, and Tory, a short, ruddy girl soldier about Briar's age. All of the able soldiers had volunteered to come along, and Briar chose five from among them. None of them had questioned her authority to do so. Tory, who never used firearms, flipped a short blade out from her sleeve and handed it to Briar.

"Princess." Isabelle gave her a level look. "Are you sure you want to do this?"

Demetri held his breath. He didn't dare ask her himself, but he was anxious to hear the answer.

"Do I want to do this?" Briar looked thoughtful, as though she was truly considering the question. Then, "No. Not really. But it's necessary, so it doesn't really matter."

Just as before, her resolve chilled Demetri. That he couldn't say why only made it worse.

Isabelle said, "Then good luck."

23

MONSTER

B RIAR RODE ON THE back of the self-propelled carriage as it trundled through the woods. Kinsley sat with her, while the others rode inside. They set out before twilight, though the dark clouds overhead covered enough of the sky that no real light filtered through the trees, bringing an early night.

They traveled north for two hours as night fell around them. It began to rain, a steady downpour in great sheets. The wind drove the rain into the carriage, and the slanting barrage blurred the forest around them. Briar and Kinsley were drenched after a short while, and as the rain-soaked forest floor churned beneath the carriage wheels, flecks of mud spattered them. Briar blinked and wiped her face, continuing her search.

She tried to keep her thoughts centered on the task at hand, and when she couldn't, she thought of Garrett, and how very dead he could be in a few days' time. For someone more emotional—someone like Garrett, maybe—that might have been a distraction. For Briar, it kept her focused. It reminded her how high the stakes were and why she couldn't fail. And it reminded her she couldn't dwell on the fact that these corpses had been people once, her family and her servants and her subjects. She couldn't think about Laurel, and how her cousin had said that sometimes, she could remember who she was.

She tried not to remember that it was her words, her careless *wish*, that had gotten them into this mess. All she wanted was to save them. Her people. Only, first she had to kill one of them.

She had to do it. For Garrett. Whatever he might have kept from her, whatever he might have said—she still cared about him. She cared about him more than she would have thought possible, for someone she had met only a couple of weeks ago.

She couldn't let him die.

Another hour passed as they traveled north. "I don't think the river's too far from here, Princess." Kinsley wiped his face with the back of his hand. The black mud was stark against his pale skin, giving him the look of a painted warrior. "Nothing yet?"

"No." Briar swiveled her head back and forth. "Maybe they're not—" She broke off.

"Briar?"

"Tell Alec to stop the carriage," Briar ordered. The carriage slowed to a halt. Briar jumped down, mud squelching beneath her boots. Her soaked clothes clung to her, rubbing at her skin in an unpleasant way.

Without the noise of the carriage wheels, the woods were quiet. The rain slowed to a drizzle. Aden and Tory spilled out of the carriage, and Gemma hung out the side door, still and alert. Briar motioned them for silence before they could ask any questions, wiped her eyes, and listened.

On her right. She turned ninety degrees. Something was moving through the forest. A slither through the wet, clumping leaves, a scraping over the sodden bramble. Not a bird or a critter; it was too large for that. Not a bear or a wolf—too noisy, too careless to be a practiced predator.

Briar peered into the darkness, but she only saw trees, lofty and thick.

"Briar?" Kinsley repeated, her name little more than a breath on his lips.

"There's something out there," she said in a low voice. "Kinsley, you stay with the carriage."

"I still don't like this," Kinsley said, though he obeyed, swinging into the elevated driver's seat. He lay out flat on his stomach and positioned his rifle to shoot.

Briar didn't like it either, but Kinsley was the best sharpshooter in Garrett's company, and while Gemma was pretty good too, she was the better tracker. Briar needed her out in the woods.

Following Briar's direction, Aden, Alec, and Tory angled out in flanking positions, creeping through the woods. Briar led them on point, with Gemma at her side. The three soldiers spread out, vanishing into the gloom.

Gemma bent to study the grooves in the mud. Her dark hair fell over her face in a curtain, muffling her voice. "The rain's muddied most of this, but something went this way. Judging by the tracks, it was on two feet, and dragging its steps."

"Corpse," Briar whispered. "Come on. Let's keep going."

They continued another couple of minutes. Then Gemma halted, crouching low. She picked something up off the ground.

It was a finger.

Briar suppressed the urge to make a face. She ran her thumb along each of her own sewn-on fingers and wiggled them, making sure she still could.

Then a black shadow leapt down from the trees.

It moved too fast to follow. Gemma went for her rifle, but she hadn't straightened before something small whistled through the air, taking her in the neck. Her eyes rolled back in her head, and she collapsed atop a blanket of grimy, dead leaves.

"Gemma!" Briar rushed forward and peered at the small projectile in Gemma's neck. It looked like...a dart?

The black shadow rustled forward. Briar spun, pulling out her knife.

"Don't be silly, princess," came a rasping voice. "You cannot kill me."

As Briar watched, the shadow began to unfurl. That's when she realized it was not a shadow, but wings. Two massive, sable, feathery wings. They unfolded like a bat's wings, and hidden beneath them was a fairy.

She was not like other fairies. Her skin lacked the greenish hue; instead, it was pale like polished ivory. She wore a tattered little dress, one that left her white shoulders bare. Her hair, neat for a fairy, was as black as her wings, as were the feathers woven into it. The only similarities she bore to other fairies were her pointed ears, her tiny frame, and her black eyes.

"*You.*" Briar barely recognized her own voice. "You're her. The dark fairy."

"My name," the dark fairy said, speaking slowly, as though Briar was too stupid to understand, "is Tenalabralilah." Her small lips stretched wide and thin. Briar thought it was meant to be a smile. "But what do names matter to monsters like you and me?"

"I'm not like you," Briar whispered. No matter how her growing symptoms belied this. "What are you doing here? What have you done to Gemma?"

"She will be fine." The fairy cocked her head to the side. "I wanted to make sure no one interrupts our little chat, Briar."

Briar had never imagined she might meet this fairy. She'd always figured her for a coward. She had cursed an infant after all, an infant who could not harm her. She had never dared show her face at the castle while Briar was alive. Then again, she was immortal and near impossible to kill. Even if she wanted to, Briar still had no idea *how* to kill her. She was helpless to do anything.

And helpless to defend herself.

Before she could think twice, Briar burst out, "Why did you do it? Why did you cast this rotting curse? Wasn't one curse enough for you?"

"*Enough*?" The dark fairy sneered. "Nothing could ever be *enough*. Nothing will ever be enough until all you humans are dead. Or subjugated beneath my feet."

Briar shouldn't have been surprised by this, but the sheer vehemence, the hatred in the fairy's voice, took Briar aback. "Then why curse me at all?" she asked, and she couldn't stop her voice from shaking. "If you want to hurt *all* humans, then why focus on me?"

"You and your curse were the object of my revenge, little princess." Her black eyes glittered in the silvery light of the moon. "My punishment for your father and the monarchs in the Glen Kingdom. For thinking they could quell *me*. For thinking their alliance could *stop* me."

The dark fairy shook her head. "Perhaps it would have been enough. That first curse. If you'd slept while all your people died, while your family died—it would have been enough." Her mouth twisted. "It was as good as killing you, after all. As far as your parents were concerned."

Briar felt cold seeping into her veins, turning her blood to ice. That was the future she'd feared. And that fear led her to make her wish, a wish she'd never meant.

"But then you fell to the curse and the entire kingdom fell with you." The dark fairy's small hands clenched into fists, and Briar imagined those long, sharp fingernails drawing blood as they dug into the palms of her hands. "I don't know how, but they were linked to you. And if they all slept and woke with you, my curse meant *nothing*. My revenge was wasted."

She fluttered forward and stopped less than a foot from Briar, who forced herself to remain still. Even though the fairy stood a hand's length shorter than Briar, she seemed like a giant, her black wings towering.

"You would all sleep a century away and wake to continue your lives together," the dark fairy hissed. "Well, I wasn't about to let that happen. So I cast a second curse. That you would rot. And the whole kingdom rotted. Each year, they rotted a little more. Each year, becoming monsters." Her lips stretched in that dreadful grimace. "Like me."

That monster inside Briar raged, warring with a part of her that was becoming lesser every day. She wanted to destroy this creature, rip her to pieces, make her hurt, make her bleed. But her humanity protested, crying out in a small voice, clinging to the last vestiges of herself.

It was that small part of her that spoke, that humanity. "I am not a monster," Briar said, a shred of despair in her voice.

The dark fairy leaned towards her. "Not yet."

There was something odd around her eye. It was so faint that Briar didn't notice it until now, with the fairy's face inches from her own. A weird pattern, like small, spidery veins, spread out from the corner of her eye. Briar didn't think they were veins though, as they were a dark, angry red.

"But you might get lucky, little princess." The dark fairy stepped back, turning in profile. Briar breathed out, low and shaky, resisting the urge to run. "Perhaps your doomed life will end before you lose yourself to the rotting. Because I'm going to kill you all. Your little prince friends. All your soldiers. Every human on the face of this earth, I will destroy."

Her words were unfathomable. "You can't. Humans and fairies have lived in peace for hundreds of years—"

"Humans and fairies have lived in a standstill," the dark fairy spat, "and an end to that standstill was always inevitable. Humans are a blight on this land, and they must be destroyed."

"Yes, well, in case you forgot, *you can't kill humans*, so—"

"I don't plan to kill any of you myself." The fairy's lip curled with scorn. "I don't need to. I might not have intended for your kingdom to rot with you, but they did. And now there's a whole army of them. An army of monsters—and I mean to unleash them."

Something icy gripped Briar at her core, but it was a strange cold. A cold that burned, like plunging into freezing water. "No. You can't."

"I can," the dark fairy said, her tone mocking. "And there is nothing you can do to save them."

"I can kill you."

The dark fairy's wings went still. Briar held her breath, waiting for a blow to drop. But then the fairy laughed, a cruel, high laugh. "*You* kill *me?* Don't you know what that will do to you?"

"Yes," Briar said. A kind of clarity came over her. In this moment, she knew she wasn't making an empty threat. She *was* going to kill this fairy. It didn't feel like a decision—more like a premonition. It should have terrified her, but she felt steady and sure. "What does it matter? I'm going to die anyway."

"Perhaps you're right." The dark fairy didn't sound afraid either. Only amused. "That is what it means to be mortal, after all. So go ahead, little princess. Come and try to kill me. I'll be at your castle, mustering my army. I'll even wait for you."

Briar narrowed her eyes. "Why go to the castle? Surely the corpses there have left by now."

"No." The dark fairy clicked her tongue, sounding annoyed. "Those *meddlers* who call themselves my brethren erected a barrier to keep your people inside the castle. A powerful barrier—but not powerful enough. Soon, I'll have the strength I need to bring it down—and then my army will be free to go where I direct them." She took a step back, her black wings bleeding into the shadows. "So come find me, princess. I'll be waiting—in that place where you slept all those years." Another step, and she was gone.

Briar breathed a tremulous breath. Her knees buckled, threatening to bring her to the ground.

Then a noise from behind drew her attention. Scraping, slithering—scraping over the forest floor.

Dragging feet. Dragging fast.

All of a sudden, Briar remembered why they were here in the dark woods and the misty rain. She leapt to her feet and spun, just in time to duck the purpled hand that swung at her.

She fell back, tripping over Gemma. The corpse that reared over her was tall and thin, with lank hair and one eye, bulging and slimy. A faded coat hung on its gaunt frame, and its trousers were ridden with holes. Its skin carried a faint sheen, like melting candle wax, but very little of its flesh had fallen away.

It looked so much like a human.

Its single eye fell on Gemma with a hunger Briar recognized. "No!" She propelled herself forward, lunging for the corpse.

It was not a human. It was a monster.

Her attack caught the creature off-guard. The force of her leap sent them both sprawling across the ground. Leaves stuck to her face as she tried to get her arm up to deliver a punch, but the corpse latched onto her arms. Her bones trembled in its grip, threatening to splinter.

But she was strong too. Summoning every ounce of strength she possessed, she wrenched her arms up, breaking the creature's grip. A backhand blow to its face shattered its nose and jaw, but before she could deliver another blow, it grabbed her by the throat and tossed her away. Little pains erupted all over her body, but they were nothing as she rolled to her feet. The corpse did the same, lumbering upright.

Using a burst of speed, Briar closed the distance between them in half a second, coming behind the creature. She placed both hands on either side of its head and *twisted*.

The corpse's neck snapped, and it fell at her feet.

Panting, Briar took a step back. At once, the pains she'd suppressed rose to the surface, bruised skin and flesh scraped raw.

Her ankle was throbbing; she'd fallen on it wrong. But she didn't have time to think about that. She needed to get the corpse, get Gemma—

A clammy hand closed around her neck from behind.

Briar tried to scream, but the sound that escaped her lips was more like a gurgle. A second corpse. She couldn't see it, but she knew it by its putrid stench, and by the strong, cold fingers wrapped around her neck. She flailed, kicking out. It was going to crush her throat like she'd done to the corpse on the train, and it might not even kill her, not like it would kill anyone else—

A shot *cracked* through the air.

The hand around her neck fell free, and Briar dropped to the ground.

When she looked, she saw the second corpse dead at her feet. *Dead* dead—a bullet had taken it through the head, and the remains of its brain and skull lay scattered across the ground, enmeshed among the wet, sticky leaves.

Briar looked around, her breath hitching in her throat.

"I hope the one you got isn't dead," Kinsley said. He lowered his rifle, peering at her from twenty paces away. "Thatcher said we needed one alive."

"No," Briar croaked. "It's not dead." Her ears buzzed from the shot of the rifle.

"Good." Kinsley reached into his coat pocket, pulling out the sedative and a syringe. "We'd never have managed two anyway. What's wrong with Gemma?"

Briar staggered to her feet. "I think she's fine. Just knocked out." Briar grimaced at the puzzled look on Kinsley's face. "The corpses weren't the only thing in these woods tonight, Kinsley."

They made it back to Isabelle's manor in the early hours of the morning, well before dawn. The air was heavy, laden with moisture from the rain and filled with earthy odors dredged from damp soil. Demetri and the soldiers met them at the manor's side door as they brought the corpse in. Alec, Aden, Tory, and Gemma were all conscious, but still a little foggy, so a couple of the others stepped forward to take the corpse from Briar and Kinsley.

"Best get him to Thatcher straight away," Briar advised. Her limbs quivered as the corpse was lifted from her. "He gave us five sedatives, and we just used the last one. Doesn't keep it out too long."

As the corpse was carried down the corridor, Demetri turned to Briar. He half-raised an arm, as though to reach for her face, but stopped and left his hand hanging awkwardly. He dropped it a second later, but the damage was done. He glanced away and asked, "Are you all right?"

Briar tried to keep her dismay from showing. "Fine. I'm fine."

Demetri looked up, his eyes searching her face.

She cleared her throat. "I'm going to see if Thatcher needs anything else from me. How is Garrett?" she asked, turning away.

"He's about the same, Thatcher said—Briar." The tips of Demetri's fingers brushed the back of her neck. Where the corpse had gripped her from behind and likely bruised her skin. "What—"

"I'm fine." Briar jerked away. His touch was light, but it felt like fire. "It's nothing. I'm fine."

She stopped by her room to change out of her muddy clothes. Her shirt clung to her as she stripped it off her skin, and her legs felt rubbed raw when she removed her trousers. Dressed in dry breeches and her old shirt, she set out for Garrett's room.

By the time she got there, the medic had taken the corpse and retreated into another room to extract its blood. Isabelle met her in the antechamber of Garrett's room. "I've been sitting with him the past couple of hours." Her voice was rough and her eyes bloodshot. "He's been in and out of consciousness. You, ah—I think you should see him."

"Why?" Briar frowned. "I mean, I don't mind, but—was he asking for me?"

"Not exactly." Isabelle had the weirdest look on her face. "Actually, I think he thought I *was* you. Or at least, I hope he did."

"Why? What did he say?"

"Never mind." Isabelle evaded her gaze. "Just—go in."

Briar was puzzled, but she shrugged and went inside.

Garrett's bedroom was lit by a single gear-bulb lamp. His bed was set in an alcove at the far end of the room. He lay beneath two thick, heavy quilts, though the collar of his shirt was damp with sweat, as were the curls at his forehead. He appeared to be asleep, though his head shifted from side to side. His face was pinched and crumpled.

The whole room smelled like death.

Briar dropped into the straight-backed chair at his bedside. She looked him over, unsure what to do. For one thing, she had never been comfortable around sick people. She didn't know what to say or do.

Garrett would know. He was so natural at caring; he seemed to understand how the people around him felt before they themselves did. He put on a cheerful face, but even in the short time Briar had known him, she'd discovered the incredible depth of feeling and vulnerability he possessed. There was something admirable about someone like that, someone who lived with such passion.

Garrett turned his head, murmuring unintelligible things.

"Garrett?" she ventured, leaning forward. "Can you hear me? Garrett?" She touched three fingertips to his forehead, then to his cheek. He was too warm, his cheeks flushed red. There was a glazed bowl of water on the nightstand beside them, and a damp rag. Briar dipped the rag into the bowl, squeezed the excess water free, and turned back to Garrett to dab at his forehead.

She felt a bit stupid at first. She had never tended to a sick person before. But this wasn't just a sick person. This was Garrett. And as she ran the damp cloth along his hairline, her awkwardness faded, giving way to other feelings.

She touched the damp cloth to his neck. Ruefully, she remembered how she had stared at his bare neck when she first met him. How strange she had found it, for all the men in her time wore high collars and cravats, covering themselves to the chin. But she preferred this fashion. Garrett had a nice neck.

What a weird, stupid thought. Briar pulled her hand away, dipping the rag into the bowl of water and wringing it out.

She tried to dab at the other side of his face, but she had to lean out too far from the chair. So she shifted, perching beside him on the edge of the bed. There was still a hand's width of space between them, but Briar's breath caught in her throat at the sudden nearness.

As she touched the damp cloth to the side of his face, he muttered again. His eyes flickered open.

"Garrett?" Briar said softly. "Are you awake?"

A small groan escaped his lips, deep in his throat. "Bri—Briar? Is that—you're here?"

"Yes." She rested the damp cloth against his exposed collarbone. It quickly warmed against his skin, infusing it with feverish heat. "I've been—I was out. With some of the soldiers. Did they tell you?"

He blinked with some effort. His green eyes were dark with fatigue. "Isabelle—she was—she said you...had gone. To find..." He coughed. "To cure me."

"Yes," she said, striving for a nonchalant tone. "And I was successful, which I'm sure comes as a surprise to no one. So we just have to wait for Thatcher to do his part and you'll—be fine." Her words wavered. "You'll be cured." None of that was untrue, so why did she feel so raw?

She hated seeing him like this. Sick, hurting. Helpless. It was only a few nights ago that their positions had been reversed—he had been visiting at *her* bedside, making sure she was okay. Offering to help her. Promising to save her. Now he was the one that needed saving. Which she had done, so long as the transfusion worked—so why was it so painful to see him like this?

Briar closed her eyes. She knew why. It was the same reason it had been painful to stand in front of everyone and hear Garrett say, *"It's not like it meant anything."* Logically, she knew she wasn't being fair. Logically, she understood what he'd meant. It was true; when he had kissed her, breaking her curse, he hadn't even known her. It hadn't meant anything.

But it should mean something now. Shouldn't it? And his keeping it from her, that meant something. Because now, she thought they *did* mean something to each other. Now, after everything, and with the possibility of what might happen lying before them—

And that was the real rub. That was why she was being stupid. Because she was probably going to lose her soul or die, and that meant *this*—if *this* even existed—couldn't mean anything.

He couldn't mean anything. To her.

"Briar," Garrett said, and she looked down at him. He groped his hand around, and when his fingers brushed her knee, she realized he was trying to take her hand. She reached out and let him wrap his hand around hers. The creases in his palm were moist with sweat. He gazed at her through pained eyes. "I—should have told you. About...waking you. The kiss."

Stones, it was like he'd read her mind. "I—oh. Well—Garrett, it's all right," Briar said, unsure how to respond. "Like you said, it didn't mean anything, did it? I know you were just trying to wake me and you did. It doesn't matter."

"No, it—didn't mean anything." His hand tightened around hers. "But that...doesn't mean *you* don't mean anything. To—me."

"Oh. Uh..." Briar fumbled for a response. Something to make him stop. He was exhausted, and feverish, and probably delirious. He didn't know what he was saying.

"Listen, Garrett." Briar tried to slip her hand out of his, already moving to slide to her feet. "You must be very tired. Maybe you should just close your eyes and—"

"I...love Snow," he said in a weak voice.

"Erm...all right. I mean, yes," she stuttered. Churlish as it was, that hurt a little. She thought he'd been about to confess something to *her*, and now he was talking about Princess Snow. "I know."

"I miss her." His gaze slid away, his eyelids fluttering. "Every day. All the time."

Briar felt her resolve to leave softening. She bit the inside of her cheek. "I know." His grip was loosening, but instead of taking the chance to pull away, she turned her hand and laced her fingers through his.

"I don't want to forget her." His voice faded to little more than a whisper. "But sometimes...I think I am." He coughed. "There are some things...they slip away from me. Like you...with your memories." His eyes sought her face. "A memory of her...fades. And the feeling fades. I can't...remember her laugh. I try, but I...can't hear it. Anymore."

"Garrett." Briar leaned in, trying to hold his gaze. "Memories do fade. You told me that, remember? It happens to everyone. It's like..." She paused, trying to come up with the right words. "We lose little pieces of ourselves. Every day, probably. But that doesn't mean those memories never meant anything. That doesn't make your love for her any less."

She hoped she'd said the right thing, the comforting thing. Like he'd done for her. She couldn't read anything in his expression. Only discomfort and fatigue.

"I still love her," Garrett murmured. "Snow." His head lolled to the side.

Briar nodded, trying to ignore the sinking feeling in her chest.

"But then," he said, his voice fading, "there's...you."

Briar's heart lurched into her throat. She half-opened her mouth, but she had no words. Garrett's eyes fell shut, his labored breathing evening out as he slept. She sat there for several minutes, stock-still. The clock on the mantel *ticked-ticked-ticked* while Garrett breathed ragged breaths, in and out, in and out. His hand was limp in her grip.

But then...there's you.

A light knock on the door startled her. Briar looked around. Kinsley stood in the doorway, his pose reluctant, as though he wasn't sure he should come in. "Pardon the intrusion, Princess..."

"It's all right." Briar gently tugged her hand free from Garrett's and stood, setting the damp cloth on the nightstand. "What is it? Is Thatcher ready to do the transfusion?"

"No. I'm afraid it's bad news."

"What?" Anxiety pooled in Briar's stomach. "What's wrong? Was something wrong with the corpse? Will the transfusion not work? Is Garrett—"

"Pardon, Princess, but it's not to do with Prince Garrett at all," Kinsley interrupted. "Prince Demetri said I should tell you. It's the djinn." Kinsley's expression was grim. "He's gone. He escaped."

24

IRREVOCABLE

DEMETRI RUBBED ONE HAND over the other, trying to resist punching something. "How could he have escaped," he muttered. "He was under guard the whole time! And there was no way out of that room."

"He's a djinn," Briar said sourly. "Whatever that means. Who knows what kind of powers he has?"

"That's what I'm trying to find out," Isabelle said. The three of them were gathered in the library. Isabelle, seated in the cushy, scarlet armchair, wore a high-necked blouse with billowing sleeves and buttons down the front. The buttons, combined with the blouse's deep navy hue, rather gave her the look of one of Garrett's soldiers in their uniforms. She had a book open in her lap and a sizable stack teetered on the floor beside her—most of which she had already gone through. "But there's just nothing about djinn anywhere. The only thing I've been able to find was in Masters' *Creatures of the Fey*, and all it contained was a vague reference to djinn being 'creatures of illusion.' Whatever that means."

Creatures of illusion. Demetri didn't know what it meant either, but he didn't like the sound of it.

"Well, it doesn't really matter now, does it?" Briar said unexpectedly.

Demetri looked at her. She stood, arms folded tightly across her chest, on the far side of the room, in front of the large bay windows. Outside, a gray rain misted down, spraying the windows with water. The rain whispered as it ghosted down from the sky, providing a soothing backdrop to their rather *un*-soothing conversation.

"What do you mean?" Demetri gripped the table behind him, leaning against it. The djinn would never not matter. His being *free* would never not matter. Not after everything he'd put Demetri through. "That devil has wrought so much havoc on our lives, and now he's free—"

"He's been free," Briar pointed out. "All this time, until he revealed himself to us. Believe me, I don't like the idea of him out there either. But we've got bigger things to worry about right now."

"Prince Garrett will be fine," Isabelle said. Her gaze was fixed on Briar, astute and compassionate. "Thatcher said he received the transfusion with no apparent side effects. He's well on the mend."

It wasn't quite as rosy as all that. Thatcher also said the healing effects of the corpse's blood wouldn't be permanent. Garrett would need another transfusion in about three weeks and would continue to need them, unless a more effective cure could be found. Even worse, Thatcher couldn't say what kind of long-term effects Garrett might suffer from the blood transfusions.

He was going to live, but the outlook was still bleak.

"I'm not talking about Garrett." Briar shifted, standing up straight. "I'm talking about the army of corpses up north."

"Hardly an army." Isabelle put her book aside. "A rabble, maybe."

Briar opened her mouth to respond, but then she clenched her jaw. "A large rabble," she said after a moment, though Demetri was sure that was not what she'd meant to say.

"Well—" Isabelle rose from her chair, smoothing her hands over her striped skirt "—I was hoping my research would narrow down what you need to break the curse, but unfortunately, it's had the opposite effect. There are about a million different ways to break curses, and even if you had the time to try them all, some of them are near impossible." She picked up a book from the gray-wood table. "Still, I'm not giving up. We have to find something."

Demetri looked at Briar, who stared hard out the window, her eyes following a raindrop as it streaked down the glass outside. She'd been very quiet since she returned from her venture in the woods last night—and, Demetri thought, very troubled.

Demetri, Isabelle, and Briar gathered with Garrett in his room that evening. Garrett, Demetri was pleased to see, was much improved—his fever gone, his strength returning. He was still in bed, but sitting upright against the carved headboard. Isabelle and Demetri sat in beechwood chairs at his side, while Briar remained standing, hovering at the foot of the bed. She was still quiet as Demetri and Isabelle chatted with Garrett, filling him in on all the (rather awful) things he'd missed. When Isabelle mentioned Briar's foray into the woods, Briar interrupted. "There's something I need to tell you all about that."

They looked at her. "About bringing in that corpse?" Demetri asked.

"No, not that." Briar's gray eyes darted among them, as though she was afraid to settle on one for too long. "I didn't want to say anything until—" Her gaze flitted in Garrett's direction. "Anyway. When I was out in the woods—before I found the corpse—" She took a deep breath. "I saw the dark fairy."

Demetri felt like there was a line of ants crawling down his spine. "The dark fairy. You *what?*" He twisted, shrugging off the shudder.

"Yes. I spoke to her." Briar proceeded to explain what the dark fairy had said. That she'd cursed Briar for some mad revenge scheme to take Briar from the people who loved her. That she'd felt cheated of that revenge and cast the rotting curse. And that she intended to start a war between fairies and humans by using the corpse monsters to annihilate humankind.

"Well—right," Isabelle said into the silence that followed. "Army. I see."

Demetri shook his head. Just when he'd begun to think that things could not get worse. He should have known better. From now on, he resolved to expect the very worst from any situation he encountered. "Well, our best recourse is still finding a way to break the rotting curse," he said.

"The other option is military force." Garrett scratched his chin, an unhappy tilt to his mouth. "Hopefully, the rider I sent to Elstra sent word to my father, but we don't know. Even if he did, it will take time to recall enough troops to send north.

Which means what we've got here, who we've got here, is all we've got."

"I don't want to waste the lives of your father's soldiers," Briar interrupted. "And I don't think we can waste more time trying to break the curse. The dark fairy could move at any time. Which means *we* have to move now—go back to the castle. That's where she'll be."

"But move to do what?" Demetri asked.

"To kill her," Briar said. "I want to kill the dark fairy."

Demetri's heart plummeted into his stomach.

"Killing the dark fairy means sacrificing your soul," Garrett reminded her.

For the first time since they'd stepped into his room, Briar looked Garrett straight in the eye. "Yes. I know."

Something black and jagged clawed up Demetri's chest. He should have realized when he said that killing the fairy was no longer an option. The look in Briar's eyes then, as though she'd been thinking through something. This was it.

He remembered what she'd said. *I have to be the one to fix it—no matter the cost.*

"You can't be serious," Demetri said. "It's madness."

"What it is, Demetri, is our only option."

"There's got to be something else we can try," Garrett protested.

Isabelle nodded. "I'm sure if we check the library, I can—"

"*No,*" Briar snapped. She came around behind Demetri and Isabelle so they had to turn in their chairs to look at her. "Our best option is to find a way to cure the corpses. And I'm not saying that because I'm one of them," she added. "I'm saying it because they're my people. My kingdom. I owe it to them to save them."

Garrett clasped his hands before him. He looked remarkably calm, considering their topic of conversation. "Losing your soul—I'm not even sure what that *means*. The queen said you'd care about nothing. She said you'd have nothing to tether you to the world, no—no—"

"No meaning to your life." Demetri's voice was hollow. "That's what she said."

Briar looked at them each in turn, as though considering. She looked wan in the hazy daylight cast through the frosted window, but somehow her ghost-like visage added strength to her. She said, "Look, I appreciate your concerns. But let me be clear. This is not a thing I'm discussing. This is no one's call but mine. It's my kingdom, and it's my curse, and I would be the one to bear the consequences, if I chose to do so. Well, I'm choosing. This is it. I know where the dark fairy is. She told me to come find her, and that's what I'm going to do."

She left the room, her fading footsteps echoing in the corridor outside.

The silence she left in her wake was dreadful. The three of them sat there, Briar's final words hanging in the air.

"So," Garrett said, breaking the quiet, "we are going to help her, right?"

Demetri managed to say, "Of course."

"Good." Isabelle straightened, tugging at her skirt. "Because if you weren't going to, I was going to have to kick you both out of my house. Princes or not."

When Briar heard they'd decided to help her, she agreed to wait another day for Garrett's condition to improve. Demetri pointed out they still had no idea how to kill a fairy, but Briar reminded him there were plenty of fairies in the same woods they were traveling through. Demetri didn't think those fairies would be keen to tell anyone how to kill them, but Briar seemed confident they would.

Garrett concerned himself with other problems. As Demetri watched him pace around his room, he said, "Assuming this fairy is telling the truth about going to the castle—"

"What if she's not?" Demetri interrupted. "I mean, why tell us where to find her anyway? And we know there are corpses all over the kingdom, not just at the castle."

"Yes," Garrett mused. "But the castle probably has the largest concentration. It's where I would start—you know, if I was an evil fairy who wanted to use a kingdom of rotting people to do my bidding. There aren't any large cities in the Mountain Kingdom, so the rest of the corpses are probably spread out everywhere. She can gather up stragglers as she heads south."

"And," Demetri muttered, "she's probably just arrogant enough to believe we have no chance of stopping her." He wasn't sure that was arrogance though. It might just be the truth.

"Briar says she has a secret way to get us into the castle, so we don't have to go straight through the front courtyard." Garrett paused, looking thoughtful. "Once we're in, there will still be a horde of corpses to deal with."

"We'll need to distract them," said Demetri. "Of course, the whole idea is to save as many of them as possible, so we don't just want to blow them up like we did before."

Garrett's eyes alighted. "No, we don't want to blow them up. Even if we did, we'd need more grenades than we have time to get. What we want to do is confine them somewhere. So Briar has time to do what she needs to."

They left the manor early the next day. It was a cool, wet morning, but the sun was bright as it crested the horizon. They gathered in the grove of elms outside the house, the trees' brittle, dying leaves providing scant shade.

Isabelle was leaving too, but not with them, much to her chagrin. "I admit that a battle against corpses is not really my cup of tea," she said, "but I could help."

"And we need your help, Belle." Garrett cupped her shoulder in his hand. "But elsewhere. I need to make sure my father is prepared if we fail here. I need *you* to make sure that telegram has gone through, and I need you to go to the capital yourself. Speak to my father. He likes you, and he'll believe you if you say this threat is real." Garrett smiled. "He finds you a much more sensible person than me."

So Isabelle set out west on horseback, accompanied by two of Garrett's soldiers. The rest of them headed north. There were only seventeen of them, though they hoped to meet up with the rest of Garrett's company in a few days—they would be coming back from the train station by now.

Autumn was well upon them, the leaves changing from green to crimson reds and tawny golds, falling from the trees. The days turned cold and dry, scenting the air with a crisp fragrance, like the first bite of an apple.

The past few days had been so filled with anxiety and shocking discoveries that the two weeks' ride north was a welcome respite at first. Demetri hadn't quite processed everything—the djinn, Garrett's near-fatal illness, Briar's venture into the woods, and her decision to kill a fairy. After about three days, though, Demetri began to resent all the time he had to dwell on things.

The arrival of the djinn and everything he'd revealed was something Demetri wanted to forget. He was frustrated he'd never received a satisfactory answer about why Dev set him free, but a larger part of him longed to let it go. If he could figure out how. He was beginning to think that if he ever wanted to find a way to free himself from that darkness, that would be the first step.

Some part of him still held the naïve belief that if he could pretend it hadn't happened, then he could go about his life like nothing had changed. As though he was still the same person he'd been eighty-two years ago. But he had a growing sense of how wrong that was. That was not the way the world worked, and no matter how he wished it, things could never go back to the way they were. The life he thought to live with Briar was gone, and it wasn't coming back.

Besides, he'd learned the danger of wishes.

Briar largely avoided him during this time, but one morning, as their horses wove a path through a close-knit stand of beech trees, she brought her horse up beside his. It was a gloomy morning, the sky overcast and the air dense and hazy. It was the kind of morning that dampened Demetri's spirits, and for that reason, he did not look at Briar as she came up beside him.

"You're still not okay with this," she said, "are you?"

It was such a stupid question that Demetri had no idea how to answer. He finally said, his eyes fixed ahead, "Do you want me to be?

Her voice was infuriatingly calm. "I'd like to know you accept it, at least."

"I'm here, aren't I?" he said dully.

"I have to do this, Demetri. It's the only option."

"It is *not* the only option." Demetri shot her a look out of the corner of his eye. "We could still wait for reinforcements from Garrett's father—"

"Bringing in soldiers just means letting the dark fairy win." Briar turned her head, surveying the woods. "It means starting the war she wants, pitting soldiers against corpses. I can't let that happen."

"Is that what this is about? Winning?"

"You know what it's about, Demetri." She sounded tired and looked it too, her eyes creasing at the corners, her mouth curving downward. "I told you, remember? Those people are my responsibility. It's not just about stopping them from killing everyone. It's about saving them too."

"And *I* told you." Demetri stared at her, willing her to turn and look him in the eye. As though the weight of his gaze could convince her. "You don't have to do this on your own. We can find a way to save you too, Briar."

"We are saving me. From becoming a monster." She shifted the reigns in her hands, the gesture restless. "Demetri, everyone else has made my decisions for me my whole life. My parents—" She faltered. "You're the only one who ever cared what *I* wanted. You're the only person who gave me a chance. Don't stop that now."

"I am *trying* to give you a chance." Demetri leaned forward in his saddle. "*I'm* not the one acting like your parents, Briar. *You* are."

Briar looked around at him, startled. "What?"

"This decision you've made," he said. "It's because you're afraid, isn't it? You said it yourself—you're afraid of becoming a monster. A *mindless* monster. You're so afraid of losing your mind that you can't see losing your soul could be so much worse. Briar, it could turn you into a monster of a different kind." His voice was earnest, rising in volume, trying to make her understand. "Think about your parents. Your whole life, they lived with you in the castle, but they kept themselves apart. That's what the rest of your life will be like if you do this, Briar."

Briar's gaze was stubborn, but she was still listening. "I don't follow."

"You heard what Garrett said." He wondered if mentioning Garrett would make her reconsider. "Without a soul, you won't care about anything. You won't *love* anyone. That's worse than losing your mind, isn't it?"

"Is it?" The uncomprehending on Briar's face was terrifying. Not the uncomprehending of a mindless monster, not the lack of recognition he'd seen before. This was a lack of comprehending around this one, basic concept—life without love. "I don't know if that's true, Demetri. I don't know who I *am* without my mind. But love..." Her voice turned sad. Sad but so, so *resolved.* "It's like you said, Demetri. I've lived without love for most of my life. I think I can manage."

She tugged at her reigns, urging her horse ahead. Demetri watched as she disappeared into the ranks of soldiers.

He did not think she'd said it to be cruel. But it hurt all the same.

25

BRINK

G ARRETT SUSPECTED ANY FAIRIES they encountered on the way to Briar's castle weren't going to be very helpful, in spite of Briar's insistence to the contrary. And his suspicions proved well warranted. What was odd about it, though, was Briar's utter lack of concern.

They made good time on their journey north. They met up with the rest of Garrett's company a couple of days south of the train station. They reached the base of the sloping mountains a week later, and set up camp in the woods to make preparations—and to speak with the fairies.

But none of the fairies who turned up to speak with them would give them information about how to kill one of them. And though Briar pleaded and cajoled, though she spat in their faces and stomped her feet at them, Garrett had the distinct impression she wasn't really disappointed. At first, he thought she was secretly relieved she wouldn't have to go through with killing the fairy. But the more he observed her annoyance with the fairies, the more it seemed like an *act*. And as he continued to observe, he noticed other things about her—an anticipatory gleam in her eyes when the fairies departed, a smug aloofness when Demetri tried to tell her "I-told-you-so."

It was like she had expected all along that the fairies would not help. It was like she had *planned* for it.

They remained camped in the woods, under the cover of soaring fir trees and sparsely green pines. The air was brisk and laden with the pine's spicy fragrance as the light of the dying sun faded from the sky. Garrett, having set up a thorough perimeter around their camp, went to make a quick round of it after dinner. Halfway through, he ran into Briar.

"Were you making the rounds too?" Garrett asked with a straight face.

"No." Briar's tone was dispassionate. "I was looking for a bedtime snack. A mouse, maybe a small squirrel."

"Are you...being serious?"

"Wouldn't you like to know?" She quirked a smile. "I just wanted to stretch my legs. See if any inspiration about how to kill a fairy would strike."

"Ah."

They walked in companionable silence. Briar tugged a spare thread on her spencer, her gaze distant. Garrett eyed Briar, trying to gauge if she really was scouting for forest critters to eat. Nearby, the off-duty soldiers nattered and chuckled and banged pots and pans as they cleaned up after dinner.

Then Garrett said, "What will you do? If we don't find out how to kill the dark fairy, I mean."

Briar's reply was flippant. "I could always wish her dead. Then maybe that djinn, wherever he's got to, will do it for us after all."

Garrett didn't respond, though her indifferent tone furthered his suspicions about her. The truth was, even though he knew the cost—even though he understood what the dark fairy was, and what would happen if she had her way—he still didn't want Briar to go through with this. When she'd first announced her intentions, Garrett had felt like he'd fallen down a deep, narrow abyss. And even now when he thought about what was going to happen, he felt like he was still falling, the sky growing smaller and smaller above him.

He supposed he would know what it felt like to hit the ground once it was over and done, once the dark fairy was gone. He didn't want to know.

He said, "Are you afraid at all? I don't mean by the possibility you might not be able to kill her—but by what's going to happen if you do?"

Briar kicked a fallen pine cone. "I do wish—" She glowered. "I am never going to use that word again." She paused, curling and uncurling her fingers into a fist. "I would love for there to be another way to do this. If I could stop her without losing my soul. But there's not. And we're out of time. So this is what I do." She looked at him sidelong. "You haven't tried to talk me out of it."

Garrett shrugged, hoping the gesture belied the crushing feeling in his chest. "It's not really my place to talk you out of anything." And that was the truth of it, no matter how it hurt. Whatever Briar meant to him, she had never been his to lose. Wallowing in his own despair was selfish.

"Maybe not." Briar stopped and stood still. Her voice was odd, hesitant and wary. "But I wouldn't blame you if you tried."

Garrett turned to her, his hands clasped behind his back. "If you don't really want to do this, then I would turn around right now and send for my father's reinforcements." He forced himself to look her in the eye. He forced himself to mean what he said, even though he could not suppress the dispirited note in his voice. "But I think you've made your peace with this and if that's so, then I understand. I understand having a duty to your kingdom. Like you said—" He tried for a smile "—it's what we do."

And he meant that. As much as it hurt, it was her choice. And he had no right to take it from her.

Briar's eyes gleamed with a wonderful ferocity. "There's another reason I want to break the curse, you know."

"What's that?"

"To cure you." She tugged at the fingers on her left hand. The nervous gesture was at odds with the determination on her face. "If I break the curse, then the corpses will turn back to people. There won't be any such thing as a corpse creature, and the venom they carry will cease to exist too. So maybe you'll be cured."

Garrett had tried not to think much on his wound, now that he was better. He'd had plenty of other worries and thoughts to distract him. But deep down, it *did* worry him.

As often as he chased death, he found he did not want to die. Not now.

Something *snapped* in the foliage beside them. They both jumped.

"Did you hear that?" Briar whispered.

"No," Garrett shot back. "I just jumped a foot in the air for fun."

"I think it came from over there." Briar peered into a thick, tangled cluster of ivy.

Garrett placed a hand on the pistol at his waist.

"Wait," Briar said to him.

A snatch of something bobbed out from the ivy. Something *orange*.

Briar took a wary step forward. She raised her voice and said, "It's all right. We're not going to hurt you. It's me—Princess Briar. Do you remember me?"

At first, only silence met her words. Then a small, hunched figure stepped out of the darkness—a fairy. A fairy Garrett had seen before. His tattered tunic and breeches were matted with leaves and dirt, and the bit of his hair that wasn't black with grime was the color of squash.

Also, he had no wings.

"There's only one way to kill a fairy," Jas said, "and it isn't easy."

"Why are you willing to tell us?" Garrett asked. "The others said no fairy would ever reveal how to kill you."

"How to kill *me* is as easy as killing any of you," the fairy Jas said. "I'm mortal now."

Garrett, Demetri, and Briar were gathered outside Briar's tent. An old-fashioned oil lamp lit their space; the fairy was adverse to anything brighter. Briar sat cross-legged on the ground, her face illuminated in the lamp's orange halo. The fairy stood facing her.

"You're mortal because of the dark fairy," Briar recalled. "That's why you're willing to tell us. Because she took your wings."

Garrett leaned against the bristly trunk of a pine tree. He eyed Briar appraisingly. The certainty in her voice confirmed what he had suspected since the wingless fairy turned up—she had been counting on him. That was why she asked so many fairies, even once it was clear none of them would share their secret—she wanted to be sure word of their intent reached Jas.

"Why couldn't we do that?" Demetri sat up straight from his perch on a mossy log. "I don't mean to be insensitive, but—what the dark fairy did, taking your wings. Couldn't we do that to her? Then she'd be mortal, and—would the person who killed her still lose their soul?"

Jas looked as though he'd suggested the sun rose in the west. "No, you wouldn't lose your soul. But no human can take the wings of a fairy. It's not possible. I couldn't either, not anymore. I'm mortal, you're all mortal. Only another fairy could do it, or, well—"

"A djinn?" Garrett filled in.

The fairy looked startled. "Yes. So unless you happen to know one of them, it's not possible."

Garrett, Demetri, and Briar exchanged vexed glances. "Well, he was never going to do it anyway," Garrett muttered.

"So that brings us back to the original plan." Briar placed her hands on her knees. Garrett had to give her credit; she didn't sound the slightest bit disappointed. "Killing her as she is. Which we don't know how to do." She tilted her head, eyeing the fairy. "Unless you tell us."

Jas eyed her right back, his expression wary and reluctant. Then he reached inside his patched, tatty tunic and brought out a white, wooden stake. It was about six inches long, knobby along its sides and pointed at its tip. When Briar only stared at it, the fairy stretched his arm towards her, nodding.

"What is this?" Briar took it from him.

"A splinter from her tree. See how it's pale like her." Jas's voice was scornful. "All fairies are born of a tree. It is forever tied to us. It lives so long as we do." He took a deep breath. "The only way to kill a fairy is to use a splinter from their own tree. You must stab her with it."

"All right." Briar eyed the stake, turning it from one end to the other. "Sounds easy enough."

"You can never regain your soul." Jas's black eyes were unfathomable in the sparse lamplight. "You know that."

"Yes." Briar climbed to her feet. "So everyone keeps telling me." Without a word of thanks to the fairy, she walked into her tent.

Demetri escorted Jas to the edge of their camp. Then the two princes gathered outside Garrett's tent with some of the soldiers to discuss strategy.

"All right." Demetri drew a hasty blueprint of the castle in the dirt. "Briar thinks the dark fairy will be in the western tower, where she slept all those years—that's what the fairy said. If she has the corpses protecting her, then I imagine many of them will be in the throne room."

"Aden and Alec, you'll be most in need of secrecy." Garrett looked between the twins. "If you're discovered, the whole plan is out the window. You acquired all the necessary supplies from the outpost, correct?"

"It's all in hand, sire," Aden assured him.

"Well in hand." Alec grinned.

"Good." Garrett rocked back on his heels. "Then it'll be my job to ensure we have the corpses' attentions in that throne room."

"Remind me again why *your* job is the craziest, most dangerous of all?" Demetri protested.

Garrett gave him an innocent look. "Crazy? I'm hurt."

Demetri looked at gruff Iain. "You've known him since he was a boy. Can't you ever convince him not to go haranguing off on these dangerous plans?"

"Never works, Highness," Iain said. "Best to just go along and protect him as we can."

"That's the spirit," Garrett enthused. For the first time since they'd begun this venture, he was beginning to feel like his old self again. He felt more sure of who he was and what he was than he had in a long time.

He wondered if Briar had anything to do with that.

"Lastly, remember we're trying to spare as many of these corpses as possible," Garrett concluded. "Don't spare one if it means your life, because they will be trying to kill and eat us. Or just eat us. Whatever. The point is, don't go for the heads if you don't have to. If Briar breaks the curse, it shouldn't matter how we've harmed them so long as they aren't *dead* dead. They'll be cured and restored to normal."

Everyone headed off to their respective tents, but Demetri lingered as the soldiers left.

"Listen," he said to Garrett. He scuffed the toe of his boot in the dirt. "What I said about you having the most dangerous task—I know you do things like this all the time and you can take care of yourself. But I'm asking you. Please be careful. Don't take any unnecessary risks."

Garrett grinned. "Demetri, I'm touched."

"I'm not asking for me." Demetri met his gaze. "I'm asking for Briar."

Garrett felt the grin slip off his face. "For Briar? What do you mean?"

Demetri hesitated. "Look, anything could happen out there tomorrow. To any of us, myself included."

"Well, *if* something were to happen to you, of course I'll look after her." Garrett clapped a hand on Demetri's shoulder. "But you'll be fine. I know you will."

"Even if I am—" Demetri squinted into the blazing campfire nearby "—she'll need *you*, Garrett. More than she'll need me. Especially if she succeeds and loses her soul. If that happens, she'll need someone to remind her what it means to feel. So you have to be careful. You have to survive this."

Garrett stared at him, wondering what exactly his friend was saying.

"Garrett," Demetri said. "I know you care about her."

Garrett dropped his hand from Demetri's shoulder. It hung awkwardly at his side. "Well, of course I care about her. After all we've been through—"

"Look, I'm not telling you what to do with your life." Demetri ran a hand through his floppy hair. "And I know things are complicated for you because of Snow. But I just need to know that—whatever happens to me—you'll be there for her."

"I can't believe this." Garrett's face was warmer than he liked. "What are you saying?"

"All I'm saying is don't die," Demetri said. "Because, Garrett—she cares about you too."

The plan was to be up at dawn the next morning. It would take them the day and part of the night to climb up the mountain. But Garrett was restless, slipping in and out of sleep. He woke once and sat straight up in his cot, thinking it must be morning. After a foggy moment, he realized it was still dark out.

That's when he realized what woke him. A noise outside.

In an instant, Garrett was on his feet. He registered the cold weight in his hand before he realized he'd grabbed a pistol. He peeked his head out the tent flap, the barrel of his gun preceding him.

Briar was outside, sitting on the ground, her legs sprawled on either side of her. Her head was bent forward as she traced something in the dirt, her hair a pale sheet in front of her face.

"Oh." Garrett relaxed. "It's only you."

Briar looked around at him.

"What are you doing?" he asked. He slipped into his boots, then stepped out to join her. "Catching a little midnight snack? Field mouse? Squirrel?"

Briar wiped a hand through the dirt, obliterating whatever she'd traced there. "Ha. Ha. It's well past midnight." She folded one leg towards her. "Near dawn, in fact."

She was right; the sky had turned the dark violet of pre-dawn. A glacial mist was beginning to coalesce around them, forming droplets of dew that clung to every pine needle, every shrub leaf, even the sides of their tents.

Briar looked up at him as he came to stand over her. She wore a long, wool overcoat and her slender brown boots. "I was just sketching. I couldn't sleep."

She pulled her other leg towards her and Garrett caught a glimpse of her bare knee. He realized she wore only her short nightdress beneath her coat.

He cleared his throat and said, "Me either. Obviously."

They looked at each other. A wood thrush trilled a long, delighted song, welcoming the early morning.

"Well." Briar tucked her hair behind her ear. "I should probably—"

"Briar," Garrett said, the words coming out before he could stop them, "I should have told you. About waking you. About the kiss."

Briar gave him the strangest look. Her forehead wrinkled, but the glint in her eyes was bated, as though she knew what he meant to say.

"I'm sorry, I know that came out of nowhere," he hastened. "It's just, tomorrow—or today, I guess—and I wanted to apologize, in case we don't—"

"No, it's just—" Briar climbed to her feet. "You already said that. You already apologized."

Garrett was baffled.

"While you were ill." She stood, brushing pine needles from her coat. "I sat with you for a while. We talked. You don't remember?"

"No." Garrett felt his cheeks warming. He vaguely remembered different visitors, but he didn't remember speaking with Briar. His mind whirled with all sorts of embarrassing things he might have said. "I, uh...apologized?"

"You said what you said just now." Her gaze was too direct, too significant. "You said you should have told me."

Garrett raised a hand to the back of his neck. "What else did I say?"

"Well." She folded her arms. He had the distinct impression she was considering what or how much to tell him. "Mostly you talked about Snow."

His heart flipped. He had not expected that. "About Snow?"

"You were afraid you might be forgetting her. I tried to—well. I tried to say the right thing."

"You always say the right thing," he said without thinking.

Briar's lips parted with surprise. It was an expression she showed so rarely that Garrett stared back at her. His gaze was drawn to the curve of her mouth, the shape of her top lip.

When he realized what he was doing, he looked away. He lifted his gaze to the sky, to the stars. Their dazzling light had begun to fade as the sun prepared to rise, but they were no less beautiful for it. Beautiful and terrible. Terrible in their longevity, their eternity. They seemed to mock him.

"Garrett?"

Garrett dropped his gaze. He flinched when he realized how close Briar stood. It was impossible not to notice what the rotting curse had done to her, the little flaws in her face. The dark circles beneath her eyes. The place at her hairline, discolored and waxy, where her skull was a little dented in.

He cherished every flaw.

"Are you all right?" she asked in a low voice.

No, he was not all right. "Yes, I, uh..." Garrett breathed in. She was so close. He couldn't decide if he wanted to step back or not. "I was just thinking about what you said. Or what I said, I guess. About Snow." He ran a shaky hand through his hair. "I do worry

I'm forgetting her sometimes. It's a terrible thing, but. Maybe it's just a part of it."

"A part of what?"

Finding you. Feeling for you. He reminded himself what was going to happen, what she was going to do, but it didn't help. It only intensified the harrowing, glorious ache in his chest. "Moving on."

Her gray eyes locked on his face. "Do you want to move on?"

Garrett considered. He thought of what the queen said, about replacing one sleeping princess with another. Snow with Briar. He knew it wasn't that simple, but he couldn't help but consider the symmetry. What were the odds, really, that he would be drawn into a quest for another sleeping princess—and that this time, he would wake her?

It probably meant nothing. After all, if Briar succeeded in killing the dark fairy, then she would lose any ability to feel or love. But before Snow had died—before she was taken from him—Garrett had always seen possibility where others saw none, and he was beginning to remember what that felt like. And that gave him hope—no, it was more definite than hope—a sense, really—that somehow, they would all come out of this whole.

"Yes. I want to move on." He was surprised how easy it was to get the words out. How true they were. "If you had asked me that a month ago, I don't know I could have said that. But yes. I'm not sure how—but I do want to." He looked her straight in the eye. "Now, I do."

Her voice was grave. "Now?"

"Yes." Garrett swallowed past the lump in his throat. "Yes, now."

26

THORNY

Demetri peered into the darkness, trying to make out the castle in the distance. He, Briar, and most of the soldiers were outside the north side of the castle village, huddled beneath a long, broken wall. Garrett and some others had gone to scout ahead. It took them the day and part of the night to get up the mountain, and now they waited beneath a heavy, orange midnight moon.

Beside Demetri, Briar fiddled with the white stake, running her fingers over its gnarled knobs. She wore a pretty new blouse, trimmed with lace on the sleeves and the bodice. It was a strange choice for battle, but the leather harness vest she wore over it was more practical. Still, even with the lace, she was a fearsome sight, bruised and dented and spectral.

"Are you afraid?" Demetri asked.

Briar glanced at him ruefully.

"I'm just asking." Demetri held up his hands.

"You're not the only one," Briar said softly. She gazed at the gouges their shoes made in the dirt. "Maybe a little. I just wish—I mean, it would have been *nice* to find another way to do this. When we met Prence and the other fairies in the woods, I told Prence they should have killed the dark fairy a long time ago. Now, if I could find a way to stop her that didn't involve killing her, I would. Not because of the consequences—just because of what it means."

"I don't understand."

Briar pursed her lips. "When I saw the dark fairy in the woods, she said I was like her. A monster. And I can't help but feel that by doing this—by murdering her—I'm proving her right."

"You're not a monster, Briar," Demetri protested.

Briar's lips lifted, a ghost of a smile. "I told the dark fairy that." The smile vanished. "And she said 'not yet.' It keeps coming back to that, Demetri. To killing. That corpse I hunted down in the woods—I didn't want to kill him either. I don't regret it. Garrett would have died otherwise, and I'd do it again to save him. But I didn't like it. Because he was more than just a corpse. He was a person, *my* person. Part of my kingdom."

"But the dark fairy was wrong, Briar, don't you see that?" Demetri pushed. "You aren't anything like her. That corpse in the woods—you said it yourself. You did that to save Garrett. Just like you're doing this to save your people. The dark fairy—" Demetri stared into the darkness. "Everything she's done comes from a place of hatred. And that's what makes her a monster."

"So the ends justify the means?"

"That's not what I—"

"I know, Demetri." Briar heaved a sigh. "I know. I just think I should be better than this. You're saying I'm not like her because of where I'm coming from. But I'm not sure what difference it makes."

Demetri said, "It makes all the difference in the world. As much as having a soul does."

He didn't quite mean to say that last bit. The last thing he wanted was to start another argument here, on the verge of battle.

"Demetri…" The look on Briar's face was curiously vulnerable. Far from the stubborn resolve she'd displayed the last time they had this conversation. "I want you to know—and it doesn't change anything, because I still have to do this—but I understand. What you were trying to tell me. And I…" She took a deep, jittery breath. "I do *care*, you know. About losing my soul. I don't want it to happen. I couldn't admit that before, I think, because I was afraid I would change my mind—and I can't change my mind."

"But you can admit it now?"

"It's just, last night—or this morning or, well—I was talking to Garrett and…" She sucked in her cheeks, as though biting something back. Her voice was so small, he could barely hear her. "I know what I'm giving up. I think I made you feel like it didn't matter. But I know it does." She smiled a smile so bleak, it looked terrible on her face. "But these are the only choices I have. Doom my kingdom and myself to a short life as mindless monsters. Or give up some part of me to save them all. And at least with the latter choice, somebody gets saved."

Demetri looked at her. She was so strange in this moment, such an odd mix of fragile and determined, fierce but wretched. And she didn't deserve this fate. She should have been bright and peculiar, everything that Briar really was, with a whole world open before her, full of possibilities.

He wanted that for her.

"Just promise me," she said, her tone considerably lighter, "that if losing my soul turns me into a monster like you said, you'll lock me up somewhere."

"Don't even joke."

"I think this is rather the time for joking, don't you?"

"With any luck, I won't have to lock you up."

"What makes you say that?"

Demetri affected a blasé tone. "There's no telling what will happen in there, is all."

When Garrett returned, he looked grim. "Looks like the way is clear of corpses or anything else," he said, "and our way in should work, barrier and all."

Demetri said, "What is the barrier, anyway?"

Garrett looked half-resigned, half-incredulous. "You have to see it."

They scurried up the hill towards the castle. The night was frigid, an early precursor of the winter to come, and the ground was packed with cold, clumpy mud that stuck to their boots. They came around the curve in the land over the crest of a small ridge. Garrett reached the top first. In the bronze light of the moon, he pointed. "Look there."

Demetri peered across the ridge.

The castle was laid out before them. The gray-blue spires of the fortress bled into the dark night sky, but the white towers, though marred with grime, stood out strikingly. The walls below were obscured, for they were entirely surrounded by the barrier.

A thick, tangled growth of black vines filled with thorns.

"Thorns?" Briar barked the word. "*That's* what the fairies put up as a barrier? *That's* keeping the corpses in?"

"I just wonder if they were trying to be funny," said Garrett.

Briar and Demetri frowned at him.

"You know, brier thorns?" he said with a straight face. "*Briar?* Get it?"

"I don't think the fairies have that sort of humor," said Demetri. "Or any humor, really."

"Never mind that," Briar said crossly. "How are *thorns* doing anything at all? We corpses don't bleed much, after all."

"There's got to be something else to them," Garrett mused. "Maybe the thorns are poisonous to the corpses."

"Let's hope they're only poisonous to the corpses," Demetri muttered.

"With any luck, we won't have to worry about them at all," Briar said bracingly. "Our way in is through here—beneath the thorns."

She led them down the ridge, following a rocky path that ended at a large, cylindrical opening in the mountain, where a steel pipe was built into the land. A mucky stream of water trickled out of this tunnel, giving off a faintly noxious odor.

"Sewage tunnel." Demetri sighed. "Wonderful."

"I never actually used this in or out of the castle," Briar admitted, "but I considered it. I studied the blueprints several times. This should lead us straight into the dungeons, I believe."

"Isn't it a bit of a security breach to have a tunnel leading from the dungeons outside the castle?" Garrett pointed out.

"Well, it doesn't lead *right* into the dungeons—but yes, it does seem a bit dodgy," Briar conceded.

They started through the tunnel, winding up their gear-bulb lanterns to light the way. The tunnel was large enough that only the tallest of them had to crouch a little, and wide enough to walk two people across. Though no one living had used the castle in years, the tunnel still smelled rank, and the water they tramped through was leaf-strewn and slimy.

"I'm never going to feel clean again," Demetri muttered.

Briar looked around with an amused expression. She jerked her head, indicating he join her at the front. He did so, as Kinsley fell back to give them some privacy.

"I was thinking about something," Briar said. She ducked her head to avoid a large pipe, and Demetri followed suit.

"More bad news?" he asked, resigned. "It's more bad news, isn't it."

"Since when are you such a pessimist?"

"It's a new thing I'm trying."

Briar shot him a droll look. Behind them, Kinsley's gear-bulb lantern gave off a small nimbus of light, illuminating her expression in snatches. "I was thinking about what Isabelle found, that reference to djinn being 'creatures of illusion.'"

"Whatever that means."

"Yes, well. Remember when Dev first turned up at Isabelle's, he was wearing one of the soldier's uniforms?"

"Ye-es."

"Well, that's what I was thinking about," Briar said. "What if djinn are creatures of illusion because they can make people see what they want? Which would mean they would have the power to disguise themselves. Which would mean, maybe, that he was actually—well—"

Comprehension dawned on Demetri with a good helping of dread. "You think he was masquerading as one of the soldiers?"

"I think it could be possible."

Demetri made a small sound in the back of his throat. It came out very like a whimper.

"I know." Briar's voice was glum. "As though we didn't have enough problems."

"Well, it couldn't have been anyone at the manor with us," Demetri reasoned. "Garrett would have noticed someone missing while we had him captive. But the men we left with the train—" He shook his head. "But they're all here now. Which means—"

"Yes." Briar tossed a glance over her shoulder. "He could be here. With us."

She didn't sound concerned, but the consternation on her face matched Demetri's feelings.

"Well, that's good to know." Demetri said lightly. "There's probably a half-crazed djinn coming along this mad venture with us. Lovely."

"Just thought I'd mention it."

"I wonder—" Demetri lowered his voice "—there *was* something weird. Something Dev said. He said he was wrong about me being the key to waking you, and that it was nice of me not to hold that against Garrett."

"*Did* you hold it against him?"

"No, of course not. That's my point."

"I don't understand."

"Because he knew that—that I wasn't upset with Garrett for kissing you. He knew that I knew."

"You knew?" Briar turned an accusatory look on him. "You knew and didn't tell me?"

Demetri coughed. "Yes, well—anyway. When Garrett told me, we were alone. And I never mentioned it to anyone. Not only that, but what the djinn said—that it was nice of me *not to hold it against him*. Those were my exact words to Garrett when he told me—that I didn't hold it against him."

"But you say you were alone." Briar frowned.

"Well—Garrett told me in the village while we were tending to Spencer. Spencer was injured of course, and I thought he was passed out cold, but he was the only other one in the room."

"So you think it could be Spencer?"

"Maybe. But I don't know for sure, and what can we do about it now, anyway?"

"Not much." Briar pressed her lips together. "Not much at all."

They spent half an hour creeping through the sewage tunnel before its oppressive, heavy stench began to lighten, letting in a trickle of fresh air. But Briar slowed as they approached the tunnel's end. "Hang on," she said. "Something isn't right."

"What do you mean?" Kinsley asked. "Do you hear something? Corpses?"

"No, it's—at the end, up ahead. I don't think we're coming out into the dungeons." She picked up her pace, trotting forward. "I think it's..."

Her voice and clanking footsteps faded as her form vanished into the darkness. Demetri and Kinsley exchanged a glance.

"I hate when she does that," Demetri said.

The two of them picked up speed to go after her. Demetri listened, but all he heard was the *plink-plink* of water dripping in the tunnel.

"Briar?" Demetri called.

She came into view at the end of the tunnel. The relief that flooded through him was short-lived. As he joined her, peering out, he realized why she'd run ahead. This was the end of the tunnel—but not the natural end. He could see most of the metal had rusted away in fragments, leaving a large, gaping fissure.

Here, about fifty feet below the base of the castle. Outside.

Demetri stared at the way up. The tunnel clearly should have continued up the side of the cliff that the castle was perched on. But it had broken off and fallen away, leaving a very steep trail up the cliff.

But it wasn't only the steep path that worried him. It was that they were outside, exposed. The thick, black thorns clustered around their only way up. Far too close for comfort. "Well," Demetri said, "we may find out if those thorns are poisonous after all."

"I can't do this," Garrett muttered. "I—can't—do this."

"You're already doing it," Briar told him, her voice firm but not unkind. "We're halfway there. If you stop now, you'll just have to hang here forever, stuck on the cliff side surrounded by poisonous thorns and a long, long drop below you."

"Are you trying to be comforting?"

"No, I'm trying to get you moving again."

Demetri adjusted his grip, peering up at the pair of them. They were halfway up the pitted bluff, using what rope they had to scale the steep, craggy path. The snarl of thorns encroached on either side of them. They had already discovered, to the dismay and death of Garrett's soldier Kelley, that the thorns were indeed poisonous. The smallest scratch on Kelley's arm left him screaming and frothing at the mouth, until he lost his grip and plummeted down that long drop. The best that could be said was it was quick—he was probably dead before he hit the ground.

Garrett was having a hard time of it. Apparently, he was afraid of heights. They'd stopped a few times already, when his fear got the best of him.

Briar, just above Garrett, spoke to him, too quietly for Demetri to hear. Whatever she said did the trick, for they were moving again a minute later, slowly but surely. Gales of wintry wind blasted them as they climbed, whipping their hair, catching their clothes. Demetri's eyes watered beneath its onslaught.

The way up ended at a rust-encrusted iron grate at the base of the castle. Briar pulled through it and emerged a few seconds later to pull Garrett through. When Demetri followed after, he found Garrett on his knees, as though he was resisting the urge to kiss the dank floor. They got him up and moved down the dark, dripping tunnel so the soldiers could climb in as well. As they all joined them, Garrett spread a glare among his company. "If any of you breathe a word of this—"

"No offense, sire," Dom said, his eyes twinkling, "but did you really think we didn't know you were afraid of heights?"

Once everyone was in, they started down the tunnel, boots tramping through water puddled across the concave, steel floor. They were beneath the castle now. A sober hush descended as they made their way in the shadowy gloom, all of them silent, save for their short breaths reverberating across the corroded pipes.

The sewer appeared to dead-end until the glaring light of the lanterns revealed a short ladder built into the wall, leading to a round door. Briar went up first and twisted the door open using a wheel in the center of it. The hefty steel door opened slowly, squeaking with old age. Briar started through, waving for them to follow.

Through the door, they found themselves in a dark corner of the dungeons, which were so like the sewage tunnels—dark, damp, and scented with mildew—that Demetri was rather glad he had never been in there before. Empty cells lined the corridors, most of the doors scarlet with rust and standing ajar. Demetri wondered if there had been anyone in here when the sleeping curse fell. If there had been, he hoped they were long gone by now.

The silence was promising enough.

They headed through the maze of cells and started up a narrow, rough-hewn staircase. The staircase emerged onto the first floor of the castle near the southern end.

Demetri followed Kinsley and Briar into the open corridor, where the floor beneath their feet changed from rough stone to slick marble. Aden and Alec were right behind him, heavy canvas packs on their backs with their necessary supplies.

"Go that way." Briar pointed down the corridor. "You remember my instructions, how to get to the kitchens? And from there?"

"Got it, Your Highness." Alec grinned and nudged his brother. "C'mon, let's go." They disappeared around the corner as

Garrett and the others came up. Once everyone was out of the dungeons, Briar led them up another stairwell to the third floor, a short ways down from the entrance hall.

"Well," Demetri said, retreating into a shadowed corner, "so far, so good."

Something fell on him from behind, knocking him down. His cheek smacked against the floor as he sprawled flat on his stomach.

He heard Briar scream his name, but all Demetri could do was struggle beneath the weight pressing him down against the marble. He felt a hot, heavy breath against his cheek, and he could smell its rancid stink. *A corpse*, he thought, slapping back with a hand to push it off him. *Don't let it bite you, don't let it bite you—*

Then the weight was gone. Demetri scrambled to his feet, spinning around and yanking his rapier out of its sheath. He got up just in time to see Briar snap the neck of the struggling corpse, and it fell to the floor in a slimy pile of bone and flesh.

"Right," Demetri said between shallow breaths. His cheekbone smarted and his chest felt shattered. "Spoke too soon."

Briar dropped her hands to her sides. "Where the hell did it come from?"

No sooner had she spoken than an ominous moan echoed into the corridor, rebounding from wall to wall. It came, quite clearly, from the entrance hall. Demetri and Briar exchanged alarmed glances as Garrett called for his soldiers, harrying them up the staircase as fast as he could.

Then a mass of corpses spilled around the corner like skittering roaches, rushing towards them.

Two of them were upon Demetri in an instant. He reacted instinctively, his terror a distant thing, though he could still feel it in the erratic thump of his heart and the fluttering in his stomach. He raised his rapier, plunging the thin blade through the open eye socket of one corpse before spinning around to knock off the grip the other had got on his arm. He pushed it back with his blade and sliced across its throat, deep enough to drop it to the floor, gagging and flailing.

The whole corridor was thick with corpses. Garrett fell back as a corpse shoved him into the paneled wall, but a few, whip-like shots from his pistol felled the monster. Then Briar appeared out of the fray. "I thought they'd be further back in the castle!" she shouted.

"Well, they're not." Garrett took the moment to reload his pistol. "Listen, you get Kinsley and get through—we'll clear a path. Don't worry about the corpses. Just get to that fairy."

Briar threw a quick look over her shoulder. When she turned back, she and Garrett exchanged an unreadable glance. "Don't die." Briar looked from Garrett to Demetri. "Either of you."

"You too," Demetri said. He wanted nothing more than to kiss her before she left. But after another quick exchange of glances with Garrett, the two of them dove back into the fighting. Garrett fired off shots to clear a path as Briar ducked, grabbed Kinsley, and wove through the corpses, using her bare fists to knock a monster aside where she needed to. Demetri followed the trail of her shining hair until a corpse darted in front of him, breaking his eye contact. By the time he fought the creature off, Briar was gone.

They fought through the corpses. The air felt thick, muggy with heavy breaths and so little room. Demetri struggled to brandish his rapier in such tight quarters, with corpses pressing in on all sides. Garrett and Spencer spearheaded their assault into the entrance hall, using repeater rifles to launch a spray of bullets into the second wave that met them. Garrett's goal seemed to be to push them back into the castle, but most of the corpses staggered through the open doors at the front, down into the inner courtyard. Demetri hardly noticed at first as he, Tory, Dom, and Wilton were covering their rear, pushing back at the corpses coming from behind. Then Demetri stumbled out onto the broad, stone steps. He looked around and saw the horde filling the courtyard.

There were at least two hundred of them. Some surged towards Demetri and the soldiers, but most turned the other way, clambering over the broken wall like ants, tumbling into the outer courtyard beyond. For a moment, Demetri forgot about the battle waging around him. He dropped his blade and stared at the corpses going out.

Out.

"Where do they think they're going?" he asked aloud, not to anyone in particular. "They can't get out yet. Not through those thorns."

No one answered him. Shaking himself, Demetri turned to look for Garrett.

A corpse leapt in front of him and punched its claw-like hand straight through his gut.

27

BURIED

GARRETT SQUEEZED THE TRIGGER on his repeater, sending a spray of bullets into the sea of corpses surging towards them. The *tack-a-tack-a-tack-a-tack-a-tack* of the gun only added to the cacophony of shooting and shouting around him. Several corpses fell to his fire, but many staggered off in the other direction. It wasn't until then that he realized most of the corpses weren't coming at them. They were scrambling over the wrecked wall into the outer courtyard. Garrett frowned, shooting a few rounds from his pistol to fell a corpse coming at him.

"Sire!" Tory spun around, dropping a corpse with a slash from each knife in her hands. Her mousy hair was a cloud of frizz around her head and her freckled cheeks bloomed red. "Prince Demetri—he's taken an injury. It looks bad."

Garrett felt like stone, frozen and heavy, seized with dread. "Where?"

They fought their way through the tide of corpse creatures, Garrett firing his pistols and Tory slashing with her knives. Evans and Finn had dragged Demetri beneath an arched stone entry into the ramparts on the eastern side of the courtyard, while Beckett and Iain defended them. They stopped shooting long enough to let Garrett and Tory by.

Inside the ramparts, a gear-bulb lantern sat on the mossy flagstones, illuminating Demetri's pallid face. He sat slumped against the grimy wall, his head rolling from shoulder to shoulder as he fought unconsciousness. Finn crouched beside him, pressing his wadded-up uniform coat against a wound in Demetri's side.

"Demetri?" Garrett knelt beside his friend, the flagstones cold through the knees of his trousers. "Demetri, can you hear me?"

"—corpses—" Demetri muttered. "Going—out..."

"You noticed." Garrett took Demetri's head in his hands, forcing him to look at him. The hair along his neck was soaked in sweat, dampening Garrett's palms. "Demetri, stay with me. You can see me, can't you?"

Demetri's eyes were glassy. "Br-Briar," he coughed.

"No, it's Garrett. Remember?" Garrett looked around. "Where the hell is Thatcher?"

"Evans went to look for him." Finn leaned back to give them room and wiped his hand across his dark brow. "No sign of him yet."

"Curse it," Garrett swore. "How bad is it?"

Finn's face was grave. He peeled back his wool coat from Demetri's side, allowing Garrett a quick glimpse of the wound. That quick glance was enough. Demetri's dark waistcoat and white shirt were a bloody, pulpy mess where his flesh had been ripped apart. "A corpse punched into him," Finn reported. "Not all the way through, but..."

Garrett ran a hand over his mouth. Outside, the sounds of the nearby fighting echoed beneath the archway, a reminder of how close the corpses were. But Garrett hardly noticed, his attention fixed on his friend. He reminded himself that Spencer had suffered a similar wound and was still alive today—or at least, he was the last time Garrett saw him, about five minutes ago. He'd made it all the way down the mountain with that wound and lived. Demetri would too. He had to.

"Corpses," Demetri muttered. His chin lolled forward onto his chest.

"Stay awake," Garrett ordered, lifting Demetri's limp, heavy head. He looked Demetri in the eye. "You have to stay awake. Just until Thatch gets here. All right?"

"Garrett," Demetri mumbled. "The corpses—"

"I know, I know, they're nowhere near where we need them. Plan A didn't work." Garrett shrugged. "No problem. There are plenty more letters in the alphabet."

"So what's Plan B then, sire?" Finn asked.

"Give me a minute, Finn, I'm working on it." He stretched up from his crouch, craning his neck to see outside. "I don't know why they're all massing here. They can't get past those thorns without—"

A low rumble interrupted him—soft at first, like distant thunder. But it quickly grew louder, reverberating off the arched ceiling. Then the flagstones beneath them gave a violent *lurch*, and Garrett reached out to keep from falling over, his fingers smashing into the stone wall.

A clammy hand grasped his arm. Garrett looked down and saw Demetri's eyes, open and more focused. "Earthquake?" he whispered.

The rampart began to shake in earnest, and this time, Garrett toppled over. He grabbed a hold of Demetri's shoulder and grappled for the wall with his other hand. "Hold on!" he yelled.

The earth groaned and heaved beneath the stone floor. The walls and the arch above them trembled, flecks of stone shaking free. Iain and Beckett stopped shooting, clutching onto either sides of the arch for dear life. Huddled in the corner with Demetri, Finn and Garrett gaped at the shuddering ceiling, expecting it to cave in on them any second.

Then it stopped. The shaking slowed, the grumbling went silent. It was a few seconds before Garrett realized the earth was still again. He took in a tremulous breath and glanced around. "Is everyone all right?" His body felt like jelly, every joint jostled, every bone rattled. "Demetri?"

"'m—gonna—be sick—" Demetri mumbled.

"Be sick, just don't die," Garrett advised him. "Briar's orders, remember?"

"What *was* that?" Finn asked. "An earthquake, up here?"

"The dark fairy," Garrett said. It had to be. Leaving Demetri with Finn, he staggered to his feet, using the wall to steady himself as he picked his way over a layer of gritty stone. He joined Iain and Beckett, both on their feet outside the archway. "The corpses—"

"They've all but forgotten us," Beckett said. "See for yourself. They're making for the outer courtyard, them's that's not there already."

She was right. The corpses spilled into the outer courtyard like a tidal wave surging over the wall. Every now and then one broke away and ran at them, but as most of the soldiers lined the rampart, they were easily taken down.

"We have to stop them," Garrett said. "I wager that earthquake was enough to break through those thorns. Gemma, Falcon," he said, and both soldiers jumped to their feet. "Follow the rampart here and get as high as you can." He scanned the dark skyline above them, noting the pointed tops of the towers against it. "Get up in those towers." He pointed to two watchtowers on either side of the wall. "Shoot down as many as you can. We have to keep them in here."

"Those two can't stop them all, Your Highness," Iain pointed out.

"I know," Garrett said. "That's why I'm going to draw them back inside. Into the throne room."

"Pardon, sire," Beckett said, her voice a mixture of polite bluntness, "but that's fairy stones crazy, even for you."

"Come on, Beckett, where's your sense of adventure?"

"Probably in the same place you left your sense of self-preservation, Your Highness," Iain observed.

"Listen, I need you two to lead the others into that horde." Garrett eyed the soldiers on the wall. "Wilton and Dom will stay here with Finn and Demetri. Kale, Spencer, and Tory will come with me. You lead the rest—" The rest being a grand total of six men "—into the courtyard. Get to the front gate and hold them off." He ducked beneath the arch to rejoin Demetri.

Finn, crouched over the fallen prince, looked around anxiously. "No sign of Thatcher, sire?"

Only then did Garrett realize he hadn't seen the medic outside. "No."

"I think I can stitch him up," Finn offered. "He'll need surgery for the damage on the inside, but if I can stop the surface bleeding—"

Demetri's eyes fluttered open. "I'm right here, you know."

"Yes, well, we weren't going to consult you about saving your life." Garrett pulled out his pistols from their holsters, spinning them open to check his ammunition. "So, Finn is going to stitch you up. I'm off to do something very important and heroic." He filled the two of them in on his plan to lead the corpses into the throne room.

"That's fairy stones crazy, sire," Finn told him.

"Do you know, that's exactly what Beckett said," Garrett said pleasantly. "Anyhow, you, Wilton, and Dom will stay here with Demetri—"

"No," Demetri protested. His voice was weak and broken. "You need—everyone. Just—leave me." He coughed, a bit of blood dribbling onto his lower lip.

Garrett crouched before him, looking him in the eye. "I'm not leaving them here to guard you, and I'm not leaving you here to die," he said, his words low and steady. "I need you here harrying the corpses at the side, making sure none of them escape. All right? So no dying. You can die on your own time, Demetri. Which is to say, pretty much never, since you're about a hundred years old and still sickeningly handsome."

"Ninety—Ninety-nine...years old," Demetri corrected.

"Whatever." Garrett removed Demetri's pistol from his holster and fumbled it into his friend's hand, closing his feeble fingers around it. He gave a sharp nod to Finn, who returned the nod in understanding. *Guard Demetri.*

"Right then." Garrett stepped outside into the smoky courtyard where Kale, Spencer, and Tory waited for him. Iain and Beckett's lot had already taken off to turn the horde back, while Dom and Wilton stood at the entryway, guns in hand. Garrett checked both pistols at his waist, adjusted the shotgun slung over his shoulder, and hefted his repeater in hand. "Let's get to it, gents. The cavalry has arrived."

"Where?" Kale asked blankly.

Garrett blinked. "What?"

"You said the cavalry has arrived."

"Yes. Us."

Kale's bearded face was puzzled. "But usually people say 'the cavalry has arrived' when someone turns up to help in a very dire situation. Like this one."

"Well, no one's coming to help us, Kale." Garrett rested his repeater against his shoulder. "We're all we've got. We are the cavalry. So. Shall we go be heroes?"

As it turned out, sending a shower of bullets into the back of the corpse horde made them very angry, which was exactly what Garrett was counting on. He and Spencer, armed with repeaters, drew their attention from the tops of the wide, stone steps. Gemma's sniper work and Falcon's flaming arrows encouraged the corpses to seek shelter, and more of them turned towards the castle once the other soldiers turned them back. After that, Garrett's job was simple—run.

He, Tory, Spencer, and Kale dashed into the dilapidated entrance hall, glass fragments snapping beneath their thundering boots. A hundred corpses poured in after them. The mad run down the length of the castle passed in a blur for Garrett, a desperate blur of corridors flying by and a barrage of gunfire. Garrett's chest burned with exertion, his arms aching from sprinting and shooting. He took out any corpses running at them from the opposite direction, while Spencer and Kale looked after their sides. Tory guarded their rear, slicing at any too close behind them.

As they approached the throne room, the two-story hall coming into sight beyond the twin stairwells, Garrett shouted, "Now hopefully not too many of them will have come around the side corridors to cut us off from—"

He broke off as a horde poured around the corner ahead from one of the side corridors.

"You had to say it," Spencer shouted. "Didn't you, sire?"

"That one's on me," Garrett conceded gracefully. He was out of ammunition for his repeater, so he tossed it and yanked his shotgun off his back, taking aim. The thunderous crack of the shotgun was lost on him, near-deaf as he was, but he felt the jolt of it each time he fired, ricocheting through his bones all the way to his ribs. They were stuck in the thick of the fray, and it was like being in a tub of molasses, their struggle to push forward slow and leaden. Corpses screamed in Garrett's ear, clawing and lunging at him. He elbowed a corpse in the face, trying to turn about. Through the mass of bodies, he saw Spencer go down beneath the throng, hollering and flailing. Stumbling free, Garrett backed into the throne room, but five corpses followed in a flash, surrounding him, hands grasping, broken teeth bared—

A shot rang out and one of the corpses went down, losing its hold on Garrett. A second shot, and a second corpse fell. Then a third and a fourth. Garrett shoved the butt of his shotgun into the last one's face, then fired his own shot into its gut as it reeled back.

He looked up, spotting a lanky figure at the top of the ballroom staircase. "Kinsley! What are you doing here?"

Kinsley scurried down the staircase to join him. "Your Highness—"

"Where's Briar?" A fistful of terror jerked at Garrett's heart, the first he'd felt since racing into the castle. "Why aren't you with her?"

Before Kinsley could answer, Kale staggered free of the fray, Tory close behind. "Sire, I advise that we run," Tory said between shallow breaths. "Now!"

They took off across the throne room, their footsteps clacking against the mosaic floor. "What if Alec hasn't got everything ready?" Kale shouted.

"Then we're pretty well dead," Garrett shouted back.

They sprinted for the back of the hall where there was a small chamber hidden behind a gilded gold wall. Tory found the door, shoving it open. They spilled into the chamber behind her, and just before Garrett slammed the door shut, Spencer slipped inside, a line of blood marking a nasty cut on his cheek.

"Where did you come from?" Garrett asked in amazement. "I saw you go down—I thought for sure you were dead."

Spencer shrugged. "I guess I just don't die easy, sire."

"No, you don't."

The chamber was a sitting room for the king and queen with a small balcony at the back, closed off by twin doors. It was a low, windowless room, filled with dusty bookcases, stained wood tables, moth-eaten armchairs, and one long, ornate credenza, tooled in gold. Tory, Spencer, and Kale began piling that furniture up against the door to keep the corpses from getting in. Garrett took a deep breath, like the first breath of a drowning man, surfacing through the water. Only now did he feel the sweat dripping down his face, the burning in his legs, a long gash down his forearm where a corpse had sliced a claw-like finger through his sack coat and shirt. "Alec should be in place," he said. He could barely hear his own voice, his ears were buzzing so badly. "Kinsley, why are you here?" Garrett's heart quaked in his chest. "Where's Briar? In the tower? Why did you leave her?"

Kinsley shook his head, his black hair askew across his brow. He looked as pained as Garrett felt. "I didn't, sire. We got to the top of the tower, but the fairy wasn't there. Briar thought she might be at the front of the palace somewhere, where she could get a good view of the walls. We headed up into the ballroom on the fourth floor, but we met a few corpses, and I'm afraid we got separated. I was trying to figure out how to get to the ballroom when I heard you lot coming down below."

"So Briar's gone after the fairy alone," Garrett said. His fear for her was a palpable thing, strumming through his heart.

Then a tremendous, tumultuous blast resounded from outside, rocking the ground and raining dust down as the pillars in the throne room exploded.

Garrett fell to the ground, his knees slamming into the floor. He threw his arms over his head as a second explosion rocked the painted walls, and then a third. He wanted to retreat to the back of the room, get as far from the blast as he could, but the ground wrenched with such vehemence that he couldn't make it to his feet. The noise was deafening as the raised corridors lining the throne room crashed into the floor below, hopefully piling up walls of rubble so thick and high that the corpses would be trapped with no way out.

Garrett wasn't sure how much time passed as they huddled in the dark, praying the ceiling wouldn't fall down on top of them. It couldn't have been more than a minute at most. Then everything went still. Garrett raised his head, blinking through a dark gray haze. Tory, Spencer, Kinsley, and Kale got to their feet, all covered in a film of dust, just as Garrett was. They all looked like ghosts. Garrett's ears rang worse than ever, and when Spencer grinned and said something, Garrett couldn't hear him at all. Spencer repeated himself, exaggerating the movement of his lips so Garrett could understand. *"Dynamite worked just fine."*

Garrett jerked his head to the side, indicating they should check. They tottered forward, pulling aside the furniture. Once it was clear, Kale pushed at the carved oak door.

It wouldn't budge. Spencer and Kinsley stepped forward to help. But no matter how they threw their weight at the door, it would not open.

The dynamite had worked, all right. They were trapped in too. Trapped, while Briar was out there facing the dark fairy alone.

28

CAVALRY

DEMETRI DIDN'T UNDERSTAND WHY he was not dead.

He'd lost consciousness, and for how long, he couldn't say. The last thing he remembered was the constant *bang!* of gunshots as corpses tried to get in beneath the rampart's arch. After Finn stitched him up, Demetri had ordered the stoic soldier to help him to the entryway. Finn wasn't happy about it, but he did it, propping Demetri up against the side of the arch. Finn had joined Dom and Wilton outside, firing at the corpses streaming towards them. Demetri fired too, though he wasn't sure how accurate his aim was, given how badly his arm shook and how dotted his vision was. Fallen corpses had begun to pile up in stacks, bottlenecking the entry, but not enough to keep the rest from them.

He remembered a screaming Wilton, poor, shy, reedy Wilton, yanked off the rampart's edge, vanishing into the clutches of the corpses. He remembered Dom wrestling with a corpse before it snapped his neck in two, leaving Dom crumpled on the floor, the perpetual smile gone from his face. The last thing Demetri remembered was Finn taking him by the arms and dragging him back into the sparse safety beneath the rampart, pulling him around a corner so he would be hidden.

Everything after that was blank. He'd passed out.

He wrenched awake when the wall began to quake, though it was only for a couple of seconds. He blinked in the silent, gloomy darkness. It took him several minutes to remember what was going on.

Briar.

Demetri struggled to rise, clutching at the rugged stone wall. The pain from his wound was staggering. He nearly passed out again from the sheer weight of it. Glancing down, he picked at the bloody remnants of his shirt.

"Finn?" Demetri called. His voice echoed into the quiet. He thought, at first, that all the gunfire had ruined his hearing. But everything was still too, no flashes of gunpowder, no movement outside. The powder residue lingering in the air, faintly metallic, was stale and old. Demetri staggered upright—or semi-upright, anyway—and tripped around the corner, coming out beneath the archway.

The remains of someone dark-skinned lay at his feet. *Finn*, Demetri thought sadly. Whole chunks of his flesh had been torn away. Weirdly numb, his mind resisting the worst of it, Demetri cast his gaze around. Another body was in a similar state on the floor—a small one that Demetri thought was Dom. He peered over the edge and spotted a paler body, Wilton.

There was still a pile of corpses at the entry. Aside from a twitch here and there, they were still. Dead or unconscious. Demetri looked out, but nothing else moved in the courtyard.

"All dead," Demetri murmured. "Why am I still alive?" He couldn't shake off the shock that he was not dead too. He thought he could hear fighting beyond the wall, in the outer courtyard. But the inner courtyard had been abandoned by soldier and corpse alike. They were all inside or at the front gate, struggling to get free.

Demetri glanced up at the looming castle. All that was left was for Briar to do her part.

A flutter of movement at the window on the top floor caught his eye. Demetri peered into the darkness and the distance. Something was moving up there on the windowsill. That would be the windows in the Hall of the Singers. Something perched there, bird-like.

The dark fairy.

If she was up there, then Briar was too.

Lurching forward, Demetri began making his way into the entrance hall, one unsteady step at a time.

29

RISING

B RIAR HAD NEVER FELT more alone in her life. That was her fault. When Kinsley vanished during that blitz attack from a gaggle of corpses, she could have tried to go back for him. But she'd continued towards the front of the castle, escaping through the etched oak doors into the drawing room.

A terrible sense of isolation struck her as the ballroom doors shut with a resounding boom. The antechamber was black as pitch, and though Briar needed no light, a warm glow would have been welcoming. She felt paralyzed. She felt like her memory was leaving her in the worst possible moment. But it wasn't her memory failing her now. It wasn't her foggy brain feeding this sense of abandonment. It was her own resolve, falling away like so much rotted flesh.

In the end, she was alone, and that was how it had to be. She had to kill the dark fairy, and she had to do it on her own. No one could help her do it. No one could shoulder the price of this murder. These were her people, and it was her duty to save them.

That's all there was to it.

Briar pushed open the door into the Hall of the Singers.

She was sure the dark fairy would come here. When they'd discovered the corpses weren't in the throne room, Briar had figured the dark fairy was going ahead with her plans to break the thorn barrier. She would need a good view of it. There was only one place in the castle that would provide a clear view, and that was the gilded balcony in the Hall of the Singers.

Briar was half-afraid the fairy would be gone and half-afraid she would not be. When she stepped into the hall, she found her latter fear had come true. The fairy was there on the balcony, gazing out the open, tri-fold windows.

The Hall of the Singers was even larger than the throne room. The dark ceiling arched high overhead, its paint faded and peeling. Three massive, candle-filled chandeliers used to hang from the ceiling, but now they lay in tangled heaps on the floor. The scent of cold and powder smoke floated in through the curved windows on a whispery breeze.

Briar crept across the hall. At first, she thought she might take the fairy by surprise. But then the dark fairy said, "I was worried that futile barrier might stop you from getting in."

"We found a way past it." Briar's arms felt rigid down by her sides.

"So did I." The dark fairy's voice was a sibilant hiss. "They were fools to think they could stop me. They cursed this castle, encasing it in thorns. So I cursed the land to break. Come and see."

Briar mounted the white oak steps with a confidence that was not real. Her boots clomped against the stairs, and a dousing dread poured over her with every step. The wooden stake, tucked up her sleeve, seemed to burn against her skin.

As she reached the top of the stairs, the dark fairy backed out onto the windowsill, where the white stone was caked black with grunge. The fairy wore a twisted smile. Briar came only as far as she needed to see. Below, the inner courtyard was empty, lit by the low, portly moon. In the outer courtyard, there was movement at the gates, though Briar could not see if they were open. And beyond the castle, the dense, knotted barrier of black thorns pressed against the walls—but not outside the gates. There was a break in the land now, a deep gorge like a scar, cut across the hills. It parted straight through the thorns, and the ridge tops on either side of it were clear as well. The dark fairy had broken the barrier, all right. And she'd split the land in two to do it.

"Your friends have been fighting my corpses." The dark fairy gazed down at the courtyard. "They led many of them inside the castle. But it's a useless attempt. They will die, and the corpses will escape."

Briar could feel the white stake up her sleeve, its knobby edge resting against her elbow. She should use it now while the fairy was distracted. But she didn't. She only looked at her. The scarlet, vein-like lines eking out from the corner of her inky black eye had spread. Now they covered the left side of her face, down her jawline, across her cheek. Briar had forgotten about this affliction, whatever it was.

"What is that?" Briar's voice felt like ice, tenuous, ephemeral. "On your face?"

The dark fairy reached up with her long, white fingers, laying black-lacquered nails against the side of her face. "It's nature's curse, little princess."

"I don't understand."

"Magic is about intention," the fairy intoned, "and you are dying, little princess, because of my curse. I did not curse you to die, but you are dying all the same. Your people are *beyond* dead." Her eyes glinted in the moonlight, which poured into the room in wide shafts. "And fairies gave their word. Never kill a human."

Before Briar could respond, an enormous explosion blasted in the distance, behind and below them. The painted walls and the paneled floor gave a colossal, turbulent tremor, and what was left of the glass in the windows burst. Briar tried to keep her footing, but as a second and third explosion rocked the hall, she fell to one knee.

There was a booming crash in the wake of the explosions. The ballroom. Part of it was supported by the marble pillars the explosion was meant to bring down. For a moment, Briar feared the Hall of the Singers would come down too. But the room stilled, everything motionless save for motes of dust drifting in the air.

Briar pushed herself to her feet. There was shattered glass everywhere, littering the floor like gleaming flakes of translucent snow. The dark fairy sat in the same place on the windowsill. If the explosion had moved her at all, Briar could not tell.

"Do you know what that was?" Briar asked. She unbound her fist and stretched her fingers wide, subtly sliding the stake down her sleeve and into the butt of her hand. She still felt hollow inside, a cavernous wasteland of the worst fear imaginable, but the explosion had strengthened her. She grasped for the resolve that got her here, all the way from Isabelle's house to the castle. "That was my *friends*," she said, "trapping your corpses in the throne room. So your army isn't going anywhere, fairy."

The dark fairy flexed her spindly fingers. "A minor complication. I will get them out."

"No," said Briar, "you won't."

She gripped the stake and summoned her speed, closing the distance between them in a whirlwind instant. She stopped right behind the fairy and plunged the stake downward, over her shoulder, aiming for her neck.

The tip of the stake was less than an inch from her target when the dark fairy reached back and wrapped her hand around Briar's wrist. The strength in that grip rivaled the strength of a corpse creature. The fairy *squeezed*, and Briar's flesh broke apart in her hand, oozing through her fingers like pale slime. Chunks of bloody sinew popped out, and then Briar heard a horrible *crunch* as her bone splintered into slivers. The pain was excruciating, white-hot, blinding, reverberating through her entire body like its own explosion. She screamed and wrenched free of the fairy. The white stake fell from her dead fingers, clattering to the floor.

Briar swayed, her legs crumpling, as boneless as her wrist. She collapsed, barely remaining upright. Sucking in shallow breaths, she clutched at her elbow and goggled at the shambles of her forearm. The back of her arm was still intact, though the flesh clung tenuously to the bone and muscle that remained. The inner side of her forearm was wrecked, a gaping hole where skin and sinew had been. Briar could see part of the bone, shattered, surrounded by jam-like gore. She drew in a ragged gasp and looked at the fairy towering over her.

"*You* would kill *me?*" the dark fairy snarled. "Did you actually think you could manage it, princess? You might have been a queen among your pathetic people, little Briar, but the truth is, you are as worthless as any of them."

It was a moment before Briar could get anything more than a whimper past her lips. "What is it—with you and humans? None of your kind—like us all that much—but you—you *hate* us—for nothing, for no reason—"

The dark fairy rushed at her in a gust of flapping wings. Briar winced and recoiled, the burst of wind stinging her eyes. The fairy stopped short, her face inches from Briar's own. "I have plenty reason." Her breath was hot on Briar's face, and Briar tried not to quell beneath the fairy's vitriol. She was like acid, spilling out, dissolving everything in its path. "I *gave* humans a chance, princess. I tried to live among them once. But everywhere I went, I was scorned. When they should have accepted me—no, when they should have *worshipped* me."

Briar gaped at her. She had *lived* among humans? Why? Just so she could be a god among them? If that was the case, then she'd been the same then as she was now—she just wanted humans beneath her, subjugated, so she could lord over them.

It didn't matter why she'd done it. There was no changing her, no convincing the dark fairy to turn from this path. That was clear. Briar closed her eyes. She felt like the entire world had dropped away, all of it, save for this one moment, this one place, only her and this fairy. This fairy who would burn the world for revenge, this fairy who would annihilate a species just to crow over their destruction. And the only way to right any of it was to kill her, and Briar had failed in that.

As though reading her mind, the dark fairy said, "And you would try to kill me. You, who were never anything more than my instrument of destruction. How will you kill me now, Princess Briar?"

"Maybe I will."

Briar's eyes flew open.

Demetri stood behind the dark fairy, the white stake in his hand.

The fairy whirled around. "*You*," she said, her voice seething. "Put that down, boy."

Demetri looked terrible. His face was gray, his waistcoat torn open, shredded and stained with blood. And he was barely standing despite his attempts to look otherwise. But he held the stake firmly, and there was no fear on his face.

"Demetri," Briar gasped, "*no*. Don't."

"Don't you know what comes of killing a fairy?" the dark fairy asked. "You will lose your soul."

"My soul's a little damaged anyway." Demetri's tone was almost amiable. "It's no great loss."

Briar couldn't let him do this. She struggled to rise. Her limbs trembled, her bones chattered, her circulation slowed, making her sluggish. Her body was an anvil. The burst of speed she'd used had taken so much out of her, and her arm vibrated with pain. Wobbling all over, she got to her knees.

"It must kill you," the dark fairy said, "to know you could have ended this from the start, boy. You were with Princess Briar when she fell to the first curse. You could have broken it the moment it began. But you didn't break the curse at all. Some common boy did, not even a true royal. So what exactly can you do, little prince? You're useless."

"I can kill you." Demetri lifted the stake.

"No," the fairy said, "you can't." She raised her hand and curled her fingers into a fist. "I curse you, Prince Demetri. I curse every bone in your hand to break."

"No!" Briar cried.

The sound of snapping bone was drowned out by Demetri's scream. The stake fell from his limp hand as his fingers bent of their own accord, twisting at ugly, unnatural angles. White bone broke through the palm of his hand. As Briar watched, Demetri *thudded* to his knees, clutching his wrist.

The dark fairy marched through a field of broken glass and gave the white stake a good kick. It rolled across the balcony, rattling until it dropped over the edge and hit the floor below with a *clink*.

"Now you only have one hand," the fairy said, matching Demetri's casual tone. "What can you do with one hand, little prince? As I said—useless."

Crumpled on the floor, Demetri half-choked, half-mewled an unintelligible response. He did not seem capable of getting back to his feet.

"And as for you—" the fairy turned to Briar "—I think it's time that—"

Briar threw herself at the fairy. She launched forward with the weight of her whole body and slammed into her, sending them both tumbling into the marble wall.

Briar wasn't sure she could stand again, but she didn't have to. She knelt over the fairy and delivered a shattering blow to her face. A rush of satisfaction surged through her when she heard the fairy's nose break with a sharp *crack*. She struck another blow, and another, and another, her knuckles smarting with glorious pain. Bright red blood stained the fairy's face, stark and vibrant. The fairy squealed, limbs thrashing, black wings pinned to the ground.

Briar could sense a familiar fog hovering at the edge of her brain, threatening to overtake her and bring on the mindless monster within. But as she delivered blow after blow, she thought of Demetri, crumpled in the corner. She focused all that violent rage, sending it through a narrow funnel, and the funnel was Demetri—allowing her to use her strength without losing control.

Suddenly, the dark fairy's wings blew forward and Briar cringed back from the blast of wind. The dark fairy took advantage of her lapse, placed both hands against Briar's chest, and gave a hard, bruising shove that Briar felt all the way to her breastbone. She rolled off the fairy, and before she could regain her footing, the fairy was on her. She lifted Briar by the back of her jacket and tossed her against the balcony's stone railing.

As Briar fell to the floor in a broken heap, a blackness, like thick tar, stole over her. A knowing rooted deep within her. And the knowing was this: she could not beat this fairy. She could not kill her and she could not stop her. It was like Jas said: she, Briar, was mortal. The dark fairy was immortal. Indestructible. She was strong, and Briar could not beat that strength.

She rose into a seated position, dizzy, her head pulsating. She tasted coppery blood on her mouth. The dark fairy approached, her bare feet crunching over shards of glass and leaving bloody footprints in her wake. Briar's gaze traveled from those feet to the fairy's sneering face. Behind the fairy, her vast, black, feathery wings loomed over them both, gently beating like the wings of a colossal bat.

Strength.

"Maybe I should kill you after all," the dark fairy said.

Briar didn't quite hear her. Two memories were coalescing in her mind, like pieces of a puzzle snapping into place. She was thinking of Jas, giving her the weapon she needed to kill the dark fairy. *"How to kill me is as easy as killing any of you. I'm mortal now."*

"Nature's curse is already taking its toll on me," the fairy mused, "and though its affliction is painful, it cannot cause me lasting harm. I am immortal."

"No human can take the wings of a fairy. I couldn't either, not anymore. I'm mortal, you're all mortal."

The dark fairy touched the side of her own face where the spidery veins covered her skin in crimson rivulets. "Yes, I will suffer. Perhaps," she murmured. "But even this cannot kill me. I cannot die. Not even if I kill you."

"It was your own fault, you know," Briar whispered, getting one foot beneath her.

"What?" the fairy snapped.

"You shouldn't have made the curse breakable by true love's kiss." Briar lifted her head. "Because you don't understand love. Why do you think that *common* boy could wake me with his kiss when he never even knew me? Because you have no concept of love. So much so that you couldn't work it into your curse, not the way you meant to."

"Even if that's true," the dark fairy said derisively, "it doesn't mean that I—"

A *shot* broke the air, the shot of a bullet. Then a second, and a third. Each one hit the fairy in the back. She screeched in pain, contorting like an insect as she reached behind her, as though to rip the bullets from her skin. A fourth bullet took her in the side as she bumbled around, and a fifth in her gut.

Demetri slumped upright in the corner, and he held a pistol in his left hand. Acrid smoke looped out of the barrel. "As it turns out," he grunted, "you only need one hand to pull a trigger."

"Foolish boy." The fairy staggered towards him. "Your weapons cannot kill me."

Using the railing for support, Briar stood. She took a lurching step.

"I am immortal," the fairy spat, "and you cannot change that. No human can."

"Maybe so," Briar said, and she leapt *up* at the fairy—onto her back, taking a wing in each hand. The weight of her body brought the fairy down, slamming her into the oak wood floor face-first. Briar dug her knee into the fairy's bony back. Her grip tightened around each wing, ruffling feathers in her fists.

"But you made me more than human," Briar said, her voice savage and low. "You made me a monster."

She began to pull.

The dark fairy's scream tore from her throat like a blade sawing into bone. Briar drew every last ounce of strength within her, and she *felt* it, a warm cascade flooding her limbs all the way to the tips of her fingers. She grit her teeth, muscles straining, and *ripped* the wings free of the fairy. They came loose and Briar stumbled back, a black wing as tall as herself in each hand.

The dark fairy lay moaning and trembling on the floor, blood seeping from nubs on her shoulder blades. Her black hair was unkempt, strewn across her face. Briar stepped around to join Demetri without taking her eyes from the fallen fairy.

"Briar." Demetri's voice was tinged with disbelief. "How—you—"

"Wait," Briar said. "It's not over yet."

"*No.*" The dark fairy got one hand beneath her, and then another. In agony, she lifted her head and got onto hands and knees. A fine dusting of glass clung to her cheek, and her black eyes burned. "No," she rasped. "It's—*not*—over. Will you kill me now...little princess?"

"I don't want to," Briar whispered, "and I don't have to."

The fairy's smile vanished. Then her eyes widened. The spidery veins stretching across her face began to spread, snaking down her neck with rapid speed. The fairy trembled violently, her teeth clacking against each other. She staggered to her feet, but her whole body was seizing up. As the veins crept down her bare arms and vanished beneath her little dress, her black eyes brightened, going red, red, red to match the disease taking over her. Where the lines marked her face, her skin began to crack like parched soil baking in the sun. By the time the veins reached her legs, her face was breaking apart, crumbling into dust. Her mouth opened in a wordless scream before it, too, crumbled away, and her red eyes bulged until they popped, blood streaming forth from the empty sockets.

Briar dropped the fairy's wings and clutched at Demetri, her fingers digging into the folds of his shirt. She watched in horrified fascination as the fairy disintegrated. Her black hair fell away, her flesh crumbled like clay. Sinew dried up until there was nothing left but a bare skeleton, which shattered into a million pieces. When all was said and done, there was nothing left of the dark fairy, save for her wings and a pile of dust.

"Briar," Demetri croaked. "How..."

"She called it nature's curse." Briar felt strangely detached as she ran over the details in her mind, marveling that it had worked. "Because the rotting curse was too close to death. She didn't curse us to die, but she cursed us to rot, and that was so nearly the same thing that nature, or whatever, struck back at her. She *meant* for me to die. She didn't think it would kill her because she was immortal—"

"—but you saw to that," Demetri finished. "How did you do it? Jas said no human could take a fairy's wings—"

"But I'm not really human anymore, Demetri." Briar glanced down at herself. "I'm—I'm—"

She lifted her arms in front of her. Her sewn-on fingers were the same, dead and sluggish—save for her pinky, which had fallen off in the struggle. The ugly gash on her left palm was unhealed. And where the fairy had crushed her arm, it was the same—throbbing, gaping, the softened flesh clinging to the bone.

"I'm a monster." *No. No.* Briar turned to Demetri, her heart stuttering in her chest. "Demetri, I'm still a monster. I'm still...this."

Demetri's eyes were exhausted and uncomprehending. Then he seemed to realize. "You're still half a corpse."

Briar nodded desperately.

"The others—the corpse horde—"

Nothing more needed to be said. Demetri slipped and staggered with Briar's support, but halfway down the stairs, he begged off, sliding down onto a step. "You—go ahead."

"I don't want to leave you—"

"Go." Demetri leaned against the railing. "You can—come back. For me."

Briar spared him one last glance and took off, half-toppling down the stairs. She tried to run despite her leaden limbs, despite her aching body. Tripping over her own feet, she burst into the ballroom.

There was little left of the ballroom—just a sliver of the dark wood floor, what hadn't fallen into the throne room below. Briar skidded to a halt at the edge. A vast rubble stretched before her, the ballroom and the marble pillars brought down by the dynamite. Beyond that wall of stone and wooden wreckage, trapped in the throne hall below, was the corpse horde.

Her people.

At first, Briar thought she had failed. She could see no change in the people below her. They were like her, but worse—rotted, discolored, flesh seeping off their bones. They were just as they had been. Unchanged, in spite of the dark fairy's death.

But as Briar looked closer, she realized something was different. Many of them were silent; none were struggling to get free, none fighting with each other. Most of them looked lost. Briar scrambled down the mountain of rubble, her trousers catching on jagged stone, splinters of wood jabbing into her palms. As she neared the bottom, she realized some of the corpses were talking to each other. Speaking in whispers and hushed tones, like one might use at a funeral. Someone far back in the hall was weeping quietly.

As Briar slid onto the floor, one of the corpses looked around and saw her. It was Laurel. The maddened, hungry gleam was gone from her eyes, replaced with something else.

Reason. And fear.

"Briar," Laurel said, those fearful, *human* eyes alighting on her. "What's going on? Why are we—what—?" She stared at her mottled hands in horror.

Killing the fairy had worked. She had cursed them to become monsters, and they weren't monsters anymore.

But they were still dead.

30

RECOMPENSE

BRIAR SAT ON HER four-poster bed, her gaze traveling around the room she grew up in. Outside, the harvest moon had set and the sun was up, bringing a new day over the ruined castle of the Mountain Kingdom.

It didn't feel like a new day. Not when everyone in the castle was still a corpse.

Briar had been over and over it, why it had worked this way. The dark fairy was dead, the curse was broken—but not all broken. As broken as it could be.

Briar slipped off the bed and crossed the room to her vanity table. She looked into the smudged mirror, studying the person who gazed back at her. Violet circles stained the white skin beneath her eyes, and a greenish bruise marred her dented temple. The dent, at least, was difficult to see if you didn't know to look for it.

She held her hands before her, studying those too. Her left palm was bandaged, concealing the open gash, and on her right hand, her three middle fingers were still sewn on. They were stiff, but curled at her command. Her pinky was gone, lost in the fight with the dark fairy.

Her gaze traveled up her forearm. The wound there was also bandaged. Briar picked at the fraying edges of the cloth bandage and began to unravel it, pulling the whole thing off. Beneath it was a wreckage of skin and sinew. Thatcher had cleaned out the shattered shards of bone, the chunks of clotted blood. But the gaping hole in her arm was still there and always would be. It didn't hurt anymore, really, but there was an inexplicable ache all the same, in the hollow where her arm should have been.

The dark fairy's death didn't cure her, nor did it cure her people. It stopped the rotting, and by extension, took away the hunger—that maddening hunger that made them into monsters and stole their sense of self. Briar should have been glad of that. She *was*—after all, her mind was intact. And her people, too, were no longer driven to mindless violence.

But it seemed a hollow victory. It wasn't enough. She couldn't understand why it wasn't enough.

She had wanted to *fix* everything.

A *tap-tap* on the open door broke through her maudlin thoughts, and she turned to look.

Garrett stood in the doorway, lit by the damp sunlight spilling into the room behind him. He looked exhausted and dirty. He'd wiped his face clean, but a sheen of smoky gray dust clung to his hair and his clothes, giving him the look of a specter. A bruise was beginning to blossom at his jaw, plum-colored and spectacular, and a long rent sliced through the sleeve of his dark shirt. But he was otherwise whole and alive.

Briar felt a knot of fear unravel in her gut, one she hadn't even realized was there. Relief coursed through her like a drug, unsteadying her.

"They got you out." She took an unconscious step forward.

"They got me out." He came into the room. He seemed to bring the sunlight with him. "Took four bloody hours. I guess the dynamite was a little more effective than I anticipated." The corner of his mouth lifted in half a smile.

Briar hesitated, measuring the distance between them with her eyes. Three steps, maybe. Before she could talk herself out of it, Briar took those steps and threw her arms around him. He was warm and solid and gritty, and as his arms came around her, she felt the tension leave his body. There was something wonderfully strange but comforting about the angles of him, the way he fit against her.

"They told me what you did," she said, her words muffled by his shirt. Beneath the caustic dust was the heartening scent of *him*, and she wondered when she'd become familiar with it. She rested her head against his shoulder, the jut of his collarbone pressing into her cheek. "Leading all the corpses into the throne hall. A little reckless, don't you think?"

His laugh reverberated between them. "I'm getting this from you? The girl who was going to sacrifice her soul?"

"Fair enough." She dropped her arms and stepped back. A layer of grit clung to her cheek.

Garrett's eyes found hers, studying, scrupulous. "They told me what happened too—some of it anyway. And I saw them. The corpses."

For the first time ever, a sliver of discomfiture woke in Briar, insidious and unwanted. She felt unsure beneath Garrett's gaze, and she stepped back, turning away. It was stupid and shallow and selfish, to be worried about how she looked—how she would always look—when her kingdom was much worse off. She had never cared how she looked anyway. It was hardly the most important thing about a person. But then, most people didn't have dented-in foreheads or sewn-on fingers. She realized the bandage for her forearm still lay on her vanity table, and she wished she hadn't taken it off.

"Why didn't it work?" Garrett asked. Judging by the proximity of his smooth, deep voice, he had moved after her. "The dark fairy is dead—why didn't it break the curse?"

"I think it did." The words were like lead in her mouth, burdensome and toxic. She perched on the velvety, mauve bed. "I was thinking about the sleeping curse. When you kissed me, you broke the curse, even though I should have slept for another eighteen years. But it didn't erase the time I'd already spent sleeping. It didn't change the past. It didn't make it so the curse never happened in the first place."

"I don't understand."

"The dark fairy cursed us to rot and become monsters." Briar dared a glance at him. She fiddled with a pearl button on the front of her blouse. "Dev told us, remember? She said, 'I curse you to rot until you are no longer human, but a monster.' Well, her death broke that. It stopped the progress of the rotting. But it couldn't undo the rotting that had already happened." She held up her bandaged palm. "I don't think this will heal—none of it will. But we won't get any worse."

"So you'll always be you." Garrett's smile was exultant. "You won't lose any more memories. You won't lose who you are."

Briar couldn't share his smile. "But some of the corpses—some of my *people*—they're too far-gone. Many of them rotted so much that they became completely lost in their own minds, and there's no coming back for them." She spoke in a low, wretched voice. "Others are more like me—they know who they are, they remember...well, they have holes in their memories, like me. But they remember the curse, everything they did—"

They remembered all of it. Briar thought that might be a worse curse.

"And the hunger?" Garrett asked. If this question made him nervous, he hid it well. "Is that gone too?"

"In a manner of speaking." Briar dropped her arm. "Eating raw flesh staved off the rotting, or at least, it slowed it. That's why it kept us mobile, cleared our minds a bit. And since the rotting stopped, the hunger is gone. But..." Briar paused. "I was exhausted after the fight with the fairy. I could barely move until Gemma brought me another raw rabbit. The *hunger* is gone, but I don't think my body will function without..."

"A raw rabbit now and then," Garrett said pleasantly.

Briar looked up at him, inexplicably annoyed. "Doesn't any of this bother you?"

"Any of what?"

"All...*this.*" She lifted her arm, displaying the gaping hole.

His face folded into an expression of genuine solicitude. "Does it bother you?"

"Well, I mean..." Briar struggled with this question. "It's all very...manageable."

"Yes, it is." Garrett lowered himself onto the bed beside her, his hands splayed at his sides. She could feel the warmth of his fingers—not touching her thigh, but near enough to feel the whisper of them. "Briar, I know you were hoping the rotting would go away, and I was too, but only for your sake. This—" Garrett reached across her and wrapped his warm, gentle hand around her ruined forearm. "I can handle this, so long as you can."

Briar looked at him. The room around them was wrapped in darkness, and the shadows cut through his earnest face. He didn't belong in the shadows, she thought, and for a second, that thought stayed her. She didn't want to drag him someplace he didn't belong. And he belonged in the bright.

But it was easy to forget that Garrett had lived in the dark too. It was easy to forget that, beneath his winsome smiles and his (sometimes lame) jokes and his exhilarated eyes, there lurked a person who had experienced unimaginable loss—not once, but twice. And that was what made him such a spectacular, perplexing phenomenon. That he could absorb shadows and reflect them back into something golden, something new, something radiant.

He was the kind of person who could withstand a little darkness.

An involuntary but welcome smile spread across Briar's face. "That's very nice of you."

"I am very nice," Garrett agreed.

"But you know, that is technically an open wound," Briar pointed out. "And your hands are rather dirty still, so—"

"Oh, right." Garrett dropped her arm like it had burned him. His hands, of course, were caked in dirt like the rest of him. "Sorry."

"That's all right." Briar stood. "I wanted to talk to Thatcher anyway. And check on Demetri."

Briar didn't see Demetri until a few hours later. Thatcher had seen to him straight away, performing surgery to stitch up the damage inside him. It took a while, but he was stable now, Thatcher reported, and should be fine after several days' rest.

Demetri's hand was a different story. Like the rotting curse, the dark fairy's death didn't fix the broken bones, and some of them had been so shattered, Thatcher was worried about them healing properly. He did what he could, but there was no telling what the lasting damage might be.

Briar visited Demetri in the afternoon, but Thatcher had well plied him with morphine, so he only woke for a short time and was very groggy. Briar wasn't even sure he recognized her.

She wandered the castle after that. She wasn't sure she wanted to talk to anyone right now, not even Garrett. After an hour meandering through dusty, gilded rooms and halls laid with cracked marble, she found herself outside on the back ramparts. The rampart afforded her a view of the sheer drop down the bluff and the low-hanging mist hovering beyond it, concealing the bottom far below. A fierce wind wailed at her as it drove through the mountains, pricking at her unprotected face. Briar didn't feel its chill, but she winced at the force of it.

"This must've been the worst place to have guard duty."

Briar looked around. A corpse girl stood at the top of the stone stairs behind her. Her black hair, streaked with gray, twisted in the wind, and her faded gown blustered at her scrawny ankles.

The girl joined her at the edge of the ramparts. Briar could see the person she'd once been, but beneath an overlay of the person she was now.

"Because of the cold, I mean," Laurel added. She lay her hands flat atop the wall's flagstones.

"I don't feel it at all," Briar noted.

"Nor do I."

"There's one advantage."

"Sure." Laurel glanced at Briar sidelong. "I like your dress."

"Likewise."

They both shared bitter smirks. Briar had bathed and changed into an old gown, a lightweight, jade-colored dress with a high waist, loose skirt, and plunging neckline. And like Laurel's gown, it was faded and moth-eaten. They were both of them relics of a time long past, and they looked it.

Laurel's gaze turned hesitant. "I asked around. About your parents, I mean. I'm sorry. No one has seen them." Laurel's fingers curled around the edge of the wall. "No one remembers—or at least, that's what everyone told me."

Briar nodded gravely. She supposed if anyone did remember seeing her parents die—or worse, remembered killing them—they wouldn't want to be responsible for bearing that news. "So they're dead." She wished her voice didn't sound as steady as it did.

"Yes."

"I know I should be—I must seem so heartless." It wasn't that she didn't care. It was just that, to her, they had been dead since the moment she woke from the curse. Though even then, she hadn't really mourned.

"Not at all." Laurel raised an eyebrow. "I don't mean because they were—well, you know how they were. But we all should have been dead a long time ago, Briar. Maybe not so long for you and me—but even without your curses, we'd have been dead some years past. Your parents even longer."

"I don't know." Briar toyed with a stray thread on the hem of her sleeve. "I'd like to think modern medicine would have us all living past a hundred."

"Instead, it's magic that's done that."

They were both quiet for a bit. A flock of birds soared out of the mist, cawing as they zoomed into the distance.

Briar said, "I'm sorry."

"For what?"

Briar fixed her with an incredulous look.

"I know *what* you're apologizing for." Laurel's tone was candid, almost brusque, and her expression said she was unrepentant about that. "But I don't think you should. You're not at fault for what happened. And you did everything you could to save us. And you *did* save us, Briar."

"Did I?"

"Yes." Laurel looked over the wall, her eyes as distant as the craggy mountaintops on the horizon. "I know you wanted to fix it all. You wanted us to go back to the way we were. And I'd be lying if I said I didn't want that too." She exhaled slowly. "We all did things. When we were flying in and out of conscious thought, one moment a monster, driven by hunger. And the next I was me, and I knew me, and there were things I could remember and things that I couldn't, but..."

Briar's throat felt full.

"I almost welcomed it," Laurel said. "Letting the fog take me over. At least then, I didn't know what I'd done." She stopped suddenly. "*I'm* sorry."

"For what?"

"For rambling on like that." Laurel sounded aggrieved. "Here I am trying to lighten your guilt, and all I'm doing is adding to it."

Briar said, "I was just thinking how lucky I was. I got the best deal out of the curse."

"Yes, you did." Laurel bumped her with her bony hip. "You slept through most of it. Lazy."

"Well, that was only because—" Briar broke off. Because of Dev. But she didn't want to talk about the djinn.

Laurel looked at her curiously but didn't ask for an explanation. She said, "If only we could sleep now. We don't sleep at all, you know. We can't even if we try. Do you sleep?"

"Not without difficulty, but yes. I get a few hours most nights."

"I suppose once the rotting has advanced enough, sleep becomes unnecessary," Laurel said wistfully. "Our bodies don't need it. It would be nice though. To rest for a bit. To escape into happy dreams. Mind you, with our luck, we'd only have nightmares." She laughed.

Briar looked at her. Her laugh was a real laugh—a bit rusty, but true and full of mirth. She wondered that her cousin, after all she had been through, could still laugh like that.

Laurel turned to face Briar. Squaring her gaunt shoulders, she took Briar's elbows in her hands. "Briar. Know-it-all, headstrong, mouthy Princess Briar, I want you to listen to me."

"I am not mouthy," Briar protested.

"Are you listening?"

"Yes," she grumbled.

"Good. I want you to look into my eyes right now and believe me when I tell you that *we are all right*. All of us. And we will *be* all right. Me, you, all the corpses in your kingdom. You saved us and we *are* saved. If not for you, we would still be monsters, and if not for you, an evil fairy would be using us to wipe out humankind."

Briar sighed. "I know."

"Good. Now I want you to promise me something."

"And you call *me* mouthy."

"Shut up and listen."

"Let me guess. You want me to promise I won't blame myself? All right, I promise. It's not rational anyway."

Laurel said, "I want you to promise me that when your two princes are ready to depart, you will leave this place and go with them."

Briar gawked at her. "Huh?"

Laurel's grip on her elbows tightened, just enough to prove that she still possessed monster-like strength. "Do you promise?"

"But—I—" Briar sputtered. "Why? I can't just leave—I finally saved us like you said, and I belong here now, ruling my kingdom—"

"If I thought you really wanted to do that," Laurel said, "then I wouldn't tell you to go. But you don't want that, Briar. You never have. You would do it, I'm sure, because you feel you must, and you would do it well probably, because you do everything well. But you were never raised for it, and I don't think you want it. I think you want to explore the world, and I think you need to explore the world. Don't stay here in this place where you were cursed and doomed."

"You were all cursed and doomed," Briar pointed out.

"This place is our home. But it was never yours, Briar. It was your prison."

A delightful ache woke within Briar. A dream she had never dared dream, a wanting she had never dared put to words. To be free of these walls forever. To explore, like Laurel said. To go to the Glen Kingdom and all the kingdoms, and to learn all the things she had missed in eighty years.

"But someone has to keep order here." Briar tried to keep the hope out of her voice. "Someone has to rule."

Laurel's smile held a wicked gleam. "Well, I *am* your cousin and your closest living relative. If you abdicated, well…"

"You would rule?"

"I will admit my asking you to go is a *little* self-serving." Laurel laughed again. "But does it matter if we both get what we want?"

Now Briar laughed too. And it felt true and mirthful; it felt like she hadn't laughed in years. She threw her arms around her cousin's neck. "Do you really mean this, Laurel?"

"Well, of course I do. You deserve some happiness after all this."

Briar drew back. "I just wish—no." She stopped short. "I'd like to do something for you. For all of you, if I could. Some last thing. Some parting gift."

"You don't think saving our lives was enough of a parting gift?"

"I meant—" Briar stopped again. She thought of what she'd nearly said, what she'd prevented herself from saying. *I just wish…*

An icy thrill slithered down her back. But if she could help them one last time...help all her people...

"Laurel," Briar said slowly, "I think there is one thing I can do."

<hr>

After working everything out with Laurel, Briar spent the next few hours sitting with a sleeping Demetri. She didn't tell Demetri or Garrett what she had planned, and she didn't intend to. She was quite sure they wouldn't approve.

Ten minutes to midnight, Briar headed out to the inner courtyard. She wore a long, wool coat over her linen dress—for decency, really, as she didn't need it for the cold. It was a breezy night, the air bearing the scent of the piney mountains and the damp mist that lurked below. Briar ducked inside the fragmented eastern ramparts and took the stairs up to the dark, paneled roof—a place where she wouldn't be interrupted. There she waited beneath the open sky, made gray by a sheen of clouds, cloaking the starry light and the moon.

"I heard you've been wanting a word."

Briar whirled around. There was a man coming down the roof towards her, a familiar man in a navy blue soldier's coat. A full beard covered most of his face. "Kale?"

Kale smiled as he approached her, and the cat-like smile was not Kale's.

"No." Briar stared, a sinking feeling in her chest. "Not Kale."

"Correct," the djinn said. "Not Kale."

"That's not what I meant. Where is Kale? What did you do to him? How long—"

"I didn't do anything to him." The form of Kale blurred and vanished into a cloud of azure smoke. When the smoke reformed, it was the djinn Dev, his sleek black hair pulled back at the nape of his neck, his dark eyes glittering.

"Kale died the first night he was here." The markings on the djinn's face flared with a cobalt gleam, washing them both in a blue light. "When he came with your two princes. He was holed up with Demetri while Prince Garrett woke you. Demetri was too busy fighting to notice when Kale was torn apart by corpses."

"He didn't notice because *you* replaced him," Briar shot back. "I've never known the real Kale, then."

"No. You haven't."

Briar pushed this to the back of her brain. She had business with this djinn, and she didn't want to spend a second longer with him than she had to. "I don't know how you knew I wanted to talk to you—"

Dev raised his eyes to the pewter sky. "I hear things."

"—but I want to make a wish."

Dev's gaze dropped to her face, rapt. "I figured as much. I must say, I'm a little surprised."

Briar gazed out at the courtyard. It was empty save for its own, gore-stained wreckage. All her people were in the castle, and the bodies of the dead had been removed. Still, she imagined she could see them there, her people, waiting.

"If I wished for the rotting to go away," Briar said, stuffing her hands into the large pockets of her coat, "if I wished for them to be normal again...to be restored exactly as they once were...could you do that?"

"No," Dev said. And though it was what Briar had expected, it still hurt to hear. "That would be asking me to break a part of a curse—no, to reverse it. I can't do that."

"You altered my curse," Briar argued.

"No. I didn't touch your curse. I just extended the same courtesy that was done to you to the rest of your kingdom. I couldn't have changed your curse if I'd wanted to."

"And of course, you didn't want to."

Dev didn't look put out by the accusation. "No. I didn't."

It was so unfair, Briar thought, that she had to turn to this creature for aid. But she'd promised Laurel. She'd promised them all.

Briar took a deep breath, closed her eyes, and said, "I wish for every rotted person in this kingdom—all who were affected by my curse—to be able to sleep. I want them to sleep for as long as they like or as short as they like. An hour, two hours, a night, a week, a year. Whenever they want. I want them to wake when they want to wake. And when they sleep, I want them to sleep peacefully and have only pleasant dreams."

When there was no response, Briar opened her eyes. She half-expected the djinn to be gone. But he stood there, a curious gleam in his eyes. "That's your wish?"

"Yes," Briar snapped. "It is."

"Very well." Dev narrowed his eyes. "And because I care about you, Briar, I will count all of that as a single wish. Which means you still have one left, should you choose to use it."

"One? What do you mean?"

"A djinn can only grant three wishes to a single person." Dev said this with a pleased expression, as though it delighted him to explain his ways to her. "It's the rules. Otherwise, a person could just go on making wishes all their life."

Briar clenched her teeth. "I won't ever make another wish of you."

"If you say so."

"Tell me something." Briar fixed the djinn with a fierce glare. "Why did you let Demetri go? After all that time? Why let him wake me? You could have used me for another eighteen years. So why?"

"I already told you."

"I want the truth this time."

Dev stepped forward. He was almost exactly as tall as she was, and he met her glaring gaze. "What I told you *is* the truth, Briar. I meant it when I said I'd grown fond of you."

"Oh, please," Briar scoffed.

Dev cocked his head to one side, and there was no mischief on his face now. "Do you know how long I usually draw on a princess's life force? No more than a few years. It drains them, you see. Eventually, they die. And they are only with me for snatches of time during their nights, when they're dreaming. But you, Briar…"

Dev's eyes grew darker, more serious. "You were cursed to perpetual sleep. And the curse kept you from dying. Sustained your life force. So you see, I've known you, dear princess—I've lived with you—for much longer than any other princess I've encountered." His tone turned thoughtful. "Perhaps that changed me a little. Perhaps getting to know you helped me see you as a person, real and true, and not just something to sustain my freedom. Can you believe that?"

Briar wanted to scoff again, but she said nothing. She didn't want to believe it. It was easier to think this creature was simply pure malice and mischief, as evil as the dark fairy.

But she wasn't sure if that was true.

"So…" Dev lifted one shoulder in an artful shrug. "Why did I wake you early? Let's just say, it was in your best interest."

Briar could not contain her sarcasm. "You think?"

"Yes, I do. Not that it was best you return to the waking world. It was best that you were *gone* from the shadow world."

"What do you mean? Why?"

"You changed there, you know." Dev's voice turned sharp. "Or didn't you notice? Did you think, when you came back from the dead, that that was a result of the rotting curse? Enabled by the abilities you gained as a corpse monster? Because if so, you're wrong about that. Your rotting hadn't progressed enough to keep you from death. You came back to life because your body healed itself once Garrett pulled that piece of wood out of you."

Briar's head spun. "But I didn't heal. I still have a hole in my torso."

A smile flickered over Dev's face. "You healed enough. It *was* the rotting that kept you from healing all the way."

"What are you saying?" Briar shook her head, trying to absorb this information. "That even if I hadn't been afflicted by the rotting curse, I would still be—I *am*—unkillable? Because of something that happened to me in the shadow world?"

"I don't know about *unkillable*. But more or less, yes, that's what I'm saying." Dev nodded. "That is why I set you free from the shadow realm. Before that place could change you any more. Damage you further."

"But if I gained some kind of healing ability, how was I *damaged?*"

Dev looked surprised. "There are all kinds of damage, Briar, that go beyond the physical. I would have thought—given what you were willing to sacrifice to kill the dark fairy—you would know that by now."

Briar bit back a frustrated response. She wanted to be done with this creature—but she had to know one last thing. "Can you still get to me?" she asked. Her voice was hard but brittle, like a thin sheet of glass. "When I sleep at night—can you still use me?"

If Dev cared at all how this notion disturbed her, he didn't show it. "Only during certain hours," he said. "But you've nothing to fear from me, Briar. I won't use you again. I promise. I told you. I don't want you to go back to that place."

Somehow, his promise did not reassure her.

31

PARTING

DEMETRI SPENT MOST OF two days in and out of morphine-induced sleep. He thought he remembered some visitors—Briar and Garrett, and Thatcher, of course. But when he woke the third morning, it was like emerging from a fog, as though the past two days had been a dream.

One of the first things he learned was that Briar was abdicating her throne, leaving it to her cousin Laurel. It was, she said, a mutual decision between them, and best for both the kingdom and herself. She intended to keep in touch with Laurel and to serve as an intermediary for the Mountain Kingdom to the outside world.

They left the castle the next day. Thatcher seemed to think Demetri could use another couple of days in bed, but they *could* go, he said, if they had to, and everyone felt they had to. Demetri was as eager to be gone as anyone else, even if it meant enduring some pain on their way down the mountain.

"Is it really okay to leave them there?" Demetri asked, as they made their slow way along the ridge. It was a bright, cloudless day, the cheery sky at odds with the bitter chill in the air. The cold bit clear through Demetri's wool jacket, intensifying the ache in his side. "I mean—the way they are?"

"They'll be all right," Briar said. "Laurel will be a good queen. She'll make sure the people who are worst off are looked after. And they all have a lot to do—negotiating with the fairies to get these blasted thorns down—" She stole an apprehensive glance at the thorns on their left, far enough away that they were in no real danger, but close enough to ensure they stepped carefully "—checking in on everyone else in the country, restoring the castle. I think that will help them—having tasks to perform."

"Yes." Demetri gazed out over the sage green hills below, their dips and rolls giving the land a lumpy, ill-formed look. "I'm sure it does."

Demetri didn't have any tasks anymore, and this had never been more apparent than it was now. Becoming king of the Glen Kingdom, marrying Briar—those things were lost to him. He'd begun to accept that. But he still had no idea what he was supposed to do instead.

Regardless, it should have been all right, he thought, as they made their slow, treacherous way down the mountain. It hadn't gone exactly as planned, but he'd done what he set out to do. They rescued Briar, broke her curse. She was awake, she was alive, and she was all right. The dark fairy was dead and the corpses were no longer a threat. It should have been enough.

But all Demetri felt was a bone-deep weariness, born from more than the wound in his side.

It took them two days, twice as long as it should have, but they reached the woodland at the bottom of the mountain. They regained their horses and the carriage there, which was a comfort to Demetri, as he and other wounded rode in it back to the train depot. Briar and Garrett checked on him often, especially when they made camp at night, but Demetri knew his quiet, one-worded responses would drive them off eventually. He wasn't trying to be cruel. He didn't want to hurt them. It was for that reason that he stayed silent and kept his distance.

The days grew short as they headed south, the sun sinking into the horizon earlier each day. Strong, wintry winds, birthed in the mountains, blustered at their backs, and the trees bared their branches, their colorful leaves blanketing the forest floor. The air was ripe with cold.

It wouldn't be as cold or windy in the Glen Kingdom, Demetri thought. He wouldn't have minded some warmer weather. But he wasn't going back to the Glen Kingdom.

They had no way of knowing if a working train would be waiting for them at the train station, and in fact there wasn't—but a train was on its way, an attendant said. Only a day away. So it was decided they would spend the night at the station.

Demetri, however, decided he would not.

Thatcher looked him over one last time. He was not happy to hear Demetri's plans. The medic conceded that he was well enough to ride, so long as it was only a few miles a day. "But the nearest town you come to, see a doctor," Thatcher insisted. "You may be a prince, Your Highness, but that's an order, I'm afraid."

Demetri managed a faint smile. "All right. And I'm not a prince. Not anymore."

He made sure all his things were packed and set to saddling a horse just outside the station's black metal fence, under the overhang of its sloped roof. Saddling the horse was not without difficulties, thanks to his splinted, bandaged hand.

He was trying to adjust a last strap when Briar and Garrett turned up, coming outside from the platform. Briar led the way, rushing towards him, her square-heeled boots clopping against the pavement. Garrett followed a step behind, but he only looked resigned.

"Demetri." Briar's voice was breathless. "Thatcher said you're leaving and I told him that couldn't be..." She trailed off, taking in the horse, saddled and packed.

"It's true," Demetri said. A weight descended on him as he faced her.

Garrett took an uncertain step back. "I'll just—I'll be—I'm going...over there," he said, gesturing vaguely. Sparing a glance for Briar, he walked a good ways off, leaving Demetri alone with her.

Briar stared at the horse, her expression complicated. Something about her eyes, troubled and storm-like, made Demetri's stomach clench.

"I don't—" Briar looked from the horse to Demetri. "You're *leaving?*"

Demetri held her gaze, difficult as it was. "I am."

"But you're still healing, you're still recovering." Briar laid a hand against the horse's side as though to keep it in place. "Demetri, you can't *leave.*"

"Thatcher cleared me to go."

"That's not what I mean." Briar came around the horse. Her hair was tied in a loose knot behind her neck and the wind whipped stray strands across her face. "Where are you going to go, Demetri? What are you going to do?"

"I don't really know." Demetri shoved his good hand in his trouser pocket. The other dangled aimlessly at his side. "That's sort of the point."

"Why can't you come with us?" Briar closed the distance between them, and her proximity was painful. "Back to the Glen Kingdom? Demetri, I know it's all different, but I don't have a home either. Garrett says we can stay at the castle. His father won't mind, he says."

"Yes, he told me. And you should go with him, Briar." Demetri forced a smile that felt like it might break his face. "There are all sorts of new things in the Glen Kingdom. You haven't seen the half of it yet. You'll have plenty to do."

"And you could too! If only you'd come."

Demetri stroked a hand over his horse's flank. Its coat was soft and cool, bristling against his palm. "The only thing I was ever meant to do in the Glen Kingdom," he said, "was rule it. I can't go back there, Briar. Not now that way is gone for me. There's plenty for you there, but for me, there's nothing."

"You don't know that. You haven't even tried."

"I'm not abandoning you, Briar," Demetri said quietly. "I hope you know that."

"I don't know that." Her voice was relentless, a blade that could not be parried. "I *need* you, Demetri. Don't *you* know that?"

Demetri attempted a laugh. "You always used to say you don't need some man—"

"I don't need some man," Briar interrupted. "I need *you*."

Demetri glanced over his shoulder at Garrett's distant form, some thirty feet away. Briar followed his gaze, then grabbed him by the shoulder, turning him to look at her. Her touch cut straight through his coat, straight to his core. "Demetri, you are my friend," she pleaded. "You were there for me when no one else was. You told me about the curse, you came to wake me. I wouldn't be here if it weren't for you, and—" She stopped, some new realization taking hold in her eyes.

"What?" he prompted.

Briar studied his face as though looking for answers there. "I wouldn't be here if it weren't for you," she repeated. "And you wouldn't be here if it weren't for me. None of this would have happened to you if it weren't for me."

"Briar, that's not—" He was going to say that wasn't what this was about, but that would have been a lie. And he thought she knew it. He thought maybe, she understood what he had only just begun to admit himself. Still, that didn't mean he blamed her. "I've told you none of this is your fault. You have to know that."

"I know," she said. "But that doesn't make it easy to forget, does it?"

"Briar, if I hadn't known you or if I had left you to your fate—I would have lived a cold, empty life without you."

"And that isn't what this is now?"

He shrugged helplessly.

"I told you that you'd changed," she said wistfully. "Remember? Back in the castle, when I first woke. And you *have* changed, Demetri. And I don't care; it doesn't matter to me. But it matters to you, doesn't it?"

Some of that darkness—the darkness that still surrounded him—dissipated. Knowing she understood, even only in part, brought some light into him. "Briar, I don't know who I am anymore—no, I don't know what I'm supposed to *do*. And I have to figure that out and I have to do it on my own."

"And you have to do it now?"

"Yes. I think so."

Briar sighed. "All right."

An unhappy silence fell between them. On the other side of the fence, the combined voices of the soldiers drifted by, a low murmur punctuated by an occasional shout or laugh.

Demetri managed to say, "I love you, Briar."

Briar bit her lip. "I know."

He smiled. "That's all I needed to hear."

Before he could turn away, she threw her arms around him. Demetri flinched, but it was not so painful as he thought. After a moment's hesitation, he wrapped his arms around her too. He committed it to memory, this moment, this fleeting piece. The press of her hands into his back. His face buried in her hair.

"Goodbye, Demetri." She spoke into his shoulder, imprinting her words there.

"Goodbye," he whispered.

After she disappeared into the station, Garrett came to join him.

"Well," Demetri said, striving for a light tone, "thank you for doing as I asked and not getting yourself killed. Although not for lack of trying, from what I vaguely remember."

Garrett rubbed a hand behind his neck. "I wasn't trying to get killed. I just did what I had to is all. So did you, in the end."

"I suppose we all do what we have to." Demetri struggled to tighten the cinch on his saddle, but it kept slipping over. He tried to hold it in place with his arm, but Garrett stepped forward and held it for him.

"Thanks," Demetri muttered. He tightened it well and good. "You're not going to tell me I don't have to go?"

"I believe I already did." Garrett grinned. "I can say it again, if you like."

"It's all right. I know I don't have to. But I need to."

"I understand."

With all the courtesy of a prince, Demetri offered a hand to his friend. Garrett took it and pulled Demetri into a quick embrace.

"Don't get into trouble on your own," Garrett said as he stepped back. "Trouble is *my* territory. So if you find any, I expect a telegram. Understood?"

Demetri, taking a page out of Garrett's book, grinned broadly. "Understood."

As he mounted his horse and set out from the train station, Demetri looked up at the sky, squinting into the sun's cold, distant light. He was alone again, just as he had been all those years in captivity. But this was the right thing, he felt. He didn't know what he was supposed to do. He didn't know how to go back to the person he used to be.

But that was all right. So long as he could find the person he was now.

32

HAPPILY

GARRETT SWUNG HIS ARM back and forth, working out the muscle. "It doesn't hurt," he admitted. "Not like it did anyway. A little sore, maybe."

"That's normal," Thatcher remarked. "At least, as normal as any of this can be."

Garrett had discovered that the reason Thatcher had disappeared in the middle of the battle was because he had gone to harvest blood from dead corpses. He had been hopeful that killing the dark fairy might cure Garrett, but he didn't want to risk Garrett's life on that hope. And rightly so, for the dark fairy's death did not cure him. Breaking the curse, they'd discovered, could not undo what had been done. The corpse people were still corpse people, and so their venom still existed.

But Thatcher felt he had enough blood to last for "about a year or so." That was hardly reassuring, and Garrett said so, but Thatcher pointed out that meant he had a year to find a true cure. "And I already have an idea," the medic told him. The two of them were in the small, square operator's office in the train station, which Thatcher had claimed for medical purposes while they were there. "There's a man in the Desert Kingdom who discovered a method for creating anti-venoms. I'm thinking this method should work for you."

"Let's hope." Garrett scratched his arm through the sleeve of his wool shirt. "Thatch, I know I'm always harping off on these dangerous quests, but—I really, really don't want to die. You know?"

"I know, sire."

Garrett pulled his gray sack coat on and headed onto the busy train platform. The train had arrived about an hour ago, and everyone was eager to be gone. Soldiers jogged up and down the platform, calling to each other as they loaded supplies. Garrett stood, breathing in the last of the mountain air. It was not as crisp as usual, but damp and scented with oncoming rain. That was just as well. With any luck, they'd be headed home in another twenty minutes. And this time without corpses sabotaging the train halfway there.

He headed aboard and wandered down the narrow corridor, ducking his head into every compartment. Near the end of the train, he found what he was looking for—Briar. She sat alone in a passenger compartment next to the window, gazing at the grim clouds outside, low and wispy in the sky. He'd given her some privacy since Demetri departed, so he knocked on the cherry wood doorframe and waited for her reaction. When she looked around and saw him, she smiled, so he took that as an invitation and slipped inside. He lowered himself onto the scarlet seat beside her, stretching his arms over his head.

"We should be off soon," he said. The train hummed beneath him in agreement.

Briar nodded.

Garrett glanced at the creased paper folded in her hand. "Another letter?"

"No." She smoothed the paper over her knee so he could see it. "Actually, this is one of my sketches. It's for a flying contraption. Want to know how it works?"

"Not really." Garrett chanced a fleeting look at the sketch. A *flying* contraption? "I mean, I'm sure it's fascinating, but—"

"—you never want to test it." Her eyes were playful and pleased in their understanding. "I know." Then she sighed.

"Still thinking about Demetri?" he queried.

Briar eyed him sideways. "Sort of," she hedged. "I understand why he felt he had to go. I've just been thinking that I should have made him go home. All those years ago, before any of it. As soon as he found out about my curse and told me, I should have thanked him and sent him on his way. But I let him stay because—he was the one who told me the truth. He was the only one trying to help me. He kept me going. Without him..." Her hand clenched over her sketch, crinkling the paper. "But he paid for it. Far more than anything I paid."

Garrett folded his hands behind his head. "He wouldn't have gone. From what he told me, he loved you long before he told you about that curse. He would never have left you." *Then.*

"I know," Briar said in a low voice. "That's the worst part."

Garrett dropped his arms. "What do you mean?"

Briar eyed him sideways again. She set her paper aside and dropped her hands into her lap. "He loves me. But I don't think I ever loved him. Not like that."

Garrett was flummoxed by this. "You didn't?"

"I know it sounds horrible."

"No." Garrett shook his head. "You feel what you feel. It's just—you care about him. I've seen it."

"Of course I care about him." She traced a hand down the length of her unbound hair, the gesture endearingly self-conscious. "But that's not the same thing. I'm not saying he never meant anything to me. He was there for me when the rest of the world wasn't. But I don't love him—not like that. I didn't even realize, not until..." She gazed out the window, and the reflection of her face in the glass was too hazy for Garrett to read it.

"Until what?"

Briar didn't answer right away. The tiny bulbs lining the corridor flared to life as the sky grew darker and gloomier outside. A light drizzle began to fall, misty rain spattering the window.

Briar said, "I've been thinking about something." Given her mock-innocent tone of voice, he judged this something was not too serious.

"And what's that?" he prompted.

"Well." She turned around to face him, one leg pulled up into her seat, the other dangling over its edge. "You did kiss me once."

A tiny hope sparked to life within Garrett. "Yes." He matched her innocent tone. "I did."

"And you remember it, don't you?"

"Of course I do."

"But," she said, inching a little closer to him, "I don't remember it."

"Well," Garrett said reasonably, "there are a lot of things you don't remember. It's a bit of a problem with you, isn't it?"

Briar gave him a little shove. "This is different and you know it. I don't remember you kissing me because I was asleep when you did it, and might I say, I think I'm being very generous in not pointing out how creepy that is."

"Creepy!" Garrett protested. "I was saving your life!"

"The point is—" Briar rolled her eyes "—you know what it's like to kiss me."

Garrett shifted around too, leaning his shoulder against his seat. He could feel the stirrings of a familiar inkling within him, the intuitive knowing he felt at the start of a quest. It felt weird here, now, when their quest was ending. But also right. Weirdly right.

"Well," he said. His voice was tangled in his throat. He leaned towards her. "I know what it's like to kiss sleeping you. I don't know what it's like to kiss waking you." He paused. "That does sound creepy, doesn't it."

"I told you." Briar shifted again. Closer now. So close that he saw things he'd never seen before. The ring of blue around the gray in her eyes. The curve of her collarbone where it disappeared into her blouse. "So the truth is, neither of us really knows what it's like to kiss each other."

Garrett's chest was a maelstrom. His heart quivered as the maelstrom tugged at it. "Right. Exactly."

"And the only way to come to any real conclusion about a theoretical hypothesis," she said, "is to test it."

Garrett meant to answer—if only to have the last word—but while his eyes were exploring the arch of her neck, Briar stole his move and kissed him.

It was unexpected. Not that she kissed him, but what it *was*. He was afraid that when he kissed her, he would think of Snow.

But Snow was his past, and this kiss was not his past. He deepened the kiss, and her hair was silk in his hands and his pulse was a hummingbird beneath her palm and her breath was a guttering candle as their lips broke apart.

He felt it all like a door opening before him, and through the door was a wide, open world. An expanse to be explored. A gleaming field of possibility and newness. This kiss was not his past.

"Well?" Briar said. Her forehead was cool against his, and her palm lay flat against his chest. "Better than kissing sleeping me?"

"Actually," Garrett said, his voice a low thrum between them, "I'm not sure."

Briar's fingers dug into his chest. "You're not *sure?*"

"No. I think I need to try again. Then maybe I'll know."

"Oh." Her hand skated up his neck and cupped his cheek. His heart quivered again. "That's logical. You can hardly make a concrete conclusion about anything after only one try."

He murmured his agreement. As he bent his neck to capture her lips, the train shuddered into movement, picking up speed as it hurtled down the tracks. Racing towards the expanse. Hurtling into the new.

Don't Miss the Next Book in the Series!

AVAILABLE NOW

Turn the page for a sneak peek!

Isabelle flinched as the splintering oak door slammed shut behind her, closing out the scowls and mutterings of the tavern workers inside. An icy gust blew past, and Isabelle shivered, pushing her windswept curls from her face. Not even her snug wool coat was enough to guard against the bitter chill of the Black Forest. The village tavern may not have been very friendly, but at least it had been warm.

This was the third village she'd come to in the past week, and so far, no one knew of a castle in these woods. But Isabelle had become suspicious of this professed ignorance. The villagers' fearful eyes and curt responses told a different story. There *was* a castle in this forest. But no one wanted to talk about it. Which did not bode well for Isabelle.

Standing outside the tavern now, Isabelle peered up at the slate blue sky. It was not dawn yet—the sun rose late and set early this time of year, especially so far north—and she wondered if she should wait for daylight before setting out. The village here was small: a cluster of houses, a business or two, and the one tavern, all pitched on either side of the road. Beyond the village, the road ended, leaving no clear way through the tangled wood.

Isabelle wound the gears on her lantern, and as the bulb flared to life, she raised it high, throwing a circle of bright white light ahead of her. The road ended, but perhaps there was a path, Isabelle thought, as she ventured past the final stone houses. The wooded land rose just ahead, obscuring what lay beyond—more forest probably. Indeed, the air was scented with the musty fragrance of cold, muddy earth and dead leaves.

Isabelle hesitated. Her lantern's cold, metal handle bit into the crevices of her palm as she shifted her grip. Sunrise must have been close, because the world around her had begun to lighten, the black veil of night lifting. But the way forward was still concealed, murkier than ever in the pre-dawn gray.

A shadow shifted ahead, something moving in the dark.

Isabelle froze. Her spine felt rigid, as though something had clamped it tight. The movement could have been anything—a hawk winging beneath the forest canopy, the wind rustling the furry branches of a spruce tree. But something about the way that shadow undulated in the gloom—with uncanny grace—put Isabelle on alert.

"Heard you're looking for the old castle."

Isabelle gave a start, her heart leaping in her chest.

A woman glided out of the forest, materializing from the darkness.

Isabelle's breath sank out of her. "*Stones.*"

"Sorry. Didn't mean to frighten you." The woman gave her the briefest of smiles, her glinting teeth a flash of white. As she stepped into the light of the lantern, Isabelle took in the sight of her. She had thick, fiery red hair, bound in a complicated mass of braids. Her skin was wintry fair, her cheeks pink with cold. And she was tall. Isabelle was tall, but thin and bony. This woman had a heft to her, a muscled litheness.

"Well?" the woman said. "Are you?"

"What?"

"Looking for the old castle?"

Hope seized Isabelle by the throat. "Yes, I am. If it's real, anyway."

"Of course it's real." The woman smiled again. There was something off about her smile—as though it meant to convey something more than friendliness. Something sinister.

Isabelle shook off a chill as a cutting wind sliced through her black coat. The mistrust of the villagers, the darkness of the early morning—it was putting her on edge. If there *was* something off about this woman, well, Isabelle knew people who lived alone could be a bit strange. She herself was, after all.

"So the castle?" Isabelle prompted. "Where can I find it?"

The woman turned, shrugging for Isabelle to join her. "There's a path you can start on. I'm headed that way my-self—I'll show you."

Isabelle followed, relieved. She'd begun to think this entire venture was a fool's errand. That the telegram she'd received had been nothing more than a cruel prank. The telegram had contained news of Isabelle's brother, claiming he was being held prisoner in an old castle here in the forest. But the details had been vague, and as Isabelle delved further into the forest, she'd begun to think it was all for nothing. But now, as Isabelle trekked up the sharp rise in the land and down a dirt path, she felt hopeful for the first time since leaving the Glen Kingdom.

The forest was formless in the early darkness, shadows blur-ring together. Bulging fir trees were like sleeping giants and bar-ren alders like twisted monsters, their branches grasping and grotesque. Isabelle kept her gaze on her guide, wary of wandering off the path. "This castle then." Isabelle stepped over a mossy rock jutting up from the ground. "It's still standing?"

"Was the last time I saw it." The woman came to a halt, round-ing on Isabelle. "If you're going there, you should know. People say the castle is cursed."

Isabelle felt an icy hand grip her heart. She was not typically a fanciful person. She believed in what was rational, what was recorded, and what could be proved. But she also knew very well that curses were real. They *had* been recorded and proved. "Cursed? In what way?"

"No one really knows." The woman studied Isabelle as though appraising her mettle. "There are all sorts of rumors. But the story generally goes that—back when the kingdom still stood—a witch cursed the last Forest king. Him and his family. Even their descendants."

A shiver rattled through Isabelle. Enough time had passed that the sun should have risen by now, shedding morning light. But the Black Forest was true to its name. The dark fir trees soared overhead, blocking out the sky. Even the bare-limbed alders loomed, their knobby branches snarling together in a tangled canopy. A thin layer of snow lay over it all, dusting the fir trees and clumping in the crevices of the alders.

"Why did the witch curse them?" Isabelle asked.

"Who knows?" the woman replied. "Some say the king slighted her. Some say they were lovers, and he broke her heart. Others claim the royal family was involved in something dark—forbidden rituals and blood magic and all sorts of madness. Some of the stories are outlandish, I'll grant you. But *something* happened that night the king fell. The stories agree on that. It was no invasion or famine that toppled this kingdom. Something struck down the royal family in one swoop. And the castle has been abandoned ever since."

There could be some truth to it, Isabelle thought, watching a tiny critter scurry across the path. There was little historical evidence to say why the kingdom fell, and no one knew what had become of the last Forest king. "And their descendants?"

"What?"

"You said the witch cursed the king's descendants as well. Or *were* there any descendants? If everyone was killed—"

"I didn't say they were killed. I said they were *cursed*. Including their descendants." The wind picked up, soughing as it blustered through the fir trees. The woman's red hair blew in the wind, but she stood still, untouched by the cold. "Some people say they fled to the mountains. But others say the descendants still walk these woods. Haunting the forest. Living out their curse." Her gaze settled on Isabelle with a smile that did not reach her cool gray eyes.

Isabelle swallowed. "So the castle itself isn't cursed then."

"I suppose not."

"And it's not abandoned anymore?"

"No. It's not. But the one who lives there now—some disgraced lord—doesn't much like visitors." The woman's tone turned bitter.

The one who lives there now. Isabelle reached for the crumpled paper tucked in her pocket, the transcript of her telegram. The paper felt brittle in her hand, the well-worn creases grown sharp. According to the telegram, her brother had stayed at the castle as a guest—until he'd done something to offend the lord of the castle. Now he was a prisoner. Though she hadn't seen him in three years, Isabelle knew her brother, and she could well believe Ansel had done something stupid or criminal. But that didn't mean she wasn't worried about him.

"Well, whatever he likes," Isabelle said, trying to make her voice light, "I need to get to that castle. So, I just follow the path?"

"Yes. Follow the path through the woods. When it ends, you've got about three miles before you reach the castle. But it's a straight shot through the forest. Due north." The woman stepped aside. "I'll leave you here. I'm headed elsewhere." A smile played at her lips as she watched Isabelle pass. "Good luck. And you really *should* try to reach the castle before dark."

Isabelle stilled. She turned back towards the woman.

"Why?" she asked.

"Oh. You know. There are those stories. The cursed descendants haunting the woods." The woman smiled. "And wolves."

"Wolves?" Isabelle echoed, trying to hide her alarm.

"Yes, they're all about this forest. And at this time of year, food gets scarce. They get hungry. But not to worry." The woman tipped her head. "You'll be fine. So long as you reach the castle before dark."

Then she was gone. Vanishing through the trees, the deep foliage swallowing her up.

Isabelle let out a long breath after she'd gone, feeling shaken. *Nonsense*, she told herself, heading down the path. *She's just a strange woman.*

Still. That didn't mean Isabelle wasn't in danger. Whether it was unfriendly villagers or the merciless winter weather—or wolves or curses or this "disgraced lord"—Isabelle knew she was risking a lot, coming here on her own. But the girl who'd sent her the telegram—a servant at the castle—had insisted she come alone.

Isabelle pressed on, following the scanty deer path through the wood. The ground beneath her feet grew soft and doughy, the untraveled path awash with fresh mud. Once or twice, the path almost disappeared, and Isabelle thought it was at an end. But then it appeared again, and she realized it had only been eaten by the forest—by the dense clusters of trees and overgrown bramble. Finally—her relief so thick it clogged her throat—she came to the end of the path. Another three miles due north, the woman had said, and she would reach the castle.

But she'd only gone about one mile when she heard it. A long, keening howl—a howl that quivered through the air and ghosted past the back of Isabelle's neck.

Isabelle's breath snagged in her throat. *Wolves.*

Another howl sounded out, and before it was done, a second one, joining the first in an otherworldly symphony. Isabelle licked her cracked lips. The stillness that had come over her seeped through her bones, settling on the inside like a hardening lump of clay. Hardening into fear.

Those wolves sounded close. Much too close.

Isabelle turned around. She scanned the forest behind her, her gaze roving over the darkening wood.

And latched onto a pair of yellow eyes, smoldering like embers in the shadows.

Isabelle's breath froze in her chest.

She turned and ran through the woods, and the cries of the wolves raced after her.

ACKNOWLEDGEMENTS

Eleven years ago, two things came together in my mind: a lifelong love for fairy tales, and a newfound love for zombies. *Rotting Beauty* was the result. *Rotting Beauty* was not the first novel I wrote, but it was the first one I took further than a rough draft. Bringing this book to publication has taken years of hard work, as well as a lot of help from others.

Thank you to all the alpha and beta readers for this novel, including Rachel, David, Fanny, Sarah, Allison, and Emilie. Your feedback has been invaluable to me as a writer and made this story what it is today.

Thank you to Nadia and all the amazing people at Miblart for designing my beautiful cover. Thank you to Saumya Singh for bringing the Five Kingdoms to life by creating the wonderful map in this book.

Thank you to Rachel, David, and Heather for all the advice and encouragement you have given me over the years. Your support means more to me than you know.

And finally, thank you to my parents. You have always supported my dream to be a published author since I was seven years old, writing stories about squirrels and jackrabbits and making them into books. Not once have you ever wavered in that support or suggested I try to be something else. Thank you.

About the Author

ELIZABETH K. KING is a fantasy and horror writer. Over the years, she has nurtured her love of monsters through TV shows like *Buffy the Vampire Slayer, Supernatural,* and *Grimm.* She spends her time writing in her gothic study and roaming the Shire (her backyard) with her cocker spaniel, Blue. She lives in Houston, Texas.

You can find Elizabeth online at www.elizabethkking. com, on Instagram @elizabeth_k_king, and on her Facebook page, Elizabeth K. King, Author.